THE CONCRETE LAWYER

Adam Barrist

iUniverse, Inc.
New York   Bloomington

iUniverse books may be ordered through booksellers or by contacting:

iUniverse
1663 Liberty Drive
Bloomington, IN 47403
www.iuniverse.com
1-800-Authors (1-800-288-4677)

ISBN: 978-1-4401-6573-3 (sc)
ISBN: 978-1-4401-6574-0 (hc)
ISBN: 978-1-4401-6575-7 (ebook)

Printed in the United States of America

iUniverse rev. date: 12/04/2009

For Joy, Alexander and Dominique

AUTHOR'S NOTE

This book is fantasy and should be interpreted as such. Not a single character in this book is real, nor is a single character in this book modeled after a real person. While I gleaned many of the ideas in this work of fiction from my experience as a practicing attorney, virtually every detail of this story is make-believe.

I feel specifically compelled to address a few issues in that vein.

In my view, the courts of Philadelphia and its surrounding counties are some of the most distinguished, honorable and just courts anywhere. I have never encountered any judges or attorneys such as the ones whom I describe in this book.

Additionally, I have never experienced, nor do I know of anyone ever having experienced, the law enforcement corruption described herein.

This book is neither a portal into my soul nor an accurate representation of how I, personally, view the world.

Please accept this book for what it I intended it to be: an enjoyable, fully invented work of fiction.

PROLOGUE

The telephone rang on an unseasonably cool Parisian Tuesday. As he sat in the apartment at his ornate Louis XV époque desk, he took the call that he had long expected, but desperately hoped would never come.

When he had started his new life several years prior, memories from yesteryear quickly faded. He reminisced of nothing from his previous existence.

Upon hearing the caller's voice, it was instantly and understandably clear that those to whom debts are owed do not just fade into the sunset. When that much money and power is at stake, such people could not be expected to disappear.

The sunlight peeked through the purple fleur-de-lys emblazoned drapes and reflected off of the gold leaf edges of the walnut desk into his eyes. The sharp brightness, combined with the message of the caller, caused him to feel an extreme nausea that he had not experienced since when he did devil's work. Because his new life was so worry free, he seldom spent a moment upset, anxious or afraid. In fact, the only concern that he possessed since moving on to his new life was that this very telephone call would come.

Judging by the look on her man's face as he spoke into the telephone, the unclothed brunette knew exactly who was calling. She also knew that her life was on the verge of changing for the worse. As she drew nervously on her Gauloise Légère and exhaled the smoke towards the immaculate 12-foot etched ceiling, she pondered whether she should, or could, extract herself from this situation. Such thoughts quickly evaporated as she realized that if she ran away, she would be caught and dealt with. When she accepted the life of near royalty many years prior, she knew that such luxuries could come to an abrupt end one day if a "contingency," as her benefactor called it, occurred.

"When is this 'messenger' coming?" he spoke into the phone.

"What does 'soon enough' mean? I'm not going to deal with this nonsense! You've found me, and I ain't goin' nowhere, so let's get this done with, so that you can take what you want and let me crawl back in my hole and enjoy what's left of my retirement. I urge you to please keep in mind that I made myself very accessible to you. I could have disappeared to a place where you could not have found me. Your interests are still viable and protected. I've acted in good faith – so don't you tell me how it's going to be," he yelled into the receiver, his face now bright red.

He looked impatiently at the brunette, and smacked his lips three times in rapid succession with his right index finger and middle finger together. She quickly obliged his request and placed a pack of Gauloises and a box of matches on the desk. With the telephone still affixed to his right ear, he looked down to the red package of cigarettes, and spoke into the phone, "Please hold on one second."

She quickly realized her mistake, but it was too late.

Clutching the brunette's mouth violently with his right hand, evocative of his former self, the silver haired man barked in horribly accented, but grammatically correct French,

"Conasse! Tu sais que je ne fume que les cigarettes américaines!"

After he shoved her towards the solid plaster wall that had stood since the 19th century, she quickly retrieved the proper American cigarettes from the lavish marble topped nightstand. With a trembling hand, she carefully placed that box in front of her man.

He lit a cigarette, inhaled the tobacco fumes, closed his eyes, collected himself, and exhaled. He picked the telephone receiver back up, and calmly said,

"I apologize for the interruption. I assume that you'll alert me the moment you know when the messenger will be arriving. I can be reached at this number – and, as I said, I'm not going anywhere – I just want to be done with this and move on with my life."

The brunette retrieved a bottle of scotch from another room and poured a stiff one into a highball glass for the silver haired man. As he hung up the phone, she handed him the glass.

"The day has arrived, my love," he said, raising his glass, "let's begin the preparations, shall we?"

CHAPTER ONE

"A.B., you there? You there, bro? Are you there? Terri, would you find out from Kristin where the hell Alex is? He was supposed to be back from court fifteen minutes ago, and I need him right now."

Nick Carlson's voice annoyed the living shit out of me, and just about everyone else who had to perpetually listen to his absurdly amplified twang in our office on a daily basis. His insistence on buzzing in on young Associates' intercom systems, by using his speakerphone, rather than lifting his telephone receiver compounded his abrasiveness.

"A.B., where you at, babe?" Now off the intercom, but still equally audible to the four secretaries and six attorneys in his quadrant of the office, he added, "God, people really gotta start stepping it up..."

"Nick, I'm here. Sorry about that."

Actually, I really wasn't sorry. I had just gotten back from a case management conference at Philadelphia City Hall and desperately needed to find out what was going on in the Phillies' matinee game against the Cardinals. By the time that I had returned from the conference, the game was already in the seventh inning. Although Kristin Fabrizzio, our 28 year-old dynamo receptionist, shouted to me on my way back in the office that the Phils were up 3-1, I needed to know the scoring details. Had Ryan Howard belted two homeruns? Was Cole Hamels in the midst of one of his double-digit strikeout performances? Was Nick Carlson really buzzing in on my intercom, when I had gotten into the office two minutes earlier and had just logged onto *espn.com* to check the goddamn score?

"Oh...I thought you were – never mind. My office, now!" he ordered.

When a Partner at Krauss, Carlson, Whitby, Miller and White directed an Associate Attorney into their office in such a tone, the recipient of the communication would jump to attention, straighten their tie or blouse and briskly walk down the hall to meet their fate. In the minds of Associates and support staff, Nick Carlson was the most feared of the Partners. He was what the secretaries called "a screamer." My idea of "a screamer" was a petite, inexperienced University of Pennsylvania freshman girl who liked to loudly call out the name of The Lord while her upperclass boyfriend taught her the ways of the world. There I go, though, living in the past again.

In any event, Nick Carlson, a 63 year-old, 5'5" prick of a lawyer, certainly didn't fit my definition of "a screamer." He may have screamed a lot, but he wasn't a screamer. He was just an asshole.

After walking seventeen feet, I was just about to enter Carlson's office when his secretary, Terri, stood up from her chair, reached across her desk, grabbed my arm and whispered, "he's in a really bad mood today – be careful." Upon offering me my due warning, she performed the sign of the cross, followed by a solemn kiss of her crucifix.

Many Jews might have been offended by the sign of the cross, but not me. Terri's words and gesture said to me, *"you're such a nice boy. I hope that he doesn't scream at you – you can't possibly deserve it. After all, you're smarter than him and in your six years of practicing, you have garnered a more comprehensive understanding of the law than Nick has in 37 years. May God be with you."*

Confident that God, Jesus and the whole crew were on my side, I ventured into the Hades of Philadelphia's Market Street legal corridor.

"Sit," Carlson directed me without so much as removing his eyes from his computer. His pensive stare at the flat screen monitor might have suggested that the man was reading an important e-mail concerning one of the "multi-million dollar" cases about which he frequently boasted. I could see, however, that he was surfing the internet, apparently looking at a mountain property for sale.

After two good minutes of staring at the familiar surroundings in his office, such as the plaque on his desk which read, "Lead, Follow or Get Out of the Way," various golf trophies and plaster airbrushed models of fish carcasses, I said, "Nick, you thinking about buying another place up in the mountains?"

"Shhh, hang on, gimme a second," he chided me, while placing an agitated right index finger to his lips. Due to the urgency of whatever inane message or task that he was about to communicate to me, I was glad that the case management conference didn't run especially late. Nicky needed my assistance, and he needed it right away. Time was clearly of the essence.

After another minute, Carlson shook his head in disdain at his computer screen, turned to me and made eye contact for the first time, stating,

"Take a guess what Dan McDougle is asking for his place in the Poconos? Seriously. I want *you* to tell *me* what you think his place is worth. You know where they live – a quarter-mile from Lake Majestic – three bedrooms, two and a half baths, tons of warped vinyl siding that desperately needs repair."

Considering that I had absolutely no idea who Dan McDougle was, and I was unfamiliar with the Pocono Mountains' geography and residential dwelling values, I really didn't know how to respond. Since everyone whom Carlson knew was either one of his schmuck, self-important golfing or fishing buddies, or a corporate executive whose ass he kissed in the hopes of gaining their company's legal business, I figured that McDougle fit into at least one or possibly both of those categories.

"Why are you looking at me with that blank, bemused stare? Cat got your tongue?"

"Ummm, O.K. I'll say one point four."

"Close. Not bad. He wants one point two for that piece of shit! God, what an ass. I used to play golf with him all the time when he was just a bottom of the barrel V.P. at SynergyUniverse

Pharmaceuticals. Now that he's hot shit, it's as if I don't exist. You know, he didn't even acknowledge my presence last week when I was sitting three bar stools down from him at the Lumberjack Tavern up in the mountains?"

Bingo and bango. God, was I good. It took me a little while, but I eventually got the point: McDougle had a *three* bedroom vacation house *a quarter-mile away* from Lake Majestic. Carlson had a *five* bedroom vacation house *on* Lake Majestic. Nick knew that I was aware of the specs of his house, since I had visited there on several prior occasions during the annual firm attorney retreat. Gosh, I'm no real estate analyst, but could that mean that Nick's vacation house was worth more than $1.2 million? Could it even mean that his vacation house was worth *substantially* more than $1.2 million?! Bravo, super lawyer! You have stuffed sea creatures adorning the walls of your office *and* you have a house in the mountains worth more than the GDP of some Third World countries. You must just wake up every day and have to pinch yourself to make sure that it's not all a dream. Now what do you want from me and why are you keeping me from figuring out how the Phillies scored their runs?

"Alright, here's the story," he began, as he stood up, put his hands together as if he were in a tee box and began playing air golf, "I played Wissahickon Valley today, and had an unbelievable round."

That he was wearing tan khakis and a striped golf shirt in an office full of suits and ties caused me to be not shocked when he indicated that he had hit the links earlier in the day. That he had played his round at the virtually all Jewish Wissahickon Valley Country Club was somewhat surprising. This emotion was tempered by my annoyance at his decision to, yet again, play air golf in my presence. Neither I, nor anyone else in the office deemed Carlson any more hip for swinging an imaginary golf club and staring out his window as if his ball had bounced off of the Criminal Justice Center 46 flights down and three blocks away.

"Rosenberger is really not a bad player, but I – I shot a friggin' 71 today," he enlightened me, almost with a twinge of annoyance that I hadn't cut him off mid-sentence to ask him what his score for the day was.

Now it made sense. I knew that prominent Philadelphia podiatrist, Barry Rosenberger, had retained the firm a few years ago to sue one of his former medical practice members for breach of a covenant not to compete. Carlson won the case, and with it, a multi-million dollar verdict and a shot of his ugly mug on the front of the city's daily legal bible, *The Legal Intelligencer*. Because of that great trial result, Rosenberger and many of his doctor friends were clients for life.

As for the "ugly" part about Carlson's mug, I have to admit that as much as I despised him, he wasn't ugly at all. What he lacked in size, he made up for with his bark and polished appearance. He was, objectively, a handsome man who commanded respect for his perfectly coiffed graying blond hair and his meticulously-appointed wardrobe. Those details caused him to exude a decidedly intelligent and successful glow.

In conjunction with his commitment to grooming and clothing, Nick made certain that he was never short changed because of his diminutive physical stature. Those doubting his greatness were presented with his ego wall of golf and fishing memorabilia and were often treated to discussions – or rather, soliloquies – about those hobbies. In Nick's mind, those harboring doubts as to his magnificence were easily reformed by those stimuli.

Nick continued, "While we were teeing off on 12, Barry tells me that he just got dismissed from some frivolous medical malpractice case, and he wants us to file a *Dragonetti* action against the Plaintiff and the Plaintiff's attorney. I told him that it was a slam dunk and that I would put one of my main men on the job."

He paused and smiled at me with his perfectly straight and snow white bleached choppers.

"That's you, ma' man! You ma' main man, aren't ya'?"

Managing a fake smile, pondering whether I was *one of* his main men or, rather, his *main man*, I shot back, tentatively,

"Indeed, Nick, I am your *main man*."

"Damn right! We (read: you) will mop the floor with that scumbag and his attorney."

Phew! I really was his main man.

Pennsylvania's *Dragonetti* or Wrongful Use of Civil Proceedings Act provides a legal cause of action to aggrieved parties who are successfully terminated from a lawsuit in which they have been named. In order to recover damages in a *Dragonetti* case, a party has the difficult burden of proving that the original suit was commenced and maintained without probable cause. Most frequently, *Dragonetti* cases are pursued by physicians unsuccessfully sued in medical malpractice suits.

"Here's the file. What do you think?" Carlson demanded.

After perusing the inch-thick materials for a minute or two, I was able to gather that in the case, Dr. Rosenberger had been accused of failing to diagnose a particular condition on a diabetic woman's foot which ultimately resulted in the woman being forced to undergo an amputation of the foot. It was immediately apparent to me that Dr. Rosenberger was voluntarily dismissed by the Plaintiff from the lawsuit without his insurance company having paid any consideration for the dismissal. However, it was further apparent that before the Stipulation of Voluntary Dismissal was executed, the case had survived a Motion for Summary Judgment filed by Rosenberger's insurance company-appointed counsel. This meant that the court had determined, as a matter of law, that a genuine issue of material fact existed, such that the case could proceed to a jury to determine whether or not Dr. Rosenberger was liable for malpractice.

Even more striking, the file revealed that the case had proceeded to a jury trial, which ended in a mistrial, as the result of the jury being unable to reach a verdict. The *coup de grâce* was that the Stipulation of Voluntary Dismissal was signed and filed only after the Plaintiff, disheartened at the hung jury, permanently relocated to Brazil, and as such, decided that she did not want to pursue the case any longer.

Translation: not only was the case against Rosenberger patently not frivolous, but he should have been thanking his lucky stars that this woman, whose foot he was responsible for causing to be amputated, tired of the legal process and decided to move on with her life.

"Uhh, Nick, I'm not sure how 'frivolous' this case is. In fact, I'm not sure that we can..."

"Like hell we can't! I told Rosenberger that the case was a slam dunk. Rosenberger trusts me and loves me. Why is the underlying case not frivolous? What the hell do you know? How long have you been out of law school, like, a week? Would you care to enlighten me with a few more of your pearls of wisdom?"

I presumed that my initial impressions of the case instantly relegated me back to being *one of* his main men, and that I was no longer his *main man.*

"Nick, the case survived a Motion for Summary Judgment, went to trial, the jury was hung, and the Plaintiff just dropped the case because she moved to Brazil."

Looking like a beaten man, primed to admit the error of his ways, Carlson paused for a few moments with his miniature jaw open. He abruptly snapped out of his daze and shouted,

"Well I don't give a fuck! We're dealing with Barry Fucking Rosenberger, one of my only clients who both pays me my full, undiscounted rate of $550.00 per hour and has never questioned a single one of my bills. It's because of people like him that allow your little Julie to drive her Mercedes SUV. You say the case ain't frivolous. I say, get your ass in your office, close the door, open that Ivy League brain of yours and think of a brilliantly creative way to make it frivolous. *Comprende?*"

"Yeah, Nick, I understand. I'll get to work."

"Hey, A.B., while you're *getting to work,* why don't you also *get to work* on bringing in some of your own business to this firm? I've been meaning to talk to you about this for a long time. Any trained monkey can write a brief or do the song and dance in front of some dumb ass jury. If you really want to be valuable to this firm, you're going to have to build your own book of business – do you catch my drift?"

"I've got a few things in the pipeline, Nick – it's just that..."

"You just keep tellin' yourself that, kiddo."

Kiddo?

"With that attitude, you'll be making the kind of money that Julie makes now, in, well," Carlson said mockingly, while looking at the ceiling, "I'm not too good at math, but, I'd say you're on pace to catch up with her current salary in about seven years. How does that make you feel as a man?"

It made me feel like grabbing the fishing reel on his desk that he used as a paperweight and bludgeoning his face with it.

"Not so great, Nick. I guess that I've got some room for improvement."

"Well, Alex, I'm glad that you agree."

Was he going to can me right there?

"I'm sorry?"

"The firm's Partners – we also see a great deal of room for improvement from you. And with the economy, and all, we're just not going to be able to give you the same raise and bonus this year."

"Nick, I'm a little confused. I know for a fact that I had the highest billable hour total of any Associate this past year – that means that I made more money for the firm than any of your other employees."

"Whoa, whoa, whoa, don't get so defensive there, Tex. Last time I checked, this was a team – and I expect you to be a team player. That means taking one for the team when the team's on a five game losing streak. Do you see what I'm saying."

I saw exactly what he was saying. Irrespective of my job performance, in light of the sluggish legal employment market, they were banking on their slighted Associates not finding employment elsewhere.

What's the difference about a smaller bonus and raise? I was pretty certain that my financial institutions would understand when I asked them if I could decrease my monthly mortgage, car lease and student loan payments. Plus, I wasn't in it for the money. I was in it for my lifelong idealistic goal of padding the bank accounts of fat cat law firm partners.

"Yeah, Nick, I see what you're saying."

"Good. You know why I love you, A.B.?"

I'm waiting with baited breath. Please tell me, Nick.

"Because I know that when I see you next, you will have a shit eating grin on your face, telling me the most brilliant theory in the world as to how we can overcome the slight difficulties presented by the factual scenario in Rosenberger's case. By the time you're done, I'll be fully convinced that Rosenberger stands to make millions off of this suit.

"By the way, since I'm trying to build up my corporate practice and distance myself from this lower end – I mean – individual client stuff, don't put my name on the pleading – just put yours." (Read: "Alex, when the attorney whom you sue is so repulsed that he elects to make it his life goal, henceforth, to ruin the legal career of the person who sued him, that person will be you and not me. Since I sign your paycheck, you really shouldn't have a problem with this prospect.")

As if in full agreement with everything in his statement, I nodded, smiled and said, "Will do, Nick, I'm all over it."

God, was I a pussy. Anything for money, Alex, anything for money.

"Well, O.K., then – off you go!"

CHAPTER TWO

"Off you go!" was Carlson's patented and most frequently used method of telling units subservient to him that he was done with them for the time being and that they should leave his office right away. When he uttered those words, it was usually done in a tongue in cheek manner, so as to sound like a 19th century British schoolmaster. Most of my fellow Associates, although as sensitive to Nick's idiosyncrasies as I, were generally not similarly offended by the "Off you go!" that followed almost every interaction with him.

What struck a chord with me about Carlson's use of that term was rooted in the fact that from kindergarten through 12th grade, I attended the ultra-prestigious Presbyterian Academy in Philadelphia's upper-crust suburbs known as the Main Line. "Presbyterian," since its founding in 1795, has, without interruption, been known as *the* finest preparatory school in the Greater Philadelphia region, and one of the finest in the country. Presbyterian's student body has always been comprised of the children of the most prominent physicians, lawyers, and business magnates in the city. In recent times, Presbyterian became the "in" school for Philadelphia's professional athletes to send their children.

Some of its faculty were from the British Isles. I suppose that their learned accents caused the school's paying clientele to feel as if they were getting value for their 15,000 1980s and 1990s dollars.

My colleagues and I always got a rise out of the foreign intricacies of the Queen's English. "Off you go, then" was one of the most ubiquitous such phrases employed by our British teachers. It seemingly had an infinite number of meanings and projected authority, intellect and arrogance – three of the virtues that Americans of any age love and expect of the British.

My teachers said, "Off you go!" in proper context, and because of their British heritage, were, in my view, permitted to do so. When Carlson said, "Off you go!" he meant it in a demeaning way, perhaps fancying himself as a British schoolmaster. Carlson, though, wasn't a British schoolmaster. He was an American douche bag.

In other words, I was intimately familiar with the genuine article, and Nick Carlson was a far cry, intellectually and socially, from the genuine article. My knowledge of such highbrow existence, though, was not rooted in generations of privilege.

During my kindergarten to 12th grade term of 1981 to 1994 at Presbyterian, compared to my classmates, I was disadvantaged. I had no trust fund, and my father had started his restaurant supply business from the ground-up, without the use of the omnipresent "family money" that nearly all Presbyterian Academy families had at their disposal. In fact, until I graduated from the University of Pennsylvania after my Presbyterian career, no member of my family had graduated college. While at Presbyterian, I actively concealed this fact from my colleagues, for fear that they would relegate me to an even lower caste than the one in which I was placed from being a Jew at a blue blooded white Anglo-Saxon Protestant institution.

As a youngster in grade school at Presbyterian, I took a lot of heat for being Jewish. I initially never understood how my classmates knew that I was Jewish. My name, Alexander Phillip Brown, was hardly Jewish-sounding, and my physical appearance, or so I was told, was decidedly non-Jewish, and almost *goy*-esque. I had straight dirty blond hair, and my nose, although not quite turned up like many of my Mayflower descendent classmates, was not typically Jewish looking. As for standing out in the locker room, I was born in 1975. At that time, the overwhelming majority of American male babies born near large cities were being circumcised. In fact, the only classmate of mine who stood out in the locker room was Pieter Van der Meer, who was born in Holland, and moved to the States as a toddler. The fact that he *wasn't* circumcised subjected him to much ridicule from his Presbyterian Academy colleagues.

During my thirteen years at Presbyterian, while my classmates progressively acclimated themselves to me and my alternate and foreign background, I too acclimated myself to their way of life, tendencies and values. Having been immersed amongst Christians for such a long period of time, I ultimately reached a point where I felt more comfortable in the school's chapel than I did in my own synagogue. This fact never seemed odd to me since, throughout my childhood, I attended synagogue services exactly twice per year, on the high holidays of Rosh Hashanah and Yom Kippur. As a student at Presbyterian, I attended chapel services three times per week, and eventually grew fond of them, committing most of the hymns that we sung to memory. I took a particular liking to the Lord's Prayer, which, without a single mention of "Jesus," "Christ," or "Jesus Christ," I considered to be a very neutral blessing that could be savored by God-fearing people of any faith.

Being socialized solely amongst Christians, once puberty arrived, I became attracted to young ladies who were Christian, rather than Jewish. In fact, since virtually every one of my girlfriends during my time at Presbyterian, and later at the University of Pennsylvania and Villanova Law School was Christian, my parents could not possibly have been surprised when I chose to spend the rest of my life with a fiery and sexy brunette law school colleague named Julianna D'Amico.

CHAPTER THREE

Carlson's comments to me about my "little Julie," her "Mercedes SUV," and the allusions to her salary resounded in my head as I set out upon my trip home to the remote Brandywine County suburbs.

I had grown to enjoy the commute, which, at roughly 45 minutes, was moderately long by Philadelphia standards. The ride in my BMW 5-Series gave me a chance to decompress from work and listen to the radio. On this evening, however, I was unable to put my workday behind me, and could not get Carlson's comments out of my head.

My wife was obviously a hot piece of ass that any sex-deprived middle-aged partner in a law firm would kill to even see in a bikini, but it seemed a tad creepy that he was referencing Julie by name and knew that she drove a Mercedes SUV. I neither concealed my wife's name, nor the type of car that she drove, but unlike my relationship with some of the firm's other Partners, my relationship with Nick was not one in which we referred to each other's wives by name or discussed the cars that they drove.

I was not ignorant to the fact that the Partners gossiped amongst each other. In all likelihood, some of the mid-level Partners figured out that my family's gross income was greater than theirs. Since most of the Partners' wives did not work, and Julie practiced in the Wilmington, Delaware office of one of the nation's largest and highest paying firms, Cartwright Stanley, the math was quite easy: add my salary to her salary. As the mega firms such as Cartwright Stanley proudly published on their websites their Associates' salaries, by level of experience, the partners at my firm could decipher, virtually to the dollar, how much money we grossed per year.

Nevertheless, the statement didn't sit well and left me puzzled. Was he saying that a 31-year old didn't deserve to drive a Mercedes? Was he saying that a woman didn't deserve to drive a Mercedes? Was he saying that if I didn't win the case for his jackass client, he would romance my "little Julie" and have his way with her in the back of her Mercedes? I wasn't going to sleep well.

Just as I prepared to merge onto the Interstate towards home, my cell phone rang. The caller ID revealed that it was Vinny Lubrano, a former classmate from Presbyterian, who called me four times per year, invariably when all of his single friends were occupied and he needed a wingman with a heartbeat to aid his never-ending quest for bimbos.

"Hello?"

"Shalom! How's my favorite Hebrew. Oh, wait a minute – I forgot – I don't like *any* Hebrews. Anyway, what's up, you fuckin' *schvartze*, why haven't you called me in, like, a year?"

"Hmmm…maybe it's because I'm a Hebrew and you don't like us."

"Dude, who pissed on your latkes? I was just kidding. I'm at the Capital Grille – why don't you meet me here? If this place is anything like it was last night, there will be chock full o' sluts with huge knishes, if you know what I mean."

Although he wasn't going to find the cure for cancer, or design NASA's next space vehicle, Vinny always found a way to be able to cleverly insult a person of any race, creed, religion or national origin in such a manner that left the recipient humored, rather than offended. In this particular instance, I had to laugh at hearing the word, "*schvartze*" come out of a Roman Catholic Italian-American's mouth. "*Schvartze*," derived from the Yiddish word for "black," is an extremely derogatory term used by some American Jews to refer to individuals of sub-Saharan African descent.

Vinny was the heir apparent to the Lubrano Concrete dynasty. Lubrano Concrete was, by far, the largest concrete construction outfit in the Philadelphia region, which included the Philadelphia five-county surrounding area, South Jersey and Northern Delaware. Lubrano Concrete constructed the overwhelming majority of concrete high rise projects in the area.

Due to the inherent delays and weather problems affecting the construction of high rise buildings, Lubrano Concrete was involved in a huge amount of litigation. I had been trying to get their business for years. I tended to subconsciously temper my efforts, though, due to Vinny's abrasive personality.

"Vinny, tonight is not the night for this. I have a dickhead partner in my office who thinks that I'm his bitch. I'm going home and drinking a bottle of wine."

"That is the most asinine thing I've ever heard you say. Do you know how many bottles of wine I have in my locker at 'The Grille?' You're coming over. You can cry on my shoulder, or in your wine, I don't give a shit. I'll even listen to your nonsense, if you would just come over and watch me get some ass."

"I wish that I could, but I've had a shit day, a shit week, and it seems as if I haven't seen my wife and kid for a month. I need to go home. Let's do it next week, or something. Sorry."

"Listen to me – your wife is a *paisan*, like me. Julie friggin' loves me. Just tell her that you're going out with me and she'll understand."

Lubrano had a point. Although Julie did not care for many of my school friends, she had a warm place in her heart for Vinny. He was very handsome, had more than a passing resemblance to George Clooney, and was charming and complimentary to her without being offensive.

"Yes, Julie thinks the world of you, and I'm happy about that – we've been through this a million times. Tonight is just not the night."

"You know, you really know how to rain on someone's parade. I wanted to invite you to the Grille to tell you that I'm hiring you to work on a new case that I have. All of those fuckin' Chanukah cards and stupid leather portfolios with your firm name on them have finally paid off. Well, since you don't want to come to the Grille, maybe I'll ask Kelli to get me the Yellow Pages, so that I can look up an attorney to hire who actually understands the meaning of client entertainment."

By "Chanukah cards," Lubrano was referring to the neutral "Happy Holidays" cards that my firm sent out to current and prospective clients each year. Since the words, "Merry Christmas" did not appear on them, Lubrano apparently deemed them as being celebratory of the Festival of Lights.

If he was serious about my representing his company, this was to be a career- changing event.

"Are you messing with me? Because if you are, I'll never forgive you."

"Come to the Capital Grille and I'll tell you about the case – we want to move on this right away."

"I'll be there in fifteen minutes."

With that, I exited the Interstate. I drove up Packer Avenue fourteen blocks, made a right on Broad Street, and headed towards City Hall with its ancient glowing yellow clock that had come to symbolize the city. In no time, I pulled up to the Capital Grille's valet area at the intersection of Broad and Chestnut Streets. If Lubrano was not pulling my leg, when I reclaimed my car later in the evening, I would be a real lawyer, instead of somebody's whipping boy. Or, so I thought.

CHAPTER FOUR

Philadelphia is a city of many, many wonderful local restaurants. From South Philadelphia's Italian red sauce joints to Rittenhouse Square's upscale bistros to Old City's trendy club-like resto-bars, one needed never look far to find a homegrown masterpiece of a restaurant.

With such wonderful domestic product, it is surprising and somewhat saddening that the best professional bar scene is at the Capital Grille, an upscale chain steakhouse on Broad Street. Literally in the shadow of Philadelphia's massive ancient, Second Empire style City Hall fortress, the Capital Grille sits in the heart of Center City's legal district. While some cities such as New York and Boston have financial districts, Philadelphia has a legal district. It is a city of lawyers, legal staff and vendors providing legal support services.

From five-thirty forward on any given weekday, the mahogany and brass bar was a virtual Who's Who of the Philadelphia legal community. Successful and unsuccessful personal injury lawyers, commercial litigators and transactional attorneys could be found there. Members of the state and federal trial and appellate bench could also be spotted at the bar. It was where lawyers brought clients to entertain them. It was also where sleezeball married attorneys took their young and attractive secretaries and paralegals, so that they could sexually harass them out of the office environment.

Lubrano was a virtual barfly at the Capital Grille. In the absence of a wife or live-in girlfriend at home, the Capital Grille, with its $49.00 Dry Aged Sirloin and $12.00 martinis, served as Lubrano's *de facto* personal caterer. Lubrano, who affectionately referred to himself as a "construction guy" (in Philadelphia-speak, a "cunn-shtruk-shin" guy) didn't exactly fit in with the typical demographic of the Grille. He didn't exactly *not* fit in, though. Individuals who pulled up to the valet stand in a Porsche or Ferrari as Lubrano usually did, did not generally encounter being denied service at this lawyer haven.

Entering the Capital Grille on a weekday evening was always an overwhelming proposition for me. It beckoned its guests through a revolving glass door. The door, a leftover from a bank which previously occupied the space, completely clashed with the stodgy atmosphere inside. Prior to reaching the revolving door, patrons were led into an enclosed foyer in which complete silence existed. Although this chamber was devoid of any sound, guests could peer through the door and see what was about to hit them.

On this night, similar to any of my other prior visits to the Capital Grille, as the revolving door opened into the restaurant, my eardrums encountered extreme shock in being transferred from an environment of total silence to an expansive hall of a hundred alcohol-affected shouting voices.

As an attractive and demure wavy red haired hostess with a name tag reading "Kelli" prepared to welcome me, Lubrano, spotting me from his catbird seat at the end of the bar, shouted, so that everyone in the bar could hear him,

"What took you so fuckin' long? That's the problem with you hourly-paid sons of bitches. You're never in a rush to get anywhere."

As usual, Lubrano was flanked on either side by a platinum blonde and a dark haired floozy. In this instance, his female companions appeared to have arrived at the Grille in a Mustang or Nissan ZX with the pale yellow license plates from the Garden State. While I hadn't seen their vehicles or yet heard a peep out of their mouths, I would have bet one of my pinkies that these young ladies hailed from either Cherry Hill or Marlton, New Jersey. Their nappy curly hair, combined with their obviously surgically enhanced breasts and gum chewing dictated that they could be from nowhere else.

"Sorry that it took me a full twelve minutes to get here from the time that you called. Due to the record-setting murder rate in the city, I've really been having a tough time getting the Philly cops to divert their resources to give me police escorts to bars and restaurants. It's such a bummer."

"Oh, *git ale-t*! You get police escorts?! That's fuckin' awesome! Are you, like one-uh-them dis-trick attorneys?" the blonde bimbo inquired.

Residents of Southern New Jersey have some of the finest and most recognizable Philadelphia accents. Distinct from other blue-collar accents of South Philadelphia, Northeast Philadelphia and Eastern Brandywine County, the South Jersey accent is truly a gem. I could be in any corner of the world and hear two words out of a South Jersey resident's mouth and be able to decipher that they hailed from east of the Delaware River.

One of the most common expressions uttered by working class Philadelphians is, "get out," a contracted form of "get out of here." To the untrained ear, the phrase sounds like, "*git ale-t*." Just as Brooklyn has "*fughetaboudit*," the Philadelphia area has "*git ale-t*." The phrase has multiple meanings and connotations and can be used in any season or setting.

For example, two forty year-old neighbors speaking about how one of the husbands on the block was caught sleeping with the babysitter: "Oh, *git ale-t!* I always knew that Mike was a pig! Tina cooks, cleans, goes to aerobics class and don't eat nothin' but *sale-itt* (salad), so she can stay in shape for him, and this is how he repays her?"

Or, the phrase can be used in a joyous, exclamatory scenario, such as, "You're havin' a party for the *Iggles* (Eagles) playoff game this weekend? Oh, *git ale-t!* We'll definitely come over. I'll paint the kids' faces green and bring my seven-layer bean dip. Do you think I should put green food coloring in it?"

Alternatively, one can use the phrase to connote a somber stance, e.g., "Kevin's father died? *Git ale-t!* That's a *senn!* (sin) It's probably a blessing, though, he was so sick for so many years."

In this case, the young lady was simply expressing shock that an acquaintance of her gentleman caller had enough clout as to be afforded a police escort when an emergency potential client representation opportunity presented itself.

"Honey, baby, do me a favor and stick to the Ketel One and Tonic, O.K.? He's not famous. He's my Jew *consigliere*, and anything that we say about you guys is subject to the attorney-client privilege, so you better be good. Why don't you go check on our table?" Lubrano ordered, obviously unaware of the meaning of attorney-client privilege.

"Aren't you going to introduce us to your friend?", asked the other young lady.

"Alex, this is..."

The first bimbo interrupted, "I'm Crystal, and this is my girlfriend, *Ale-eey* (Ali)."

"Oh, *git ale-t! Ale-ixx and Ale-eey!* I think that we're gonna hit it off," the police escort girl interjected.

Just for kicks, I asked, "what part of Jersey are you guys from, Cherry Hill?"

Ali responded, without hesitation, "I'm from Mount Laurel, but Crystal is from Cherry Hill. How'd you know?"

Lying through my teeth, I responded, "I've got lots of relatives from Cherry Hill and I recognized the accent."

"Oh, *git-ale-t!* Did they go to high school at Cherry Hill East or West?"

Visibly agitated, Lubrano directed, "Enough with the chitchat! Check if the damn table is ready – I'm dying of hunger."

As Team New Jersey bounced away in their painted-on cocktail dresses, Lubrano grabbed my arm and demanded, "Why are you fucking with them? They're going to catch on. You're a Main Line Jew – they know that neither you nor any of your extended family would ever set foot in New Jersey, other than to get cheap full service gasoline."

"Vinny, I'll shut up, but you're grossly overestimating the intelligence of these women."

"Whatever, dude. I banged the shit out of them last Thursday, and you'll be happy to know that they passed both of the Lubrano compatibility tests with flying colors."

That Vinny had engaged in intercourse with two women simultaneously was far from front-page news. In fact, his stories of sex with *multiple* partners were more the norm than the exception. I was so desensitized to these conquest stories that I seldom experienced even a ping of jealousy when hearing about the acts in which no self-respecting suburban wife would engage. As for his "compatibility tests," they were quite simple: fake knockers and no pubic hair. If an attractive woman with an IQ of below 70 possessed those two attributes, she had a fighting chance at landing one of Philadelphia's wealthiest and best looking bachelors for the evening.

Gazing towards the hostess stand, I observed Crystal motioning us over us over with her right index finger while contorting her body in such a manner that her manufactured cleavage became accentuated. While Lubrano was not the type of person who would immediately move when gestured by a woman, for him, food took precedence over the need to play hard-to-get mating rituals. As such, he promptly directed that the bar tab be transferred to the dinner bill and pushed me with both hands toward the hostess stand.

When we arrived, Vinny kissed Kelli on an area of her face that was not quite her lips, but not quite her cheek, either. After the exchange, he said, "Kelli, sweetie, tell my Jewish friend that if I weren't such a high roller here, you would have given our reservation away a half hour ago."

Genuinely charmed by this buffoon, she responded, "That is true, you do come here quite a bit and the staff only has complimentary things to say about you."

"That's what I thought. How's the porterhouse tonight?"

As if a) it were different from any other night, or b) she knew. The woman was paid to look sexy, smile and record the names of patrons who wanted to eat dinner, in that order.

"The chef told me that it's superb tonight."

"Alright – I'll hold you to that. I'm gonna have a three pound lobster, too. I'll talk to you after dinner."

On the way to the table, walking past the mahogany wine lockers, Ali contributed, "That hostess is such a friggin' tramp. She shouldn't be flirtin' wit' the guests. Like, she's a restaurant hostess for a living. None of the successful businessmen who come here would ever consider hookin' up wit' her."

Having known Ali and her sidekick for all of seven minutes, I couldn't say for certain that she wasn't in Forbes Magazine's *World's 100 Most Powerful Women* list, but I might have been inclined to bet against it. In fact, the odds were pretty good that Ali's pocketbook and necklace, bearing the Gucci and Tiffany & Co. logos, respectively, were purchased with either a revolving credit line with a balance in excess of $10,000.00, or by a married Plaintiff's attorney in his late 40s, eager to compensate the young New Jerseyan for sexual favors. Unlike Kelli, who worked for a living, I strongly suspected that Ali spent her days waking up at mens' houses or hotel rooms at 11 a.m., going to the tanning salon, reading celebrity gossip magazines and shopping on the internet with money that she didn't have.

Once we sat down at the table, Vinny immediately summoned our server. "Darrell, here's what we're gonna do: I wanna do two crabmeat cocktails for the table. Give us the clams casino. You got Blue Point oysters tonight?" Darrell enthusiastically nodded, while penciling down Vinny's directives. "Good. Bring us an order of them. Bring the gals a couple of those salads that you make, and what else do we need to start with?"

"Mr. Lubrano, last week, you enjoyed our jumbo prawn cocktail."

"O.K.. Bring us two of those, but do me a favor – call them 'shrimp' next time. I come here enough that you don't have to blow smoke up my ass. We're gonna do a bottle of *Voove*, also. Just get it out of my wine locker – you know where it is. Bring my friend a bottle of Manischewitz, while you're at it."

"Mr. Lubrano, I'll have to talk to the sommelier, but I'm not sure that we have that wine…it *is* a wine, isn't it?"

"Darrell, Darrell, Darrell! I know that you're an African American, but you mean to tell me that you've never heard of the finest Jewish wine in the world? It tastes like a combination of cough syrup and dogshit – I think that you'd like it."

Darrell politely laughed, likely saying to himself, "You piece of garbage. If you weren't a 25% tipper, I would tell you to piss off."

"I'm messing with you! Just bring us the apps and the *Voove*, then we'll talk about steaks and lobsters after that."

When the word first came out of his mouth, I wasn't quite certain to what he was referring. The second time around, however, I knew exactly what he was trying to say. He wanted a bottle of Veuve Cliquot champagne. As someone who had spent a considerable portion of his life in France, hearing his tortured pronunciation of the brand made my stomach turn. Even though I would ordinarily correct someone who so butchered the French language, Lubrano had a fragile ego. One comment taken the wrong way could cause him to change his mind about giving business to my firm.

"So, what's up, *consigliere*? Did I interrupt your evening of ambulance chasing by asking you to break bread with me and two smokin' hot girls?"

They giggled in unison and Crystal sarcastically pled, "Oh stop it – we're not *just* 'smokin' hot.' Ali has her dental hygienist certificate and I'm going to paralegal school next year. Also, I'm not sure if I ever told you this, but the Dean of Princeton Law School was, like, practically begging me to apply. I was like, 'why would I go to law school and become a lawyer when I can make, like, basically the same amount of money as a paralegal or a court reporter.'"

There were so many things wrong with Crystal's statement that instead of responding, in the hope of numbing my agitation, I chugged, in one gulp, the flute of Veuve Cliquot that Darrell had just poured for me.

While Lubrano and his unrefined union labor minions might have found these two artificially bronzed, surgically enhanced hussies attractive, I did not. In fact, their sheer existence was already appalling to me. Moreover, since Princeton does not have a law school, I seriously doubted whether anything that came out of their mouths was even remotely rooted in fact. It wasn't that I *completely* doubted the veracity of Crystal's statement – I'm sure that there was some truth to it. For example, she probably gave oral sex to a Rutgers University professor at some point, who, in an attempt to stroke her ego, probably told her that she was so bright that she should consider applying to law school.

After politely informing Vinny that I could hardly be classified as an "ambulance chaser," since my practice was generally limited to high exposure complex commercial litigation, he responded, "Relax! You've been nothing but a stick in the mud since you walked in here." Now whispering, he added, "You're putting the girls on edge. Let them say their stupid shit. Just don't pay attention to them. If your *addytood* keeps me from getting laid tonight, you'll never get any legal work from me."

"Alright, fine, I'll be nice." I said. "So what is this case about?"

"My dad and I will make an appointment and come see you in your office this week, but in a nutshell, our lumber subcontractor on the Breezeview Plaza job fucked us big time. They've constantly delivered late to the site, and half the time, the wood is not up to snuff to use for concrete forms. Long story short, their lateness and other fuck-ups caused us to be unable to meet the general contractor's deadlines, and we've been penalized by the g.c. to the tune of $1.9 million. So, to make up for that, we've backcharged the lumber sub $1.9 million, and have obviously refused to pay them the $1.2 million that they say we owe them. So, I want to sue them in Brandywine County before they sue us", he said, slurping two Tabasco and horseradish laden oysters back to back, not once taking his eyes off of the bounty of food before him.

"Normally, we wouldn't backcharge one of our suppliers so much money. There are only so many lumber suppliers out there, and we need people to work with us in the future. We're not going to let these pricks do it this time, though. They fucked up too bad on this job and I don't like their fuckin' *addytoods.*"

Hearing Lubrano's pronunciation of "attitudes," while using my silicone princess tablemates' accents as a reference, reminded me of how atypical he was during his time at Presbyterian. Although he grew up in Gladwyne, the most posh of all Philadelphia suburbs, at heart, he was a pizza sauce-stained "wife beater" undershirt-wearing *goomba* from South Philly.

Vincent Lubrano, Sr., who went by "Vince" had hit the big time with his construction business and moved the family to the Main Line around the time that Vinny and I entered kindergarten at Presbyterian together. Despite spending his entire pre-collegiate academic career at such a bastion of upper crust, blue blood, white bread Protestantism, Vinny was fundamentally a South Philly city kid, who, in spite of his good looks which made him popular with the ladies from his adolescent years forward, never truly fit in at that institution.

"Hmmm, that sounds like an interesting case. Why do you want to file suit in Brandywine County? The job was in Philly."

"Because the lumber company is from Brandywine County, and we've run out of judges in Philly and Winslow County. They don't play ball anymore – it's not like the old days. They're all prejudiced against us and make us lose every case."

The prospect that the Lubranos had "run out of judges" in Philadelphia County, where 72 judges are on the bench and in Winslow County, where 26 judges are on the bench, was a disturbing statement. If they had fallen out of favor with all or many of those judges, I wasn't so sure that anything that I could do could help them.

Even more disturbing was the "play ball" comment. What did he mean by that? Was he suggesting that Lubrano Concrete had previously coaxed judges into ruling a certain way? The comment did not sit well with me. Although I had heard myths about particular judges who had it out for a specific attorney or party, I was pretty sure that it was impossible for an entire county bench to collectively disfavor one attorney or party.

Nevertheless, under the state court venue rules, suit could properly be filed in Brandywine County, but it seemed extremely illogical to sue a Brandywine County Defendant on its home turf, when at least two alternate venues were available. To that end, I suggested,

"Brandywine County would be a God-awful venue for you. They do not take kindly to foreign businesses or individuals. And yes, even though your main office in Winslow County sits about fifteen minutes by car from the Brandywine County Courthouse in Weston, you are as much of a foreigner there as someone from Nepal. I think that the first thing that we should be doing is to..."

"What did I just tell you? We'll talk about this when my dad and I come to your office."

With that, my cell phone vibrated and its display revealed an incoming call from Julie. I excused myself to the men's room and took the call.

Cutting to the chase, Julie asked, "How's your dinner? Did you get Vinny to sign a fee agreement yet? Don't take any retainer less than $15,000.00, or your firm will end up getting stiffed. When are you going to be home? You are aware that you have a wife and child, right?"

"Julie, I'm here on business. Trust me, I would much rather be with you and Charlie, rather than with this idiot and his harem..."

From time to time in a man's life, as words are leaving his mouth, he immediately regrets uttering them and would give anything to be able to immediately retract them. This was one such occasion. Although Julie was not the jealous type, she would definitely pounce on this opportunity.

Laughing, she continued her cross-examination, "Oh, I see, so the two of you have *women* there. Well, that certainly alters things a bit. I apologize – I take back what I said earlier about how you should be home with Charlie and me. I wouldn't want you to squander this opportunity. So take your time, enjoy your steak and expensive wine and I'll wait up for you. Only problem is that it's getting a tad chilly in the house, so I'll have another layer of clothes on when you get home – probably one of your heavy sweatsuits. In case you're interested, I'm not wearing anything right now, so I guess that you're missing out. Listen honey, I don't want to keep you from your...what did you call them, your harem? Where are they from anyway? Jersey or Northeast Philly? Did you bring condoms? If we're going to have one or more additional women in our marriage, I'd kind of like to not get herpes, gonorrhea, or worse, so make that sure you double bag it, O.K.?"

"Julie, please don't do this to me. I'm struggling right now and you're not helping things. Do you honestly think that I want to be here? I'll be home at about 10:30 p.m. Don't wait up."

Once again laughing, this time, more sardonically, "Honeybuns, I don't think that you'll have to worry about that tonight. I'll be deep into a dream about the Neiman Marcus handbag department in fifteen minutes. Nightie night!"

As she hung up, I felt a sharp pain strike me between the eyes, signifying the beginning of an intense alcohol-assisted headache. I was going to be in trouble for doing absolutely nothing wrong. I had to deal with Lubrano's idiotic antics in the hope of getting his business, and now Julie was on my case. Didn't she realize that if I landed Lubrano Concrete, I would be well on my way to making enough money where she could "retire," and care for Charlie and any other children that we had down the road? I splashed some water in my face, ran my hands through my hair and returned to the table.

"Were you giving birth in there?" Lubrano demanded.

"The little lady ain't happy, Vinny," I responded.

"Let's take a walk."

As we walked to the front door, he began, "Listen, I feel for you. I shouldn't have brought you here tonight. Why don't you take off and we'll talk later this week. You're seriously cramping my style and are preventing me from working my mojo with the girls. So, I'm gonna let you off the hook. Go home to your wife and I'll be in touch."

I shook Vinny's hand and walked out the revolving door, hoping that I hadn't blown my chance to represent Lubrano Concrete and jump start my career.

CHAPTER FIVE

On my way home from the Capital Grille, I attempted to call Julie to let her know that I would be arriving earlier than expected. When she did not answer, I figured that she was on the phone with her mother discussing a shopping emergency, and therefore could not be bothered by having to answer the "call waiting" beep. Such emergencies apparently occurred with great frequency on Long Island. Whether it was a major sale at Fortunoff's or the opening of a new store at the Riverhead outlet mall, shopping emergencies trumped most other things, and, most assuredly, a telephone call from a husband.

Immediately after leaving a message for Julie, I received a call from my college freshman year roommate, Eric Markowitz.

Since he was practicing medicine in suburban Pittsburgh, I seldom saw him anymore. We spoke on the phone about four times per year, usually to discuss a Flyers' trade or free agent signing. With the benefit of caller I.D., upon answering the phone, I demanded, "Don't tell me that we got Peter Forsberg back!"

"No, not quite..."

"Tell me that they got Rod Brind'Amour back!"

"I've got better news, actually."

"You tell me your good news, but after you do so, I'm gonna tell you even better news."

"Well, I doubt that, but here goes: Rachael is three months pregnant."

"Mazel Tov! I'm so happy for you," I said.

"Yeah, I kind of figured that you would be – you're the first person other than my parents whom I've called."

"You cut me off. What I was going to say is that – well, don't get me wrong, I'm happy for Rachael – I know how much she wanted to be a mom, but I'm really happy for you, in particular."

In typical dry, devoid of sense of humor doctor fashion, he responded, annoyed, "Uhh…I don't understand, we're having this baby together, why wouldn't you be happy for Rach, too?"

"Can you please hear me out, instead of jumping all over me, like you've been doing since freshman year? What I was going to say before you so rudely interrupted was that I would like to congratulate *you* for finally finding your dick. I know that you tried hard to find it during your four years at Penn, but those bio and organic chemistry lectures got in the way. This is a tremendous development for you. Do you guys know who the father is, yet? If you're stumped, I could probably think of five or six…well, seven or eight guys who might be candidates."

Once again, in textbook doctor style, Eric added,

"Do you understand that what you have just said makes no sense? You're congratulating me for 'finding my dick,' and have therefore, at least implicitly, acknowledged that it was I who impregnated my wife. Then, you proceed to ask me if we know who the father is. Those two statements run precisely contrary to one another. Let me ask you this: how did you pass the bar exam? Forget that, I'll go you one better – how did you even get into Penn?"

"Oh, I guess you're right. I hereby retract the second comment. I was just being a jerk. I'm glad that you finally found your dick. Period. Is that better?"

"Much better, now what's your good news?"

"I'm suing a lawyer on behalf of a doctor who was supposedly wrongfully sued."

"Not many things could be better news for me than my wife being pregnant with our first child, but what you just said fits into that small category. Tell me the details – I love it."

Eric was probably only half kidding. Everything that he had done in life up to and including the present, was aimed at becoming a wealthy physician. Due to a recent nationwide explosion of off the chart verdicts in medical malpractice cases, liability insurance was more expensive than ever for doctors to maintain. In many states, including Pennsylvania, doctors were faced with the prospect of not being able to operate an adequately profitable practice in light of rising insurance premiums and sometimes felt compelled to move their practices to other states. Eric resented the fact that he might have to move to another state in which to practice if he was to earn the high income for which he worked so hard.

"My firm represents Barry Rosenberger's practice..."

So as to carry out the American Jewish tradition of claiming to know every other Jew this side of Tel Aviv, Eric interposed, "Sure, I know Barry, he's a great guy. Proctologist out of Jefferson Hospital, right? My dad used to play tennis with him."

"Actually, he's a podiatrist out of Pennsylvania Hospital, and he doesn't play tennis, he plays golf. But what's the difference, colons – feet, it's basically six of one, a half-dozen of the other."

Trying to save face for losing this game of Jewish geography, Eric asked, half befuddled, half annoyed, "You might want to check on that, I'm not so sure."

"O.K., I'll call him right after I'm done with you and ask him to check his Board certification diploma, to see whether he may have forgotten what his specialty is. You're right, it's probably easy for doctors to forget whether they spend their days examining bunions or sticking their fingers up peoples' asses," I added, antagonistically.

"In any case, here's the deal: Rosenberger got sued for malpractice after he allegedly failed to diagnose a condition that caused a woman's foot to be amputated. After the case proceeded to a trial which resulted in a hung jury, the Plaintiff decides to up and move to Brazil, effectively giving up on the case. After she moved, she authorized her attorney to voluntarily dismiss the case. Oh, and here's the kicker: before the case went to trial, Rosenberger's attorneys filed a Motion for Summary Judgment which was denied. This means that the court determined, as a matter of law, that there was a material issue of fact for the jury to determine at trial. Translation: the underlying case was, almost by definition, not frivolous. Yet, this jackass partner in my firm is insisting that I sue both the Plaintiff's attorney and the Plaintiff from the underlying case."

"That's so funny – my dad is starting a new prepaid legal defense program for doctors, and he's looking for a firm to work with. I would have mentioned your name to him, but I didn't know that you handled cases involving docs."

Eric's father was the venerable, Dr. Sanford Markowitz. "Sandy," as he was known amongst his fortunate inner circle, was one bad Heeb. Using the small fortune that he had accumulated by being the only cardiologist within a 20-mile radius in a remote area of Berks County, Pennsylvania, Sandy had realized a large fortune in the real estate world. He eventually came to own half of the county. With his white balding comb-over hairstyle, a Cuban cigar perpetually emanating from his scowling mouth, a pinky ring on either hand, and gold-rimmed prescription sunglasses that he wore indoors and outdoors, the man simply projected an air of arrogant wealth.

Reluctantly, I suggested, "Interesting, tell me more."

"It's pretty simple. Every doctor whom he knows is fed up with the insurance company attorneys who are appointed when they get sued. The insurance companies hire cheap attorneys and they end up settling even the most frivolous of cases, so as to prevent runaway juries. The result is that the insurance companies penalize the doctor, regardless of whether the case had merit. The doctor is either assessed a huge increase in his malpractice insurance premium, or has his coverage dropped altogether. Basically, since those shitbag attorneys work for the insurance companies, they serve their interests, instead of the interests of the doctors. Also, they're getting paid hourly and not based upon the result of the case, so they have no incentive to push for a case to be dismissed, even if that case is frivolous. Hell, the insurance company attorneys *want* the case to go all the way to trial, so that they can make the most possible money."

"Tell me something that I don't already know."

"Here's how it works: each subscriber pays $2,500.00 per year. If they're sued, they get the services of a competent attorney who isn't captive to the whims of the insurance company."

After having heard Eric's summary of what I had expected to be a cockamamie scheme, I was quite pleasantly surprised. While I knew that Sandy had excelled in the real estate arena, his track record in other entrepreneurial fields was not quite as remarkable. The last time that I had sat down with Sandy was at Eric's 30th birthday party, a year or so prior. At that time, he had bragged to me about how, during the preceding year, he had lost "in excess of *sevvvvvvvven figures*" investing in a carbohydrate-free sucking candy and environmentally-friendly disposable diapers. Since he was just investing in those items just as a "*kibitz*" that would have advantageous tax consequences for him, he didn't mind losing the money.

So naturally, when I heard Eric describe his father's very creative and potentially profitable idea, I was more than surprised.

"Sign me up. Tell him that I'm interested. Should I call him tomorrow?

"Yeah."

"Does he have a name for this pre-paid legal program?"

"It's called Physician's Justice."

CHAPTER SIX

After hanging up with Eric, I felt legitimately excited about the prospect of bringing Sandy Markowitz's new company into my firm. It sounded like a novel idea that might generate some serious interest from the medical community.

I had talked with Eric so long on the phone that I was exiting the Interstate when our call was finished.

Upon winding my way for a few more minutes through the woods, I arrived at our house. Strangely, when I pulled the car onto the driveway, I noticed that our bedroom light was not illuminated. I immediately suspected that Julie had planned a romantic homecoming for me. Although it was not something that she did much of anymore, when we were younger and wilder, Julie would, from time to time, surprise me with a bedroom full of candles, wearing her birthday suit.

She had most frequently pulled that stunt when she wanted to buy an expensive pocketbook or similar item, and felt the need to butter me up, so that I couldn't say "no." In this case, however, I was struggling to remember whether she had talked about buying such an expensive item. Maybe I wasn't giving the young lady enough credit. Maybe she simply wanted to make love to her soon to be famous husband who was about to land Lubrano Concrete as a client.

As I opened the front door, I did not hear the voice of the late great Barry White emanating from our stereo speakers. Nor did my olfactory senses detect the odor of the Bath and Body Works candles that she so loved and I so hated.

In fact, the only item out of the ordinary that I noticed was a stack of what looked to be blankets on the couch. As I inched closer, I saw that Julie had left for me a bed sheet, an old comforter, two pillows, a bottle of Advil, toothpaste, a toothbrush and a suit with an accompanying shirt and tie. Attached to the bottle of Advil was one of Julie's elegant pink personalized Post-It notes that contained the printed notation, *"From the Desk of Julianna Brown."* Her message read,

> *"Thinking of you…Hope that tomorrow morning your back doesn't hurt from sleeping on the couch and that your head doesn't hurt from the booze. Love ya'!"*

To top it off, she sealed the note with a kiss in her red lipstick.

I had a dedicated wife. Even while punishing me, she was still concerned about my well-being. Though I didn't deserve to be punished for anything, I was more humored than angry about her decision to relegate me to sleeping on the couch.

Since the beginning of our courtship, some seven years prior, I had averaged about one couch relegation per 18 months. Initially, the act did not sit well with me. I was raised in a patriarchal family in which the sheer idea of my mother telling my father to sleep on the couch was inconceivable.

However, as time passed since Julie and I had begun dating, I learned that shortly after each couch relegation, she, out of guilt (and, perhaps subconscious nervousness that I would lose my cool and abandon her) gave me earth-shattering sex. While the sex in our marriage occurred with respectable frequency and was good, our post-fight sex was on a different plane. So, having been through this drill before, and cognizant that I didn't do anything to warrant being directed to sleep on the couch, I knew that Julie had started a game of cat and mouse foreplay, which would result in my getting laid in the near future. Tomorrow, I would pretend to be apologetic for going out to dinner with a potential multi-million dollar client and the bimbos, and she would give me a talking to about how it seemed that I didn't want to spend time with my son, and all would be better.

If I was going to be forced to sleep on the couch, I was damn well going to enjoy myself, though. Although I wasn't a big hard alcohol drinker, tonight seemed like an appropriate night to hit the good stuff. When I leaned in this direction, Dewar's was my poison of choice. With three ice cubes in a highball glass, the strong and oaky stuff made me feel like a lawyer.

And so, I dimmed the recess lighting in our family room, turned on Comcast SportsNet's Sports Nite to catch the lowlights of the Phillies' 9th inning implosion, and sipped my lawyer juice.

Before I knew it, I was on my fourth Dewar's and was watching the Harry Kalas and Lenny Dykstra-narrated VHS tape entitled, "Whatever it Takes, Dude!" chronicling the Phillies' wild ride to the 1993 World Series. I was going to be in pain tomorrow and going to work would not be fun. What kind of a lawyer would I be, though, if I couldn't execute my duties in a proficient manner with a stinging scotch hangover?

CHAPTER SEVEN

The next day, I arrived at the office at 9:15 a.m. Although I generally did not like to get in any later than nine, if questioned, I was sure that Walter Krauss or even Nick Carlson would commiserate with my plight of having to sleep on the couch the night before, which indirectly resulted from my pursuit of an extremely legitimate client development activity.

I snuck in the back door and scurried into my office in stealth mode, so as to avoid detection. As soon as I rested my briefcase on my leather executive chair, Kristin spoke over my telephone intercom, "*Ale-ixx? Ale-ixx*, are you there?"

Kristin was about as South Philly Italian as they came, and was smokingly hot, to boot. She had a naturally tanned complexion, which perfectly complemented her dark brown curly hair. When I and the other males in the office were lucky enough, Kristin straightened her curls, rendering her such an absolute knockout that on those days, it was legitimately difficult to concentrate on the business of lawyering.

While I wasn't a smoker anymore, and tended to be repulsed when others smoked, there was something *sexissimo* about Kristin's pack-a-day Marlboro Red habit. When returning to the office after lunch, I sometimes spotted Kristin standing outside the entrance to our building at 16th and Market Streets, screaming into her mobile phone and puffing away on a Marlboro. She would always interrupt her angry rant, metamorphasize her growl into a sweet-as-spumoni wide tooth bearing smile and pay me a greeting. A typical scene would be:

"Annamaria, don't even get me started on Nicoletta, did you see what she wore to Aunt Lucia's 65th birthday party?! Her fat ass is lucky that that tent she was wearin' didn't bust at the seams. I can't believe that Johnny D'Alessandro hooked up wit' her down in Wildwood. What a fat fuckin' whore that slut is...oh hi, Ale-ixx, how was lunch?"

After she greeted me, I would usually head through the revolving glass door into the building lobby and give a backward glance to catch a free, unobstructed look at Kristin's posterior, which was typically covered in some sort of black stretchy material that showed off her extremely flattering lower curves. As for her upper curves, I was pretty sure that her breasts were surgically enhanced. If they weren't, the woman was truly talented. She was about 5'2", weighed no more than 90 pounds and had, what I judged to be large C or small D cuppers. Regardless, she worked the dangling-crucifix-between-the-cleavage gimmick to perfection. Apart from the largeness of her assets, the golden symbol of Christianity acted as a tractor beam that lured all onlookers hypnotically to her chest.

"Yeah, Kristin, I'm here, who's on the phone? If it's not an emergency, I'm going to have to ask you to take a message. I'm afraid I had a few too many last night and I'm not feeling so hot."

"Ohhhhhh...that's a *senn*! I'm gonna have my mother bring you some of her stracciatella soup for lunch. It always does da' trick. Youse boys – youse just never know when enough is enough. I had three-a-them vodka Red Bulls last night at Chickie's and Pete's and I feel as sober as Father Donato at Sunday Mass. Don't worry, the soup will cure you all up. Any case – ain't no one on the phone. Vinny and Vince Lubrano are *here* to see you."

I momentarily lost feeling in my limbs.

"What?! You must be kidding with me!"

"You mean you didn't know they were coming? They seemed pretty sure they had a meetin' wit' you. I put dem in da' main conference room."

Now, at a whisper, Kristin continued, "Is da' younger one married? I didn't see no weddin' ring? He's fiiiiiiiiiiine, and he's *uhh-tail-yinn* (Italian) too!"

As Kristin confirmed the Lubranos' presence in my office, adrenaline shot through my system and counteracted my lingering alcohol withdrawal nausea.

"Kristin, he's not married – can we please deal with that later. I need you to work a little South Philadelphia magic, if you know what I..."

"*Ale-ixx,*" she said, with as sophisticated a tone as she could muster, "have you no faith in the great Kristin Fabrizzio? Fix your hair, splash a little *wooder* (water) on your face and come into the conference room in four minutes. I'll take care of everything."

Actually, I had as much faith in Kristin as anyone could possibly have in a receptionist. She was an absolute ace who looked the part, sounded the part and acted the part. Clients loved calling the office to speak with her before she passed calls along to the appropriate attorney, and clients loved even more coming to the office to see her in person. As for the "fix your hair" comment, she was quite mindful that personal appearance was important to clients of law firms. Although she had never previously heard of the Lubranos or their company, she had correctly surmised that they were potential clients who could do wonders for my young career. Kristin wanted me to succeed.

Following Kristin's lead, I hung my suit jacket up on the hook behind my office door, went to the men's room, straightened my tie, and replaced the piece of hair that was out of position. I then made my way to the main conference room. Before I entered, I saw, through the glass doors, what appeared to be Kristin placing a plate of pastries on a table adjacent to the long conference table. She was bending over to adjust the pastries while calculatedly juxtaposing her butt in such a way as to give both of the Lubrano men a pristine view.

Before I could utter a word after walking in, Vinny shouted, "Don't you fuckin' work for a living? It's nine fuckin' thirty. You're lucky that we didn't leave and go to the Jones Williams firm already – you know they're right next door?! I told you that we were in the market for a new lawyer and you can't even get to your office by nine o'clock. You're lucky that Kristin here is Italian and had these cannolis – from Termini's, I might add – here for us, or we would have been gone already. What is it with Jews? You don't mow your own lawns, and you think that clients are going to wait all day for you."

"Hi, Mr. Lubrano, it's so great to see you, thanks for coming in this morning. Gosh, it's been a while. And, Vinny it's been a while since I've seen you also – what's it been, about nine hours? I wish that you had told me that you were going to come in today. I just returned from City Hall. I had to handle a discovery motion there this morning. Had I known that you were coming in, I could have asked someone to cover the motion for me."

"Oh, that's a *senn*," interrupted Kristin, coming to my rescue, "I forgot that you were arguing that motion this morning – I should have seen it on your calendar and told these gentlemen."

"Kristin," Vinny demanded, with a smile, "I don't know a motion from a potion, nor do I care where he was this morning, but don't you realize that Alex is hung over beyond belief? How that's possible, I don't know. He was my guest last night at Capital Gri…"

Vince Lubrano interrupted his insolent son and stated in a calm, calculated and deliberate manner,

"Alex, we're glad that you could meet with us on such short notice. Vinny tells me that you have a good amount of experience in construction law. We are unhappy with our current attorneys and are looking to begin anew."

As Vince paused, Kristin inquired, "Is there anything else that I can get youse gentlemen? I gotta get back to da' reception desk."

Sarcastically rude, Vinny pressed, "Well how 'bout a double espresso? Can you get me a double espresso, now that I have a cannoli?"

Without missing a beat, Kristin responded matter-of-factly, with a seductive smile, "Is a crab's ass watertight?"

Laughter erupted from the Lubranos as they watched her pasta-fed buns exit the room. With that brief moment of levity, my heart rate, for the first time since entering the conference room, crept below 150. For a second, I relaxed, thinking that the meeting with the Lubranos would be a pleasant one. I envisioned Vince telling me in a complimentary tone that since he had known me through Vinny from the time that I was a young child and was confident in my intellect and intensity, he would have no doubt that I could effectively serve Lubrano Concrete.

Instead, as the conference room door closed when Kristin left, the smiles turned to stoic poker faces. Vince immediately opened the dialogue by saying, "Alex, we're changing lawyers because I'm sick of getting ripped off by the big white shoe firms in this town. Their partners charge me $575.00 per hour for work that I know some pimple-faced punk out of law school is doing. Even if we get a good result in court, the legal fees create a losing financial proposition. So, that brings me to you and your firm. Vinny tells me that you do a good bit of construction work and that your firm is smaller than the Jones Williamses and Cartwright Stanleys of the world. So, I was thinking..."

Clearly lacking mental equilibrium from the effects of the Dewar's from the previous night, and with my head positioned fully up my ass, I interrupted the powerful and feared Vince Lubrano in mid-sentence, saying, excitedly,

"Mr. Lubrano, you have made the right choice. Frankly, I'm not sure how the Jones Williamses and Cartwright Stanleys stay in business while firms like mine purvey the same high-quality services and charge a fraction of what they charge. I think that you're going to be happy with..."

Vince, with a reddened face and a right index finger pointed across the table at me, angrily interjected, with sweet ricotta cheese cannoli filling noticeably smudged beside his lips,

"I think that you're going to shut your trap until I'm done speaking. Strike one was keeping us waiting this morning, and that was just strike two. What's strike three gonna be?"

Looking at me as if I were the cretin and not he, Vinny pointed a finger to his head, as if to say, "Think before speaking, dumb ass! No one interrupts my father."

Vince continued, as his face returned to its normal color,

"Since Vinny thinks that you might be a good fit for us, I'm going to cut to the chase, so that strike three doesn't happen. You're going to sue Bicentennial Lumber Works for me before they sue my company. Even though our claims are superior, I don't want to be in a situation in which I have to counterclaim against them after they sue us. The jury always sides with the party that sues first and interprets counterclaims as being unsubstantiated posturing. In exchange for your services, we are going to pay you, and you only, $325.00 per hour. You will be free to involve any other attorney or paralegal from your firm on this case, but I'm not paying a penny for their services. If you attempt to mask their billable time under your name, I *will* know, and you and your firm will be terminated immediately. You will then have to sue us for your fees. I'm not paying any more than a $10,000.00 retainer. If you accept these terms, Vinny will have the file couriered to you today. You will review the file, prepare the Complaint and will have it filed by the end of the week. Do you accept these terms?"

With my heart almost visibly pounding through my custom made shirt, and a bead of sweat slowly running down the side of my face, I responded, "Mr. Lubrano, this is such a tremendous opportunity for me and the firm. I would love to be Lubrano Concrete's lawyer in this case and in many cases in the future. The problem is that I don't make the decisions about fees and retainers. Plus, we would have to do a conflict check to determine..."

With half of a cannoli in his mouth and powdered sugar coating much of his chin, Mr. Lubrano interrupted,

"Alex, my friend, we are at about strike two and seven eighths. First of all, don't worry about the conflict check. I did my own conflict check and you guys are OK. There is no conflict of interest in this representation."

Vince then shoved another whole cannoli into his mouth, stood up and motioned his son to do the same. As he began to walk towards the doors to the conference room, he said, sternly, "I'm calling Walter Krauss later today and I'm going to tell him that we were in his office this morning, ready to retain you guys, and all you did was interrupt me and make excuses as to why you couldn't represent the largest concrete construction contractor in the entire tri-state area."

Kristin stood at the door to the conference room, holding a silver tray containing Vinny's double espresso. With a quick hand gesture, I motioned her to not bring the tray into the room.

"Mr. Lubrano, please let me assure you that Krauss Carlson would relish the opportunity to represent your company. I hope that you did not interpret my comments as trepidation towards this relationship. It's just that I need to speak with..."

"You need to speak with no one. Here's the deal: accept my proposition right now and you'll be a very important person in two years time. Your name will be in *The Inquirer* twice a fuckin' week every time I have you file an injunction against someone. Jim Gardner will be mentioning your name on Action News and your mother will be blushing when her friends congratulate her at her bridge game for having such a famous son. Now, do you represent Lubrano Concrete or not?"

Pins and needles radiated to every extremity in my body and I felt like I could lose control of my bladder any second.

"It would be my pleasure. We have a deal. No need to call Walt Krauss. I'll speak with him."

"Good. As I said, Vinny will courier the case materials to you. That Complaint will be filed by the end of the week."

I shook hands with Mr. Lubrano and then with his son. After the exchange, Vinny asked, as if this marble floored and oak walled law firm were a dentist's office, "Who do I get the parking validation stamp from?"

"Uhh, Vinny...we actually don't validate parking."

Befuddled, Vinny responded, "You don't...what the fuck... we just told you that we're retaining you, and you don't validate parking?"

"Vinny, we're not a restaurant – we're a law firm. I wish I could..."

"What is it with you? Jews are so money driven, yet you don't even get into the office until 9:30 a.m. I banged those two chicks from last night until four in the morning. I slept until 5:00 a.m., was in the gym by 5:15 a.m. and was on one of our construction sites by 7:00 a.m. You've gotta show me a little more."

Grabbing his son's left tricep from behind, the elder Lubrano instructed, at an audible whisper, "Vinny, don't worry about the parking – put it on your corporate card."

"O.K.," Vinny added with a poisonous smirk, "I'll just deduct the Liberty Place parking fee from your first bill."

I politely giggled as if to signify that I would happily acquiesce to paying for his parking fee. In actuality, I was about to get my ass handed to me. I didn't have the authority to agree on behalf of the firm to pay for his parking fee, let alone to agree to represent Lubrano Concrete under Vince's dictated terms. I, a peon sixth year Associate, in a firm full of multi-million dollar verdict victors, had just agreed, on behalf of the firm, to represent a client under certain terms without discussing those terms with a Partner. Even if the terms of the representation would turn out to be acceptable to the partnership, I was still in extremely hot water for being so presumptuous as to assume that an Associate could sign up a client without previously checking with a higher-up.

While grappling with that reality, I was still digesting the Lubranos' directives. Vince's comment about having performed his own conflict check was disturbing to me. There were two ways that Vince's statement could have been interpreted. He may have been just blowing smoke, as if to say, "conflict check – shmonflict check – who cares if you have a conflict? I'll pay you enough to forget any ethical concerns that you have." Alternatively, it was possible that he had somehow obtained a list of the firm clients, likely illicitly, and determined that the firm would have no conflict with the representation. Neither proposition was particularly appealing to me.

As the Lubranos entered their elevator, I silently wondered whether I had just scored a major coup that would advance my career or whether I had committed a major mistake that would endanger any hopes that I had to become a young Partner.

Sensing my pensive apprehension, Kristin took it upon herself to soothe my nerves. "*Ale-ixx*, what were *youse* talking about in there and how come they didn't stay long enough for their espresso?"

"Kristin, since when do we have an espresso machine in the office?"

Leaning on the reception desk in a manner perfectly calculated to expose a significant portion of cleavage, and tapping her teeth with her pen in a most seductive manner, Kristin responded,

"*Ale-ixx*, my dear, you never give me my due credit for the ingenuity that I possess."

Baffled that she used the words, "ingenuity," and "possess" in a sentence, I grinned at her with approval. She continued, with her beaming blue eyes, "I'm friggin' *Sale-th* (South) Philly *uhh-tail-yinn* – I have been trained to create espresso where there is none. You put double coffee and one-half *wooder* in the coffee maker, garnish with a lemon peel and *voilà*, you got espresso."

Genuinely impressed, I then asked, "O.K., that's very creative. Would you now mind telling me how you came up with these cannolis that are apparently from Termini's?"

"Oh, you just got lucky wit' doze. Today is Denise's birthday, and I picked up the cannolis at – you guessed it – Termini's Bakery in *Sale-th* Philly. We were gonna celebrate her birthday this afternoon but your clients kinda ate *dem* cannolis."

Expecting her to politely decline, I said, "Kristin, I'm going to make it up to you, since you hooked me up. At lunch, I'll take a cab down to Termini's and will get you replacement cannolis, biscotti and whatever else you want."

"Damn *shhh-trait* you will! You're also going to pick me up *linguine con vongole* at Dante and Luigi's. I'll call the order in because you won't know what the fuck you're askin' for."

Adoring her sultry petulance, I couldn't feel slighted that she was speaking in such a tone to me. She had saved my ass and had displayed tons of moxie in doing so.

"Not a problem, Kristin. I won't forget this."

"Don't mention it. *Ale-ixx*, do me a favor, though. Do something nice and romantic wit' Julie this weekend. You need to relax. I can see that them Lubranos are makin' you tense. You've just brought the firm a major client. Go celebrate."

In my warped egocentric mind, I interpreted her act of invoking Julie's name and suggestion that I romance Julie over the weekend as being a thinly veiled come on. Maybe she was fantasizing about my romancing her. In actuality, I was likely just fantasizing about her fantasizing about my romancing her. Reality didn't bother me, though – such delusions kept my job interesting.

In any event, I would have loved to have relaxed with Julie, as Kristin had suggested, but tensions were about to rise on another front and there would be no time for leisure.

CHAPTER EIGHT

By the time that I had made my way back to my office, the nausea symptoms had returned to properly compliment my splitting headache. The mail had already been delivered and was resting on my chair, next to where I had previously placed my briefcase. As I leafed through it, I noticed sets of voluminous interrogatories and requests for production of documents in three separate cases. I had also received requests for admissions in another case. The receipt of these documents guaranteed that my next working month would be a very busy one. My nausea increased.

I also noticed the ominous sign of the illuminated red light on my telephone handset. I had voice messages waiting for me.

Once I punched in my security code, the pleasant automated female voice informed me that I had four messages. The first, recorded at 6:57 a.m. by Vinny Lubrano stated,

"Brownie! It's 7 a.m., man. I fuckin' double teamed those girls last night, no thanks to you. I did some crazy shit with them – you have no idea. Listen, I think that my Dad and I might want to come in today to talk about that case. Let me know what your schedule is. Later."

The second, recorded at 8:15 a.m., also from Vinny, stated,

"Dude, where the fuck are you? Call me the fuck back! My Dad and I are coming down there at nine. If you're not there, we're goin' down the street to Jones Williams, O.K.?"

I was able to ascertain that the third message was from Vinny by virtue of the robotic lady telling me that the caller's phone number matched that of Vinny's cell phone. The message, left at 9:05 a.m., consisted only of a click.

The robotic lady then spoke the caller identification number for the fourth message. The number of the caller was from the suburban Philadelphia 610 area code, but I did not even remotely recognize the digits that followed the area code. The message, spoken in a deep, guttural male voice began, after two throaty coughs and a clearing of the phlegm from the airway,

"I know, Gloria, I did call his office, he's not answering! Maybe he stepped up from his desk! Jesus Christ, do you think that it's possible that the kid might have to use the restroom once in a while?"

Another voice, this time one which resounded in an authoritative, female tone, spoke from the background,

"Sanford, what the hell is the matter with you?! Eric gave you his cell phone number too. Why don't you just call that?"

The male voice returned, *"Gloria, shut up! Is this the answering machine? Well, if I'm being recorded, Alex, this is Dr. San...it's Sandy Markowitz, Eric's father. I'd like to speak with you about something. Please call me back at 610-555-57...Gloria, what's our new home phone number again?"*

"SEVEN! FIVE! FIVE! SEVEN!"

"Right-o....610-555-5775...O.K. talk to you later..."

"Sanford, I said SEVEN! FIVE! FIVE! SEVEN!"

"Gloria, that's what I said. Stop listening to my...[click]"

Good God. After being emasculated by the Lubranos, I was being harassed, via a telephonic recording by a geriatric Jewish couple. Knowing that Sandy had retired several years ago and that he spent most days playing mahjong and trading securities on the internet, I was quite confident that he was waiting, literally, next to the telephone for my call. Hoping to do a *mitzvah* for an elder, I immediately called back the "7557" number, believing that Gloria Markowitz, rather than her husband, was correct.

"Hello?" A sweet female voice answered, sounding nothing like the woman whose voice I had just heard.

"Hi, Mrs. Markowitz it's Al..."

"*Alick-zannnnnnnnnn-durrrrrrrr*, honey, how are you? How are mom and dad? They must be on cloud nine with that little *shayna punim* Charlie. Did you hear the wonderful news? My baby is having a baby! *Oy, gut!* I can't wait to pinch that baby's little cheeks!"

"Mazel Tov, Mrs. Markowitz, I'm so happy for..."

"Gloria, GET OFFFFFFFF THE PHONE!"

"Sanford, you're being very rude. I'm going to the mall with Harriet. I'll bring dinner home later. If you want lunch, just look in the..."

"GET THE HELL OFF THE PHONE!!!"

"O.K., O.K., Alex, honey, send mom and dad my love and give that little Charlie a hug and a kiss for me."

"I certainly will, Mrs. Markowitz."

"Are you off? Is Gloria off the phone?"

"I think that I heard a click."

"I swear to God – that woman is going to give me another coronary and I'm just going to collapse and die one day. Just collapse and die! Why you young kids feel that you need to get married is beyond my comprehension. In my time, we got married so that we could get laid. Now, kids are screwing at age 15. It's a different world."

I offered a forced laugh. He continued,

"Eric tells me that you've developed a new hobby of suing lawyers."

Seeking to correct his erroneous understanding of the extent of my experience in handling Wrongful Use of Civil Proceedings cases, I responded,

"Dr. Markowitz, I wouldn't exactly call it a hobby. One of the Partners in my firm has a client who believes that he was wrongfully sued in a medical malpractice case. Between you and I, I actually hold some doubts as to..."

Clearly agitated, he swiftly interrupted,

"Nonsense! All medical malpractice lawsuits are frivolous! Who the fuck is going to deliver your wife's next baby when you scumbags have driven every single OB/GYN out of the state? What goddamn 19 year-old Pakistani would you trust to operate on your kid's eye after some punk in the schoolyard threw a rock at him? Huh? What's that? I don't hear you responding. Do you know that I just read in a publication that 83% of all medical malpractice cases are eventually thrown out of court? I also read somewhere that out of the last 20 $1 million-plus med mal verdicts rendered in this state, the juries were bought in 17 of them. *Se-vennnnn-teeeeen!* Why do you think that I got out of the business, huh? Some jackass on welfare whose life I saved decided that he didn't like the scar that a surgery left. So guess what he did? Guess!"

"Do you want me to, uhh, do you want me to answer?"

"No, I want you to pull on your pud. Yes! Answer me!"

"I would guess that he sued you."

"You would guess correct, then. He sued me, the insurance company gave me some 26 year old so-called *lawyer* who didn't know his ass from a hole in the wall. Long story short, he couldn't even get the case thrown out of court. He wanted to settle for $75,000.00 and I refused to sign off on it. Case goes to trial and the jury comes back with an $825,000.00 verdict against me. The insurance company dropped my coverage two weeks later, basically forcing me out of the profession. My attorney told me that he was 99% sure that the jury was paid off. What do you make of that?"

What I made of that was that Sandy Markowitz was a deeply delusional and humbled person, on top of being a typical doctor.

In my experience, however, no doctor since the time of Hippocrates, had ever believed that he or she had committed malpractice. Sandy was no exception. As a product of being at the very top of their classes from kindergarten through undergraduate school, I found members of the medical profession, most of the time, to be egomaniacs who rightfully believed that they were more intelligent than any person not in their profession. This reality explained Sandy's spouting out of patently bogus statistics concerning the ratios of dismissed lawsuits and instances of jury tampering. No person with a high school education could have possibly believed the statistics that Sandy was offering. That he was trying to convince a practicing lawyer that those statistics were accurate resounded in sheer arrogance and bordered on absurdity.

Although Philadelphia's juries routinely awarded some of the highest and most outrageous verdicts in the country, I doubted that the extent of Sandy's alleged malpractice in the case that he described consisted simply of leaving an unsightly scar. I was willing to bet that he had left an instrument sticking in the patient's heart or that he had severed one of his ventricles. Nevertheless, due to the business opportunity that he was about to pitch to me and my desire to keep my relationship with Eric intact, I was not prepared to bring the inconsistencies laden in Sandy's story to his attention.

To that end, I simply responded,

"Tell me about it! I'm in a damn dirty profession. I should have done the smart thing and gone to medical school."

"What, so you could spend a half mil on your education and not make a respectable living until you're 34, only to find out that the malpractice premiums require your wife to shop at J.C. Penney's and for you to only be able to afford to eat canned beef stew for dinner? It ain't peaches and cream, *boobie*. Even though you're forced to whore yourself as a scalawag depraved shitbag every day, you still make a nice living and drive that 5-Series. Eric would love to drive a car like yours. Do you think that he can afford it with all of the shit that's going on?"

Almost at the same level as their obsession with Chinese food, American Jews were highly preoccupied with what cars their peers drove.

After it was apparent that I was not going to respond to his last remark, Sandy cleared his throat, switched to a softer tone and stated,

"I'd like for you to meet me and one of my business partners, George Ridgeway, for lunch at the Perennial Club." With a snicker, he continued, "Before you say anything, don't worry, they're not going to check your pecker for circumcision at the door. They've been letting Yids in for a few years now, since their membership has been suffering."

I responded, "Great, I'd love to. I think that I have some availability during the middle of next week. Let me check with my secretary, though – she handles my calendar."

"You have some availability at 12:30 today. And cut the crap about your secretary. I knew you when you were a snot nose 18 year-old freshman at Penn who banged whatever slop was left on the ground at four in the morning when the fraternity party was ending. I'll see you then. Oh – be prepared to turn on some of that Presbyterian Academy charm. George Ridgeway is an old school Brandywine County *goy* who has his first scotch of the day with his ham and eggs. He'll appreciate that shit. See you later, *boobie.*"

Having heard George Ridgeway's name for the second time, I was certain that I knew him from somewhere. Was he a parent of a Presbyterian student? Was he a television personality? For the life of me, though, I couldn't place where I knew him from. Before I had a chance to ask Sandy, he had hung up the phone.

CHAPTER NINE

What a morning it had been. Arriving at the office with a raging hangover, having slept on the couch at the direction of my angry wife, the stars didn't seem to be aligned in such a manner that I would have expected to have banked two major clients by lunchtime. Although my hangover symptoms had nearly completely faded, the prospect of discussing with Walter Krauss the two new clients whom I had signed up without approval of any partner was a daunting proposition that made me feel uneasy.

Compared to Carlson, Walt Krauss was a decent guy. Compared to Carlson, though, Slobodan Milosevic was a decent guy. Nevertheless, I had a fair amount of respect for the guy. He was a hard ass when you screwed something up, but if you did your work in a professional manner and billed your 2200 hours per year, Krauss treated you justly. Plus, it was tough not to respect a man who had pursued in excess of 20 jury trials to verdict during his 30 years in practice. The cases that he had taken to verdict were not penny-ante rear-end motor vehicle accident cases. Krauss' clients were strictly of the commercial litigation variety. Most of his cases involved businesses in high-profile disputes reported in the local and national media. The high amount in controversy in Krauss' cases allowed him to bill his clients an obscene rate without their batting an eye. Companies being sued for or seeking to recover tens of millions of dollars tended not to complain when a lawyer's bill for a half million dollars arrived, regardless of the outcome of the case.

Despite being in my sixth year of practice, I tended to be shy when it came to entering the Managing Partner's office. Krauss did not aim to intimidate, but it was hard not to be wary when speaking with the man who had the final say on what your yearly bonus and raise would be, and when you were to be considered for partnership. This occasion was different, though. I walked down to Krauss' office with a swagger. There were some pretty big hitters at the firm, but I was pretty sure that none of them had gained two new large clients since the office lights were turned on this morning.

When I arrived at Krauss' open office door, I could see a telephone receiver protruding from the side of his balding gray head. Normally in such an instance, I would wait outside his door until he was finished with his call. In this case, however, the triumphs that I had realized thus far during the day caused me to have the confidence to mosey on into his office and plop myself on his leather couch. As I sat down and air released from the cushions, the scent of leather flowed through my nostrils. Moments like this made me enthusiastic to be a lawyer. The prospect of one day achieving the smell of leather in a corner office the size of Rhode Island with a view of Logan Circle and the Philadelphia Museum of Art and its Greek pillars in the distance was what all those years of toiling late at night in college and law school were all about. Some of my law school contemporaries wanted to achieve justice for indigents or be responsible for setting the next important Supreme Court precedent, while they worked out of a windowless office at a low paying firm. I was more than happy to forego those lofty goals in order to one day hopefully smell leather and have an inspiring view of the City of Brotherly Love.

Krauss clearly did not realize that I had been reading The Wine Spectator with my legs crossed on his couch for over three minutes. After he shouted into the phone,

"If you don't want to disgorge the documents then we'll see what Judge Lees has to say about it. I've been practicing in this town longer than you've been alive, you piece of shit. And I'm gonna tell you something: paybacks are a bitch. Good day, son," and hung up, he turned around and was startled to see me.

"Oh, Alex – I didn't realize that you were here. What do you need?"

Normally, I would have responded rapidly and nervously with the reason for my visit. Today wasn't one of those days, though. I was on top of the world and was going to ride the wave until I was put in my place.

"This article says that there are a few 2002 Barbarescos that are ready to drink now, and are virtually indistinguishable from some of the high-end Barolos from the same year."

Apparently piquing the interest of a self-proclaimed wine-nut, he defiantly responded,

"Tell me something I don't fucking know! I've been hoarding the shit since it came on the shelf. I don't need The Spectator or some guy who just got his bar ticket to state the obvious for me. How can you beat a wine that sells for $35.00 and tastes identical to a wine that sells for $250.00?"

Changing his tone from enthusiastic to agitated, Krauss continued,

"I'd love to chat about your newfound oenophilia, but I bill $600.00 per hour – $50.00 more than Carlson if you're keeping track – and I can't charge my clients for educating you about wine. So, let me cut to the chase: I'm very happy that you're bringing Lubrano in. They'll be a nice client for you. Just make sure you don't fuck anything up for them or else you won't get a second chance. Only problem is that when I fuck something up for one of my clients, they either want to negotiate the bill down or fire me outright. If you fuck up, your arms will be used to support the foundation of that new condo they're building just south of the Walt Whitman Bridge, and your legs, ass and balls will be reinforcing the 17th floor of the office tower they're building on Market Street. Hah!!!"

After Krauss spoke those words and cracked a smile for the first time since I entered his office, as a means by which to stroke his ego, I feigned bewilderment as to how he learned that the Lubranos were in the office and that I had made a deal with them. In actuality, I wasn't surprised that his office moles, who included support staff, attorneys and even security personnel on the ground floor of the building, had made him aware of the Lubranos' presence in the office. As for my signing Lubrano up, Krauss probably figured that there was no other explanation for my act of confidently parading into his office. After all, had they come to visit me concerning representation and I failed to get the deal done, I most assuredly would not have been so bold as to read a wine magazine in his office while he was taking an important call.

"Walt, how did you..."

"Because I know *everything* that happens here, Alex. Don't you know that by now?"

With my charade still alive, I added, "Walt, I should never have underestimated you."

"Alex, Rule Number One: never underestimate the man who signs your paycheck."

With his mouth open and his eyes fixed on the ceiling, searching for something witty to categorize as "Rule Number Two," at least four seconds passed before I jumped in to save him from further embarrassment.

"Walt, I need to talk to you about what rate we'll be charging them."

"Jeez, that's funny. I'm not sure if you've checked my profile on the firm's website recently, but I'm the Managing Partner. Generally, the Managing Partner decides what rates the firm is going to charge clients, not vice versa. But please, counsel, enlighten me."

God, did I hate it when lawyers called other lawyers, "counsel," or "counselor." In this case, Krauss was clearly trying to sound like one of the characters on *Law and Order* or *Boston Legal*. He just sounded like a putz, though.

"Walt, they were going to walk out the door if I didn't agree..."

"If you didn't agree to WHAT! Let me ask you something. Why do you think that they came to you? Because they trust you and they know that you are going to treat them as your number one client. Do you think that they get that same attention at the big firms?"

Pausing, and staring at the floor, knowing full well that he was dead-on, 100% correct, I muttered, "I got fucking played by them."

Surprisingly, Krauss stood up, smiled widely, extended his hand to shake mine, and said laughingly, "Like a fucking violin, my boy. Like a fucking violin."

"I'm such an ass."

"No you're not. I don't have asses working for me – I only have good lawyers working for me and you're a good lawyer, Alex. You just got your cherry popped in losing a fee negotiation with a client. Trust me, it will happen again. You'll be better prepared next time, though."

Expressing my gratitude for softening the blow of this humbling experience, I offered, "Thanks, Walt."

"Don't mention it, kid. Now what's the damage?"

"I committed to a $10,000.00 retainer and $325.00 per hour."

Once again nervous that Krauss was going to throw me out of his window, and down 46 flights onto 16th Street, I waited while he clasped his hands, stared away from me and finally said,

"Well, that's not *horrible*. We usually bill you out at $350.00. They would have paid $400.00 per hour if you hadn't been a pussy. Here's what we're gonna do: you're gonna win this case, and you're gonna win it good. You're gonna bill the hell out of the file, so that we can make up the difference between the $325.00 and $400.00. After you kick ass for them and the case is over, you're gonna send them a letter, saying that your rate has been raised to $425.00. That's still $50.00 per hour cheaper than what the Associates your age are billing at the big firms. When the retainer gets below $2,500.00, you get it replenished ASAP. Are we done here?"

"Actually, Walt, believe it or not, right after the Lubranos came in, I think that I may have secured another client. I'm going to have lunch with the potential client now at the Perennial Club..."

As I was about to tell Krauss about the Physician's Justice concept, Kristin piped in on the intercom,

"Mister K-rail-sss, excuse me, I have Ryan Watson on the phone for you from the Aston Martin dealership. He says that it's about service being done to your car."

"Alright, Alex, we *are* done here. I need to take this. Listen, good job. Don't sweat the fact that you completely botched the fee negotiation. Do me a favor and make me some money on this case. By the way, don't try ordering gefilte fish at The Perennial Club. They might catch on to you."

As I walked out of Krauss' office, I felt greener than the color of a drunken tailgating idiot's painted face in the Lincoln Financial Field parking lot at 10:00 a.m. on an autumn Sunday before an Eagles game. I didn't even recognize the "fee negotiation" as having been a negotiation at all. What Krauss had said made perfect sense, though. I was a hell of a lot cheaper than the big firms, and they knew that I would treat them like *numero uno*.

Boy, did it suck to know that one had been had by a couple of unsophisticated construction goons.

CHAPTER TEN

The Perennial Club was founded during the Revolutionary War as a society dedicated to supporting the policies of George Washington. Its illustrious 175,000 square foot French Renaissance building sits at the intersection of 18th and Locust Streets in Center City.

Until the late 1980s, The Perennial Club's membership had been comprised of an almost homogeneous affluent white male Protestant body of people. Until that time, though, being an affluent white male Protestant did not guarantee one to be admitted as a member. Extensive background checks had been conducted upon prospective members that included, among other topics, measures to determine applicants' political affiliations, family history and financial position. Needless to say, those ascertained to have even minimally left-leaning sympathies or interests, or were determined to be from new money, were denied admission.

As the Clinton years approached, much of the Old Guard had died off, and a more liberal mindset began to grip the nation. At that time, a veritable armageddon occurred, which saw an upheaval of The Perennial Club that left the club a shell of its former self. A few non-ethnic looking, hyper-wealthy Jews were let into the club. Shortly thereafter, one or two power-wielding blacks were admitted.

Almost simultaneous to the admission of the club's first minorities, The Perennial Club began to hemorrhage older members who were dismayed over the infiltration of undesirables at their beloved club. This effect began to snowball in the mid-1990s, when members of the elite all-Jewish Spruce Club began to defect from that club to The Perennial Club, where they were now welcome. Successful Philadelphia Jews relished the fact that they could now eat, drink and entertain in a place that was once, in their minds, a microcosm of American post-World War II anti-Semitism. This migration resulted in the closure of the Spruce Club in 1997. As the Spruce Club, at its peak, maintained a membership of 1,000, its closing was accorded much attention in the Philadelphia social scene.

I had always found the transition of Jews from the Spruce Club to the Perennial Club to be most ironic. Many of the Jews making the move condemned all things *goyim*, from Miracle Whip on Wonder Bread sandwiches to hunting game. Yet, these same Jews, by virtue of their joining the Perennial Club in astounding numbers, apparently had inwardly longed for that which they outwardly scorned.

When the Spruce Club closed once and for all, many of its remaining members joined the Perennial Club. At that point, around the turn of millennium, a significant portion of The Perennial Club's members who followed the fundamental old-money right-wing tenets of the club evaporated. With some exceptions, The Perennial Club, today, has been transformed into a young, new-money, relatively progressive thinking club for Philadelphia's businessmen and businesswomen.

So, while I found Sandy's comment about circumcision and Krauss' comment about gefilte fish at least marginally humorous, I did not believe their points to be well-founded in light of the current climate of the club. In fact, on the two prior occasions during which I had visited The Perennial Club, I was the guest of a Japanese former law school mate, and a female Greek Orthodox court reporter trying to solicit my deposition business. On neither of those occasions did I feel discriminated against. Then again, with my WASP-like physical appearance and manner of speaking, I would have been unlikely to be detected as a Jew anyway.

As I entered the main Locust Street entrance of the Perennial Club, I thought to myself how, notwithstanding the revolution amongst the membership ranks, the beautiful and imposing inner design of the building remained very much apparent of being a haunt of old school wealthy blue blooders. After walking up the curving staircase that led into the club, I was met with marble floors, deep wooden décor and portraits of important looking people adorning the walls.

Upon my entrance, I was greeted by a sickly, emaciated black man who appeared to be in his late 70s or early 80s. A tag which was crookedly affixed to the left breast pocket of his tuxedo bore the name, "Wells." I guessed that that was his first name rather than his last name.

As I approached to within three feet of him, Wells apparently not recognizing me as a member, demanded, "May I help you, sir?"

"Yes," I responded, "I'm here to meet Mr. Markowitz and Mr. Ridgeway for lunch."

"You here for Mr. Ridgeway, then. Ain't no Markowitz a member here. We got a Berkowitz, a Derschowitz and a Markstein. Ain't no Markowitz – you here to see Mr. Ridgeway."

"O.K., thank you. Where might I find Mr. Ridgeway?"

"He in the Lombard Room havin' lunch."

"Where is the Lombard Room?"

Clearly frustrated with my questions, Wells responded, "Same place it always been – they ain't move it."

"Sir, you'll have to forgive me, I've only been to the Perennial Club a few times and I'm not sure where the Lombard Room is. Can you point me in the right direction?"

Without uttering a word, Wells contorted his body in what appeared to be painful fashion and pointed behind his body to the left, looking at me as if I were a flaming idiot. I thanked him and walked in the direction that he had suggested.

After about fifty or so feet, I came upon a dining room labeled on the outside as the "Lombard Room." I quickly recognized Sandy Markowitz sitting at a table with another gentleman whose back was facing me. Distinguished looking wood, silver, mirrors and drapes abounded.

When Sandy saw me walking slowly towards the table, he motioned me over with a stern look, continuing a conversation with his table mate. As I arrived at the table, Sandy stood and shook my hand, stating,

"Nice to see you, Alex. Thank you for joining us today. I'd like for you to meet George Ridgeway. This is his place."

I might have been more impressed with that comment several years prior when The Perennial Club was still an ultra-exclusive establishment and undesirables such as myself were not permitted to roam its halls. Nowadays, though, unless someone was about to tell me that Ridgeway owned the real estate upon which the Perennial Club sat (which, in light of its historic value and prime location, was probably worth 75 to 100 million dollars), I was not going to be impressed.

Mr. Ridgeway finished a sip of a scotch-looking drink, turned to me and extended his leather-looking hand in my direction without standing. As I caught a glimpse of George Ridgeway, my heart skipped a beat.

The sight of this man was genuinely startling. With his ice blue eyes and contrasting reddened war torn face, which bore clear signs of years of alcohol abuse, he looked like a sinister bad-guy linchpin character from a second-rate movie. After wiping his mouth with a cloth napkin and clearing his throat, with sickly mucous audible, he offered,

"Alex, George Ridgeway, very nice to make your acquaintance, son."

When he spoke, his yellow and black crooked teeth had confirmed for me that in addition to a significant portion of his life being dedicated to alcohol consumption, Mr. Ridgeway had apparently also dabbled in cigarettes and black coffee.

"And it's a pleasure to meet you, Mr. Ridgeway," I said, still in awe of his disquieting appearance that was half-latter year Jack Palance and half-latter year Jimmy Stewart. After I had stopped looking for the Rawlings insignia on his body and was sufficiently convinced that I was seated adjacent to an actual living human being and not a piece of talking leather, I took notice that his right hand was involuntarily trembling. Judging by the looks of this guy, I was inclined to believe that his hand motions were the result of his waiting until 12:00 p.m. to have a first drink, rather than of some neurological disorder.

Ridgeway looked over my left shoulder and motioned with his middle finger and index finger, apparently summoning someone behind me to the table. I prayed that he wasn't directing his twin brother, the grim reaper to approach. Thankfully, the person who arrived was a woman in her late 60s with a name tag that read, "Doris."

"Delores, hon, we're in hurry, doll, so we're just going to go ahead and order."

Ridgeway sounded pretty confident, so I opined that the waitress' nametag, which appeared to be about 17 years old, contained a misspelling, rather than Ridgeway having misspoken her name.

"Alex, get whatever you'd like, but the soup and sandwich are world class here."

Not seeing a menu in front of me, I must have had a puzzled look on my face, because Delores, with discontented body language, waddled her well-nourished buttocks that were roughly the size and shape of the back end of a 1970s era Volkswagen Bug to the other end of the room to retrieve a menu.

When she returned, I was pleased to learn that there were actually multiple types of soups, sandwiches, salads, and even some hot platters. Seeing that both Ridgeway and Markowitz were champing at the bit, I glanced quickly at the menu and ordered a chicken salad sandwich and a Diet Coke.

When it was Sandy's turn, he questioned, "Let me ask you this – your roast beef platter – does that come with potatoes?"

"Yes, sir."

"What *kind* of potatoes? I knew that it came with potatoes – it says it right on the menu. I meant what *kind* of potatoes!" Markowitz barked, as if Delores were out of line.

"Whipped, sir."

"Alright, then I'll substitute some plain pasta for the potatoes."

Visibly fatigued, Delores responded,

"Sir, I'm afraid that we don't have pasta. I can give you navy beans, red cabbage, brussel sprouts..."

Interrupting, Markowitz ran his hands through his scant hair, and crossly stated, "Forget it. I'll be on the toilet all night. Just bring me the roast beef and put the gravy on the *siiiiiiiide!*"

Still looking at Markowitz with contempt, Delores asked, "Mr. R?"

"The soup and sandwich, Delores."

"And another Cutty Sark, Mr. R?"

"Good God! I'm low, aren't I?!" Ridgeway said, with a drunkard's laugh, the hairs on the bridge of his nose rising at attention. He pointed towards me with a shaky finger and a sly smirk, "My attorney here must have finished off my drink while I wasn't looking. Damn parasite lawyers – that's why I got out of that filthy profession. Too many drink stealing scoundrels like this one here."

With that comment, I counted three separate people, two of whom were in old school Philadelphia lawyer tortoise-rimmed glasses, turn towards Ridgeway inquisitively. Ridgeway challengingly raised his empty glass towards his admirers and shook the ice cube remnants, as if to say, "You want a piece of this, you candy ass?"

As a significant portion of the Perennial Club's remaining membership base was comprised of attorneys from Center City's old-line firms who didn't find lawyer jokes funny, Ridgeway's comments were undoubtedly interpreted as being uncouth and in bad form. Since he was making the comments in "his place," I surmised that he didn't give a shit that they were ill-received. In fact, having known Mr. Ridgeway for a grand total of eight minutes, I was fairly confident that this man would have told Queen Elizabeth to fuck off if he didn't like the way that she was looking at him.

Without wasting any time after Delores left, Ridgeway began, "Alex, do you know who I am?"

Trying to decide whether or not he was asking a trick question, I paused and mumbled some incomprehensible sounds until he cut me off.

"Does my name sound familiar to you, son?"

In fact, it did. Ever since Sandy had mentioned his name earlier that morning, I was struggling to figure out from where I had previously heard his name. Until he asked this question, though, I had concluded that my hangover was causing my brain to function in a less productive fashion than usual, and that I was simply creating a false memory.

"Actually, George, it does. Did we have a case together at some point? Did you have any grandchildr...err...children who went to Presbyterian Academy?" I asked.

His neutral look turned to an angry frown, which caused me to believe that he wasn't used to being addressed as "George" by young whipper snappers.

Taking a healthy gulp of his newly replenished Cutty Sark, he said, matter of factly,

"I'm quite certain that we did not have a case together. I've not been practicing law for the past eight years since they had me retired." He paused and then asked, "Ring a bell?"

It actually did ring a very strong bell at this point, but I still wasn't sure where I knew his name from.

Markowitz looked on with a proud and menacing smile, as if he knew what Ridgeway was about to say. Ridgeway proceeded,

"Here's how you know me: Office of Disciplinary Counsel v. Ridgeway."

As he sat back in his chair and smiled at me with one side of his mouth, again exposing his decaying teeth, my heart dropped, and I lost my breath for several seconds. His prior initial smirk now transformed into raucous evil laughter, as I turned as pale as a ghost. Markowitz joined in the laughter. I began to feel as if I were the victim of some cruel joke devised by these two obviously disturbed old codgers.

"George, I think that our young friend may have just shit himself. Your reputation certainly precedes you."

While Ridgeway poured several splashes of sherry into his snapper soup, I was afforded a few seconds to reflect upon what I knew about the case of Office of Disciplinary Counsel v. Ridgeway.

Few law students remembered names or holdings of specific cases that were taught in law school, however <u>Ridgeway</u> was an exception. *Everyone* who attended a Pennsylvania law school or who attended law school out of state and studied for the Pennsylvania bar exam knew about the <u>Ridgeway</u> case. It contained some of the most outlandish set of facts of any case in the history of Pennsylvania jurisprudence.

As I remembered, the case began after a Plaintiff's attorney, who, apparently, was George Ridgeway, had a personal injury case dismissed when a Brandywine County judge sustained the Defendant's preliminary objections. The preliminary objections were granted after Ridgeway stubbornly refused to amend his client's Complaint so that it conformed to a relatively new Brandywine County local procedural pleading requirement. The requirement had been previously challenged in another case as being unconstitutional, and was ultimately upheld by the Pennsylvania Supreme Court two years prior.

But for Ridgeway's procedural blunder, the case would have been an absolute surefire multi-million dollar victory. His client, a 45-year old mother of two, had been paralyzed when a drunk driver rear-ended her vehicle while it was stopped at a red light. Civil cases seeking to recover for personal injuries from a drunk driving accident were often futile because the offender usually had little or no insurance and no personal assets that could be attached upon a verdict being rendered. This case was different, though.

Ridgeway's client had been hit by a Rolls Royce driven by the CEO of a locally based international plastics manufacturer. Prior to the accident, the Philadelphia Inquirer had estimated his net worth at $1.5 billion dollars. So, in addition to the more than adequate insurance coverage that the potential Defendant possessed, he had an obscene amount of personal assets upon which a judgment could be executed. Even though Brandywine County was known as a conservative venue, the facts of the drunk driving case absolutely shocked the conscience, such that had the case proceeded to trial, a verdict in the tens of millions was not out of the question.

Seeing millions of dollars in contingency fees slipping out of his hands and a likely malpractice suit against him on the horizon, Ridgeway had desperately filed a Motion for Reconsideration of the court's Order. The Motion did not address the legal merits of the dismissal, but, instead, alleged that the trial judge, Judge Newton, harbored a several decade-long personal vendetta against Ridgeway, dating back to their time in the Public Defender's Office together. Ridgeway maintained in the Motion that over a period of years, Judge Newton had turned the Brandywine County Political Machine against him, making it impossible for him to practice law in his home county.

According to my law school professor who taught us about the Ridgeway case, the Brandywine County Political Machine was a lonely remaining bastion of sinister government that had not been present in any American major metropolitan area for the past 50 years. Conspiracy theorist that she was, my professor, while not knowing the basis for Ridgeway's claims of a concerted plot against him by the Brandywine County judiciary, nevertheless advised her students that Ridgeway might not have been as off base as he appeared. She shared with us that there really was a "Brandywine County Political Machine" that not only hand-selected its judges and other elected officials, but that closely controlled their agendas once they were in office.

At the time, I remembered dismissing what my professor had said as typical disgruntled rhetoric from someone who was upset that the mean salary of her students in five years would be double hers. Meeting Ridgeway in the flesh did little to change my prior opinion.

In any event, as I recalled, Judge Newton not only denied the Motion for Reconsideration, but penned a sharply worded published opinion that called into question Ridgeway's fitness to practice law, and all but accused him of having committed malpractice on behalf of his clients.

While the preliminary objection ruling was under appeal in Superior Court, Pennsylvania's intermediate appellate court, the case took a turn for the bizarre. After a late dinner at a restaurant in Center City Philadelphia, Ridgeway walked back to where his car had been parked. The journey to his vehicle required that he walk through Philadelphia's "Gayberhood." During his westbound walk on Walnut Street, he stumbled upon a familiar face walking eastbound on the same side of the street.

George Ridgeway, minding his own business, came face to face with his nemesis, Judge Newton, right there on Walnut Street. Instead of wearing his black robes and holding a gavel, Judge Newton was wearing a black leather vest and chaps and was holding the hand of a similarly dressed man. A sixty-something devout Catholic, and family man, Judge Newton had not previously disclosed his homosexual tendencies to anyone.

The next part of the story was subject to divergent accounts. What is undisputed is that days after the "Gayberhood" encounter, Ridgeway, draped in an American flag, appeared outside the Brandywine County Courthouse in Weston, PA, holding a sign that read, "Judge Newton is a Corrupt Homosexual." It is further undisputed that Ridgeway, and his sign, appeared on the front cover of the Brandywine County Daily Post the following day. Within the week, Judge Newton came clean concerning his sexual tendencies, admitting during a live television news conference, that he was a "proud competent gay jurist." During the press conference, he was flanked by his wife, children and the other 26 judges on the Brandywine County bench.

What is disputed is that according to Ridgeway's account, Judge Newton, when he encountered Ridgeway in the Gayberhood, offered him $25,000.00 in exchange for his silence. Judge Newton claimed to have come clean, immediately upon seeing Ridgeway, requesting only that he not expose what he had seen until Judge Newton had had a chance to first tell his family. Judge Newton vehemently denied offering Ridgeway any money.

Within weeks after his display in front of the Brandywine County Courthouse, charges were brought against Ridgeway under the Pennsylvania Rules of Professional Conduct for intentionally making a false statement about a sitting judge. While Judge Newton did not dispute that he was a homosexual, he fervently disputed that he was a "corrupt" homosexual, as declared by Ridgeway's sign.

An Office of Disciplinary Counsel panel ultimately ruled that the corruption allegations were reckless, unfounded and vexatious, and recommended a disbarment of Ridgeway. Ridgeway's high-priced attorneys were unable to persuade the Pennsylvania Supreme Court to reduce the penalty to a suspension from the practice of law for a period of years.

The <u>Ridgeway</u> case was universally taught as an illustration that under the Pennsylvania Rules of Professional Conduct, ordinary First Amendment rights were a bit murky when it came to making public inflammatory statements about judges.

When I finally caught my breath and regained my composure, all that I could think of to say was, *"You're* 'Ridgeway' of <u>Office of Disciplinary Counsel v. Ridgeway</u>?"

Hyper-sarcastically, he replied, "Sandy, we've got a genius on our hands."

"Wow, it's really a pleasure to meet you," I added, as if star struck, "They really railroaded you, didn't they? Is it true what I've heard about the 'Brandywine County Political Machine'?"

"Young man, you can't even begin to imagine." He said, while chewing on a large piece of turtle flesh from his snapper soup, "What they taught you out of the casebook ain't the half of it. Let me ask you, what do you remember from that case?"

"Uhh, it's been a while," I responded, "but I know that you and Newton had a history dating back to the P.D.'s Office, he screwed you on a case, you saw him holding hands with his gay lover in Center City, he allegedly tried to bribe you, you held up an inflammatory sign outside the courthouse and ended up getting disbarred."

"Pretty good. Now let me tell you what you don't know. Not only did Newton bribe me, but I took the money – all twenty-five grand of it. He had to borrow the money from that judgette, Mary Elizabeth Rolston, because he had a honey of a gambling problem to complement his buggery habit." In a vociferous tone, he continued, "I guess you're wondering why I'm admitting to you, a complete stranger, that I've committed a felony, right?"

I assumed that I was one step ahead of Ridgeway. I figured that he was going to tell me that he had just retained me as counsel, and as such, I was prohibited, pursuant to my duty of confidentiality, from disclosing the admission to anyone, even law enforcement authorities.

I figured wrong.

"If you're thinking that the attorney-client duty of confidentiality is what makes me feel secure in disclosing this information to you, then you're wrong. I couldn't give a shit if you repeat what I've told you to CNN. If I were ever proven to have accepted the bribe, it would necessarily mean that Newton would be proven to have offered it and that Rolston was part of the conspiracy. They would both be taken down from the bench and shockwaves would be sent through the county. So, everyone knows that I'll never get busted for accepting a bribe because neither Newton nor Rolston would ever corroborate the story."

"Why did Judge Rolston give him the money?"

"Because that's what they do in Brandywine County. They take care of each other. Newton, several years ago, transformed her from a Clerk in the Prothonotary's Office into a bloody COMMON PLEAS JUDGE!!! The woman couldn't get a job out of law school, so she went from menial job to menial job in the courthouse, until Newton took a liking to her and moved her up the ladder. And, you better believe that when Newton called the heads of his political party and directed them to endorse Rolston, they hopped to it. Newton was one of the best fundraisers the party had until it came out that he liked to take it up the ass. The man had so much power, though, that even after he came out of the closet, he kept his seat on the bench. Is that the least bit baffling to you?"

Ridgeway was now foaming out of both sides of his mouth. With his snapper soup finished, he was now chowing down on his liverwurst sandwich, the sight of which made my hangover symptoms return. This man was diabolical.

Why the hell had Sandy Markowitz, an exceedingly successful physician and businessman, mixed himself up with this nut?

Responding to Ridgeway's query, genuinely fearful that red beams were going to shoot out of his eyes and melt me, I managed a meek, "Indeed it is."

"O.K., bucko, then we're on the same page. This leads me to why we've brought you here today. Being semi-retired as I am, and having exposed the Brandywine County Political Machine for what it is, I've had to find new things to crusade for. You see, my daughter lives in north-central Pennsylvania. About two years ago..."

He paused, his face became even redder than its normal state, and tears began to flow. After composing himself and wiping the tears away with a handkerchief, he continued,

"About two years ago, her eight year-old son – my only grandchild – out of nowhere, couldn't catch his breath, his face became flushed and his lips turned blue. My daughter rushed him to the hospital, which was only about ten minutes away. When they got there, he was still conscious, but they had no cardiologist on call. They ended up sending him in a helicopter down to Hershey, but it was too late. He was gone. Mitral regurgitation. Here's the pisser: two years prior, a cardiology practice consisting of three doctors that used to offer its services to that hospital flew the coop. Each of them had been hit with frivolous medical malpractice cases during the preceding years that caused their insurance premiums to skyrocket. After a while, they couldn't afford to make a living and opted to pick up and move across the New York border to a hospital in Elmira.

"If there were a cardiologist at the hospital near my daughter's home, my grandson would still be alive today. Instead, the multi-billion dollar trial lawyer lobby in this God forsaken state allows those frivolous cases to proceed. The Plaintiff attorneys love it because the state of the law here creates very lucrative results for them. The defense attorneys love it too because even though they regularly get whacked for multi-million dollar verdicts, the never-ending flow of cases keeps their kids in private school. The upshot is that our doctors are leaving and we're all suffering."

I sensed a tinge of jealously from Ridgeway towards lawyers who, unlike him, didn't have their law licenses revoked and were earning a robust living.

I gently responded, "George, I heard about something called the MCARE Act that was supposed to limit frivolous cases in

Pennsylvania. Hasn't that helped cut down on the malpractice cases and keep the doctors in the state?"

His somberness, abruptly transforming into anger, Ridgeway snapped,

"That's the problem! The trial lawyers' lobby has inundated the media with that bullshit. The MCARE Act requires that Plaintiffs in med mal cases file a Certificate of Merit. All the Certificate of Merit needs to say is that the Plaintiff's attorney has received an opinion from some whore doctor certifying that malpractice has been committed."

He was a madman, but the Physician's Justice program, nevertheless, sounded like something that might generate interest from pissed off physicians across the state. Most importantly, I saw dollar signs in my future.

"So where do I come in?" I asked.

"It's an easy concept, Alex. Like Sandy told you, the docs these days feel like the deck is stacked against them. They get sued frivolously and the insurance company hires a half-rate attorney to perform damage control. Even in the most frivolous of scenarios, do you think that the attorney hired by the insurance company is going to be pushing for a dismissal of the case?", he challenged me.

"No. A dismissal of a case means fewer billable hours." I responded.

"Sanford, we've got a fucking Rhodes Scholar in our midst."

Frustrated with his ass-backwards way of thinking and insulted by his sarcasm, I had had about enough of George Ridgeway. I had already scored one major client for the day and was flush with confidence. While I wanted to represent Physician's Justice, I wasn't about to let some elderly has-been speak down to me.

When I lost my composure, I had little fear of what the consequences might be. Lubrano Concrete was already in the bag. The worst thing that could have resulted from my outburst was that Ridgeway would have told me to leave his club. That prospect did not particularly frighten me. In the best case scenario, Ridgeway would have formed a high opinion of me, as being someone who stood up for what he believed in and would be a zealous advocate for his new venture.

At a whisper, so as not to offend other, more significant, patrons of the Perennial Club, I said,

"Listen, you miserable old fuck. I'm really sorry to hear about your grandson. That's a heartbreaking story and I can't even begin to imagine what you and your family have gone through. But I am not about to sit here and take your self-serving sarcastic offensive bullshit. You want me to serve as Physician's Justice's counsel? Fine. I'll consider it. But don't insult me. I'm a graduate of the Presbyterian Academy and of the University of Pennsylvania. I'm a smart and competent motherfucker. You may have years on me, but that's about it."

I stood up from my chair, not having touched my chicken salad sandwich and started to walk away. As I took my first step, my body was pulled back by Ridgeway grabbing my left arm and Markowitz grabbing my right arm. Markowitz asked, "Will he do?"

Ridgeway responded, with fervor,

"Unquestionably."

Breathing heavily and agitated, I asked,

"Were you acting like an asshole just to test me?"

"No, Alex. I really am an asshole. Ex-wives have said so and the courts have said so. That issue is immaterial. Sandy said that you were a stand up, hard-nosed bulldog. Now that I know that there's some truth to that statement, I would like to extend an offer for you to serve as counsel to our new venture."

Not liking this guy one bit, but feeling guilty for possibly letting Sandy down, I responded, "Gentlemen, I really need to get back to the office. Let me think about things a bit and I will get back to you."

"O.K., Alex," Sandy added, "I should warn you, though, we have seven other firms who are begging to get this gig. Tell the crew back at your office that we need an answer ASAP."

Apparently, by virtue of Sandy having made that statement, he did not take me for a particularly intelligent person. That reality depressed me. I did some hard introspection and wondered what I had done to make these people think that I was a half-wit.

"George, thank you for lunch. Sandy, it was great seeing you. Please give my best to Eric."

With those parting words, I left the Perennial Club and headed back to the office.

CHAPTER ELEVEN

I had some major ass kissing to do. Julie's act of relegating me to the couch was serious business. She wouldn't stay mad forever, but if I wanted to get back into our bed, and, moreover, her pants, action would be necessary. To that end, I telephoned an old friend from Presbyterian to help me out.

While Brian Humphrey always seemed a tad effeminate while we went to school together, no one ever would have thought that he would be the one person out of our graduating class of 93 students to proclaim his homosexuality publicly. He was one of a select few people from our class who had attended The Academy for 13 years or longer. Like me, he was a lifer.

I took a particular satisfaction in mocking my longtime friend for being gay. It was not an act of homophobia; it was a just fun thing to do.

After I dialed and the phone rang a few times, a flamboyant, bitchy sounding male voice answered, "Huuuuuuh-low – Roberto Brian Florists, can I help you?"

Seizing the moment, I couldn't help myself. In my best Harvey Fierstein accent, I said,

"Uhhm yes, I told my boyfriend, Bruce, that he had big thighs. I'm not sure why he was offended because I meant it as a compliment, but I need the perfect thing to make him forgive me. Can you gays...err...guys help me with something like that?"

"Brown, what the hell do you want – some of us work for a living – don't you have an ambulance to chase?" He responded.

"Alright, *touché, pédé*," I added.

Turning the tables, he said, "You know how hot I get when you speak French."

"Brian, I think that I just vomited in my mouth. Why would you say something like that to me? Plus, '*pédé*' means 'faggot.' I was trying to insult you." I added.

"Well, the joke's on you because all it did was get me excited. Why would you call me and waste my time when I have flowers to arrange?"

Grappling with the seemingly impossible fact that I played offensive line on the eighth grade football team next to someone who now arranged flowers for a living, religiously watched Rachael Ray, and had a Latin lover named "Roberto," I changed to a more serious tone,

"Brian, I need you to send flowers to Julie at her office. You have my credit card information. Just put something together and charge me whatever is appropriate – unless, of course, you already maxed out my credit card stocking up on KY jelly, in the event that there is a worldwide shortage."

As I was speaking into the phone, Nick Carlson made a thumb and pinkie finger sign to the side of his face, to suggest that I should call him when I was off the phone.

Brian responded, "What did you do this time, you bastard? Please don't tell me that she caught you fucking your nineteen year-old paralegal."

"Brian, I resent that. You know damn well that my paralegal is in her late thirties."

"I'll take care of it. I'll pick out a cute necklace and put it in with the flowers, too."

"Let's not get carried away. I didn't fuck up that badly. I just came home late after having dinner with Lubrano last night."

"God, he is so hot. Is he still gorgeous? I haven't run into him for years."

"Brian, I'm now actually feeling physically ill – and I'm not even joking. You're just trying to agitate me at this point."

With that comment, he erupted into a very non-gay, masculine laughter, that reminded me of the old days when he was just one of the guys.

Amping up his bitchiness, he snapped, "Alright, I'm done with you. Don't be such a cheap son of a bitch. You've got yourself a nice little trophy wife. We really don't know what she sees in you, but she's yours nevertheless. I don't care how big the fuck up was, she's still pissed at you. She's getting a necklace with the flowers. You might even get laid tonight."

Following his logic, I responded, "Fine. Do what you need to do. Thanks, man. Listen, after Julie gets the flowers and she's speaking to me again, I'll have her call you to set up a dinner with all four of us."

"Good idea. Ciao. Gotta run," he said as he hung up the phone.

The "four of us" referred to myself, Julie, Brian, and his "partner," Roberto Maldonado. Julie loved evenings out with "the ladies." For Julie, dining with "the ladies" was like dining with two of her girlfriends. They would talk about the latest celebrity gossip, decorating ideas, and whatever fashion *faux pas* were occurring in the particular restaurant in which we were dining.

Brian better have been right about the necklace getting me laid.

CHAPTER TWELVE

Although Carlson had directed me to buzz him once I was finished with my call, I nevertheless felt compelled to walk down to his office to address whatever issue he had. This decision was half based on the premise that I felt it ridiculous that some people chose to communicate within an office by intercom when, after a three second walk, a face to face conversation could occur. My decision was also half based on my desire to contravene his direction to me. I didn't generally have a big problem with authority, when the person asserting the authority was the same person who signed my paycheck. I did have a problem with bullies, though.

So as to subtly communicate to Carlson that I would not be bullied by him, I periodically purposefully did not follow his directions. This was one such scenario. Instead of calling him via the intercom so that he could use his bully pulpit to bark orders at me using his speakerphone, I made the eleven pace journey down to his office.

When I arrived at his office, I knocked on the door twice and entered before being invited in.

Startled, Nick asked, "I thought that I asked you to...never mind. Just, uhh, shut the door and take a seat."

I obliged.

"Alex, my boy," he asked, "let me pose a few questions to you."

Since my billable hour total from the previous month was a very respectable 216.8 and I hadn't missed any deadlines that I could think of, I was perplexed as to what subject matter Carlson was prepared to bust my balls about.

"First," he began, "what did the chick look like who you banged last night, and does she have a sister? Second, how did Julie find out? And, third, why in God's name were you spotted at The Perennial Club eating lunch with George Fucking Ridgeway today?"

Carlson had overheard me ordering flowers for Julie and probably assumed that I was caught with my pants down, therefore necessitating the flowers. As for being detected at the Perennial Club in Ridgeway's presence, it was immediately apparent to me that someone in the Lombard Room had recognized me and, horrified that I was dining with someone as notorious as Ridgeway, called Carlson to tell on me. While a few years earlier in my career, I might have stroked Carlson's ego by allowing him to tell me about his far-reaching allies all over the city, I was unwilling to do so on this occasion. I therefore didn't start my answer by asking Nick how he had known that I was with Ridgeway.

Instead, I simply responded, "Nick, I was wining and dining a potential client last night, who incidentally, I signed up a few hours ago. I got home really late last night, and Julie's pissed. I just sent her flowers to get back in her good graces. No banging of other women took place."

"You sure? You know you can talk to me if things aren't right at home," he replied.

Nick Carlson was about the last person with whom I would consider discussing any problem, let alone a domestic problem. Furthermore, as I knew that he couldn't care less about anything affecting me other than how much money I was making him, he clearly had a veiled agenda, namely banging my wife.

"Nope, but thanks for asking," I responded in a fatigued tone.

"Aren't you curious how I knew that you were eating with George Ridgeway?" he asked proudly.

"Nick, I saw five or six attorneys at the Perennial Club whom I've had cases with. One of them must have recognized me and called you, right?"

Baffled that I was able to deduce such a simple concept in such short order, he shot back, irritated,

"Well, just remember that I have people all over this city and beyond who respect me and who let me know right away if something or someone with whom I am associated is...is...doing something fishy."

"Nick, there was nothing fishy about the meeting. I didn't know that he was *the* Ridgeway of <u>Office of Disciplinary Counsel v. Ridgeway</u> fame."

"Well, Mr. Ivy League genius, he *is* that Ridgeway. Now what the hell were you doing breaking fucking bread with that asshole – in The Perennial Club, of all places, where you demonstrated to the whole city that Krauss Carlson associates itself with suspended reject lawyers who have a habit of defaming members of the bench?"

"Nick, it was nothing, really," I began, with Carlson glaring at me as if he were an elementary school principal and I had just hit a girl, "a family friend, Dr. Sandy Markowitz, is partnered in a new program with Ridgeway called, Physician's Justice. It's pretty simple: Doc pays a set fee per year to belong to the program. If he gets sued, he gets personal counsel, provided by the program, to work in conjunction with his insurance company-appointed counsel. Markowitz and Ridgeway are looking for a firm to provide the personal counsel services to its subscribers. That's where we would come in."

"Alex I'm gonna tell you this once and only once: George Ridgeway is a certifiable, Class A lunatic. You don't have the slightest fucking idea what this guy is all about. I know people in Brandywine County who have told me some serious shit about this guy. Before he got his ass suspended or disbarred or whatever, he was one son of a bitch of a lawyer. He used to have an office in Weston, right next to the courthouse. His partner was Jim Winston – a real bullheaded Brandywine County power broker blowhard. Winston had so much power in that county that when he drove his Ford Crown Victoria through the window of a bedding store while shitfaced, he didn't even get charged by the police. They wrote up the incident report indicating that he hit a deer! A deer in the middle of the Borough of Weston. They might as well have said that he hit a camel! The man was so well connected that the bedding store owner was practically apologizing to him after the accident for having his storefront so close to the street. Winston took a nice souvenir from the accident though. He was left with a severe limp because his left leg was broken in something like 14 places."

This information did not surprise me. From what I had heard about how things worked in Brandywine County, I believed every word of what Carlson, usually full of shit, was telling me. He continued,

"Ridgeway always resented Winston for the power that he wielded with the judges, County Council members and civic leaders. Winston got tons of lucrative easy municipal work from his contacts. Ridgeway always arrived in the office earlier and left later than Winston. Ridgeway toiled away at his five million bullshit slip and fall cases, while Winston was three sheets to the wind, teeing off on the golf course by 1 p.m. every day. The final straw occurred after Ridgeway lost his license. Ridgeway had settled some humongous personal injury case that brought in a $10 million fee for their firm. While he settled that case before he lost his license, the terms of the General Release were not agreed to until after his license was revoked. So, once the settlement proceeds came in, Winston refused to distribute a penny to Ridgeway, based on Rule of Professional Conduct 5.4."

What a ballsy conniving son of a gun this Winston was. Now I felt a tad bit of empathy for Ridgeway. Pennsylvania Rule of Professional Conduct 5.4 provides that an attorney may not share fees with a non-attorney. Since Ridgeway was not licensed, he was, technically, not a lawyer, and apparently according to his former law partner, was not permitted to receive any of the proceeds from his own case.

Carlson continued,

"Ridgeway hired a lawyer who immediately filed for a temporary restraining order in Brandywine County to enjoin Winston from moving the $10 million and to compel Winston to place the money into an escrow account. Now, here's the kicker: Ridgeway files the friggin' TRO paperwork. When do you think that the hearing was scheduled for?"

"Well, in any TRO that I've filed or that's been filed against one of my clients, a hearing was either scheduled that day or the following day," I responded.

In fact, temporary restraining orders, unlike preliminary injunctions or permanent injunctions, were aimed at maintaining the status quo and preventing irreparable harm. While monetary harm alone was not, in theory, sufficient to cause a court to order injunctive relief, in a scenario in which a party was alleging that another party was going to abscond with $10 million, a temporary restraining order would normally be heard and granted with 48 hours.

"How does *two weeks* sound to you?" Carlson asked, smirking and reclining in his desk chair.

"It sounds like the fix was in," I responded, matter of factly.

"You bet your ass the fix was in, but you have absolutely no idea to what extent. The TRO was filed on a Tuesday. As I understand it, after Ridgeway's attorney didn't hear from the Court Administrator by the close of business on Thursday, he called over there. The Court Administrator claimed there was no record of the document having been filed with the Prothonotary, even though Ridgeway's attorney had a time-stamped copy of what was filed. They then told him that he had to re-file the document with the Prothonotary, which he did on Friday at 9:00 a.m. Hearing nothing by the close of business the following Monday, and unable to get a live person to speak with him from the Court Administrator's Office, Ridgeway's attorney goes all the way up the ladder and writes a letter to the President Judge of the Brandywine County Court of Common Pleas, Tom Koziara. That was a bad move, because if they truly believed that there was hanky panky going on, Koziara was the wrong guy to approach, as he was probably in on it. He was long rumored to have been on the payrolls of the unions and others, and was the biggest political hack in the whole county. Anyway, Koziara, two days later, pens a nasty-gram outlining the impropriety of the mere act of contacting him, when the proper course of action would have been to wait until the Court Administrator took action. The next day, Ridgeway's attorney gets a call from the Court Administrator stating that a TRO hearing could not be scheduled until the following week because Winston was on a hunting trip and would not be back until then."

"Wait a minute, TROs are regularly heard and granted *ex parte*, without the respondent being there," I said, in disbelief.

"No shit, Sherlock, last time I checked, I've been practicing law for three decades longer than you. Would you care to enlighten me on any other topics?" Carlson barked.

"No, Nick," I replied, with disgust.

"Well, as it turns out, Winston was on a hunting trip alright, a pretty damn exotic hunting trip – in Kenya. Only problem was that by the time the hearing actually took place and the TRO was granted – without Winston in attendance, of course – the bank account had already been liquidated, and Winston was probably sucking on barbecued cheetah ribs in Kenya. The epilogue to the story is that Ridgeway never saw a penny of the money, but Winston ultimately got his. A few years after he disappeared, Winston was found dead in Spain. His body was beaten so badly by robbers that the only way that he was able to be identified was by his passport which was in his pocket. The dumb ass muggers took his pocket money and credit cards, but didn't take the one item that could have gotten them the most value – his American passport.

"The story was all over the TV news and in the papers. Ridgeway, steadfast as ever, gets interviewed on Action News and says that he was certain that there was a God and that by Winston being brutally maimed, his prayers were answered. He went on to say that his only regret was that he couldn't have killed Winston himself."

Carlson, now at full laughter, continued, "Alex, my bro, this is the guy with whom you want to get involved in a business venture?!"

With the last of the alcohol leaving my system in the form of heavy perspiration on my brow, I came to the halting realization that I would be ill-advised to recommend that the firm take on the Physician's Justice program as a client. Ridgeway was bad news all around and seemed to find trouble wherever he turned. Judging by the number of enemies that he apparently possessed on the bench and bar, it seemed imprudent to associate myself with him and possibly jeopardize my career.

To that end, I confidently asserted, "Nick, I think that I've heard all I need to hear. There's no way this firm should be doing business with that maniac."

I envisioned that Carlson would be content that he had convinced me so easily. He wasn't. Instead, he was in the mood to play games with me.

"So," Carlson said, "is that it, counsel? You gonna give up after I told you a few things about Ridgeway's past? If a multi-millionaire business owner came into the office saying that he got sued for sexual harassment, are you gonna refuse to represent him if he admitted to you that his pinched his secretary's ass every morning? Hell no! You're gonna charge him $450 an hour and zealously represent him, and prove that that stupid bitch is a liar!"

Now, I was confused.

"You're gonna take this representation and you're gonna make this firm some money. If it backfires, it backfires. It's only your ass and your career. Don't sweat it," Carlson said with an ominous smile.

"Alright, you have hours to bill. Why can't you ever hit 225 hours? When Walt and I started this firm, we used to compete as to who had the highest billable hours total. One month, I edged out Walt 326.2 to 326.1. You guys should start competing like that. It would be healthy to have competition like that, no?

"Off you go."

"O.K., Nick, I'm certainly up to the task if you think that this representation is worthwhile," I stated tentatively, not knowing what was going to come out of his mouth next.

"Great, goodbye. Didn't I say 'off you go'? That's your cue to scram. I've got to call Kevin Donaghey from Maxus Industries about our fishing charter tomorrow morning. Shut my door on your way out."

I should have shut his face in the door on my way out. As I left his office, I fantasized about one day having ten clients like Lubrano Concrete and Physician's Justice so that I could start my own firm and not have to be subservient to assholes like Carlson.

CHAPTER THIRTEEN

My head was spinning from the events of the day and I needed to blow off a little mid-afternoon steam. So, I found myself in the grungy depths of Suburban Station at the Turf Club. The Turf Club is an off-track betting facility where one can place pari-mutuel bets on horse races held throughout the country. I resorted to this hell hole three or so times per year when the going got really tough. On this day, the going had gotten really tough.

The Turf Club was a virtual Hall of Fame for Philadelphia degenerates. At any given time, the number of healthy teeth in the establishment rarely rose above the number of pennants that the Phillies have won since the team's inception in 1883.

Incidentally, that number is seven. And yes, I'm talking about *that* 1883 – the one occurring 18 years after the last shots were fired at Appomattox Court House.

There were all types of trash in the Turf Club – white, black, Asian, Latin – men, women – you name it. Although a citywide smoking ban had been enacted in Philadelphia several years back, and the Turf Club adhered to the ban, the smell of cigarette and cigar smoke was still noticeable, having infiltrated the walls, ceiling and furniture prior to the ban.

Notwithstanding the shady clientele, I was hardly the only patron wearing a suit. A few unshaven bottom feeding criminal defense-looking attorneys lined the bar drinking Budweiser bottles, and watching the sixth race at Gulfstream (or, in Philadelphia-speak, "Golf-shtream"). A few copy service runners were sitting at a table, following the seventh race at Belmont.

I knew that the guys at the bar were criminal defense counsel by the way that their top shirt buttons were undone and their ties loosened. They were blue collar lawyers and looked about as comfortable in their suits as they would have looked five minutes before their vasectomy procedures. Detecting the copy guys was a bit more simple: they were standing next to their dollies. Copy guys in Center City were omnipresent. Toting bankers' boxes filled with their law firm clients' copy jobs, they too wore suits, albeit extremely cheap ones.

I had learned to play the ponies from Julie's father, Louie D'Amico, a Brooklyn native. Louie was about as great of a father-in-law that someone such as myself could ask for. He was a retired high school teacher who told dirty jokes, pinched his wife's ass in plain view at family functions, perpetually smelled of coffee, and, most importantly, loved baseball. Sure, he was a former Brooklyn Dodgers fan turned New York Mets fan, but how could I fault him? He was passionate about his hometown team, just as I was about my beloved, much maligned Phillies.

The very first time that I was invited to Julie's parents' house was during Easter Break, while we were in law school and had been dating for only a few months. After we arrived and I had ungodly amounts of cheeses, sopprasetta, and pizzelles shoved down my throat, Louie grabbed my arm and said in perfect Brooklynese, with a large chunk of sausage stuck in his front teeth,

"You eva play da' ponies? Listen, I'm gunna take you ova ta OTB. Ya' watch da' races and bet on da' horses dare." After a short but deafening argument ensued (New Yorkers, and, especially, Long Islanders, are really, really loud), during which Julie and her mother, Stella, castigated Louie for even making such a suggestion, I jumped in and indicated a desire to go to the off track betting parlor. As unappealing as the prospect of going to OTB sounded, I figured that I could get in good with Julie's dad if I followed his lead.

After Louie gave me a crash course in exactas, keying, and wheeling, I was hooked. Unlike casino gambling, betting the horses seemed to be a more cerebral, and moreover, enjoyable way of losing one's money. I found dissecting the horses' past performances in the Daily Racing Form to be fascinating and challenging. Thus, each and every time that Julie and I visited her parents' house, Louie and I went to OTB, thereby insulating me from trips to the mall with her mother and sister. While we often got into heated arguments during our OTB encounters concerning such issues as whether Steve "Lefty" Carlton or Tom "Terrific" Sea-vuuuh was a better pitcher or whether the '80 Phillies or the '86 Mets were a better team, the time we spent together betting the ponies was very useful for purposes of bonding.

On this day, though, I didn't have Louie to lean over and tell me who the "freakin' lock of the day" was. I did, however, have the benefit of an inebriated man plopping down next to me and circling in black ink on my opened page of the Racing Form, the seven horse, Roddy's Hair, a four year old gelding who was running in a $43,000.00 Allowance Race at Belmont. As each of his unsolicited words exited his mouth and I received wafts of his alcohol breath, my hangover symptoms resurfaced to a greater degree.

"I saw dat horse run dale-n in *Baldy-more* at Pimlico *lass* year. One uh dem trainers toll me dat da jockey was holdin' 'em back on purr-puss fer money. Ain't no one beatin' his ass tuh-day. I'm bettin' da' house on it. Look at doze odds – a horse dat good goin' off at 12 ta' 1 – you'll make a mint!" he said, with his drunken eyes hidden in his opaque prescription lenses. I noticed that his hair, clumped together in black and gray greasy bunches, had likely not been washed in well over a week.

"Thanks, pal. I'm all set. You have a nice day," I brusquely retorted, as he walked over to another unwelcoming subject to perpetuate more unseemly nonsense.

After I was able to somewhat politely shoo away the vagrant while narrowly avoiding his gin and tonic spilling onto my left shoe, I made a selection for the Belmont race. My choice was not based upon the empirical data that I had garnered from the Racing Form, but rather upon what I could decipher about the man who tried to pick Roddy's Hair for me. As this guy was a downtrodden loser who had probably drunk and gambled away everything of import that he had attained in his life, when I looked seven minutes into the future, I could not see this man winning the race. I could see him *nearly* winning the race and losing in heartbreaking fashion. So, I threw out what logic and the Racing Form told me. Quite confident that Booze Man's horse would finish second, I made a $35 bet, taking a $5 exacta with all of the seven other horses in the race finishing "on top" and Roddy's Hair finishing "beneath." Thus, if Roddy's Hair finished second, I had the exacta.

I walked up the betting window, said,

"Belmont, five dollar exacta, all with seven," grabbed my tote ticket from the clerk's machine and retook my seat.

With six minutes until post time, I figured that I would check my Blackberry to see what crises were awaiting me back at the office. As I pulled the handheld device out of my side suit jacket pocket, several patrons looked over at me, snickered and pointed towards me. Nestled between two routine conflict check e-mails from our office manager was the following subject line,

```
Brown, Julianna A. - They're Beautiful!
```

Before I opened the e-mail, I knew that all was forgiven. The e-mail read,

```
Honey, Princess Brian
really outdid himself
this time! Three dozen
red roses and diamond
earrings that are one
carat apiece. I love you!
```

I quickly wrote back, not buying her story, but willing to let her get some mileage off of the joke.

```
What?! Please tell me
that you're kidding.
I told him to keep it
within reason.
```

Thirty seconds later, Julie wrote back,

```
Oh, I guess that the
three dozen red roses
and earrings were meant
to go to your mistress
and I was supposed to
receive something less
significant. Oh well,
I'm glad that Brian
mixed it up. Her loss is
my gain. Won't she be
disappointed when she
gets the crappy present.
```

As the game was quickly becoming unfunny, I shot back a message that read,

```
Ha ha ha. What's the
damage…really.
```

She responded,

```
A dozen roses, and a
David Yurman bracelet.
They're beautiful – and
you're forgiven.
```

One of my favorite attributes about Julie was that no matter how mad she was, generous gifts thrown in her direction always alleviated whatever damage I had done. In my experience, nothing with the name, "David Yurman" affixed to it cost less than $500.00, so the price of forgiveness and associated night of sex wouldn't come cheap. Ah, what the hell. She was no longer pissed at me. Who could put a price tag on that?

My return message read,

```
Glad that you liked it. I
told Brian that it had to
be David Yurman, or else
it just wouldn't do. I
know that you're pissed
about last night, but the
dinner turned out to be
quite fruitful - I signed
up Lubrano Concrete
today.
```

As the gates opened at Belmont and the ponies were off, Julie wrote back,

```
Great news! Have you
decided what you're
buying me with the huge
raise that they're going
to give you after your
first monthly bill to
Lubrano nets the firm
$100,000.00? J.K. - the
Yurman bracelet and the
flowers will do for now.
But, I'll let you buy me
dinner tonight.
```

As the horses were nearing the one-quarter pole, with Roddy's Hair's previous five length lead rapidly shrinking, I responded,

```
How 'bout after dinner,
you let me make you a
sinner?
```

Since the time when I began to date Julie, I always derived secret pleasure in knowing that she had to have been committing some sort of deadly sin by permitting a non-Catholic, let alone a Jew, enjoy carnal knowledge of her. For shits and giggles, I periodically liked to remind her of her transgressions in that regard.

As the horses crossed the wire, with Roddy's Hair and Crafty Weasel finishing so close that a photographic review was necessary to determine the victor, Julie wrote back,

```
Depends on where you're
taking me to dinner. I'm
not feeling like much of
a sinner right now ;)
```

Before responding, I waited to see the outcome of the race. Crafty Weasel was a 25-1 shot. If the photo finish revealed that he had eked out a victory over Roddy's Hair, I was about to come into enough money that would more than pay for a dinner for two in any restaurant in the city, including Le Bec Fin, Barclay Prime or Butcher and Singer. While the Belmont officials mulled over photographic results, Booze Man was already launching f-bombs and other miscellaneous nonsensical, inane statements, such as "Youse're ale-t of yer minds! Duh seven horse won by a foot!"

This was clearly not the case, as the video replay, which had been shown about ten times, left any objective onlooker confounded as to who the winner was. Based upon Booze Man's comments, though, I had never been so confident of a gambling triumph in my life.

As the neon sign on Belmont's tote board that read, "PHOTO" was switched off, and was replaced with an illuminated sign that read, "OFFICIAL" my new wealth was confirmed. The order of finish read,

5
7
3
8

A still photo was shown on the board, demonstrating that Crafty Weasel, did, indeed, edge out Roddy's Hair by the slimmest of margins. The two dollar exacta paid $348.20, making my five dollar bet worth $870.50, for a net of $835.50. Not bad for a few minutes worth of work. Booze Man didn't seem to be as content as me.

After shouting, "Fuckin' fixed! Youse're all crooks!", he ripped up his tickets and wandered into Suburban Station, probably to check the phone booths' change return compartments for enough money to make more bets.

After I collected my winnings, I wrote back to Julie,

```
What will dinner at Rouge
get me?
```

Sure, I could have taken her to one of the ultra-ritzy establishments with my newfound riches, but dinner at the chic and reliable culinary marvel on Rittenhouse Square would more than do the trick. Plus, she didn't know about my winnings, and she did make me sleep on the couch the previous night. In light of that ill-advised decision, she couldn't be pampered too much.

```
Ooooh - you really aren't
taking any chances that
I might feel too tired
for lovin' when we get
home. Rouge it is. See
you there at seven. It's
a date. Love you baby, J.
```

What I found funny was that had I not pissed her off by coming home late the previous night, the flowers, bracelet and fancy dinner would not have materialized. Moreover, the virtual certainty of my getting laid that night would not have materialized either. So, in essence, by breaking the rules, I was in prime position to get rewarded.

Life really was comical sometimes. As I left the Turf Club with sixteen fifty dollar bills and change stuffed in my Bally billfold, I pondered whether Julie and I would always play these games. I hoped that we would.

CHAPTER FOURTEEN

Rittenhouse Square is a breathtaking oasis adjacent to the Market Street legal corridor. Its large size amasses four city blocks, and is lined with numerous benches and grassy areas. Yuppies walk their dogs and lovers of all ages walk hand-in-hand for hours on end, enjoying the splendors of this refuge from the stresses of city life. The Square is bounded on four sides by expensive housing, hotels, retail stores and restaurants. Prior to the mid-1990s, while still a swank residential address, Rittenhouse Square had little in the way of retail business or dining. In the mid-1990s, anchored by Rouge, a French style bistro with indoor and outdoor seating, Rittenhouse Square became a hotbed for Philadelphia's elite to see and be seen.

On this warm late Spring evening, I arrived at Rouge at 6:45 p.m., in the hope that I would already have secured a table by the time that Julie arrived. When I arrived at the maître d' podium, I was greeted by a woman who appeared to be in her early 40s, but wanted onlookers to believe that she was in her mid-20s. With readily apparent salon-colored shoulder length red hair and ridiculous looking collagen enhanced lips that frowned at me as I approached, I bid the woman an enthusiastic,

"Hello, there! What a beautiful evening, huh?"

"How can I help you, sir?" she responded as if I were not only wasting her time, but the time of restaurant's cooks, wait staff and bus staff.

"Well, my wife and I are meeting for a romantic dinner tonight and would love to be seated outside on 18th Street. I didn't call ahead for a reservation because this was a last-minute arrangement, but do you think that you would have any..."

"I've got a one hour wait for our inside dining room and a two hour wait for outside. If you would like, I can put you on the list and you can have a seat at the bar," she snapped.

As I thought over the options that she had presented to me, I gazed into the dark restaurant's white marble bar area and carefully pondered my decision. Seated at the bar were the usual run of the mill thirty- and forty-something rich divorcée "Cougars" looking for young meat, and immaculately dressed husband-hunting twenty-somethings who lived off of credit cards. While the Cougars would have undoubtedly engaged me in interesting conversation until Julie arrived, the twenty-somethings would not have even glanced in my direction, as I stood below six feet tall and would, therefore, be deemed unsuitable for marriage and, moreover, conversation.

I wanted a seat outside, and I wanted it right then. Undeterred by the hostess, and fearful that Julie's good mood might turn sour if she arrived and were faced with an extended wait for a table, I reached into my billfold, retrieved one of my new fifties, folded it four times and placed it in between by thumb and index finger. I stated with a smile, extending U.S. Grant in her direction,

"I'd really like to be seated now. Can you make that happen?"

"Yes, I actually think that I can," she responded, while taking the bill and briefly examining it to confirm its authenticity. With two menus in hand, she walked me to a prime location in the outside seating area and said, with a genuine smile affixed to her face, "I hope that you and your wife have a wonderful evening. Kendra will be with you shortly. Enjoy!"

"Thank you."

When the hostess graciously made herself evaporate, I sat back in my chair and gazed across the street to the goings on in Rittenhouse Square. With the sun still shining down on the frolicking lovers and Frisbee tossers on this high 70 degree early evening, I quickly concluded that my fifty dollar investment was a wise one. With the uncertainties of life, I thought of how insignificant, in the long run, fifty dollars was.

A very chipper waitress arrived to take my drink order while I waited for Julie. Kendra was a trim young lady with a brown bob cut and eyeglasses that nicely complimented her look. I ordered an Amstel Light for myself and a soft drink for Julie who only drank alcohol on rare occasions. As I uttered the words, "Diet Coke," to Kendra, Julie arrived, out of breath, in a dark suit, looking stunning. She dropped her briefcase, sat in her chair and said, "Actually, I'll have a chardonnay." Kendra pleasantly took the order and walked back into the restaurant.

It was immediately apparent to me that prior to leaving her office, Julie had applied a fresh coat of make-up, with extra amounts around the eyes as she knew that I liked. That effort, in itself, was a tremendous turn on to me, and signaled that she was excited for our romantic evening without Charlie, who was staying with my parents overnight.

"The bracelet is gorgeous. I really have great taste, *n'est pas?*" I asked sarcastically.

"Well," she responded coyly and sexily, "you may not have great taste in jewelry, but you're the hottest guy at this table. Plus, if you did have good enough taste to pick out this piece, I might be worried about you."

We shared a laugh and I kissed her on the lips as a salutation. After we engaged in some small talk for a few minutes about our respective days at work, Kendra returned with our drinks. With my glass raised for a toast, I said, "To us." We clinked glasses, I kissed her lips again, and we gazed out onto Rittenhouse Square.

Rouge harkened me back to my days as a young man living in Paris. The café tables were arranged in such a manner as to allow two people at a table to sit next to each other, rather than across from each other. This allowed Philadelphians to take part in the most Parisian of pastimes: people watching.

With its sprawling Benjamin Franklin Parkway that was modeled by French urban planner Jacques Gréber after the Champs-Élysées in Paris and a history of Général Lafayette crucially aiding George Washington during the Revolutionary War's Pennsylvania campaign, Philadelphia shares a storied bond with Paris and the French. In spite of this bond with its

European sister, Philadelphia cannot easily be confused with Paris. Nevertheless, Rouge and a few gastro-bars scattered throughout the city sufficed to address the homesickness that I frequently felt for the City of Light.

As the sky began to darken on this gorgeous Spring evening, Julie dined on seared tuna and I on steak frites. While we ate, I enjoyed watching numerous men walking by our table and gazing at my stunning bride. Most of these men looked handsome and successful. Many husbands in my position might have felt bothered or even intimidated from the glances of the passers-by. Not I, though.

The fleeting looks were not lost on Julie. When one particular dark haired six foot three GQ-looking subject admired my wife's cleavage, Julie caught me noticing him noticing. With a brazenly seductive grin, Julie asked,

"Jealous?"

After taking a second to decide how I should respond, I stated,

"No. Not at all."

"I find that hard to believe, honey," Julie said, adjusting herself so that I was provided with an even better view of her chest.

"Why should you find that hard to believe? In 90 minutes, that guy and all of the others who have walked by gawking at you will be sitting in some bar arguing about politics or spouting out their pseudo-intellectual views on how to make the world better." After I took a long sip of my Amstel Light, patted my mouth with my napkin and reclined in my chair, I continued,

"In 90 minutes, I'll be between two sweaty sheets having sex with the woman whose knockers this series of men have been struggling to get a glimpse of."

My comment prompted an obligatory "Stop that!" from Julie, but I knew that she both enjoyed the glances of the men and my self-assured response even more. She glowed for the rest of the wonderful evening – all the way to our cozy bed at home.

Although we had been married for over five years, nights such as this made me feel like a young romantic from my earlier days. On nights such as this, I agreed with Ernest Hemingway's observation that Paris was truly a moveable feast.

CHAPTER FIFTEEN

When I arrived in the office the following morning, four banker's boxes were stacked on my two client chairs. Affixed to one of the banker's boxes was a white envelope with a return address design in the top left hand corner that contained Lubrano Concrete's logo – a cheesy stylistic rendering of the company name with an image of a crane with the American and Italian flags waving from the top. I opened the envelope expecting to find the agreed-upon $10,000.00 retainer check. What I found was, indeed, a check. The check was made out for $9,000.00, rather than $10,000.00, however. A yellow Post-It note was attached to the front of the check. It read,

Get working. Don't lose. – Vinny.

I immediately recognized the thought process behind the $1,000.00 haircut applied by the Lubranos. They knew that since our meeting, I had likely gotten the firm partners excited about the prospect of adding such a high-profile name to their client list. They were correct in that regard. They also knew that paying $1,000.00 less than the agreed-upon retainer figure would not be enough to cause the firm to rethink the representation. They were further correct in that regard. Finally, they knew that engaging in such gamesmanship would be a message that Lubrano Concrete and not Krauss Carlson would be in the driver's seat in this relationship. Three for three.

I wasn't going to let the haircut applied by the Lubranos bother me. $9,000.00 was in the door and I had work to do. The prospect of perusing roughly three thousand pages of contracts, change orders, delivery slips and architectural renderings didn't seem all that daunting since I had a well-rested, clear head, unlike the previous day, when I had to deal with a raging hangover.

I hadn't said a word to Terri about my having to review this wealth of documents and crank out a Complaint within 24 hours time. However, in a manner known only to old-school top notch secretaries, Terri was aware that today was a day in which I needed nurturing. After she gathered that I had had enough time to review my e-mails, she came into my office with a Dunkin' Donuts Box O' Joe that contained enough black coffee to serve a thirsty construction site, and a box containing 16 Butterscotch Krimpets – my absolute favorite of the Tastykake lineup.

With a succinct "Give 'em hell!" she left me alone and closed my door.

I put my phone on its "Do Not Disturb" setting and dove right into Box #1, which consisted of all of the correspondences between Lubrano Concrete and Bicentennial Lumber.

As an unpleasant surprise, I quickly realized that on no occasion had Lubrano advised Bicentennial in writing that its product was late or otherwise non-conforming. This reality probably meant that Vinny and Vince were lying through their teeth to me about the backcharges and simply wanted to get out of having to pay Bicentennial in full. More good news: ample evidence in Box #3 pointed to the general contractor not having penalized Lubrano Concrete one cent during the course of the job. To compound things, Lubrano appeared to have been paid in full by the general contractor. These facts caused major problems with my ability to prosecute this case.

Under Pennsylvania's Contractor Subcontractor Payment Act, contractors are required to pay their subcontractors when the contractors, themselves, get paid by the project owner. In this case, it appeared that Lubrano was getting paid at regular intervals throughout the job by the general contractor, but simply failed to pay their subcontractor with the same frequency, or at all. A counterclaim by Bicentennial would expose Lubrano's liability under the Contractor Subcontractor Payment Act.

The one silver lining that I saw was that Lubrano appeared to have paid its employees and equipment suppliers more than it should have, in light of the length of and scope of the work. I could make a marginally colorable argument that Bicentennial's latenesses and non-conforming deliveries caused Lubrano to incur excess labor and materials costs. It would be a stretch, though. All that argument would do would be to cover my ass so that I didn't get sued for filing a frivolous lawsuit. In light of the facts, as they were presented to me in the documents, there was no possible way that this litigation would end with Bicentennial paying Lubrano, rather than Lubrano paying Bicentennial. I was going to file a Complaint, Bicentennial's counsel would file a counterclaim, and I would get laughed out of court. I was going to lose my first case for Lubrano convincingly.

Before I knew it, the sun had stopped reflecting off of the Comcast Center into my office, and nightfall had arrived in the City of Brotherly Love. My office appeared as if a bomb had exploded in it. Coffee stained papers were strewn all over my desk and Tastykake wrappers littered the floor near my trashcan. It was 8:00 p.m. Twelve hours had passed since I had entered the office this morning and I had just finished reviewing the documents that the Lubranos had provided to me. I had a six count Complaint to draft by morning, the secretarial support had left for the day, and I was coming down from my day-long sugar and caffeine high.

It was going to be an all-nighter, and I needed to apprise Julie of this reality. After gaining forgiveness for my transgression of two nights prior, I was about to be put in the doghouse once again. I picked up the telephone receiver and dialed home.

"Honey, why are you not in your car already?" she inquired, recognizing the caller ID.

"Jules, I'm going to be watching the sunrise from my office. I just got done reviewing the docs and now I need to draft the Complaint. Please don't give me grief about this. I'm really on the edge now and I'm about to snap. I just screamed at the cleaning lady for vacuuming too close to my office door," I responded theatrically, hoping to preemptively avoid a guilt trip and garner some sympathy at the same time.

My hyperbole worked, as Julie responded, comfortingly, "Shhh, honey, I want you to take a deep breath and collect yourself. I want you to go downstairs, walk around the block, take a nice few deep breaths, come back upstairs, and go right back at it. You're not thinking with a clear head right now and you need to take a break."

Hiding the elation associated with my not being in trouble, I calmly responded, "O.K., I guess you're right."

"Wrong. You *know* that I'm right. One other thing: make sure you order something expensive for dinner, since Vinny is going to end up paying the bill. O.K., I'll leave you be. Call me tomorrow morning once everything is done. The Complaint is going to be brilliant because you're a brilliant attorney – with a great ass, I might add. Talk to you tomorrow. I love you."

"Thanks for the pep talk. Love you too."

God, was I lucky to have such a nurturing wife. A tad overbearing at times, but, nevertheless, a sweetheart whose companionship I felt lucky to have.

CHAPTER SIXTEEN

"*Ale-ixx? Ale-ixx?*" a very loud voice spoke over the intercom, "You ain't in yet, are you?"

With drool running down the left side of my face and a carbon copy of a Bicentennial Lumber delivery ticket stuck to the right side of my face, I raised my head from my desk, disoriented, and managed,

"Hello? Hello? Who's there? Kristin, is that you?"

"*Ale-ixx!* Did you sleep here last night? What did you do to Julie?"

Ever groggy, looking at my watch, I responded,

"Kristin, I finished the Lubrano Complaint 45 minutes ago – that's why I fell asleep on my desk. Everything's fine with Julie, thank you very much."

"Well, excuuuuuuuuuse me, Mr. Man! I'm sorry that not everyone can work as hard as you!" Kristin chuckled with her cigarette enhanced raspy voice, "Speaking of Lubrano, Mr. Concrete Buns is on the phone for you. Did he say anything about me the other day? He is so hot – you need to set me up with..."

"Kristin, can you please pass him through? We don't date the clients here, O.K.?"

"Who pissed in your corn flakes this morning? O.K., here he is."

"Thank you."

"*Consigliere*, what a nice surprise to see that you decided to work for a living. Let me guess: your alarm clock malfunctioned and went off three hours early today. Am I right? Am I?" Vinny asked.

Unwilling to bite my tongue, I shot back, while pulling crud from my eye, "Vinny, your telephone call woke me up. I slept in my office last night, reviewing..."

"Hey, man, don't blame me because Julie makes you sleep in the office when she wants to have sex with her six foot eight *schvartze* boyfriend. Maybe if your dick weren't so small, she wouldn't force you to leave the house once per week."

As his insult was genuinely and uncharacteristically creative, I couldn't play the "Don't talk about my wife, you sonofabitch" card, but he still needed to be chided for mocking my work hours.

"As I was saying, I slept in the office reviewing four boxes of your documents and drafting a Complaint, which, incidentally, is masterful, given the shitty set of facts in this case. That's why I'm in the office so early – because I never went home last night. And to answer your question, no, my alarm clock didn't break, you moron."

Fearful that I had crossed the line, by invoking the issue of his intelligence, I tentatively awaited Vinny's response.

Agitated, he snapped, "What do you mean 'shitty set of facts?' You have no fucking idea what you're talking about!"

"Actually, I do," I began, with an audible laugh, knowing that it would piss him off, "this is what I do for a living. Why could I find no written evidence of Lubrano Concrete informing Bicentennial that the lumber was late or substandard?"

"Because we've been in this game for more than 30 years and that's not how we do business. Everything is verbal. There's no need to write down a complaint that we have with supplies – do you know how much time that would take?"

"I understand that. But how is that going to look in front of the jury? People like me, who have never worked in the construction industry are going to be sitting on your jury. Trust me, they'll want to know where the documented written backup is."

"Alex," he said calmly, as if following the instructions of a therapist who was counseling him on how to control his anger, "I'm only going to tell you this once: you prepare the legal documents, and I'll do all of the theorizing. When I want your opinion, I'll ask for it. Remember, you work for me, not the other way around."

Seeing that he was the one paying the bills and I was the one who was sending the bills, I begrudgingly responded, "O.K."

Suddenly cheery, he said,

"Good. How do we get this thing filed."

"We'll need to meet up today, so that you can sign the Verification at the end of the Complaint. Once you sign, I can have it filed and served right away."

"Good. I'll swing by later and sign it."

"When is 'later?' I'll need to have copies made after you sign it, so I need to know w..."

" 'Later' means that I'll come to your office when I feel like coming to your office. You worry too much. Take it easy, O.K.?"

"O.K., I'll see you later."

CHAPTER SEVENTEEN

The couple sat on a park bench, underneath a fir tree at lunchtime on a Tuesday in the Place des Vosges, on Paris' Right Bank. As the young brunette sobbed, the silver haired gentleman seated to her right grasped and gently rubbed the top of her right hand.

Since the telephone call had come and it was clear that they had been found, the couple could no longer speak about important issues in the apartment any longer, for fear of the most important secrets being revealed. As such, they were forced to journey into public places, usually outdoors, to engage in conversation.

The Place des Vosges, an 18th century residence for French nobility in Paris' Marais district, was enclosed on four sides, with a public garden in the middle. Due to the fact that both tourists and locals frequented the Place des Vosges, the couple, especially at this time of day, could easily intersperse themselves with the crowd and go unnoticed.

Notwithstanding his relative comfort level in knowing that the Place des Vosges' park benches were not similarly bugged as the apartment, he took precaution to prevent any potential lip readers from intercepting their communications. The gentleman covered his mouth with his palm as he spoke. He instructed the brunette to do the same.

"*Ma chérie*, this is the last time that we will be seeing each other until he arrives. You will not return to the apartment under any circumstances. You are not to telephone me or communicate with me by e-mail. Jean-Jacques Daigneault will...strike that – what's his name?"

"*Il s'appelle, Gilles* Daigneault. *Gilles.*"

"Whatever – I could never pronounce that name – no wonder I forgot it. I'm calling him Gil. In any case, Gil will courier my handwritten messages to you, if any. Once you receive a message, you will burn the message. If you need to contact me, you can send Gil back with a handwritten note. You will not leave the country house in La Pomponnette unless directed by me. Is that understood?"

"Yes, I understand what you say. I just am afraid zat I'm never going to see you again." She said, in a greatly embellished pouty, tearful voice.

Knowing that her preference was that she next see him on a coroner's photograph, he nevertheless acted as if she were sincere.

"Honey, I'm a survivor – you know damn well that I'm a survivor. Ain't nothing gonna keep me from returning back here in one piece, so that I can take you to the far reaches of the earth and make mad, passionate love to you in every land that we conquer."

She immediately stopped crying, pondering the gravity of the possibility that he had just mentioned.

"Darling, do not look down. Two minutes after I walk away to the right, you will take the bag at my feet and walk away to the left. You will get in the vehicle that I have left parked on Rue Saint Antoine, and you will drive to La Pomponnette. You will speak to no one, even if spoken to." Extending his left hand without facing her, he said, "Give me your mobile phone." After she obliged, he continued, "This will both save you from temptation and hamper any efforts to track you. The land line at the country house will still be active. You will make no outgoing calls. You will handle the incoming calls that we previously discussed. "

"But what if I need to…," she began, diffidently.

"Didn't you just hear me?!" He screamed, showing his fierce and capricious temper, "You 'need to' nothing. The only thing that you need to do is to sit in the country house, read, watch TV and eat. Gil will be bringing you all of the provisions that you require. End of story."

He looked over both shoulders, fearful that his short tirade might have blown their cover. It hadn't. Feeling fortunate that they were not detected, he decided to wrap things up and be on his way.

"*Chérie*, I am about to leave you. The bag at my feet contains what's left of my assets after I had to empty the rest into that little expenditure that we discussed. I am giving it to you for safekeeping because I trust you. Of course this goes without saying, but if I sense at any point that you have designs on betraying my trust, I will do whatever is necessary to protect my retirement plan. While I am confident that you are content to share my wealth once this calamity is over and order has been restored to our situation, I am not stupid enough to ignore that you may be tempted by others to betray me. Before I leave you, I warn you that if you do betray me, the fate that you will suffer will be far greater than death."

As the silver haired man stood up and walked towards the south exit of the Place des Vosges, he left a black alligator skin briefcase next to the brunette's feet. She tentatively pushed the bag closer to her body with her foot, lifted it with both hands and put it to rest on her lap.

She glanced at her watch, so as to be able to gauge when the two minute period was to begin. She watched the gentleman walk away out of her peripheral vision. He didn't turn around.

CHAPTER EIGHTEEN

"Ale-ixx? Ale? Huh-low?" Kristin's voice resounded over the intercom, ever flirtatiously.

"Kristin — I'm here — I was just taking a sip of my coffee. Sorry that I wasn't quick enough for you."

"That's O.K.. Listen, your boy, Muscles Marinara is here."

"Who?"

"You know — Concrete Buns — he's here right now."

"Are you joking with me? That jackass was supposed to give me ample notice." I said, increasingly agitated over my new client's antics. "I guess that it doesn't matter, though. I made my final revisions to the document and Terri has the cover sheet and the Sheriff's service form all ready to roll. Alright, no sweat. Can you put him in Conference Room 4, and tell him that I'll be out in a few? If he pulls that shit about the espresso again, feel free to tell him where he can shove the espresso, O.K.?"

"Ale-ixx, he's not in our lobby. He's downstairs on Market Street in a car — a very loud car. I could barely hear what he was saying. I did hear him call me 'sexy,' though."

"Jesus Christ," I said, resting my forehead in my right palm, briefly envisioning a forthcoming lawsuit.

Even though we had known each other for over a quarter century, Vinny apparently felt as if it were necessary to exert his power over me by forcing me to take the elevator down to meet him in his car, so that he could review the Complaint and sign the Verification that was necessary for filing. The joke was going to be on him, though. As long as he was paying his bills, I would refuse to get upset about his antics. After all, at $325.00 per hour, his act of forcing me to take the elevator down to meet him would cost him at least another $32.50, or maybe as much as $65.00, depending upon how fast the elevators were running. A small consolation, yes, but that reality was enough to temper my angst for the time being.

When I arrived at the bottom floor of my office building, our trusty security guard, Meldrick, who always seemed to have a clever greeting or dirty joke for me, was not even looking in my direction as I approached him. He was staring out onto Market Street, where a crowd seemed to be gathering. As I caught a glimpse of the crowd, I knew that there could be but one explanation: an accident involving a SEPTA mass transit bus. As there were, literally, thousands of attorneys who walked up and down the Market Street legal corridor each day, I knew that if I had arrived nine seconds after the accident, I would have been too late to beat another attorney to the victim or victims.

Approaching the glass doors leading onto Market Street, what I saw was quite surreal and looked more like a festive scene than one in which people were clamoring to assist catastrophically injured people. Secretaries smoking outside the doors were smiling and gazing towards the street at some sort of spectacle. A male Asian tourist was taking a photo of his female companion next to a vehicle on the street that was emitting a significant amount of exhaust. As I made my way through the revolving door, I was greeted with an obscenely loud sound of a car revving its engine.

Pushing my way past the crowd of onlookers, I saw Vinny Lubrano seated in a pristine looking cherry red Ferrari 612 Scaglietti. Wearing silver rimmed sunglasses and holding his cell phone with a leather driving glove, he spotted me walking towards the car.

"Good thing that I have absolutely nothing to do today because otherwise, I would have gotten pretty pissed off that you made me wait down here for a half hour!" He shouted, as at least 25 people looked on. What an unbelievable asshole.

"Get in the car."

As I opened the door, the smell of soft handcrafted calf leather made me immediately forget how much I currently loathed the person sitting in the driver's seat. Good God, what a vehicle.

"When did you pick this up?"

"Last week. Put your seatbelt on, we're late."

"We're not late at all. Just sign the Verification, I'll take it upstairs, Terri will make all the copies we need, and I'll have it filed and served today," I said, pulling the document from the yellow envelope.

"Didn't I tell you that you need to chill out? You're going to be dead before your 35th birthday," he said, smirking, as he peeled out across 16th Street towards City Hall.

Struggling to catch my breath, as Vinny shifted from second into third, I asked, "Where are you going? Can't I take the test drive later?"

"I need to make a stop first, and you're coming with me. You work for me now."

Although he was, in large part, joking about my working for him, the comment, which I had now heard for a second time, was nevertheless disturbing to me. I was captive in Vinny's Ferrari against my will, when I had numerous obligations back at the office. As he drove the beast one quarter revolution around City Hall and onto Broad Street, I knew that we were headed to South Philly. Given that the only significant businesses between Center City and the Delaware River were about 20 funeral homes and the stadiums that comprise the Sports Complex, I was relatively certain that Vinny was taking me to the Phillies' matinee game against the Cubs. Since nothing involving Vinny Lubrano could surprise me at this point, I was also not ruling out that he was going to take me into the basement of the Massimo A. Fasano Funeral Home, to show me the bullet riddled body of a union boss that he had just commissioned dead.

As we proceeded down Broad Street, Vinny barked into his cell phone,

"You tell that piece of shit that if he files a worker's compensation claim, I'll make sure that he's really disabled – tell the rest of those fucks to get back to work and to not cut anymore thumbs off!"

"Everything O.K.?" I cautiously inquired.

"No, Alex, everything is *not* O.K.. You have no fucking idea what I go through on a daily basis. This pussy ass union carpenter cut part of his thumb off at my jobsite. Ten to one, he was trying to light up a cigarette at the time. I'm gonna get another worker's comp claim filed against me now. Do you know what my friggin' worker's comp insurance premium was before this thumb incident? This thumb is going to cost me thousands of dollars. It's nearly impossible to make a buck in this business with the insurance companies extorting us."

Well isn't that ironic – an unscrupulous Italian-American concrete construction company owner claiming that he is the victim of extortion by an insurance company. The fact that his vehicle was worth more than a typical North Philadelphia city block slightly diminished the sympathy that I felt towards his plight.

After turning left onto Pattison Avenue from South Broad Street, Vinny drove the Ferrari into a section of the Citizens Bank Park parking lot labeled, "VIP AND RESERVED PARKING PASSES ONLY." He handed a pink ticket that read, "RESERVED PARKING" to an attendant who directed him to the left. Vinny, immediately thereafter, drove to the right, in the direction of a sign that read, "PHILLIES VIP PARKING." An attendant at the entrance to the VIP lot immediately adjacent to the stadium approached the Ferrari's window and asked, "Sir your VIP pass, please."

"I've only got a Reserved pass, my friend, but I can't park this car in that other lot – I need to park it in here."

"Sir, I cannot let you in this lot if you don't have a pass. There are only a certain number of allotted spots in the VIP lot, and if you take one of those spots, a VIP pass holder will be denied his rightful parking spot."

"Listen buddy, let's be honest. Neither you nor I give a fuck about the poor asshole who will be denied his VIP spot. Take this twenty dollar bill, shove it up your ass, and let me in the parking lot before I really start to get pissed off." Vinny said, handing a twenty dollar bill to the attendant.

"Thank you, Sir. Enjoy the ballgame."

"Actually, here's another twenty – I'm going to need two spots today."

"Well, I'm not sure –" The attendant said, while holding two twenties as we drove past him, into the VIP area.

After parking diagonally across two spots, Vinny led me into the Diamond Club entrance of Citizens Bank Park. At the gate, he flashed our tickets, and we were directed down a flight of stairs adorned by framed jerseys of the Phillies whose numbers had been retired by the team, Richie Ashburn, Jim Bunning, Steve Carlton, Robin Roberts, and Mike Schmidt.

The Diamond Club is comprised of several rows of seats directly behind home plate that are segregated from the rest of the stadium. The seats themselves are padded and have more legroom than the common seating areas. Diamond Club ticketholders also have access to an exclusive indoor restaurant and bar area.

Despite the fact that the Star Spangled Banner was playing when we walked into the stadium, signaling the imminent beginning of the game, Vinny elected to sit in the indoor area instead of going directly to our seats.

"Let's have a drink. I need to decompress a little bit after dealing with this worker's comp bullshit." Vinny said, as we approached a hostess stand.

Seeing Vinny walking towards her, a pleasant, but ordinary looking young lady who could have been no more than 20 said, smiling,"Mr. Lubrano, your usual table this afternoon?"

"Do I know you? Where's Tiffany? She always seats me," Vinny fired back, clearly upset that his usual hussy was not present to stroke his ego.

"Tiffany only works night games, I'm sorry that –"

"Listen, I'm having a really bad day. Get us seated, and have Gianna bring me a Ketel One up with a twist."

"I'm sorry, but Gianna is not working today, either. She's at her grandmother's funeral."

With his face reddening, Vinny, now with a sarcastic smirk, said,

"Tell you what – why don't you bring me the fattest, ugliest and most obnoxious waitress that you have on staff here. Tell her to make sure that she sneezes in every drink that I order today too, O.K.?"

Genuinely frightened by this volatile lunatic, the hostess, with tears welling in her eyes, was frozen, unable to utter a single word in response.

Perhaps feeling slightly embarrassed, Vinny, in an effort to avoid creating an even larger spectacle, grabbed two menus from the side of her hostess stand, handed them to her and said,

"Everything is going to be just fine. Cheer up, sweetie, Chase Utley is going to go five for five today – you heard it here first. Do you like Chase Utley?"

With color returning to her face, she responded,

"Oh my God, I adore him. He's the best hitting second baseman of all –"

"That's just great," Vinny interrupted, "would you be kind enough to show us to our table?"

With the smile once again leaving her face, the hostess led us towards a table at the center of the Diamond Club's bar and restaurant area.

"What's the matter with you?" Vinny asked, seeing that I was disturbed over what had just occurred, and, moreover, being taken away from my office when I had a major filing (incidentally, his) to accomplish by 5:00 p.m.

After taking a moment, I responded,

"Number one, why did you have to speak to the hostess like that? She's just a kid, and you've probably scarred her for life. She didn't do anything wrong, aside from not having fake tits and gobs of makeup caked on. Number two, I am wearing the same suit that I wore yesterday because I was writing and revising your Complaint all night and into the early morning, so that it could be filed today. Number three, I've been asking you to take me to your company's Diamond Club seats since this park opened in 2004. Why have you chosen today to take me?"

"It's my business how I choose to deal with people. My father has a certain way of doing things, and I think that his formula has been pretty successful. We've been around for 30 years for a reason. Don't you tell me how to operate. You see how I talked to that geek? That geek is going to tell her boss and all of the other hostesses. You wanna bet that the next time I come in here, they have Tiffany, Gianna, or someone with a half-decent rack to greet me? I pay a lot of money for these seats and I drop a lot of money on food and booze in here.

"To answer your other question, we don't need to file that thing today. I talked to my dad about it last night at dinner, and we've decided to wait until next week to file. Bicentennial's owner, Kevin Muldoon, is going fishing off of Hatteras next week. We want the thing filed while he's down there, so that we get to ruin his vacation."

The rage that infiltrated my body after Vinny's statement was so extreme that I considered cracking the glass case next to our table containing a Mickey Morandini bat, extracting the bat, and clubbing Vinny with it. The thought of my family obligations to Julie and Charlie ultimately convinced me to not inflict physical harm upon my new client, though.

As I had come to learn, there truly was no such thing as a free lunch. If I wanted to reap to financial rewards associated with representing Lubrano Concrete, I was going to have to deal with Vinny's antics – including those antics that caused me to unnecessarily sleep in my office.

Once I cleared my head and determined what mindset I would have to adopt henceforth, Vinny seemed a lot more tolerable to me for the rest of the afternoon.

Utley didn't go five for five as Vinny had predicted. He went four for six, with a walk-off homerun in the bottom of the eleventh inning.

It began to occur to me that although Vinny wasn't particularly smart, things tended to turn out as he wished.

CHAPTER NINETEEN

During the week following the Phillies game, calm was restored at the office for the first time in a while. The Lubrano Complaint was filed in Brandywine County, and service was promptly made by the County Sheriff upon Bicentennial, while its owner, Kevin Muldoon, was out of town. At the same time, the firm's New File Committee approved the representation of Physician's Justice, under a $350.00 per hour rate for Associates and a $450.00 per hour rate for Partners. After being able to convince Sandy and George that I, and not the Partners, would be doing the overwhelming majority of work on the Physician's Justice files, they agreed to the fee structure. George's sole remaining condition for signing the fee agreement was that I deliver it to him in person at his office in Weston. Seeing that he was about to sign a contract, agreeing to pay a very good rate to my firm, I complied.

Ridgeway's "office" was located just down the street from the Brandywine County Courthouse on Oliver Street in Weston. Outside the door, four screws that I surmised had been used to support the sign that once bore the name of Ridgeway's now-defunct firm were bolted into the wooden entryway.

When I opened the door to his office, it became immediately clear that no law firm or any sort of business had been actively operating out of the site for a very long time. At an empty reception desk covered in warped earth tone Formica sat a pot of soil which looked as if it had once housed a fern of some sort. Some of the soil was scattered on the ledge next to three stacks of what appeared to be utility bills. Four computer monitors sat at the receptionist's desk, with their cords exposed, confirming that they were not attached to any machines. A trashcan overflowed with Dunkin' Donuts coffee cups and several extremely weathered-looking copies of the Brandywine County Daily Post.

The small waiting area consisted of six cigarette burned and otherwise tattered fabric chairs, circa 1982. Stacks of banker's boxes, labeled "RIDGEWAY WINSTON & PHELAN – ATTORNEYS AT LAW" effectively hid the unsightly chairs. It didn't take a lawyer or a genius to figure out that the boxes held Ridgeway's old files from the disbanded firm of Ridgeway Winston & Phelan.

While I was admiring the scenery and contemplating how a once successful attorney could have been reduced to such a sad and putrid existence, I was startled when a voice no more than four inches from the back of my head exclaimed with exuberance,

"Counselor, so nice of you to make the journey out to the hinterlands of Brandywine County. I hope that you brought your passport!"

Ridgeway extended his veiny sun-spotted twitching hand and displayed his mouth full of twisted yellow and black dentistry. I shook his hand, not having yet caught my breath.

"Look like you've seen a ghost," Ridgeway said, clearly satisfied that he was able to catch me off guard.

"No, not at all. It's great to see you, George. And coming to see you in Brandywine County is really no problem – I actually live in Thornley Township, Brandywine County."

"That's not Brandywine County! Your voting card may say Brandywine County, but you live on fucking farmland that was bought and developed by some out-of-towner. Out by where you live, the hot political issues are rooted in how to dispose of the horse and cow shit in an environmentally-friendly manner, right?"

"George, I'm really not involved in nor interested in politics, let alone Brandywine County politics."

"Well, you should be! Do you know how much corr..." He sharply stopped himself and then reduced his rant to a whisper, "Do you know how much corruption is still present on that bench?

115

They're all on the take – either directly from litigants or indirectly through the special interests. What the hell is wrong with our system that major corporations are allowed to donate millions to a judge's or a congressman's campaign? What do people think these donations are for – the companies being so rich that they need to throw their money away? Hell no! The donations are a legal, thinly veiled means of effectuating bribery. And why do you think that I'm whispering to you? They've got my office bugged."

As politely as possible, I wiped my face of the saliva that had been spit on me from the time that he reduced his voice to a whisper. During our meeting at the Perennial Club, I had gathered that Ridgeway was a maniac, but this most recent diatribe convinced me that Ridgeway was also a paranoid egomaniac.

"They" bugged his office? "They" are all on the take? I was tempted to remind him that his entire ordeal in which he had lost millions of dollars began when he committed malpractice by obstinately refusing to conform to a simple procedural pleading requirement. I felt like telling him that just because a particular judge ruled in conformity with the law in such a way that made Ridgeway look very, very bad, didn't necessarily mean that that judge or the rest of the Brandywine County bench was corrupt. As far as the bugging of his office was concerned, the man truly needed to get over himself. Nevertheless, due to his age, I was willing to give Ridgeway a free pass. Perhaps early onset Alzheimer's disease was causing his dementia.

Choosing to simply not respond to his rant, I placed my briefcase on the receptionist's ledge, opened its latch, pulled an envelope out and said, "George, I've brought two original fee agreements for you to sign. This is the language that you and Sandy agreed upon with my firm. As you can see, Nick Carlson has already signed..."

"Not so fast, counsel. We need to kick off this business relationship properly. I'm taking you to lunch around the corner."

Having another meal with George Ridgeway was on my to-do list in between going to a Justin Timberlake concert and getting punched in the balls by Mike Tyson.

"George, I'd love to, but I really need to get into the office. Since I live nearby, I didn't go to the office this morning – I came straight here. Maybe we can meet up another – "

Interrupting me while grabbing my left shoulder and pushing me towards the door, he responded,

"Nonsense. That excuse might have passed muster before you worked for me, but no more. We're just going over to the Brandy Wine House for a sandwich. It's settled – I'll treat you to lunch – unless of course you want to pick up the tab – which wouldn't be the unclassiest of gestures, considering my new little venture will be paying your firm more in a month than most American families make in a year."

"I'd be happy to treat to lunch, George."

"Well, if you insist, I'm not gonna say no!" He added with a laugh, once again displaying his revolting set of choppers.

During the minute and a half walk to the Brandy Wine House, Ridgeway made small talk with me about how Weston had become a ghost town since the advent of multi-vehicle families and working mothers. Judging by his tone, Ridgeway seemed to find both such developments to be objectionable. According to Ridgeway, in the good old days, those living in and around Weston worked in Weston. He added that although Philadelphia was just twenty miles away, it might as well have been a foreign country for Weston residents. Now, Ridgeway professed, Weston was a one horse town in which virtually every person employed within the borough limits either worked at the courthouse or at a business servicing those who worked at the courthouse.

Indeed, during the course of our short walk, every business that I saw was either a law office, a court reporting agency or a printing service.

When we entered the Brandy Wine House, I felt as if I had taken a step into 1965. With the exception of a bus boy who I saw milling about, virtually all patrons and staff of the bar-restaurant were Caucasian. Moreover, from what I could see in my brief cursory glance, only three females were in the entire establishment. One was behind the bar, wearing a white blouse and a black vest and two more were sitting at a table in the bar area.

Several men were wearing sear sucker suits, many with bowties. The place looked like you could go to the bar, order an Old Fashioned, a Sidecar, a Tom Collins or a Rob Roy, and the bartender would not need to consult a book to prepare your drink. This didn't look like the place where one could find a microbrewed beer or a designer vodka.

The intense smell of cigarette smoke shocked me as I followed Ridgeway into the bar area. Although Brandywine County had not yet followed Philadelphia's lead with a smoking ban, most bars and restaurants near my house prohibited smoking on their own accord. Even in the bars and restaurants near my house that permitted smoking, perhaps one or two patrons might have been smoking at any given time. At 12:10 on a weekday afternoon at the Brandy Wine House, roughly 80% of the clientele had a cigarette in their hand or mouth.

I expected Ridgeway to lead me to one of the many tables in the bar area. Instead, he directed me to the very end of the bar itself, near the entrance to the kitchen. The perch that he chose was positioned in such a way that he could see all patrons as they entered the building. As I sat down on the maroon Naugahyde covered wooden barstool, I admired the artifacts that hung on the wall in the very dark room. Interspersed amongst the various stuffed animal heads were items such as a United Way Certificate of Appreciation plaque from 1982, a gavel signed by Judge Hamilton Stephenson, who had been dead for many years, and a Game Ball from the Franklin Green High vs. Smith Hill High football game from 1979. In short, the place desperately needed a makeover, but that reality didn't seem to be keeping anyone away.

Within seconds after we sat down, a fifty-something gaunt barmaid with sickly, straw-like bleached blond hair and a weathered face slowly walked over, and, with an indifferent expression, asked, "Your usual, Mr. Ridgeway?"

"No, Darlene, I better not. Is there any way that you can give me a non-alcoholic Cutty Sark on the rocks? Try running the liquor through that strainer gizmo that you have behind the bar," he said, in a hacking laugh, as he pulled a soft pack of Dorals from his inside pocket.

Unhumored, Darlene, without so much as feigning laughter, turned to me and asked,

"For you, sir?"

"A Diet Coke with lemon, please."

After blowing a waft of sub-premium smoke out of his mouth, with no effort to avoid doing so in my direction, Ridgeway stated,

"I always love coming in here to see the looks on attorneys' and judges' faces as they try to avoid making eye contact with me. Everyone who you see in this room is either a lawyer, judge, or works for a lawyer or a judge. I know 90% of these assholes and each of them hates me for a separate incident or incidents that occurred during the past 45 years."

Instead of being embarrassed or insulted that these people harbored such ill will towards him, judging by the demonically content expression on his face, Ridgeway seemed to be getting more than a kick out of it.

He continued, "Look at Judge Young over there. Since I sat down, he has actually contoured his body away from me. And look at Jerry McMonagle, I've seen him wipe sweat from his forehead with his handkerchief thrice since we walked in. He's still pissing his pants from when I threatened to kill him in front of the jury after I realized that he had withheld a key document from me during a trial in the mid-seventies.

"Also, there's one character over there who is simply staring daggers at me and isn't the least bit bashful about doing so. That's Geraldine Finnegan, Judgette Rolston's longtime deputy slash toady watchdog. She is loyal as they come to her boss, and would probably take a bullet for her."

While I chalked up Ridgeway's comments about Judge Young and Jerry McWhatever to his delusional paranoia, he seemed to be right on target about this Geraldine character. She was unabashedly staring nastily in our direction, and whispering to her tablemates while doing so. While I could not make out her words, they were clearly not complimentary. This woman looked as pissed off and vindictive as would a woman who had run into her ex-husband in a restaurant seated with a supermodel.

Darlene brought our drinks and asked what we would be having for lunch. After Ridgeway ordered a hot carved ham sandwich, and I a turkey club sandwich, he began,

"Alex, my boy, you can't even begin to imagine the shit that I've been through in this town over the years. I could bore you for hours about it all, but I'll spare you today. Let's talk about important things – like, for example, me. I think that in order to make this relationship a successful one, I need you to first tell me what Walt Krauss and Nick Carlson have told you about me."

Knowing that this lunatic was a lot more experienced at lying than I was, the thought of attempting to convince him that neither Krauss nor Carlson had said a single word to me about Ridgeway's dubious past quickly evaporated in my head.

"George, I'd be lying if I told you that nobody at the firm said anything to me about your trials and tribulations..."

"Well, Alex, the last thing that I'd want to do would be to make a liar out of a lawyer, so I'm glad that you've decided to be up front with me. Now," Ridgeway continued, taking a long drag of a Doral, "who said what about me? I'll tell you whether it's accurate or not."

"Respectfully, George," I began, "it really doesn't matter who told me what. But, if you really want to know what I was told, here it is: As I understand it, after your license was revoked, your former partner refused to distribute your portion of settlement proceeds from some monster personal injury case. I think that it was $10 million, or something. You then filed for a temporary restraining order to prevent him from absconding with the dough, but didn't get a hearing until two full weeks later. By the time the TRO was granted, your ex-partner was using his newfound wealth to bet on the leopard races in Kenya."

"Not bad. Either Walt Krauss or Nick Carlson has a damn good memory. Except Jimmy Winston fled to Sénégal, not Kenya. It's amazing that that gimpy bastard could flee anywhere. After his car accident, it took him two hours to walk to the friggin' john.

"Also, he stole a little under $12 million from me, not $10 million – but what the hell's the difference? The case was <u>Washington v. Home Warehouse</u>. My client was an 18 year-old black kid from an awful neighborhood in Brandywine City. The kid had just graduated from high school with a 4.2 GPA. He was also the all-time leading rusher on his school's football team and had secured a four year full academic scholarship to Harvard. He was going to play ball there. He probably could have played at Penn State, but his mama made him choose Harvard for the academics. Two days before he was set to leave for Cambridge to begin summer practice, he goes to one of those big-box Home Warehouse stores. The idiots at the store forgot to chain off an aisle in which a forklift was operating. The poor bastard wanders down the aisle looking for a desk lamp, and the forklift drops a skid full of boxes holding light fixtures on his head. Not only was he rendered a quadriplegic, but he had severe brain damage and would never be able to speak again in his life. On top of the obvious pain, suffering, and loss of life's pleasures, my experts put his lost future earnings at $40 million and his future healthcare expenses at $18 million. Home Warehouse wanted no part of the bad press or risk of an absolute runaway jury. They settled with me for $37 million. After the costs and medical liens were taken out, my cut was going to be about $12 million.

"So now you're enlightened. What else did you hear?"

"I also heard that Jim Winston was found dead a little while after he disappeared," I added, hoping to elicit more juicy details.

"Thank The Lord, you heard right," he began, with a brightening clenched face after drinking his entire glass of Cutty Sark in one fell swoop and slamming it to the gnarled wooden bar. "Having $12 million in Sénégal was like having $12 trillion in the U.S. The man apparently lived like royalty there, buying up politicians like he was so accustomed to doing here. The Sénégalese kept him safer from the American authorities than the Taliban did with Osama bin Laden.

"He got stupid, though. After years of living in the Third World, he somehow got himself into Spain – I think he wound up in Valencia. After he was in Spain for a little while and was able to avoid capture, he got cocky. He began to frequent some of the high-end restaurants and bars and word started to spread about who he was and how much money he had. With an American accent and an angry drunken demeanor, Jimmy undoubtedly stood out. And if you think that I'm an obnoxious drunk, you should have seen Jimmy. I'll bet you anything that after a few cocktails, half of that damn town knew about how much money he had. One morning, Jimmy was found bludgeoned beyond recognition. They took whatever money he had in his wallet, his clothes, and for good measure, his eyeballs. They didn't take his passport, though. His passport was found in his rear pocket, and was used to identify him. Otherwise, nobody ever would have known that Jimmy Winston had died, and his legend would have probably lived on forever."

Partially zoning out after Ridgeway dispassionately mentioned the bit about Winston's eyeballs being harvested, I had to request a clarification.

"George, did you say that they took his *eyeballs* out?"

"Oh, hell yes – here, take a look. One of my people at the FBI gave me a copy of this picture. I guess that he felt bad for me after all that Jimmy put me through."

Without missing a beat, Ridgeway reached into his pants pocket, and retrieved a folded up 3" x 5" photograph from amongst what appeared to be credit cards. It was presented to me in a similar manner as a proud grandfather would show someone a picture of his grandchild. He made no effort to shield the photo from anyone else sitting at the bar and placed it right under my nose.

What I saw was sickening. The photo, which I surmised was taken by Spanish law enforcement authorities at least 24 hours after the killing, displayed a ghostly white partially-clothed man with an open mouth and dark crimson blotches where his eyes normally would have been. Judging by the manner in which his arms and legs were bent, it was apparent that rigor mortis had set in. I pushed my sandwich to the side after I decided that I was no longer hungry.

"Why didn't they just rob him and kill him and be done with it? Why did they have to take his eyeballs out?" I asked.

"You want my guess?"

"Please indulge me, George."

"Happily. When you're in the market for a built-in cabinet and the cabinetmaker is giving you his sales pitch, he brings a booklet full of photos of his handiwork for you to see. When you're surfing the internet for mail order brides, those women have multiple pictures of themselves posted. You catch my drift?"

I thought that I did. "Do you mean that the mafia had a hit out on him, and they ripped his eyeballs out to send a warning to people loyal to him?"

"Not exactly, but you're on the right track. I think that he was just in the wrong place at the wrong time. But whoever killed Jimmy knew that their bad ass quotient would be significantly raised if they were able to let it be known amongst their criminal brethren that they extracted a rich American's eyes from his head," Ridgeway said, forthrightly.

At that moment, as I was trying to imagine what it would be like to have my eyeballs ripped from my skull, a very distinguished looking woman entered the Brandy Wine House. Clad in a dark pantsuit, with a gold necklace and lightened short hair shellacked with hairspray, she strutted into the room with a confident air suggestive that she owned the place. As she walked through the bar, virtually all onlookers paid her a greeting. She happily returned each greeting with a smiling salutation. Based upon such behavior, I had absolutely no doubt that this woman was a judge on the Brandywine County bench.

"Well look what the rabies-afflicted cat dragged in," Ridgeway said with his biggest smile yet. As the words left his mouth, the woman began to sit down at the table occupied by Mean Geraldine. Once Geraldine whispered a few words into her new table guest's ear, the distinguished looking woman rose back to her feet and looked towards us. She then began to walk in our direction. Ridgeway whispered to me out of the side of his mouth, without taking his eyes off of the figure who was approaching us,

"Get a load of the balls on this broad – she's gonna walk right over here!"

"Who is she?" I whispered back to him, but it was too late.

Wiping his face with his napkin and rising to his feet, Ridgeway exclaimed, "Well, hello, Your Honor, what a nice surprise. It's been a while."

"Yes, George, it has. How are you doing?" The woman responded, with about as fake an expression on her face as could possibly be imagined.

"Thank you for asking. I'm doing well, under the circumstances. I just had cataract surgery, prostate surgery is next and my doc tells me that I still drink and smoke too much. Enough about me, though, let me introduce you to one of the finest young attorneys in the state. And I'll have you know that he neither drinks *nor* smokes. Alexander Brown, this is the Honorable Mary Elizabeth Rolston."

"It's a pleasure to meet you, Judge." I uttered as politely and professionally as I knew how, desperately attempting to control my desire to strangle Ridgeway.

"And it's a pleasure to meet you Mr. ...Brown, is it?"

Ridgeway jumped in,

"Yes, Judge, Alexander Brown. He's my head counsel in an absolutely wonderful and innovative new venture that I've become involved in. With the medical malpractice crisis in this state forcing all of the best docs to Jersey, New York State, Ohio and even West Virginia, I've set up a prepaid legal service whereby once a paying physician-subscriber gets sued, they receive the services of Ol' Alex here, in addition to the attorney appointed by the insurance company. This way, attorneys filing frivolous cases against one of our docs will get double teamed, in a sense, and be pressured into dropping the case. We call it 'Physician's Justice.'"

"*Physician's Justice.* How lovely! What a novel idea." The judge responded in a manner that was equally sarcastic and patronizing.

Either not getting the hint or not giving a hoot that Rolston was unimpressed, Ridgeway responded,

"Judge, it really means a lot to me that you think highly of the program."

"Well, George and George's 'head counsel,'" she said, derisively, "I really do have to be getting back to my table. I only give my staff 45 minutes for lunch, and I wouldn't want to have to dock their pay on my account."

At first, I thought that she was making a self-important joke, typical of many judges. Based upon her facial expression, though, she was dead serious.

Watching the judge walk back to her table, Ridgeway, now visibly gushing and unable to contain his glee, said,

"I sure as hell showed it to her! She's been indirectly on the payroll of the Plaintiff trial lawyers' lobby for years now – and I tell her that I'm starting a program to put the Plaintiff attorneys out of business. God, do I love it! Darlene, let's fill up the Cutty Sark, hon."

Yeah, and in the process, you implicate me and do a great job of endearing me to Her Honor, you decrepit old egocentric zealot.

Handing my credit card to Darlene, I said, "George, I really do need to be going. I've got a shitstorm waiting for me back at the office. Can I get you to sign the fee agreements, so that I can be on my way?"

"That's fine – Darlene, bring me a Michelob chaser before you run his credit card – just keep everything on the same tab," he said, pathetically, while signing the agreements. "Counsel, you don't mind, do you? I figure that I might as well get my money's worth, since the good people at Krauss Carlson are treating to lunch."

Treating you to *lunch*, George. No one said anything about you going on a midday blotto bender.

"It's my pleasure, George," I responded, finding it hard to believe that someone of his ilk, who had practiced law successfully for so long, was pushing the envelope on the generosity of a baby lawyer, 40 years his junior.

Before I walked out of the Brandy Wine House, Ridgeway said, with an ominous wink of the eye, "Don't let me down, counsel. We're going to take the world by storm."

As I walked past Judge Rolston on my way out, I noticed her looking back towards Ridgeway, where I had previously been sitting. The judge was going to have the pleasure of watching Ridgeway get obliterated in my absence.

I stepped out of the Brandy Wine House and had fresh, carcinogen-free air flow through my lungs for the first time in a hour.

CHAPTER TWENTY

Under the Pennsylvania Rules of Civil Procedure, a party alleging that another party has breached a written contract must attach a true and correct copy of the contract to the Complaint. Nineteen days after the service of the Lubrano Complaint was made upon Bicentennial's owner, I learned, for the first time, that Terri neglected to attach the contract to the Complaint when she filed it with the court. It was an honest mistake on Terri's part, but nevertheless, one that initially caused me a certain degree of humiliation.

The fact that we filed the Complaint without the contract attached created a basis upon which Bicentennial could file preliminary objections. While the overwhelming majority of Pennsylvania attorneys in such a situation would have simply brought the omission to their adversary's attention so that the harmless mistake could be corrected, Bicentennial's attorney, Tim Shaughnessy, chose instead to file lengthy preliminary objections with a ten-page memorandum of law.

I had never previously litigated opposite Tim Shaughnessy, but after asking around the office, I had gathered that he was a run-of-the-mill lifelong Weston practitioner in his mid-50s, who seldom ventured outside of Brandywine County. Since, under the Rules, his preliminary objections would be instantly nullified once I filed an Amended Complaint with the contract attached, I found his action to be rather curious. Filing preliminary objections in such a scenario was the act of a know-it-all first year attorney, not of a seasoned veteran in the industry. Karma, as had been said, was a boomerang. It was a useless act of gamesmanship for which I planned to exact revenge at a later date.

Nevertheless, the joke was on Tim Shaughnessy. This litigation had just begun and he had unnecessarily caused his client to incur around $5,000.00 in legal fees by filing the preliminary objections which would soon be rendered moot. The only drawback for me was that I would be forced to embarrassingly tell Vinny that the contract was not attached. Also, in connection with the filing of my Amended Complaint, I would need Vinny to sign a new Verification to be attached to the back of the document. Since he was not an attorney, and a rather dense human being to boot, I feared that once I told him of the blunder, he would not understand that the error was harmless and would react emotionally.

In an effort to immediately face the music, I left a phone message for Vinny just after learning that the preliminary objections had been filed. One of Vinny's only redeeming qualities was that his neurotic tendencies caused him to either answer his cell phone whenever I called, or return my call within five minutes.

Today was no exception. After leaving a message for him at 2:33 p.m., our fill-in receptionist, Maria, buzzed in through my intercom, at 2:36 p.m., "*Ale-ixx*, you have a telephone call from Vinny Lubrano. May I send it through?"

I hated the days when Kristin was either on vacation or called out sick. Her sultry South Philly blue-collar voice was such a turn-on every time she buzzed in with a call for me. On this day, Kristin had called out sick and Maria DellaVecchia, another subject indigenous to South Philly was manning the phones in her absence. As a 40-something matronly-type who was famous for her meatballs, Maria's phone voice didn't really cut it for me.

"Yes, Maria, please do. Thank you." I said, as I braced myself for the tongue lashing that Vinny was about to administer to me.

"Ummm, hello, this is Ethel Goldenbergenstein," he began in a whiny mock geriatric Jewish lady accent, "I just got back from the supermarket. I tried to buy three tomatoes but the stupid *goy*

128

at the register charged me $2.49 a pound, when the sign clearly said that the tomatoes were $2.39 a pound. I was cheated out of 22 cents and I want to sue that supermarket for false advertisement and consumer fraud. Can you represent me? I'd be willing to give you a pot of kreplach as a retainer. If you really want to drive a hard bargain, I suppose that I could throw in some delicious prune hamentashen. Do we have a deal?"

A female voice in the background said,

"Stop that! You're so mean!"

Vinny responded, "I'm gonna be meaner in five minutes when I have my way with you again."

"How the hell do you know what kreplach is?" I asked, "I guess that we're taking the day off to continue last night's activities? Who's the flavor *del giorno*?"

"Oh, *consigliere*, I really think that you'll like this one. She's a firecracker."

"Don't you dare!" I heard a laughing voice say in the background.

"Vinny, I've got some mildly bad news and some good news. My support staff forgot to attach the contract to the Complaint, so we'll need to file an Amended Complaint and I'll need to get you to sign another Verification, which I'll attach to the back of the document. The good news is that Bicentennial's counsel probably spent about five grand filing preliminary objections, and the net result is that once I file our Amended Complaint, the preliminary objections will be rendered moot."

"Why do you have to say 'rendered moot'? Why can't you just say that 'the preliminary objections are going to be meaningless once I file the Amended Complaint'? Remember, I knew you when you were shitting yourself three times per day in kindergarten. I'm not impressed by your fancy words."

"Gotcha. I'll still need you to sign the Verification."

"Alright, then bring it to me now. I'm going to *Veggis* tomorrow for two days for a conference and to play some golf. I won't be able to sign it while I'm gone."

"Not a problem. Terri will print it out and my courier can have it over to you in about 45 minutes. Good thing I caught you before you left for Las Vegas."

"Alex, we seem to be having a disconnect about what I expect customer service-wise from this relationship. I didn't say 'have your courier bring it to me', I said that I wanted *you* to bring it to me. Besides, it's almost 3 p.m., – you've worked a full day. What time did you get in today, 11 a.m.? That's a hard day's work for a lawyer. You haven't seen my new place yet. Come on over, I'll sign what I need to sign, and we'll go get some drinks, *capische*?", he said, fancying himself as Don Lubrano, the head of the Lubrano crime family.

"Vinny, I'm not sure how to break this to you, but you're not my only client. I have obligations at my office and I can't just leave at 3 p.m. to go drinking." I said, anticipating his unwelcoming response.

"Alex, I'm only gonna tell you this one more time: you work for me now. I know that they don't teach you about client development in law school, but you're a sharp guy, so I would have thought that you would have picked up on the concept by now. Lemme tell you all you need to know about client development. When a client asks for a document to be personally delivered by his attorney, rather than by a courier, you do it. In fact, you do it fast. To be honest, you flat out suck at client development and you've been a disappointment to me during our brief business relationship so far."

While I wanted to throw the phone through the window, I knew, at the same time, that he was testing me to see how I would react. He knew that I had pissed off Julie on the night of the Capital Grille incident, and he knew that I had slept in my office preparing a Complaint that ultimately did not have to get filed on a rush basis.

So, I decided to react in a manner that would both preserve my dignity and not damage the client relationship.

"I'm getting in a cab now, and I'll be over in fifteen minutes. Between now and then, why don't you go fuck yourself?"

I hung up as he was trying to say something. Telling an Italian-American to go fuck himself was not quite the equivalent of telling an Italian-American to go fuck his mother. The two insults were not far from each other, though. I was proud of myself.

By virtue of having cursed at him, he would either gain more respect for me or fire me. I was fairly confident that he wasn't going to fire me.

CHAPTER TWENTY-ONE

The Palazzo at Washington Square was the largest residential condominium in Philadelphia. Recently completed, it was a behemoth, by Philadelphia standards. The modern cylindrical shaped building towered over quiet Washington Square, and existed as a sharp contrast to nearby Independence Hall and its surrounding historical monuments.

As the concrete construction contractor on the Palazzo job, Lubrano Concrete stood to make in the tens of millions. So, before ground was broken on the project, when various entities, including the federal government filed suit to prevent the supposedly unsightly building from defiling the historical area, Lubrano Concrete was forced to exercise some political muscle. While I was never clear on the details, I remember that the story of the lawsuits to block The Palazzo made the front page of the Philadelphia Inquirer one day. Just two weeks later, the government and the other suing parties did a complete about-face, dropping their lawsuits and touting the project. Editorials and reader letters that ran in The Inquirer during the ensuing weeks openly mocked the power that Lubrano Concrete wielded. In such pieces, the federal government was portrayed as having cowered when faced with the possible retribution that Lubrano Concrete was apparently threatening.

In any event, the project was completed on time and Lubrano was reported to have made a mint in performing its duties. As Vince frequently did, whenever negotiating a contract for a residential high-rise, he was able to secure one of the building's units for his personal use. Since Vinny had tired of the 2,200 square foot penthouse at the Lubrano-built Villas at Lombard, in which he had lived for a whole 18 months, Vince gifted to Vinny his 3,000 square foot penthouse at the Palazzo.

Occupying more than one-half of the entire 42nd floor of the building, I had heard that the condominium was breathtaking, and a bachelor pad of epic proportions, at that. So, even though I was agitated that Vinny had summoned me in the middle of the day, I was at least moderately curious to see what his new digs looked like. Plus, I was also very interested to see what the latest Lubran-ette looked like.

After I paid the taxi driver his $6.00 fare, I walked towards the entrance of the building, where a clean-cut Latin man clad in grey suit opened one of the ten foot glass doors and greeted me,

"Welcome to The Palazzo at Washington Square, Sir."

Although it was just after 3 p.m., inside The Palazzo at Washington Square, it looked like nighttime. The decor was overwhelmingly minimalist. Black granite abounded, as far as the eye could see. From the front door to the reception desk, which was straight ahead, 100 feet away, three gargantuan stylistic burnt orange lighting fixtures were spaced evenly apart on the ceiling. Despite their size, they emitted an incredibly small amount of light.

Water gently poured down the walls into pools that seamlessly met the smooth slate ground. With the exception of a massive five-foot tall Buddha-looking structure that stood at the center of the long hallway, no artwork adorned the lobby. A very noticeable sweet and woodsy cologne scent pervaded the room. I had absolutely no doubt that the scent had been pumped in to complete the intended effect.

Once I made my way to the reception desk, and before I was able to ask how I could find Vinny's condominium unit, a gorgeous smiling natural blonde with a German accent welcomed me by saying,

"Good Afternoon, Mr. Brown. Mr. Lubrano is waiting for you in Penthouse Four." Motioning with her left hand, in a manner as contrived as a flight attendant administering a pre-flight safety presentation, she continued, "To your right, you'll see the elevators. Once in the elevator, press the 'P3-P4' button, right above the Number 41 button."

Thanks for the education, Frau Sexy, I thought, as I caught a glimpse of her pushed-together breasts, which were nicely exposed, by virtue of her having chosen to wear a white blouse with the top three buttons undone.

While I was not impressed as Vinny had hoped I would be by the reception lady knowing my name as I walked in, I nevertheless appreciated the effort. Why he felt that he had to impress me after all of these years was perplexing. I knew that he was rich and that he commanded respect from others because of his resources. Further, he knew that I knew this. Maybe Frau Sexy was part of the whole presentation. Perhaps I was going to ascend to his ivory tower, and he was going to tell me that Frau Sexy was the mystery woman whose voice I heard over the phone earlier in the day. Better yet, maybe he was going to show me photographic evidence of the same.

The Palazzo's elevator did not disappoint. Consistent with the lobby's furnishings, the elevator was inordinately dark, to such an extent that I could barely view my watch when I checked to see if I was arriving within the time parameters that I had previously given to Vinny. Different from the lobby's black on burnt orange on black ambiance, the elevator had burgundy velvet walls with dark brown wooden accents. Most noticeably, though, the scent pumped into the elevator was different from the sweet and woodsy cologne scent. The aroma in the elevator was distinctly floral perfume-like.

The finishing surreal touch of the Palazzo experience was a Muzak version of techno house music pumped into the elevator's speakers. The shame of the whole situation was that I was certain that some highfalutin design firm had been hired to account for every last detail of the building's appearance. In all likelihood, a mid-20s stylish mousy spectacled woman and a mid-40s bald gay man were probably sitting at a conference table with a set of blueprints and one suggested, "Hey, I have a great idea! Let's make the place so dark that people won't be able to see their wristwatches two inches from their face. I bet that if we pump techno music and perfume into the elevator, the building will be a hit, and we'll win all kinds of awards!" I felt like I had entered an alternate universe.

Upon exiting the elevator at P3-P4, I entered a very long and dim hallway of what appeared to my untrained eye to be unimproved concrete. But for the framed black and white photographs which were drilled into the walls with heavy-duty construction grade bolts, and the ritzy-looking light fixtures, I would have thought that this particular floor was still under construction. At one end of the hallway was a door that read, "PENTHOUSE 3," and at the other end, a door that read, "PENTHOUSE 4."

As I walked toward Penthouse 4, I was able to take a closer look at the photographs. From the elevator to Vinny's door, the sequence of photos illustrated different stages of the construction of The Palazzo, from earliest to latest. By the time that I had made my way to Vinny's door, I was presented with a nauseating image, in contrast to the otherwise tasteful previous photos. The final photo, apparently snapped at the moment that the last beam was being placed on the building, showed a shirtless Vinny atop the structure with One Liberty Place and the Comcast Center in the background, flexing his arm muscles, as if to signify, "*I* built this thing!"

Although he was a detestable person, I had to hand it to him. Any of the half-wit ladies whom he brought into his lair would have been awed by the picture. The picture undoubtedly lessened the efforts that he would have to exert to bed any female guests about to wander through his door.

I rang the doorbell, but after thirty seconds, no one answered. Upon ringing the bell a second time with no answer, I turned the polished gunmetal doorknob, opened the door and walked in. I was immediately greeted with a smell that was all too familiar to me, having lived in a fraternity house for the better portion of my collegiate career. The joint reeked of a humid pheromone-laced sex scent. The smell could not be confused with any other odor on the face of the Earth. Quite apparently, between the time that I had hung up the phone on him and now, Vinny and his guest had decided to get back to business. Evidently, my theory about Frau Sexy being the mystery woman was misplaced – unless, of course, she had a super high-speed elevator which went directly into Vinny's condo, allowing her to beat me upstairs. I wasn't fully ruling out that possibility because when it came to clever ways of getting laid, Vinny was one of the world's grand masters.

A full view of the living room and adjacent kitchen immediately induced my jaw to drop. Floor to ceiling windows in a horseshoe pattern provided stunning south, west and north views of the city on this very clear day. To the south, the Sports Complex, the Delaware River and Camden County, New Jersey were visible; to the west, Philadelphia's skyscrapers and, in the distance, the University of Pennsylvania's Franklin Field; and to the north, Temple University, nestled amongst the North Philadelphia war zone.

When I had finished gawking at the outside view, I took notice of the Brazilian hardwood floors, dark leather couches, what appeared to be at least a 60 inch plasma screen television, dual three foot tall wine refrigerators and granite countertops, which sat atop the cherry wood cabinets.

In my preoccupied state, I did not hear Vinny approaching.

"So, you like?" he said, nearly causing me to jump out of my wingtips.

"I didn't even hear you coming," I responded, out of breath from shock.

"That's a good way to get ambushed. For your own good, pay attention next time."

"Jeez, the place is great. You've really outdone yourself this time. Are both of those things wine fridges? Do you put both red and white wine in there, or just white. I guess that since so much sunlight comes into this place, you really need to keep the wine..."

"Why do you think that you can take my Lord and Savior's name in vain? It's always 'Jeez' this and 'Jesus Christ' that with you."

"What hell are you talking about?"

"You just said 'Jeez' two seconds ago."

Here we go again.

"Can we cut the shit, please? I need to get back to the office." I said, handing him a yellow envelope containing the Verification form that I needed him to sign for the Amended Complaint.

"Don't you want to know who my female guest is?" he inquired at a whisper.

"Since it's not the German chick from downstairs, I'm probably not interested. She's one of your garden-variety fake-titted New Jerseyans, right."

"No, actually not. Plus Katarina is from Köln, not Germany."

"Vinny, Köln *is* in Germany."

"No it's not – I'm pretty sure that it's in France. Why do you think that all of the *cologne* comes from France? I thought that you were smart. Why am I paying you?"

Lowering his voice to a barely audible level, he continued,

"If you must know, I fucked Katarina last month in the building's public Jacuzzi *while she was on duty!*"

Pretending as if I were not impressed, I pulled my Mont Blanc out of my suit jacket pocket, handed it to him and directed him to sign the Verification form.

"Don't you want to see this place that I built? You just walked in the door. Have a cocktail, and I'll sign this before you leave."

"Why can't you just sign it now? I'll stay for a few minutes – just please sign the damn thing."

Leaning down to sign the document with my pen, he uttered,

"You really need to chill out. Now you're starting to put me on edge."

Retrieving the document and pen from the table, now relieved, I said,

"Thank you very much. Now, that wasn't so hard, was it?"

As I placed the document back into the envelope, Vinny said slyly,

"I'll give you an 'A' for effort, but your attention to detail sucks."

Knowing immediately that he was up to some childish and ill-timed prank, I once again pulled the document from the envelope and looked at the signature line. He had signed, in cursive, "Irwin

M. Fletcher," in reference to Chevy Chase's character in the film, Fletch.

Livid, feeling as if this latest act was the last straw, I demanded,

"What the hell is the matter with you? Don't you realize that you're going to have to pay me to take a cab back to the office so that I can get another Verification and bring it back here? What you've done is disrespectful and rude. I don't have the luxury of having my daddy as my boss. When we're all finished here, you will have wasted an hour and a half of my time, and I'm going to have to explain to Walt Krauss that I couldn't do one of his assignments because you called me over to your condo so that you could sign a Verification form with the name of a movie character. I no longer want to be your attorney and I'm not so sure I still want to be your friend."

Confidently strutting towards a bottle of Ketel One resting on his countertop, he spoke, while turned away from me,

"Baby, why don't you come out here and calm this boy down."

Just what I needed – to be forced to talk to some trashball who was actually more stupid than Vinny.

Then, a voice that I immediately recognized bellowed from behind me,

"I don't want to come out, I'm scared. I think I'm in big trouble."

Not believing that he possibly had the nerve to screw this particular woman, I turned around with a disapproving expression on my face, ready to confront her. Vinny Lubrano was the devil incarnate.

She was unable to look in my eyes, instead choosing to look at the Brazilian hardwood.

"I know I messed up, Alex, I'm sorry. Please don't hold this against me – it just happened," she said, with her damp hair tied back in a ponytail, wearing mesh shorts and an oversized weathered tee-shirt that read, "PRESBYTERIAN LACROSSE." The cool temperature in Vinny's condo aided my ability to detect that she was not wearing a bra.

"It just *happened*? Do you know how wrong this is? Goodbye. I'm gone."

"Hold on," she said, "I can log into the firm's server from here and just print out another Verification. See, all that worryin' for nothin'," she added, with her signature tooth bearing smile and flirtatious eye wink.

Relieved that Kristin had a very feasible and attractive solution, I sat down on a rich leather chair, unbuttoned my top button, loosened my tie and directed Vinny, "Make me one of those drinks while you're at it, dickface."

"Now that's the Alex I like! There may be hope for you after all," Vinny said, as I shifted from dismay to acceptance of the situation. As he shook the vodka and whatever else in a silver colored martini shaker, I couldn't figure out which element of this train wreck was more disturbing: the fact that my firm's receptionist had called out sick for the sole purpose of having a daytime romp with my client, or that my client was now banging my firm's receptionist.

Despite the fact that I wholeheartedly disapproved of the arrangement, if Krauss, Carlson or anyone else at the firm had learned that one of my clients was having sex with the staff on company time, my ass would be grass. Although the term, "sexual harassment" did not get too much publicity in Kristin's home of South Philadelphia, where the men worked and the women cooked, cleaned, went to church and had babies, the prospect of the firm getting sued was hard to ignore. Once Vinny inevitably decided that he was no longer interested in Kristin, which, depending on how good in bed he rated her, could have been anywhere from one to four months down the road, Kristin would get very upset. While I did not believe it to be in her makeup to allege that the firm (i.e., me) was sanctioning the sexual harassment of an employee by a client, the firm's management would punish both me and Kristin if they learned of the liaison.

As I was chewing on one of the olives from the martini that Vinny had handed to me, my neuroticism temporarily subsided, as I realized that there was little that I could do about the situation. The fact that the very sexy Kristin, who was wearing 65% less clothing than I was accustomed to seeing on her, was standing a few feet away from me helped calm my nerves.

As Vinny and I drank our martinis and watched ESPNEWS on the ungodly large television screen, Kristin had wandered back into Vinny's bedroom, presumably either logging into the firm's database, or tying herself up for another round with the King of Concrete.

"So, did I do good?" Vinny wondered aloud.

"Did you do good? What you did was put me in a very precarious situation. Do you know what kind of a predicament I'm going to be in when you decide that you don't want to sleep with her anymore?" I said, consuming more of the martini, which seemed to flow down my throat like fiery water. "Staff members of law firms are not supposed to sleep with clients of law firms. Period. I'm not going to sit here and get mad at you because all that is going to do is to stoke your irrational tendencies. Hell, if I keep talking, I bet that you'll have Walt Krauss' wife under your sheets by night's end."

"Is his wife hot? How old is she? Do you think he would raise the rate that you guys are charging me if he found out?"

We shared a laugh. The idea of Walt finding out that a 31 year-old unsophisticated client of mine was banging his wife was quite humorous.

"Alex, you have no fuckin' idea what this little receptionist of yours is like. I mean, if I told you some of the things that she does, it would blow your mind. She absolutely cannot get enough. And, get this. After you drive her home, she's going shopping in the Italian Market and coming back here and making manicotti and brascioli. And, I kiddingly said that I wouldn't have sex with her again until she cleaned my condo in her bra and panties. So, guess what she agreed to do? She's bringing all kinds of cleaning supplies from her mother's house, like a feather duster and a mop and shit!"

Unbelievable. The guy was so tired of laying women in every conceivable fashion that he was forced to make his mates act out his housecleaning fantasies in order for him to get off.

"Hey," he continued, "since you're taking her home, you should just drive her to the Italian Market, too. You can join us for appetizers. Why don't you pick up some nice prosciutto, parmigiana, olives and peppers at DiBruno's. I just had a case of unbelievable Dolcetto delivered – so make sure that you get the most expensive prosciutto, or else the wine will lose some of its flair."

Incredulous that he could honestly believe that I would even consider abetting Kristin in her day of hooky, or that I would run errands for him in the Italian Market, I was motionless, with an expression devoid of any sign of life.

Before he had a chance to ask me why I was not responding to his suggestions, Kristin wandered back out, this time, holding an 8 ½" x 11" sheet of paper, and sporting a refreshed coat of makeup. Her mesh shorts, which had been shortened by rolling the elastic waistband, noticeably exposed a greater portion of her upper thigh area.

"Yous're in luck. I was able to print the Verification. Now *Aleixx* doesn't have to go to the office to print another one up", Kristin said, with a glimmer in her eye.

"O.K., Alex sign the Verification, and get the thing filed tomorrow. Why don't you two get moving? I'm hungry for brascioli."

He wouldn't give up.

"Vinny, do you understand what the Verification form is? It's your certification that everything contained in the pleading is true. I can't sign your name to that document." I responded.

"Listen," he shot back, "it doesn't matter who signs it because if somebody says that what I'm verifying in the Complaint is not truthful, I'm gonna tell them that you put me up to it, so what's the difference?"

While he was trying to be funny, having known him for most of my life, I knew that he was 100% serious. Vinny would not hesitate to throw me under the bus, or, for that matter, sue me, if he didn't like the result of the litigation.

"I have a solution," Kristin piped in, "gimme your driver's license." I knew exactly what she was up to.

"What'll you do for me?" Vinny replied.

"I won't kick you in the stones – that's what I'll do. Now gimme your friggin' drivers license."

Vinny slowly walked to a wooden table next to the leather couch, picked up a crocodile skin billfold, pulled his Pennsylvania driver's license out and flung it across the room at my receptionist. It amazed me that he had the gumption to act in such a manner towards a woman whom he fancied. It amazed me even more that Kristin seemed very much to be eating up every bit of it.

After she studied the signature that appeared on his driver's license, she took a pen that was resting on the countertop and, without hesitation, signed Vinny's name on the signature block. To my untrained eye, after examining the Verification and the driver's license next to each other, I detected virtually no difference. Apparently, neither could Vinny.

"That's incredible," Vinny exclaimed, taken aback, "how the hell did you do that?"

"I can do a lot of things," Kristin retorted, tapping the pen against her teeth.

I always found it uncanny how legal secretaries could so convincingly replicate their bosses' signatures. I guess that such ability was akin to their lawyer bosses being able to determine, in a millisecond's glance, the particular cut of underwear that they were wearing on a daily basis.

"O.K., I've got what I need. I hope that the two of you enjoy each other's company. Kristin, this never happened. If confronted about this situation, I will deny everything, understood?"

"Whatever you say, *Ale-ixx*," she responded with a sarcastic cackle.

As I opened the front door to let myself out, signed Verification in hand, Vinny shouted towards me,

"Whoa, *consigliere* – aren't you gonna stay to get the full tour of my place?"

Refusing to be baited into learning of and seeing additional items which might later place me in a compromising position, I neither answered nor turned around to acknowledge his inquiry. Surprisingly, Vinny allowed me to leave the condo unimpeded. In a shocking development, he had apparently decided, at least temporarily, to value our little piece of litigation more than busting my balls.

Indeed, Vinny's allowing me to depart without hindrance permitted me to file the Amended Complaint that afternoon. Upon returning to the office, I handed off the Verification to Terri, who attached it to the Amended Complaint and dispatched our courier to make the 20 mile journey to the Brandywine County Courthouse in Weston.

At my request, our courier called me personally that evening to confirm that he had filed the document at 4:57 p.m., just minutes before the court's Prothonotary's Office closed. While it would not have been the end of the world if the courier had not been able to file the document until the following morning, that he had done so that evening allowed me to decompress and feel a sense of relaxation for the first time since the Lubranos' case had come into my life a few weeks prior.

With no valid basis upon which Bicentennial could file further preliminary objections, I would simply wait until Bicentennial answered the Complaint and responded to my written discovery, which, at this point, consisted of interrogatories and requests for production of documents. While the case figured to heat up once those responses were served and depositions were scheduled, I would have a several month reprieve from the Lubranos and their case. God, did that feel good.

CHAPTER TWENTY-TWO

After a relatively relaxing summer weekend on Long Island at Julie's parents' house, involving a barbecue, a beach visit and the obligatory trip to OTB with Longshot Louie, I returned to the office on Monday completely refreshed. At no point during the weekend did I think about my discontentednesses of being Vinny's bitch and being irreversibly entrenched in a business relationship with a disgraced former member of the Pennsylvania Bar.

Although I had only been out of the office during the two weekend days, the break was so mentally therapeutic that upon my return, I felt like I had been gone for a week. Using past experiences as a barometer, though, I should have known that my refreshed feeling would not have lasted very long. While I was exchanging the usual first-day-back-from-the-weekend pleasantries with Terri, learning of the results of her 12 year-old son's baseball playoff game, Kristin piped through Terri's intercom,

"Hey, Ter – I didn't see you come in. How did Bobby's baseball playoffs go?"

"They lost, but he went 7 for 10 in the two games over the weekend. He cried all the way home from the field, but we took him to get *wooder* ice and he forgot about the whole thing."

"Oh, poor thing," Kristin whimpered, "that's a senn. What a cutie pie."

As I began to walk back to my desk, Kristin continued, "Ter, do you know where Ale-ixx is? I buzzed him in his office and he wasn't there. He's got a phone call."

Far be it from me to believe that if Kristin had someone holding on the line for an attorney that she should have not engaged in small talk with Terri. Now that Kristin had a small amount of dirt on me, namely that I knew that she had called out of work under false pretenses to have sex with my client, I was not primed to push the issue with her.

"Kristin, I'm right here. I'll take the call back in my office. Who's calling?"

"*Oh, hi, Ale-ixx. Ummm, it's some bitchy lady from a judge's chambers.*"

Good Lord, this was all that I needed. In my experience, employees of judges' chambers in every state and federal jurisdiction were universally rude. They were rude because they could be rude without fearing the loss of their job. Most such employees had their jobs by virtue of patronage. Although employees of judges' chambers were not well paid, they knew that they had their jobs until retirement age. As an added perk, they were given license to be snippy during telephonic and in-person communications with attorneys and those attorneys' support staff.

Knowing Kristin and her South Philadelphia fieriness, she had likely sniped back at whatever judge's secretary was calling.

"Thank you, Kristin. Would you be kind enough to enlighten me as to which 'bitchy lady' from which judge's chambers is on the phone?"

"Oh, I forgot. I think that it begins with an 'R,' though. Maybe Judge Rollins, or Rodman, or something."

"Kristin, I only have one case with a judge whose name begins with an 'R,' and that's Judge Ramage in Bucks County. Why are they calling me? I settled the <u>Soderstrom</u> case two months ago and the Release is signed and the settlement funds have been paid. They must need a time-stamped copy of the Order to Settle Discontinue and End for their records. Can you do me a favor? Can you ask if that's why they're calling and, if so, tell them that Terri will send out a copy of that document in today's mail? It's too early for me to deal with those idiots in Ramage's chambers."

"*Ale-ixx*, it's definitely not Judge Ramage's chambers calling because the caller ID says 'Brandywine County Government,' not 'Bucks County.' And, I'm almost totally sure that cunt said she was calling from a Judge Rollins' chambers."

Knowing that none of the judges on the bench in Brandywine County were named, "Rollins," I chalked up Kristin's confusion to the fact that she was more concerned with Terri's son's Little League playoff games and having sex with my top client than she was about ascertaining the identities of those calling the office. Since my lone case in Brandywine County was the <u>Lubrano v. Bicentennial</u> case, and per a notice that I received immediately after filing the initial Complaint, Judge Peter Branson was assigned to the case, I was virtually certain that his chambers were calling – most likely to request a courtesy copy of the Amended Complaint. Most judges did not wish to receive so called "courtesy copies" of filed pleadings. Others, however, insisted upon it. I had never previously been before Branson, so I had no way of knowing what his preference was.

Once back in my office, Kristin sent the phone call to me. After a half ring, I lifted the receiver and announced, in my deepest attorney telephone voice, attempting to inject some levity into my initial contact with Judge Branson's chambers,

"Hi there, this is Alexander Brown. Let me take a wild guess. I forgot to send Judge Branson a courtesy copy of the Amended Complaint in <u>Lubrano</u>. I am *so* sorry – it must have been an oversight. I had instructed my assistant to do so, but – well – it must have fallen though the cracks. These things happen some times. I will have my courier bring you a copy within two hours if that's..."

Curtly interrupting me, the woman began,

"Attorney Brown, this is Geraldine Finnegan from the Honorable Mary Elizabeth Rolston's chambers at the Brandywine County Court of Common Pleas in Weston..."

Although I had no mirror in my office, I was pretty sure that my face had turned white. I felt pins and needles throughout my body and I was not breathing. She had to have been calling to tell me that Rolston wanted to chat with me. The chat would be to inquire as to whether I knew of Ridgeway's past, and to caution me to discontinue my business relationship with him. My paranoia was realized. Holy shit.

"...I would like to first begin by telling you that I found your receptionist to be exceedingly uncouth. I am a 13 year veteran of this courthouse, and have worked for four of the most well-respected judges on the bench in this esteemed building. I cannot and will not be spoken to by some Philadelphia firm's receptionist, as if I'm calling from a court reporter's office. I demand respect. If your receptionist won't give me that respect, perhaps she would like to speak with Judge Rolston, herself."

I wasn't sure what Kristin had said to her, but she had evidently pissed her off and pissed her off good. I wondered, though, where a judge's secretary got off talking to *anyone* like that, let alone to an attorney.

Continuing, the judicial secretary Nazi said, "I would further point out that allowing a judge's chambers to wait on hold for one minute and forty-seven seconds is entirely unacceptable, and I will be addressing the issue with Judge Rolston this morning."

After briefly collecting myself, I cleared my throat and set out to perform some damage control.

"Ms. Finnegan, I cannot tell you how embarrassed I..."

"Counsel, I am *Mrs.* Finnegan – I'm not quite sure how the women in Philadelphia choose to live their lives, but out here, those of us who are married and lead wholesome lives, aren't afraid to say so," she said, as if Brandywine County were located in a similar proximity to Philadelphia as Iowa. I was beginning to get the feeling that Mrs. Finnegan didn't much care for the city slicker attorneys from 20 miles away, who dared attempt to seek justice in her judge's court. I was also becoming pretty sure that Gloria Steinem types were not terribly welcomed in Mrs. Finnegan's courtroom.

"My apologies, Mrs. Finnegan. As I was saying, I am horribly embarrassed that our receptionist spoke to you that way." Quickly fabricating a lie in an attempt to smooth things over, I continued, at a whisper, "Between you and me, you are not the first person who has said something negative about our receptionist, Ms. –

err – Miss Fabrizzio. It's become a recurring problem and I fully intend to address the subject with our office manager. I can't thank you enough for bringing this issue to my attention."

"FAH-BREEZE-EE-O," she repeated, as I could hear the sound of a pencil scribbling Kristin's name on a piece of paper. "The young lady's Christian name, counsel?"

Was this loon serious? What was she going to do, put her on the Brandywine County black list? I had had just about enough of this obnoxious pompous witch. I might have been willing to take this shit from a judge, but I was not willing to do so from someone who had likely been kicked out of Archbishop Paone High School for either getting caught smoking too many times, or getting pregnant too many times. It began to dawn on me that Mrs. Finnegan was the nasty looking character whom I had seen whispering to Judge Rolston in the Brandy Wine House.

The funny thing was that I didn't even care. I had exactly one case in Brandywine County and didn't plan to have many more in the foreseeable future. Judge Branson was my judge in the Lubrano case, and I had no reason to take nonsense from some other judge's secretary. I hadn't completed four years of college, three years of law school and six years, and counting, of taking law firm partners' shit, to have to listen to the garbage coming out of this self-righteous idiot's mouth. I had reached my boiling point.

"Did you ask for her *Christian* name? I'm not sure how *Ms.* Fabrizzio's first name is, in any way, relevant. Ma'am, can I help you with something because, believe it or not, I'm a fairly busy individual, and I have clients who are counting on me this very second."

"I beg your pardon," she began, as if she were scolding one of her children, "I will not be spoken to in such a tone!"

"Mrs. Finnegan, I'm a working person just like you. I am neither attempting to undermine you nor waste your time. Please extend me the same courtesy. I told you that Ms. Fabrizzio would be dealt with. This issue is now over. Was there a reason for your call?"

"If that's your position, then fine. And yes, you can be assured that Miss Fabrizzio *will* be dealt with."

This woman couldn't possibly be for real. Was she going to summarily sentence Kristin to death and have the Brandywine County executioner pluck her from her cigarette break and immediately take her to the gallows?

She proceeded, "Attorney Brown, I actually did call for a reason, other than to get insulted by a disrespectful receptionist and an equally disrespectful city-lawyer. I was calling to let you know that Judge Rolston will be hearing argument on the preliminary objections in the <u>Lubrano Concrete</u> matter tomorrow morning at 9:00 a.m. in Courtroom 5. For the benefit of your client, I would suggest that you undergo an *addytood* adjustment between now and then. Judging by what I've seen and heard from you so far, I wouldn't imagine that you would take the time to look at the judge's procedures in *our* county local rules, so I'll enlighten you so that you do not unnecessarily delay the proceedings tomorrow. The moving party, Mr. Shaughnessy, will have five minutes to present his argument. You, sir, will then have five minutes to rebut. That's it. Decorum will be observed at all times, and this will be nothing like the free-for-all that you're used to in Philadelphia. Is that understood?"

I had, once again, stopped breathing, and my testicles had crawled up inside of my body. This had to be a joke. This was not possible. Judge Branson was the judge in the <u>Lubrano Concrete</u> case! They couldn't just change judges on the fly, could they? Moreover, the preliminary objections were, according to the Pennsylvania Rules of Civil Procedure, moot. I had filed an Amended Complaint – the preliminary objections were no longer at issue! What the hell was this woman talking about?!

Fully convinced that Mrs. Finnegan had misconstrued the reason why the judge was summoning counsel to court the following day, I decided to have a little fun with her and make her feel like the idiot she was.

"Mrs. Finnegan, I think that there must be some misunderstanding here. I filed an *Amended* Complaint. In Philadelphia County, Allegheny County, Lackawanna County and every other county in this Commonwealth, and, yes, even Brandywine County, that means that the preliminary objections are *moot,* as in NO LONGER AT ISSUE. I tell you what – how 'bout I fax you a copy of my time-stamped Amended Complaint. That way, you can be sure that it was filed, and that there's no possible way that a preliminary objection hearing could be scheduled for tomorrow. When you're done reading my fax, I want you to explain to Her Honor that you called an attorney's office, obstinately insisting that that attorney was supposed to appear in court tomorrow for no reason!"

Sarcastically laughing in a devilish tone, Mrs. Finnegan responded,

"Sir, Judge Rolston has your Amended Complaint. And Sir, she knows the Rules of Civil Procedure.

"You won't concern yourself with why she's hearing argument tomorrow – but rest assured that she knows what the Rules say. Good day, Sir."

As she hung up the phone, I immediately sensed that I should have employed a slightly more conciliatory tone with Rolston's toady. I had crossed the line and would be paying for it in a big way tomorrow and beyond. If the judge didn't already detest me for my association with George Ridgeway, she would undoubtedly detest me now. I was a city slicker who had spoken down to a hard-working, patriotic civil servant. I fully embodied what Brandywine Countyans detested about outsiders, even though I, myself, was technically a Brandywine Countyan.

Quite unsettling was the notion that Rolston's decision to hold argument on the preliminary objections was not the product of an office mix-up. She had received a copy of the Amended Complaint from the Prothonotary, alright – she had just apparently chosen to ignore its effect, as dictated by the Pennsylvania Rules of Civil Procedure.

Even more unsettling was the notion that this case was stripped from Judge Branson and transferred to Judge Rolston for no immediately apparent reason. When judges retired, become debilitated or died, cases would transfer to another judge. Absent such an extenuating circumstance, new judges were simply not assigned while a case was proceeding. The reality that Judge Rolston had seen me in George Ridgeway's presence just a week prior caused me great trepidation in my attempt to believe that there was a legitimate reason for the change in judges. These developments were very unwelcoming.

In the best case scenario, I was getting "homered" by a judge who knew that I was not a Brandywine County practitioner, and who wanted to fuck with me a little bit to get her jollies. In the worst case scenario, I was now deeply entrenched, as a key piece in a politically-charged crusade ordered commenced by a nameless faceless member of the Brandywine County Political machine.

CHAPTER TWENTY-THREE

Chemin des Grès was a quiet country road in the eastern Paris suburb of La Pomponnette. There, at No. 1121, was a large tan brick Provincial style house with a massive dark blue hipped roof. Tall second floor shuttered windows breaking through the cornice gave the residence an air of distinction and affluence. A wrought-iron gate affixed to stone columns guarded the entrance to the estate. On one of the columns, chiseled into a slab were the words, "RES IPSA LOQUITUR." Beyond the gate was an expansive circular driveway that led to the house. Two oak trees which predated the French Revolution stood in the grassy area that the driveway encircled. A Citroën C4 Coupé was parked in front of the estate.

The brunette, who had been occupying the house alone – or usually alone – for three weeks, sipped her coffee methodically while perusing the pages of the two newspapers that were delivered to the house each morning, *Le Figaro* and *L'Équipe*. A sliced baguette and a glass jar of artisanal strawberry *confiture* that she was too depressed to eat, lay on the table next to the newspapers. She desperately tried, but could not ignore the piece of scrap paper with a pencil-written message which read:

011-1-610-555-0393 – BOSIE? BOSSY?– CHEF DE POLICE

She replayed the telephone message for the fourth straight time, and wondered whether her guardian angel had truly arrived or whether her loyalty was being tested by her benefactor.

This is your guardian angel calling. I know that you've been mistreated. I've got the deal of a lifetime for you. All your troubles are about to disappear.

How could she not at least call this mystery man back? How could she betray her benefactor?

This is your guardian angel calling. I know that you've been mistreated. I've got the deal of a lifetime for you. All your troubles are about to disappear.

All day long, she tried in earnest to ascertain whether she would be more likely to live if she returned the call or if she didn't return the call. She could no longer deny, though, that her comfortable life had ended and that there would be no going back to the security and affluence to which she had become accustomed.

Was this her escape?

She smoked Gauloises and stared at the foreign telephone numbers.

CHAPTER TWENTY-FOUR

Since it was a glorious warm summer day, I parked my car in Weston's municipal parking deck, about three blocks away from the courthouse, instead of trying to find a spot on the street closer to the courthouse. Not wanting to show up late before a judge who already hated me, I made sure to arrive fifteen minutes early. Weston's rush hour, which consisted of an electric trolley running along Keystone Avenue, dropping off twelve court personnel, almost tripped me up. In spite of rush hour, I still made it past security and to the door of Courtroom 5 by 8:47 a.m.

I opened one of the double doors leading into the courtroom and was greeted with a gorgeous expanse of patterned blue and gold carpet, a dark wooden jury box and brass chandeliers. Courtrooms such as this made one truly feel like a lawyer.

Interestingly, on the wall behind the bench rested a giant circular sign which carried the Brandywine County coat of arms. Since I was accustomed to seeing behind the judge's bench the Commonwealth of Pennsylvania coat of arms in state court and an imposing eagle grasping arrows and olive branches in federal court, the display of the Brandywine County symbol struck me as being odd. Given what I had come to learn about the Brandywine County bench and bar during the past several weeks, I was inclined to believe that the gesture was a calculated thumbing of the nose at the rest of the state.

Hoping that I was able to conceal the stars in my eyes, I walked gingerly past a swinging wooden door that separated the gallery from the area reserved for attorneys. Since there was only one other person in the courtroom, a geriatric looking character wearing a blue blazer with the same Brandywine County coat of arms on the breast pocket and the words, "TIP STAFF" printed below, I wasn't all that concerned at having appeared in awe of my surroundings. As I approached closer to where the old geezer was sitting, I noticed that he was either fast asleep or dead. Given this person's advanced age, I was not in a position to believe that one possibility was more likely than the other.

I placed my trial bag on the table closest to the jury box marked, "PLAINTIFF," on the right side of the room facing the bench. As I unloaded the voluminous documents that I had brought with me, I noticed a trial bag resting on the defense table. A light beige suit jacket was draped over the chair at the defense table. While I was a novice in the arena of Brandywine County practice, it seemed quite strange that the owner of the article of clothing, undoubtedly my adversary, Tim Shaughnessy, chose to remove his suit jacket. Both common sense and experience taught me that an attorney was never to remove his suit jacket anywhere in a courthouse. Maybe there was no hook in the stall in the men's room, therefore Shaughnessy had nowhere else to leave his coat.

While scribbling some last minute notes for arguments that I had intended to make, I heard raucous laughter in a male voice, emanating from behind a wooden door next to the judge's bench. I was hoping dearly that the voice was that of Judge Branson, and that the whole transferal of the case to Judge Rolston was scrapped. I prayed that Branson came through the door while Tim Shaughnessy was still in the bathroom. God, would that have been great. When Branson asked me if I knew where my adversary was, I would be able to offer some subtle barb about my being on time and Shaughnessy being late.

Someone exited the chambers door, but by putting two and two together, I was able to decipher that this person was not Judge Branson. This particular individual, whose back was facing the courtroom when the doors opened, was wearing light beige pants that matched the jacket resting on the back of Shaughnessy's chair. Completing the outfit were a heavily starched white shirt, a solid red tie and red suspenders with images of the scales of justice throughout.

Still laughing, and facing chambers, Tim Shaughnessy, in a most pandering manner, said,

"Oh, Judge you're too much! I wish that I could have seen that Defendant with my own eyes when you handed down the sentencing. I bet you anything he won't be stealing baby formula for a loooooooooong time! Oh, gosh, that's too much." Before shutting the door, he added, "O.K., then – I'll see ya' in a few."

As Shaughnessy turned around and caught view of me, his brownnosing jubilation was instantaneously transferred to a serious, brooding gaze. He either didn't like my ensemble of a blue shirt with a white collar and French cuffs, and complimenting pale yellow tie and charcoal-colored Hickey-Freeman suit, or he simply didn't like me. Judging by the look on this guy's face, it was definitely a combination of the two.

Once he was ten feet away, he extended his hand and walked towards me. As we engaged in a firm handshake, he projected, with a booming voice,

"Alexander, Timothy Shaughnessy. It's pleasure to make your acquaintance."

Shaughnessy was roughly 6'2', and had red curly hair, and the obligatory ruddy, alcohol abuse-affected face that every male over the age of forty-five seemed to possess in this county.

"Nice to meet you as well, Tim. Actually, it's just 'Alex.'"

"I appreciate that, Alex, but in this courtroom, you'll want to call yourself 'Alexander,' when the judge asks for your appearance."

"Thanks for the tip," I responded.

"Well, hello, Timothy!" said the previously sleeping tip staff official.

Shaughnessy turned around, and without so much as saying "pardon me," he exclaimed,

"And hello to you, Francis Xavier! You're looking well. How have you been?"

He looked anything but "well." In fact, he looked as if he could kick the bucket at any given time. The minimal white hair that he still possessed was horribly out of place, and appeared as if he had stuck his finger in an electrical socket immediately after rolling out of bed. He had more hair growing out of his nose than I would have on my upper lip if I didn't shave for three weeks. Gigantic hearing aids that looked as if they were manufactured in the late 1970s adorned both ears. While he was standing twenty feet away from me and I couldn't tell for certain, I was willing to bet that his breath was rancid.

"Did you hear about Johnny Mac, Frank?" Shaughnessy asked.

"Oh, Timmy, my heart goes out to his family. He's too young for cirrhosis. What is he, 52, 53? That's just awful."

"I know, I know," Shaughnessy responded, with both hands over his heart, "I was just talking to the judge and she said that he was before her last week and looked quite ill. What a hard working attorney he is. This is just a shame."

Apparently, Shaughnessy was not bashful, in the very least, in volunteering that he had just engaged in an *ex parte* communication with the trial judge immediately before a hearing. Notwithstanding the proscription of such behavior in the Pennsylvania Rules of Professional Conduct, and the dictates of common sense, "Timmy" didn't seem the least bit uneasy about having just been in Judge Rolston's chambers.

After he was done chitchatting with Mr. Death, Shaughnessy came back in my direction, this time wearing an arrogant smile.

"I bet you're wondering why we're here today," he asked.

After he made his statement, I was under the impression that he would offer a subsequent statement, advising me exactly why, in his belief, Judge Rolston decided to hold argument, even after the Preliminary Objections were mooted. He offered no such clarification, though.

Instead, he said, surreptitiously,

"Welcome to Brandywine County."

He wasn't saying, "Welcome to Brandywine County," in the sense of, "Gosh they really do things weirdly here, we all have to deal with it, so don't sweat it." He was saying, "Welcome to Brandywine County," in the sense of, "You don't know what you're in for, young'n outsider. Might as well quit now."

157

An instant later, a hand poked out from behind the judge's door and made some sort of coded gesture to Mr. Death. Death then rose to his feet, quicker than I might have imagined that he would be physically capable, attempted to pat his hair into place, buttoned his polyester blazer and bellowed,

"All rise!"

Immediately thereafter, the chambers door swung open, and Judge Rolston entered the courtroom in her black robes. She looked as pleasant as could be and nodded at both Shaughnessy and me. Thank God. Maybe I was just psyching myself out and wasn't as screwed as I had previously thought.

Following roughly five feet behind Judge Rolston was the very snide looking Geraldine Finnegan. Even while carrying a two-foot high stack of documents and walking towards the bench, the disgruntled clerk managed to keep her nasty and disapproving eyes affixed to me. This was not going to be fun.

I thought that Mr. Death's cameo was finished after "All rise!" Apparently, though, I was wrong. After once again fruitlessly attempting to pat his hair into place, Mr. Death shouted, in a vintage blue collar Brandywine County accent,

"*Oy-izz! Oy-izz! Oy-izz!* the Court of Common Pleas of Brandywine County is now in session, with the Honorable Mary Elizabeth Rolston presiding. All having business before this Honorable Court may come forward. May God save the United States of America, may God save the Commonwealth of Pennsylvania, and may God save this county."

There were several humorous elements of Mr. Death's little announcement. However, two in particular stood out. First, "*Oyez! Oyez! Oyez!*" was pronounced, "Oy-YEA," rather than "Oy-IZZ." Mr. Death was trying to sound sophisticated, but, instead, sounded like ignorance personified. The sad part was that he had probably been mispronouncing "Oyez" since the time that he was hired as a Tip Staff member, which likely occurred upon his arrival back from the Korean War. Second, "*Oyez! Oyez! Oyez!*" was how the United States Supreme Court began its court sessions. The Brandywine County Court of Common Pleas, which heard civil trials consisting 90% of personal injury lawsuits, was not the

United States Supreme Court. As such, the *"Oyez! Oyez! Oyez!"* and "God save the United States of America" business was just a tad over the top.

I must have been the only one who thought that Death's little speech was bullshit, because Judge Rolston didn't take her eyes off of the courtroom's American flag while it was transpiring and Shaughnessy looked like he was on the verge of tearing up.

Immediately after Mr. Death was finished, Judge Rolston firmly demanded,

"Counsel, please give your appearances."

Before I responded, I noticed that there was no court reporter or even a tape recording device in the courtroom. In the absence of either, the proceedings could not be recorded. The judge could have shot me with a bow and arrow, and there would be no record of it.

Confounded, I responded,

"Alexander Brown from the law firm of Krauss, Carlson, Whitby, Miller and White, on behalf of the Plaintiff, Lubrano Concrete Corporation."

"Thank you counsel, and this Krauss, Carlson, Whitby, Miller and White – is that correct? – is located where?" The judge asked.

"Uhhh, at the corner of 16th and Market Streets."

"*Uhhh*, Counsel," she began mockingly, "you're just going to have to be a *little* more specific. You see, we don't have a 16th Street or a Market Street in Weston, Pennsylvania – you know, the town in which this courthouse is located? So, I'm not sure if you're from Harrisburg, Williamsport, Altoona or a different universe – there are *a lot* of 16th Streets out there and *a lot* of Market Streets out there." She was overtly toying with me as Shaughnessy and Mean Geraldine cackled.

Even though my firm name and full address appeared above the case caption of the Complaint, which I could see was in her hand, I was still bound to respond respectfully. I wasn't dealing with an insolent clerk – I was dealing with a sitting Court of Common Pleas judge who could, almost single-handedly have my law license rescinded.

"I apologize, Your Honor, my offices are located in Philadelphia."

"I presume that we're talking about Philadelphia, *Pennsylvania,* and not Philadelphia, *Mississippi.*"

"Yes, Your Honor," I answered, with a grin, as I pondered what the consequences would be if I threw my pen at her.

"O.K., then, PHI-LUHH-DEL-PHEE-UUH," she said, as she scribbled, presumably, the word, "Philadelphia" on her note pad.

"Since we've decided to dispose of all decorum and formalities, would it be O.K. if I just called you 'The Concrete Lawyer', counsel?"

I was beyond fucked.

Shaughnessy and Mean Geraldine laughed again in unison.

Trying to not appear disturbed, I answered approvingly, "That would be just fine, Your Honor."

"Mr. Brown, I must confess that I was truly touched to learn the other day that you neither drink *nor* smoke."

Hoping to appear as if I could take the ball busting, I replied,

"Thank you, Your Honor. I must confess, though, since we're in a court of law, that I do have a drink or two, every so often."

"Mr. Brown," she said in an annoyed tone, "The court is not particularly interested in your proclamations of alcohol consumption. This is a respected court of law, NOT a fraternity party. You will treat it as such."

"Counsel, your turn," she said, sarcastically batting her eyes and smiling at Shaughnessy wide enough to expose two aged leathery dimples on either cheek.

"Thank you, Your Honor. And, may it please the court, Timothy Joseph Shaughnessy the Third of the law firm of Meehan Shaughnessy and Sullivan, Brandywine County Bar Number 483, representing Bicentennial Lumber Works of Stillman, Pennsylvania. Good morning, Your Honor."

God, did I want to vomit. Shaughnessy was bidding her a good morning, as if he had developed amnesia and didn't remember sharing Wawa coffee and doughnuts with her a few minutes prior. Also, as if Rolston didn't already know that Tim Shaughnessy was a home boy, he tackily recited his Brandywine County Bar

ID number and mentioned, in passing, that his client was based in Stillman, a blue collar Brandywine County stronghold, whose businesses contributed heavily to judicial elections.

"And, Good Morning to you, Mr. Shaughnessy," she said, beaming.

After pulling what appeared to be the Preliminary Objections from one of the folders that Mrs. Finnegan had placed before her, Judge Rolston put on her bifocals and began to read the document. After perusing it for about three seconds, Judge Rolston, apparently having seen enough, ripped her bifocals from her face and demanded,

"Mr. Brownstein, can you please tell me what we're doing here today?"

Was that supposed to be a trick question? For starters, my name wasn't Brownstein. Additionally, I should have been asking her what we were doing in court, since my Amended Complaint had made the Preliminary Objections moot.

"Actually, Your Honor, my name is Brown – Alexander Brown. As far as why we're in court this morning, I really have to confess that..."

Interrupting me, as Shaughnessy was visibly biting his bottom lip to prevent himself from erupting in laughter, the judge blurted,

"Are you sure? I could have sworn that you said 'Brownstein.' Well, I *used to* have a dentist named 'Brownstein,' and let's just say that that didn't turn out well. You see these two teeth in the back of my mouth?" she said, opening her mouth wide enough to bob for apples, "He put a bridge in back there and I was in excruciating pain for *three weeks*." She spoke the latter part of the sentence holding three fingers in the air. Simultaneously, Mrs. Finnegan, her loyal lap dog, mouthed the words, with a compassionate look, "That's a sin."

"I hope for your client's sake that you're a better lawyer than he is a dentist," Rolston continued, without the slightest hint of concern that she had defamed someone in open court. Then again, there was no court reporter recording the proceedings, so what was the harm?

"I'm going to give you the benefit of the doubt, counsel. The Presbyterian Academy, The University of Pennsylvania – Hooray! Villanova Law – ehh, so-so."

While I was not surprised that Judge Rolston had pulled my bio off of the firm's internet website, I was quite surprised that she acknowledged having done so. In theory, neither my academic pedigree, nor any of the other items listed on my bio should have been of any consequence in her courtroom. In theory, though, my adversary should not have been cavorting with the trial judge immediately before a hearing, or at all.

At that point, I told myself that it was time to stop living in a fantasy world. There would be no justice for an outsider such as myself before this sad excuse for a judge on this or any other day.

"Mr. Brownstein, I'm going to be perfectly blunt with you – this case belongs before the PAA, not before this court. I try commercial dispute cases all the time, and you know what I end up with? I end up with a jury that is more often asleep than it is awake. Juries want slip and falls. Juries want medical malpractice cases in which a six month old child is left fatherless. Juries want blood and gore. They don't want to hear about change orders and backcharges. Do you see what I'm saying?"

I saw exactly what she was saying: she didn't know shit about the subject matter of this case and didn't want to suffer the embarrassment of having one of her home-cooked rulings reversed by the state's appellate courts.

The PAA is the Pennsylvania Arbitration Association, a private non-court-affiliated arbitration forum. Many construction contracts and employment agreements dictated that all disputes be resolved via binding PAA arbitration. In other words, in such circumstances, parties signed away their right to pursue legal action in a court, in favor of the PAA forum. Theoretically, is was less expensive to adjudicate a case in the PAA, but its rulings were notorious for "splitting the baby," or rendering a verdict that was equally pleasing and displeasing to both parties.

Lubrano Concrete and Bicentennial Lumber did not have a PAA clause in their contract, and, accordingly, the parties were free to resolve their dispute in a court of law. Judge Rolston seemed to be suggesting that the parties voluntarily remove the case from her court and place it before a binding PAA arbitration panel. I was certain that the Lubranos would not be interested in such a proposition.

Responding to Rolston, I said, tentatively, knowing that I was about to incur her further wrath,

"Your Honor, respectfully, there is no arbitration clause in the contract and my client has no interest having this case heard by an arbitration panel that will do nothing more than split the baby. It is my firm belief that a jury will compensate my client more justly than a tribunal of arbitrators will."

Staring away from the attorneys and not taking her eyes off of her fingernails, Judge Rolston retorted,

"Mr. Brownstein, when I practiced law and I began a point by saying 'respectfully', I was diplomatically telling the recipient that he or she was wrong. You have just told me that I am wrong. Thank you for your opinion, sir. But, in actuality – "

Interrupting the judge, I said,

"No, no, not at all, Your Honor, I did not mean to convey that at all. What I was trying to say was that – "

Now looking at me with mean and angry eyes, she exclaimed,

"Shut up, Mr. Brown! Just shut your mouth and try to act like a lawyer – as hard of a proposition as that may be for you!"

Now that I had gotten her good and pissed, she apparently felt compelled to dispense with the name calling and refer to me as "Brown," instead of "Brownstein."

The fact that she was describing what she used to do when she "practiced" was nothing short of hilarious. While Ridgeway was a head case, I tended to believe what he said about Rolston having never practiced law and working menial courthouse jobs.

"You know what we're going to do, Mr. Brown? We're going to implement the Hinson Rule." She began, as Shaughnessy looked on, smirking, clearly understanding what the "Hinson Rule" was. At least one of us did.

"You're gonna get your jury trial, alright. Guess who's gonna sit on your jury, Mr. Brown? Twelve people who went to Darden High, Brandywine City High and Monsignor Tocchetti. They aren't going to be any more impressed with the fact that you were fed with a silver spoon, went to Presbyterian Academy and Penn, than I am. I'm setting trial for – Mrs. Finnegan, when is my next available trial date?"

Dutifully and promptly, Mrs. Finnegan responded, at a whisper. "January 2, judge."

"January 2, it is. Good day, counsel. You are excused," she said, as she stood up. Before walking into the door leading to her chambers, Rolston exchanged some lighthearted words with Mrs. Finnegan. After they were done speaking, the judge regained the serious look on her face, hunched over and looked straight down. For a moment, I thought that my prayers had been answered and this woman was suffering a stroke or a heart attack right there in the courtroom.

When she put her hands together, as if holding a golf club, I knew that she was not about to die, though.

She was playing air golf, right there in the courtroom. In my head, I asked God to strike me down right then and to take me from this miserable world. The most important case of my career was in the hands of not just an unqualified political hack, but an unqualified political hack who played air golf. I silently condemned myself for applying such a double standard, but watching a woman playing air golf was even more difficult for me to stomach than watching a man playing air golf.

After following her imaginary ball as it sailed away, she uttered in typical asinine golf humor,

"Mr. Shaughnessy, I do hope that you bring a worthy partner to the upcoming Member-Guest. My swing is nothing short of phenomenal right now."

Shaughnessy quickly responded,

"I can see that from here, Judge. Looks like I don't have a shot this year."

What a crock of shit. The judge and my adversary were club mates. The first thought that crossed my mind was that I should immediately file a motion for the judge to recuse herself, in light of the obvious preexisting relationship between her and Shaughnessy. I quickly quashed that thought, realizing that this judge was not assigned to this case by mistake. She took over for Judge Branson because someone within the system wanted Judge Branson replaced by her. Although I could create a valid issue for a future appeal by filing a Motion for Recusal, the act of filing such a motion would make the judge hate me even more than she already did. Since the motion would be summarily denied, I didn't immediately see the point of pursing such a course of action.

The bigger problem rested in the trial date that she had allocated. Scheduling a trial for less than a half-year away on January 2nd was absurd. Cases of this magnitude required a discovery period of at least one year. Written discovery would need to be propounded, in excess of 20 depositions would need to be taken, and documents from many, many non-parties would need to be subpoenaed. What was more disturbing than the abbreviated discovery period was the fact that Shaughnessy didn't seem to care. He would need to take as much discovery as I, in order to successfully defend his case. I was now quite certain that Shaughnessy was confident in his client's position for reasons other than the merits of the case.

Playing it cool, pretending to not be affected by what had just occurred in Judge Rolston's courtroom, I walked out into the hallway towards the court exit with Shaughnessy. I had hoped that, as a sign of good faith, he would attempt to console me.

After walking about thirty feet next to Shaughnessy, without him saying so much as word, I decided to inquire,

"So, are you and Judge Rolston golfing buddies? That must be a great way for you to get a perspective of what's transpiring in the Brandywine County Court system. I guess I'd probably need to be a member at your country club, too, to know what the 'Hinson Rule' is, huh?"

Unhumored, Shaughnessy shot back, not inclined to answer all of my inquiries,

"You could hardly call us 'golfing buddies'. We happen to be members at the same golf club, and that's about the extent of it."

Sure, that's the extent of it.

"Say, Tim, which club do you belong to? Whispering Creek? Glen Oaks? Underhill?"

Shrugging me off, he answered, "It doesn't really matter, Alex. If you're thinking of joining, there's a whole arduous process that you have to go through. Maybe we can discuss it when the case is over. Listen, don't get yourself all upset about what just happened in the courtroom. The same thing happened to me when I was just starting out in this profession. I'm not sure what you're thinking, but this county works a certain way – don't think for a second that you're being singled out. When it comes down to it, it's sometimes just easier to be a white-haired Irishman in this county than a – a – youngster."

He did not intend to convey the "youngster" comment in an assuaging way. He intended to speak down to me. Also, I found it odd that he was referring to himself as an Irishman, when I didn't sense even the slightest Irish accent. All that I could detect was a stale Brandywine County inflection.

Ever curious, I responded as sarcastically as I could muster,

"Oh, I didn't realize that you were Irish. I never would have been able to tell from your accent. You cover it really well. You must have come over to this country as a young boy, no?"

Shaughnessy's face turned bright red. I was mocking him. He knew that I was mocking him. For a brief second, I thought that he was going to take the fighting stance of the Notre Dame mascot and challenge me to an old-fashioned donnybrook. After his face returned to its normal color, he responded in a perturbed tone,

"I'm an Irish-*American*, Alex."

"Oh, I'm so sorry! I thought that you said that you were *Irish*. My wife always tells me that I should get my ears cleaned out. Times like this really make me think that I should heed her advice."

"I did say that I was Irish – which, around these parts, means that one is Irish-American."

Feeling that I hadn't quite gotten my full mileage out of my smart-assed line of questioning to my adversary whom I so despised for having an improper "in" with the trial judge in this case, I asked, dramatically feigning naïveté,

"O.K., I must confess – now I'm confused. So in *these parts*, what does one call someone who is an Irish national, visiting here on vacation?"

Shaughnessy, out-smartassing me, responded with a smirk,

"A tourist. Based upon your questioning, I'm guessing that you're not Irish."

"I'm still a little confused about what constitutes an 'Irishman', but I've only been to Ireland once, so I don't think that you could classify me as being 'Irish'."

"Well, what are you, then?"

Not quite finished having fun, I answered,

"Do you mean nationality? Well, my passport says that I'm American. My parents were born in Philadelphia. Their parents were born in Philadelphia, and I'm pretty sure that their parents were born in Philadelphia. So I guess that I'm just *American-American*. Is there such a thing? Does that answer your question?"

It clearly did not answer his question. As he stared at me with his white face that was adorned with numerous broken blood vessels in the area of his nose, he was thinking something like,

"You disrespectful little shit. I was practicing law before you were born. If I could get away with it, I would drop you, right here and now."

Now, outside of the courthouse, Shaughnessy, extended his hand and, without responding to my previous comment, said,

"Good day, Alex. I'll be in touch."

After we shook hands, Shaughnessy didn't have very far to walk. In fact, after traveling approximately fifteen paces, he had reached his late model metallic gold Ford Taurus in an area directly in front of the courthouse with a signed designation that read,

**COURTHOUSE STAFF
PARKING ONLY. VIOLATORS
WILL BE PROSECUTED!**

Yeah, I really was fucked.

CHAPTER TWENTY-FIVE

Once I retrieved my vehicle from the area designated for non-cronies, I made my way down Brandywine Boulevard for about a mile and a half, until it intersected with the Interstate. Upon journeying onto the federally-funded Interstate, I felt as if I had extracted myself from a lawless, Wild West environment. It seemed incredible to me that in less than a half-hour, I would be in Center City Philadelphia. That such blatant, overt and unlawful favoritism was displayed in a suburban jurisdiction just 20 miles from the nation's fifth largest city was incomprehensible to me.

It wasn't as if I were an Armani suit-wearing Los Angeles attorney with slicked-back hair, who had filed suit in a jurisdiction well out of his realm. I was a Philadelphia-based attorney who had filed suit in a county bordering Philadelphia.

The Philadelphia skyline soon came into view. At that moment, an odd emotion overcame me. The feeling was similar to that which I had experienced during the times in which I had traveled to Europe. During a trans-Atlantic journey originating in the northeast United States, one boards an aircraft in a metropolis where American English is spoken and gas guzzling SUVs dominate the thoroughfares. Seven hours later, one is transplanted into an alternate culture in which the inhabitants speak a different tongue, and all of the cars are of the econo-box, fuel-efficient variety.

When I saw the Philadelphia skyline, I felt as if I had been rapidly transferred back home from a very foreign, scary place.

Since I was on official firm business and knew that I would be reimbursed, I opted to splurge and park my car at the One Liberty

Place garage, where the daily parking rate was $34.00. While New Yorkers might consider such a daily parking rate in the very heart of the business district to be a steal, by Philadelphia standards, 34 bucks for a day of parking was extraordinarily steep. What the hell did I care, though? The Lubranos were paying.

As I exited the elevator and prepared to walk into the office, I saw, through the office's clear plate glass entryway into the reception area, the image of an extremely irate Kristin screaming at somebody on the phone. My worrisome instincts told me that Vinny had already done something bad – very bad – to her, which had brought about the screaming. In twenty minutes, I would be in Walt Krauss' office explaining to him why I had facilitated a client's efforts to sleep with a member of the staff, thereby subjecting the firm to civil liability. As I neared the office door, Kristin was not only performing her patented pissed off South Philly-girl head and upper body gesticulation, but she was doing so with an unlit Marlboro Red clamped in between her right index and middle fingers, which were adorned with white and orange polished three-quarter inch nails. Knowing Kristin, these signs pointed to her anger level being at nuclear meltdown stage.

I held my breath and walked in the door, afraid of what I was about hear of Kristin's argument with Vinny.

"No, you did *not* just say that, you motherfucker! Don't you friggin' talk to me like that, or I'll come over there and kick your ass!" She shouted, with a red face and flaring nostrils. If at all possible, she was hotter while angry, than while not angry.

Walking past the polished marble reception desk, with all intentions of simply ignoring Kristin and her conversation, she stopped me in my tracks. As if a different person had entered her body, she immediately lost the angry puss, put on one of her famous flirtatious receptionist's greeting faces and said,

"Oh, hi, *Ale-ixx*! Weren't you going to say 'hi' to me? That's not very nice, you meanie. *Hail* was court? Did you win?"

Confused, I said,

"I'm sorry, Kristin – you seemed to be a little preoccupied – I didn't want to disturb you."

Holding her hand over the mouthpiece of the phone, she whispered,

"Oh, that's just my dad on the phone. He's such an asshole! He told me that he ain't gonna cover the insurance co-pay on my birth control pills no more if I keep missin' mass on *Sundee*. I'm a friggin' awesome Catholic. I miss, like, one mass and he's ready to disown me. My older sister is, like, 29, has three kids from three different dudes, and he still pays the co-pay on her birth control pills – so I just don't want to hear that shit."

"Thanks for the info, Kris. I really need to be getting back to my office."

"O.K.. Bye, *Ale*."

Thank God. Lubrano hadn't yet Lubranoed this particular woman. I would definitely make it a priority, though, to advise my top client that he might want to consider using multiple forms of birth control when having sex with my receptionist in the future.

After passing Kristin's desk, I swung by the break room, grabbed a decaf – black – and entered my office and turned on my computer. With a few exceptions, such as the recent Lubrano Complaint drafting all-nighter, I only drank decaffeinated coffee. I had converted to decaf a few years prior, when, during a three week trial, I had overdosed on coffee and stress and began to experience heart palpitations. Never wanting to again experience that feeling of knowing that I was about to die, and that in six months time, Julie would be screwing somebody better looking and more successful than I, I had resolved to drink only decaf thereafter.

I sipped my decaf and began to review the seven e-mails that had accumulated while I spent the morning in that foreign country, 20 miles away. Three e-mails were from a firm advertising attorney continuing education seminars. One e-mail contained an electronic notice of Judge Keenan scheduling a Rule 16 Conference in one of my New Jersey federal court matters. One e-mail contained the following stern warning from our office manager, Connie Borkowski:

```
to those who been leaving
old and smelling food in
```

```
the frige, please note that
such practice is strickley
forbidding, and every friday
from now on the frige will be
emptyed. those continuing to
leave theyre old food in the
frige will have to reporte to
Mr. Krauss. thank you for your
consideration, Connie :)
```

Even more disturbing than the notion that the firm was paying an office manager to police the company's refrigerator, was that Connie was actually a high school graduate.

Another e-mail was from Nick Carlson, who advised, to all firm Associate attorneys and Paralegals,

```
YOUR BILLABLE HOURS ARE
DUE IN THE COMPUTER
SYSTEM AT THE CONCLUSION
OF EACH DAY. I HAVE
MADE THIS POLICY CLEAR,
TIME AND TIME AGAIN.
NEVERTHELESS, CERTAIN
ASSOCIATES AND PARALEGALS
HAVE EITHER CONSCIOUSLY,
OR SUBCONSCIOUSLY CHOSEN
TO DEFY MY ORDERS. THOSE
OF YOU WHO KNOW ME WELL,
KNOW THAT I REFUSE TO BE
DEFIED. I AM A VETERAN
OF 26 JURY TRIALS. IN
THOSE TRIALS, I AM 25
AND 1. I DON'T ACCEPT
PERSONAL FAILURE AND I
DON'T ACCEPT FAILURE
AMONGST THOSE AROUND ME.
DO NOT FAIL ME. DO NOT
TEST ME. FROM THIS POINT
FORWARD, THOSE FAILING
```

```
TO ENTER THEIR BILLABLE
HOURS IN THE COMPUTER
SYSTEM BY THE END OF THE
DAY WILL BE ASKED TO
STAY HOME THE FOLLOWING
DAY AND THINK ABOUT WHY
THEY COULDN'T FOLLOW THIS
SIMPLE INSTRUCTION. AFTER
A SECOND OFFENSE, THE
OFFENDER WILL BE ASKED
TO GO HOME AND TO NOT
RETURN. START STEPPING
IT UP, PEOPLE. BE GUIDED
ACCORDINGLY. N.C.
```

Nicky sure had a way with words. Ironically, though, after receiving his e-mail, at least half of the Associate and Paralegal staff would place calls within 24 hours to head hunters, in the hope of obtaining alternate employment.

There were diplomatic and effective means by which to remind employees that billable hours were to be timely entered. Nick was apparently unfamiliar with such means. Paradoxically, between two and three employees would likely end up resigning because of his e-mail and the firm would be forced to pay tens of thousands of dollars to head hunter firms to replace those employees. Moreover, tens of thousands of more dollars would be wasted training such new employees until they became financially productive. So, in summary, by virtue of Nick displaying such bold and impressive bravado in his "respect me" e-mail, ostensibly for the purpose of generating money for the firm, the firm would undoubtedly be set back in excess of $100,000.00.

My final e-mail appeared to be of the scam variety from one of those Nigerian or Congolese Ponzi scheme groups that lures you in with the promise of a nine-fold return on your investment then steals your kidneys, or something. The message was curious, though, because the firm's SPAM filter caused me to seldom receive unwanted e-mails. Also, unlike the SPAM e-mails that I often received, this one was addressed specifically to me, and was written entirely in French. It read:

```
à: Alexander Brown, Avocat à
la Cour
Krauss, Carlson, Whitby,
Miller and White, Cabinet des
Avocats
1601 Market Street
PHILADELPHIE
ÉTATS-UNIS

Objet: Prendre un avocat

Monsieur:

J'ai besoin immédiatement
d'un avocat à Philadelphie
pour m'aider avec un procès
international complexe.
Cet avocat doit avoir une
expertise dans le droit de
la construction et doit être
immédiatement disponible. Je
peux proposer des honoraries
élevés. Veuillez me contacter
immédiatement par téléphone
à +33-1-42-51-17-03, si
vous désirez de plus amples
renseignements.


Veuillez agréer, monsieur
l'expression de mes
salutations les plus
distinguées,
Jean-Luc LE GUEN

LE GUEN, S.A.
230, RUE DES BERNARDINS
75005 PARIS
FRANCE
```

The e-mail, from a Jean-Luc Le Guen in Paris, indicated an immediate need to hire a Philadelphia-based attorney specializing in the area of construction law, to assist with a complex international lawsuit. It further indicated that excellent legal fees would be paid in exchange for the services rendered.

After fully ruling out that the e-mail was garden variety SPAM, I considered that it had to have been a cruel joke played by one of my fellow Associates. The Associates in my office knew that my career goal involved the far-fetched fantasy of one day opening up my own firm, with offices in both Philadelphia and Paris. Plus, with the two new clients that I had brought in, I was ripe for a humiliating practical joke from my jealous colleagues. Moreover, in light of the current political climate, I took a lot of heat for being a francophone and romanticizing about French history, culture and food. When I was first hired by the firm, some of the Partners even took to calling me, "Inspector Clouseau," based upon the numerous references on my résumé to previously studying and working in France. However, pranks were very uncommon and highly frowned upon in our extremely uptight office.

I began to weigh the possibility that the e-mail was a legitimate solicitation from a French businessman in need of a lawyer in Philadelphia. To test this theory, I performed a Martindale-Hubbell internet search of French speaking Philadelphia-based attorneys who specialized in construction litigation. Surprisingly, only three names popped up after the database had concluded the search. One of the names was yours truly. Another one of the attorneys, Nicodemo Fregosi, had died about a year prior, while in his late 80s. I knew that he had died because he was a marginal celebrity in Philadelphia, having served as counsel for many alleged mafia-connected construction outfits. His death was a matter of public interest and was reported in the local newspapers and on television.

The final attorney whom the search yielded, was a rotund looking, acne-afflicted creature by the name of Brenda Berkowitz. In addition to Brenda apparently pushing three bills, Martindale-Hubbell listed her as having graduated from law school just one year prior.

So, if this Le Guen were looking for his attorney on Martindale-Hubbell, where many sophisticated clients found their attorneys, and he plugged in the search criteria of a Philadelphia-based French speaker who specialized in construction law, he would have found a dead guy, a fat and ugly female novice and me. I liked my chances of competing for business against those two people.

The e-mail was not a joke – my ship had come in.

Flush with adrenaline, I closed my office door, finished off my decaf, took a deep breath and readied myself to call Monsieur Le Guen. It had been so long since I had dialed an overseas number, that I had to stop and think what code I had to dial before punching in the number that had been furnished to me in the e-mail. *Was it "001," or "011"?* Upon deciding that "011" seemed a bit more familiar, I nervously tapped the number into my phone. I dialed, "011-33-1-42-51-17-03."

After a three second pause, I heard an odd click, followed by the foreign, yet familiar steady buzzing. This buzzing on European telephone systems was markedly different from the ringing heard on North American telephone systems after placing a call and prior to the party on the other end picking up the call.

After two and a half buzzes, a voice on the other end picked up and said,

"Âllo, c'est Véronique."

Obviously, I had dialed the wrong number. "Véronique" was clearly a woman – and a very sultry sounding woman, at that. If she was Monsieur Le Guen, then something was seriously wrong.

Embarrassingly, I responded, indicating that I had dialed the wrong number and was trying to reach Jean-Luc Le Guen,

"Je m'excuse – je pense que j'ai mal composé – j'essayais à contacter Monsieur Jean-Luc Le Guen."

I felt like such a blithering idiot. If I had dialed a wrong number to someone in the States, I would not have given a hoot and would have moved on. In this case, I was inexplicably horrified at having dialed the wrong number of someone in France whom I would never meet, and who didn't even know who I was.

Instead of hanging up, the woman chose to continue a discourse with me, saying, *"Non, Monsieur Brown, c'est le bon numéro – you aahv dialed zee correct number."* I could have been mistaken, but this woman was giggling seductively at me. I had to get my head out of the gutter – this woman was clearly Le Guen's secretary, or if I had called his home, it was his wife. One wrong statement or intonation could result in my blowing this opportunity of a lifetime.

Sounding like a nervous fool, I explained that I had expected a male voice to answer,

"Je suis désolé – je m'attendais à entendre une voix masculine."

"Zat eeze O.K., Monsieur Brown. You deed nut know zat I wood be answering. Your French is impeccable – much better zan we aahd expected. Fantastic."

"Alors, merci bien, Véronique, err, Madame, err, Mademoiselle...," I began, not knowing whether I should call her by her first name, the matronly, "Madame," or "Mademoiselle," which was generally reserved for unmarried younger women. This confusion represented one of the things that puzzled me about the French. Why did they always keep Anglophones guessing?

Sensing my confusion, Véronique interrupted me, sparing me from further mortification.

"Ahh-lexx, you can call me Véronique if I can call you *Ahh-lexx.* Eeze zat a fair condition?"

"Uhh, certainly – I think that that's more than fair, Véronique."

"Alors, Ahh-lexx, let's get down to business, shall we?"

"Please."

"O.K., zen – Monsieur Le Guen eeze not ear to speak wiss you, but he aahd anticipated your call and directed me to let you know zee details of zee representation. I am Véronique Lescure, Monsieur Le Guen's personal assistant. Monsieur Le Guen is zee owner of Le Guen, S.A., a manufacturer of tower cranes for construction projects. You, of course, have heard of zee company?"

"Of course, gosh, it's an honor that you're calling me," I responded, without ever having heard of a company with a name even remotely sounding like Le Guen, S.A. I did, however, know that "S.A." meant *Société Anonyme,* and was often used as a suffix after the names of French companies, similar to the way in which American companies place "Inc." or "Ltd." after a company name.

"Good," she responded, "zenn you are in advantageous position already. Zee company entered into a contract wiss Jennings Concrete – a company out of zee Philadelphie – uhh, how you say, *banlieue*?"

"Suburbs," I shot back.

"*Exactement.* Thank you – yes – a company out of zee Philadelphie suburbs. We enter into contract wiss zem for us to sell zem two tower cranes, totaling 1.4 million U.S. dollars. After we have fabricated and were ready to ship, we get call from Jennings Concrete and zey tell us zat zey no longer want to buy. Zeeze were very special, particular tower cranes made for a very odd job zat Jennings was to build. Because of ziss, we cannot resell zemm."

I knew Jennings Concrete well. In fact, they were Lubrano Concrete's primary competition in the Philadelphia Tri-State area. This was incredible. Once the Lubranos found out that I was suing Jennings Concrete for something – anything – they would be kissing my feet. I would be Lubrano Concrete's attorney for life because of this.

Véronique's story was in line with what I had heard from not just Vinny, but from other attorneys and people in the construction industry. Jennings was notorious for stiffing their subcontractors. According to Vinny, Lubrano Concrete was able to take over Jennings as the highest volume concrete construction contractor in the region, simply because Jennings had double-crossed so many contractors that they could often not find enough subcontractors willing to provide it with the necessary materials to build its projects.

Trying to sound as if I knew what the hell I was talking about, and taking a wee bit of exaggeratory license, I responded,

"Véronique, I have to tell you that this is not a surprise to me. I have seen those jokers at Jennings Concrete do this time and time again. I'm so sorry that this happened to you. My only regret is that I wasn't able to warn you before you contracted with them."

"God, zat makes me so mad," she responded in her raspy Parisian accent. Despite the clear presence of long-standing cigarette smoking habit apparent from her voice, I was nevertheless quite confident that this woman was no older than 30. I caught myself, yet again, wondering what she looked like.

Véronique continued,

"Zey seemed so nice when we agreed to make zeeze cranes for zem – and now zey just refuse to pay us."

"Well, Véronique, it's a good thing that you called me. This sort of work is my bread and butter." Again, with more than a little hyperbole, I continued, "I've made a career out of holding companies like Jennings accountable. Trust me – when I get done with them, they'll think twice about stiffing someone again."

"I like your *énergie*, Alex – you will be good for us," she said, tantalizingly, once again forcing my mind off of business and into other arenas. "Now eehrze what we aahv to do. We need to win zee race to zee courthouse. Jennings know zat we going to sue zemm, so we need to move on ziss right away, before zey sue us in France. As you undoubtedly know, zee logistics and tax consequences of winding up in zee French court system are very unfavorable to us."

"Of course," I responded, once again without any idea of what she was talking about. At first glance, regardless of how the French courts resolved civil cases, it seemed quite odd that Monsieur Le Guen would go to the trouble of finding foreign counsel and litigating a case in a foreign country, when he could easily file suit on his home turf and hail Jennings into court in France, forcing Jennings to hire French counsel. In any event, I wasn't eager to complain.

Véronique continued,

"You can file suit in Philadelphie federal court, no?"

"I can absolutely file suit right here in Philadelphia's federal District Court, the United States District Court for the Eastern District of Pennsylvania. Jennings' operations are located in this District and the dispute is with your company, a foreign entity. And, the matter in controversy exceeds $75,000.00, so yes, the elements of what we call 'diversity jurisdiction' will be satisfied and the suit will be able to proceed here."

"Good. I want you to make sure zat Judge Haslett is assigned to this case. You have had good fortunes with him before, no?"

Now things were starting to get a tad creepy. Véronique was correct. I had had good fortunes – very good fortunes – with Judge Haslett in the recent past. About a year back, on behalf on one of Carlson's insurance company clients, I had gotten a multi-million dollar "bad faith" suit tossed out of court at the inception of the case on non-substantive, procedural grounds. Judge Haslett authored a 65-page opinion dismissing the case. Since I had briefed and argued the Motion to Dismiss, my name appeared on the opinion. Lawyers with access to Lexis Nexis or Westlaw could have easily found the opinion online in a matter of seconds. It seemed exceedingly odd that Véronique, presumably a non-lawyer, and a foreigner at that, would know of that case.

"Véronique, unfortunately, I cannot select what judge is assigned to this case. There are currently 36 judges sitting on the federal District Court bench in Philadelphia. The selection of the judge is done completely at random, by the Clerk's Office."

"Well, do you know anyone at zee Clerk's Office who can make sure zat Judge Haslett is – never mind – zee judge doesn't matter."

Thankfully, she cut herself off before asking me to exert sway in the Clerk's Office.

"Eeze zeese case interesting to you?" she asked.

Oh, maybe just a little interesting – the same way that learning that I had the winning Powerball ticket might have slightly piqued my interest.

"Absolutely. I would love to be able to work with you and Monsieur Le Guen," I responded.

"Good, I wanted to hear ziss. You will mitt in person wiss Monsieur Le Guen ziss Friday, yes?" She asked.

"Uhh," I said, scanning my calendar, curious as to why her boss was going to make a transatlantic journey to meet me, when he could simply send me everything I needed either electronically or via overnight courier, "looks like...I'm...yep, looks like I'm free on Friday."

I would have been free for her on Friday even if the Phillies wanted to sign me for a one-day contract to play on that same day.

"I imagine that he'll want to freshen up from the long flight in his hotel before we meet, so, shall we book something in the late afternoon or evening? Also, I might suggest that he stay at either the Ritz-Carlton or the Westin. They're both within walking distance to my office and are wonderf..."

Véronique responded in an almost child-like laughter,

"No, no, you silly! In France, zee hired company come to see zee client not zee reverse. Monsieur Le Guen is very old fashioned. Monsieur Le Guen eeze not coming zare. You, Alex, ahre coming eehr."

Wow. I was coming eehr? Was this woman serious? Was Le Guen really going to pay thousands of dollars for me to fly to *Paris* on a day's notice for a meeting to discuss the details of a case that was to be filed in *Philadelphia*? Did Le Guen realize that he would be paying an hourly rate for my travel time? Did I have an ethical duty to tell Véronique that her boss could litigate the case more cost-effectively by filing suit in the French court system? I would give her one bit of caution to satisfy my conscience.

"Véronique, this is a tremendous opportunity, and I have no doubt that I would be able to serve you well. I feel compelled to advise you, however, that you may be making a mistake by not bringing this case in the French court system. By filing in France, you would be forcing Jennings Concrete to hire French counsel and venture into uncertain territory. I have been involved in cases in which a Defendant has ponied up money for the sole reason of not wanting to litigate in a foreign state. In this case, we're talking about a foreign country, so it seems apparent that..."

Véronique, unpredictably annoyed, snappily responded,

"Mr. Brown, you may rest assured zat we aahv considered all of zeeze factors. Do yourself a favor and let us decide where suit is going to be filed. Zare are about 10,000 other lawyers in your city who would kill for zee opportunity to represent a sophisticated foreign client for 500 U.S. Dollars per hour. Shall I go back to searching Martindale-Hubbell for another lawyer?"

F-F-F-F-F-Five hundred an hour? I thought silently to myself, as my eyes involuntarily rolled back into my head. I must have been in shock because at some point, Véronique chimed in,

"Mr. Brown – *âllo? Âllo?* Are you zare?"

"*Oui, oui, je suis là* – yep, I'm here, sorry."

"I imagine zat you will require a retainer. How much, please?"

Not wanting to sound like an amateur, I shot for the stars, expecting to be knocked down considerably.

"Well, Véronique, for a case such as this, involving a foreign client with whom this firm has not previously dealt, we need to make certain that we are protected. I would need to ask all of the Partners, but I think that we will require no less that $30,000.00 to get started."

"I don't aahv time to wait for your Partners, Mr. Brown," Véronique responded, still maintaining the curt persona that so contrasted the flirtatious tone that dominated the beginning of our conversation. "I will wire $50,000.00 into your firm's account within the hour. After we get off of zee phone, you will please e-mail me zee wiring instructions. Air France aahz a flight leaving Philadelphia tomorrow at 6:45 p.m., getting in to Paris at 8:25 a.m on Thursday, and US Airways aahz a flight leaving Philadelphia at 6:15 p.m., getting into Paris at 7:55 p.m. Ziss way, you will have a day to adjust to zee time change before your meeting wiss Monsieur Le Guen. Now, which flight would you prefer?"

Still feeling as if I needed to pinch myself, I answered,

"Uhhh...whichever, I suppose."

Once again chipper, Véronique replied,

"Air France, zenn. Zee food and wine are better. O.K., zenn, it's a date. I will e-mail you my contact information. As soon as you e-mail back to me zee wiring instructions, I will direct our bank to wire $50,000.00 into your firm's account. Once I have completed your travel reservation, I will e-mail zat to you as well. Have you any questions for me?"

"Uhh, not really..."

"O.K., zenn. Zee next time I see you will be in Paris. I eagerly anticipate it. Bye, bye, Mr. Brown."

"*À plus tard*, Véronique."

As I hung up the phone, I felt as if I had hit the progressive jackpot on a slot machine. By the close of business, the firm would be $50,000.00 and one international client richer. In 24 hours, I would be in an airplane over the Atlantic, at the request of a client who had searched me out. If I wasn't hot shit yet, I was damn close.

Taking Le Guen, S.A., Lubrano Concrete and Physician's Justice into consideration, I was on a pretty good goddamn roll. The days of Carlson and the other asshole partners bossing me around were going to come to an abrupt end. If all of my new projects worked out the way that I had hoped, I would soon be the one calling the shots.

CHAPTER TWENTY-SIX

The rapture of knowing that I was hand selected by a major French business to pursue a significant lawsuit had overcome me. I was well-aware that the sole reason that I had been chosen was because I was virtually the only attorney listed on Martindale-Hubbell in Philadelphia with the client's required credentials. I refused to let that small bit of reality deflate the ego trip that I was experiencing. After all, I did make the conscious decision several years prior to learn and master a foreign language. Sure, I had chosen to become fluent in French solely as a vehicle by which to impress the babes. None of that mattered now, though. I was in a very good position to originate more fees this year than a good number of the firm's partners – mainly because I was unique in maintaining a fluency of the French language.

Taking Julie to Paris with me was a forgone conclusion. There was no possible way that she would idly stand by at home while I gallivanted around the globe. Plus during our many prior trips to Paris together, I had converted her into a Francophile – no easy task for a Long Islander who, prior to meeting me, couldn't pronounce the letter, "r."

So, almost immediately after getting off of the phone with Véronique, I telephoned Julie at her office to tell her the good news. Once she picked up on the other end, I announced with an unambiguously romantic tone,

"Jules, darling, I have very good news for you. Guess where I'm taking you..."

In her patented brash New York dialect, Julie interrupted,

"Who the hell have you been on the phone with for the past 15 minutes? I kept calling your office and Kristin told me that Terri told her that you were on a 'very important call.'"

I found it absolutely staggering how secretaries and receptionists were able to ascertain the importance of a particular call. In this case, my door had been closed while I was talking to Véronique, so it was inconceivable how anyone would have known who I was talking to and what my conversation consisted of. Nevertheless, both Terri and Kristin were correct in believing that my telephone call was of great consequence, and that I should not be interrupted. Unbelievable.

"Well, Kristin was right. I *was* on a very important call – which concerns the good news that I was about to tell you..."

"Honey, my good news is *way* better than your good news," Julie said, ultra-enthusiastically, as if she were about to tell me that Saks Fifth Avenue was having a clearance sale.

"I seriously doubt it, but shoot," I said.

"Listen. To. This." Julie began with her usual dramatic flair, "I just got a call from some man at a child talent agency. He somehow got a hold of one of Charlie's Christmas pictures from last year that the photographer took for us. I think that he saw the one with Charlie in the lederhosen that we bought for him in Germany..."

"Do you mean the lederhosen that we paid 125 Euros for in Munich – the ones that he wore for that one Christmas photo session and will never wear again? I just want to clarify – are those the ones that you're talking about?"

"Shut up, smartass. You're going to eat your words because those 125 Euros turned out to be a very good investment."

"Julie, I know what you're going to say, and you can forget about it. We're not signing Charlie up for child modeling. It's an absolute scam – they tell you that your kid should be in Gerber ads and then they make you pay $1,500.00 for a photo portfolio. Don't you pay attention to any of the news reports about this garbage on TV?" I said, extremely frustrated that a person as intelligent as Julie could have such a paucity of common sense. I silently repeated my longstanding prayer to God that my children received Julie's looks and my wit. My favorite way to call Julie's lack of coherence to her attention was to temper my insult with a compliment.

"Julie, honest to God, how could somebody so beautiful be so naïve? Did you, for one second, consider that this guy was a scam artist? You're a lawyer, for God sake – you're supposed to doubt everything that anyone says to you and then investigate as to whether they're telling the truth. Where did this pervert get Charlie's picture from? I'm calling the police."

"You're not calling anybody, you asshole. This guy's company is paying us $25,000.00 *up front* for Charlie to appear in a Fidelity Healthcare commercial, which is being shot three days from now."

In disbelief, I asked,

"What do you mean, 'up front'? If you tell me that you gave that crook the routing number on our bank account for him to wire money, I think that I may actually stab myself in the neck with this letter opener that I'm holding."

"By 'up front', I mean that he's sending a courier over by the end of the day with a cashier's check in the full amount. Do you want to apologize to me now, or later tonight, while you're rubbing my feet for an hour?"

"An hour?"

"Yes, an hour. Calling me 'naïve' gets you an hour. This is not a negotiation."

"I didn't call you 'naïve'. I was just saying that – "

"Alex, why don't you just shut the hell up and quit while you're behind, O.K.?"

God, did the gruff New York bitchiness ever turn me on.

"Well, fax me the contract – I want to see what this is all about."

"Alex, darling, there *are* no catches. They're not even asking us to sign a contract."

"Wow, well I guess that that does kind of beat the good news that I had."

"Honey, I'm sorry for stealing your thunder. What was your good news? Did you win a motion, or something?" Julie said, somewhat apologetically.

"Oh, nothing really. I just got a call from a French tower crane manufacturer that looked me up on Martindale-Hubbell. It seems as though I'm the only French-speaking attorney in Philadelphia who specializes in construction law. They want to pay me $500.00 per hour to sue Jennings Concrete – Vinny's biggest competitor – in the federal court system."

"Oh my God, honey, you're on such a roll. Does this mean that I can retire and have more babies?"

It was astounding to me how many women in America put themselves through the hells of law school and incurred six figures in student loan debt, only to opt out of the profession. Although Julie enjoyed her job, she fantasized, like many other working mothers, about being a stay-at-home mom.

"Let's not get carried away, please. You haven't heard the best part yet, though."

"It gets better?"

"Yeah, it gets a lot better. The client, this Jean-Luc Le Guen, wants me to fly to Paris tomorrow night to meet him to discuss the specifics. Guess who's coming with me?"

"Alex, I can't!" Julie exclaimed, as if the wind had been let out of her sails.

"Of course you can. My parents will take Charlie to the photo shoot. What's the big deal?"

"The big deal is that the only rule that the talent scout gave was that for insurance purposes, all children whom they shoot have to be accompanied by their parent. He told me that I needed to bring Charlie's birth certificate to prove that I'm his mother."

"What the hell does 'insurance purposes' mean?! Tell this asshole that you're a lawyer and that he doesn't know what he's talking about. I'll prepare an affidavit for your signature, attesting that you consent to Charlie being photographed. Trust me, it will do. You're coming to Paris with me. We're going to have a blast."

"Alex, this was the one thing that he insisted upon, and he said it about seven times – he was starting to sound like a broken record – 'The child must be accompanied by his parent. The child must be accompanied by his parent.' Alex this is *twenty five grand.*

We'll be able to put away the money to pay for almost two full years of Charlie's education at Presbyterian."

The woman had a point. Plus, I wasn't going to push the issue. There were some definite positives associated with my going to Paris alone. For starters, going alone would save me about two grand in whatever shopping Julie would have done. Further, since I wouldn't be spending my free time inside of stores, I would be afforded the opportunity to wander around the city and revisit and reminisce at some of my old stomping grounds.

"O.K., Jules, you win," I said sarcastically, "I'll just have to go to Paris alone. I'll be thinking of you while I'm cruising past Hermès and Christian Dior on Rue du Faubourg Saint-Honoré."

"Good. And you can get me a friggin' nice present while you're at it."

She was jealous as hell and I loved it.

"I'm gonna leave work early tonight because I have to get home to pack."

"Good. That means that you can bring a pizza home."

"O.K., fine. Love ya."

"I love you, too."

Ten seconds after hanging up with Julie, my direct line, which bypassed the receptionist's desk, rang. I figured that Julie didn't want the secretaries to start gossiping about how she called a hundred times per day, so she opted to call my direct line. I assumed that it was Julie calling back to tell me about another detail concerning this child modeling scam.

After picking up the receiver, I said,

"Jules, I'm *really* trying to get out of here as soon as possible. Can we discuss this when I get home?"

"Uh – I'm sorry, I must've called the wrong number. I was lookin' for Lawyer Alexander Brown."

The voice was not Julie's, but apparently that of a middle-aged African-American man.

"I'm sorry, sir, I thought that you were someone else. This is Alexander Brown. How can I help you?"

"My name is Leon Richardson. I need representation. I was walking through an intersection in Weston a few months ago and some guy in a Corvette ran a red light and hit me. I fractured my skull and these doctors say that I've got something called neurocognitive impairment. I don't know what the hell that is, but all I know is that I spent three weeks in the hospital, and now I can't remember what I did five minutes ago."

"I'm terribly sorry to hear that, sir. I'd like to learn more about this. Can I ask you first, though, how were you referred to me?"

CHAPTER TWENTY-SEVEN

While putting on my suit jacket as I readied to leave the office for the evening, the gravity of what I had agreed to do for Leon Richardson began to fully sink in. I was not thinking coherently when I accepted his proposition, and I had made a grievous error that, if detected, would cost me my job and my license to practice law. Why those realities did not occur to me during our conversation was a mystery to me. In any event, I would call Mr. Richardson back tomorrow before our scheduled appointment and tell him that I had reconsidered and that I was not interested in his offer. I had not done anything illegal or unethical yet, and this disaster could be nipped in the bud. As such, I was not going to let my curable indiscretion ruin my evening.

Before I left to go home, I made a pit stop in the firm's men's room. One of the joys associated with working at Krauss, Carlson, Whitby, Miller and White was that any time nature called, I was able to relieve myself in a marble floored, brass fixtured palace that oozed old school Philadelphia lawyer.

In addition to the rich marble and brass, the firm's men's room had a host of grooming amenities, such as a Barbicide jar containing black hair combs soaking in blue-green liquid, an aerosol can of Consort hair spray, Q-Tips, and a bottle of Listerine mouthwash with a stack of plastic cups beside it.

Although I had been with the firm for several years, every time that I took a swig of Listerine in the men's room, I had to pinch myself. The luxury of working in a place that provided its employees with mouthwash never ceased to tickle my fancy.

This night was no exception. Feeling like I was on top of the world, a 31-year old about to travel overseas to bring some lucrative and sophisticated business back his firm, I decided to splurge on the amenities. After indulging in my usual Listerine routine, I cleaned out the ears with a Q-Tip or two, and finished off by combing toxic blue disinfectant into my hair, with a lengthy poof of Consort.

Fully groomed, I exited the building, just in time to avoid being detected by the troupe of paralegals who were recruiting people to go out for cocktails. I had promised Julie that I would be home early and didn't want to let her down on this occasion, since I would be leaving for Paris tomorrow and wouldn't see her and Charlie for several days.

Barely avoiding the paralegals, I exited the building, quickly retrieved the Bimmer from the parking lot, and was on my way home.

I loved driving home shortly before dusk on warm summer nights such as this one. A strip of highway exiting the city snaked artfully beneath the Ben Franklin Bridge and provided a glorious view of the waning sun glistening off of the Delaware River. With the temperature still in the low 80s, I decided to open the moon roof so that I could breathe in the splendid summer air.

Within minutes, I was passing Citizens Bank Park. The remarkable design of the stadium allowed passers-by on the Interstate to see the humongous Phanavision scoreboard from the outside. Viewing on the scoreboard that Shane Victorino was at bat, I quickly tuned my radio to 1210 AM, so that I could catch up with the game already in progress. After quickly learning that the Braves had put up a six spot in the top of the first, I switched to music, so as to not put a damper on my otherwise happy and monumental day.

While crossing the Girard Point Bridge, I saw airplanes taking off and landing at Philadelphia International Airport, to the left side of the road. Seeing the airport reminded me that in just 24 hours, I would be relaxing on an airplane, on my way to Paris to meet Jean-Luc Le Guen, the man whose business would transfer me from a piddling clueless young lawyer into a well-respected and accomplished bona fide Philadelphia lawyer.

About 25 minutes after leaving Philadelphia proper, I had made my way onto State Route 927. Driving on State Route 927 was easily the least favorite part of my daily commute. The westbound portion of the divided highway bottlenecked, after a one and a half mile stretch, from two lanes into a single lane. Most people drove over-aggressively on this stretch of road, so as speed up and get ahead of any tractor-trailers. Those stuck behind a tractor-trailer, who followed the road the full nine miles up to the intersection with State Route 612, could expect an extra five minutes to be tacked onto their commute.

Shortly after entering State Route 927, I approached a tan Chevy Impala that was stopped on the shoulder. As I was about to pass that car, it began to accelerate. The manner in which the Impala's idiot occupant was driving the car was startling to me because he was traveling almost directly beside me at the same speed. The moron, whom I could see closely enough to be able to decipher that he had a cheesy 1970s-like porno movie mustache, looked at me, smiling, as if me wanted to race. After I accelerated, he pulled right behind my Bimmer and was maintaining an uncomfortably close distance to my back bumper. Either this asshole was worried about being behind me for nine miles up to State Route 612, or he was simply some piece of white trash messing with a guy in a BMW.

In either case, the guy's act of riding my bumper made me uneasy. In my earlier days, I would have jammed on the brakes, to see if he could avoid hitting me in time. Something told me not to do that on this occasion, however. So, instead, I pulled into the right lane, so that he could pass me.

As if his bumper were locked to mine, the Impala driver immediately shifted to the right lane behind me. I then turned back into the left lane, only to see in my rearview mirror that I was still being followed – this time with highbeams shining in my direction. This was becoming very unfunny, very quickly.

I decided to pull into the shoulder, so that this jackass would pass me once and for all.

Only he didn't pass me once I pulled into the shoulder. He followed me onto the side of the road. At that point, I made a conscious decision to try to outrun this psycho. It appeared that he was not just trying to mess with me. For a reason that was not immediately apparent to me, this person seemed to know who I was and wanted to do harm to me.

At the exact time that I decided to try to outrun the other car, in my rearview mirror, directly behind my car, I saw something startling – a red strobe light inside the Impala's windshield. The smiling mustached psycho was actually a police officer.

As both my car and the unmarked police car stopped, Porn 'Stache illuminated his blinding post-mount light on the side of his squad car. With my window open, I held my hand over my side view mirror to block the dizzying light. Since I was driving a BMW, the policeman probably knew that I had placed a premium on my time away from my job, and therefore he decided to take his sweet old time in coming to greet me and welcome me to lovely Lower Salem Township.

What an anti-climactic ending to an otherwise great day. I was about to be given a 200-plus dollar ticket for violating whatever portion of the Pennsylvania Motor Vehicle Code that Porn 'Stache could conjure up. This was not the first time that I would be receiving a ticket for a traffic violation that I did not commit. I had come to accept the fact that police officers in jurisdictions everywhere, tended to pull drivers over indiscriminately when they needed the numbers to fulfill their monthly quotas. The unfounded violations did not bother me as much as they did when I was a youngster. Since I violated speed limits and made improper lane changes on a daily basis and ran red lights on an almost daily basis, I rationalized my occasional traffic citation as being a tax which allowed me to drive as I pleased. Plus I was silently patting myself on the back for my decision to not join the paralegals for a drink. Had I opted otherwise, the insignificant summary offense that was about to be handed to me could have been a DUI. It was therefore hard for me to get overly upset about having been pulled over.

Since I lacked a vagina, I knew that there would be no talking Porn 'Stache out of the ticket. So, when I saw him approaching in my side view mirror, clad in a coordinating brown uniform with a short sleeved shirt, tie and all of the trimmings, I simply held my driver's license, registration and insurance card out the window.

Once the officer arrived at my passenger side window, he ripped the documents out of my left hand, squatted down so that he could see me, and said, with his face ten inches away from mine,

"Evening, counselor, welcome to Lower Salem, Brandywine County. Since you've just handed me everything that I was prepared to ask for, I'll assume that you've been through this drill before. And...well gee whiz...," he continued, squinting his nose, and strongly inhaling, such that several of his mustache whiskers actually entered his nostrils, "smells like you been havin' a good ol' time tonight. I guess that 'xplains the swervin' out *dare*. How much you had to drink tonight, counsel?"

There was something very wrong about him knowing that I was an attorney. Although he could have run my license plate prior to pulling me over, no information possessed by the Pennsylvania Department of Transportation could have told him that I was an attorney. Perhaps the suit and tie gave it away. As far as the alcohol, I surmised that the Listerine, still fresh on my breath after having gargled with it 25 minutes prior, was causing Porn 'Stache to believe that I had just put down a few. I was hardly worried because if necessary, a field sobriety test would prove to him that I had not drunk a single alcoholic beverage that evening.

"Officer," I said, "I have drunk no alcohol tonight. You must be smelling the Listerine that I just rinsed my mouth out with."

"You *just* rinsed your mouth out with Listerine? Yeah, and I'm *Dunn-o-Vinn* McNabb. I might have bought that story if you were drivin' in to work, but it looks to me as if you're drivin' home *from* work."

"That's just the thing, officer, we have a bottle of Listerine in my firm's men's room. I just freshened up before I left for the evening."

"Oh, is that so? Did you change your tampon while you were at it?" He responded angrily. "Give me your fuckin' keys and keep your hands on the steerin' wheel where I can see 'em. Don't move them hands 'til I tell you it's O.K. to do so. And I ain't playin', neither."

After I timidly obliged the officer's demands, he slammed the keys on my roof so strongly that there was no possible way that the keys had not caused a dent or paint chip. While startled, I wasn't terribly concerned. After the Philadelphia Inquirer and Channels 3, 6 and 10 had reported the unnecessarily harsh and unfounded treatment that was being administered to me, a completely sober and compliant subject, the Lower Salem Police Department would be paying for the repair to my car and a whole lot more.

The keys on the roof bit was too funny. If he were truly concerned that I was going to drive away, he would have taken the keys with him. In this township, an N.R.A. bastion, standard operating procedure was probably to shoot anyone who reached for the keys on their roof. So, in essence, Porn 'Stache was testing me, hoping that I elected to not obey his command.

After about twelve minutes of sitting in his squad car, presumably running my driver's license, Porn 'Stache returned. He once again squatted down, and asked,

"Counselor, what do you have to say for yourself?"

Before responding, I thought closely about what my response should be. Well aware of my rights, unlike the overwhelming majority of the people whom this dipshit had pulled over, and knowing that I had done nothing wrong, I answered succinctly,

"Officer, I have not had a sip of alcohol for the past six days. The only reason that I was 'swervin' ' as you have characterized it, was because you were following me from lane to lane. At the time, I didn't know that you were a police officer. Frankly, I thought that you were some deranged individual, trying to run me off of the road. Please either administer me a field sobriety test, or allow me to go home. I have a wife and a child who are counting on me to bring dinner home for them."

"Well, isn't that sweet, a family man!" He said, laughing mockingly. "As much as I would like to see your sorry ass trying to walk a straight line in them wing tip jobs that you're *prob-lee* wearin', my orders are to take you to the station."

Was this asshole planning on arresting me? Why was he talking about going to the police station? Baffled, I asked,

"Sir, am I being arrested? Because if not, I'm driving home."

He responded, again with a laugh, "Let me put it to you this way – you're comin' back to the station with me one way or another. I'd be happy to cuff you and throw your ass in my car. If you'd prefer, though, you can follow me to the station. You have exactly five seconds to respond. If I don't hear the words, 'Officer, I would prefer to follow you back to the station, rather than gettin' my ass cuffed', I will rip you out of this car. The five-seconds begins now."

It was now clear that I was now the subject of some sort of dirty pool activity. The lawyer in me suggested that I should tell Porn 'Stache to fuck off and allow myself to get arrested and cuffed for committing no crime whatsoever. This would exacerbate the damages that I would be claiming in my forthcoming civil rights lawsuit filed against the Lower Salem Police Department. My practical side, which was prevailing, told me that I should just follow this guy back to the police station. If I didn't, he would have to come up with an excuse as to why he arrested me. It seemed plausible that he might plant drugs on me or say that I lunged at him. I needed neither of those accusations in my life at this point. To that end, I politely responded, within his five second timeframe,

"Officer, I would prefer to follow you back to the station, rather than gettin' my ass cuffed."

CHAPTER TWENTY-EIGHT

As usual, she spent the early part of the day in the expansive backyard, with her newspapers and coffee. Unable to muster any interest in the rapidly increasing *taux de chômage* or the weekend's upcoming exhibition soccer match between Paris Saint-Germain and Chelsea, Véronique mindlessly stared towards the adjacent swimming pool. The sun glistened off of the small waves created by the warm summer wind, which provided her a relaxing pause from her otherwise anxiety and paranoia-ridden life.

She felt hopeless, as a prisoner in her own home. If she left, with or without the money, her benefactor would know, and she would be dead within 24 hours. This was not the life that she had envisioned for herself.

Just a few years prior, she was a blossoming university student at the prestigious *Sciences Po* in Paris' 7th Arrondissement. Her dreams of one day becoming a lawyer stopped abruptly on the fateful evening when, while minding her own business, having a glass of wine after class, she met him at a café near the Place d'Italie.

Having been abandoned by her father as an infant and being raised in poverty in St. Ouen by a drug abusing mother, Véronique was immediately taken when this man provided her with material possessions that she did not previously know existed, as well as paternal support and guidance. Furthermore, as she was deflowered by him, she maintained a certain sentimental and emotional connection to him. When she thought of leaving him, this emotional connection, even more than her fear of being physically battered, caused her to not betray the man who had given her so much.

Yet strangely, the most enjoyable part of her day was when Gilles, the handsome confidant of her benefactor, couriered the daily written message and accompanying provisions to her. She did not so much look forward to receiving the letter and occasional fresh roses, as she did the sight of Gilles. She often thought to herself whether she might have met, and ultimately married, someone like Gilles, had her benefactor not barged into her life when she was in such a vulnerable state.

She kept telling herself that if she accepted the offer, it wouldn't be long before this crisis was over and she was in a pleasant, safe place in a remote part of the world, where no one could threaten her well-being. In the same vein, however, she carefully considered the dire implications of botching her task.

She lit a Gauloise, and propped her legs on an adjacent chair. She looked at the French sky and pondered her options as she inhaled and exhaled cigarette smoke.

Her quandary required no further deliberation.

CHAPTER TWENTY-NINE

The Lower Salem Police Department looked almost exactly like what I had always imagined. In fairness, since I do not practice criminal law, nor did I ever expect to get pulled over for a bogus DUI, and subsequently be asked to follow the charging officer back to the barracks, I had never really previously considered what the Lower Salem Police Department looked like. However, on the three minute ride from where I got pulled over on State Route 927 to the police station, I formed an image in my head of what the place looked like, and I was pretty much on-target.

Outside of the entrance to the police station was a flagpole which displayed both the American flag and a green flag bearing the Brandywine County coat of arms. Inside, the lobby was so well-lit by fluorescent rod lighting that my eyes involuntarily squinted. White linoleum tile flooring, reminiscent of the basement of my college fraternity house (minus the loosely moraled women), gave the place a particularly governmental feel. A framed picture of the late Ronald Reagan hung on a wall, flanked by two more American flags.

Porn 'Stache held his arm around me as if I were a flight risk, and directed me towards a bulletproof glass window. After a few lockstep paces, Porn 'Stache and I arrived at the window to see a morbidly obese woman in a uniform sitting in a chair on the other side. My first instinct was that I felt a great deal of empathy for the chair upon which she was sitting. Her buttocks overhung the ends of the chair by four inches on either side. Rolls of back fat, covered by her poly-cotton mix uniform shirt draped over the seatback.

Despite the words, "No Smoking" being posted in at least six separate locations throughout the lobby area, the woman behind the glass puffed an extra-long cigarette. As I looked in her direction, she unflinchingly tapped the cigarette in a black ashtray, which sat next to a pack of Newport 100s. At that point, I noticed a nametag on her uniform which read, "WISNIEWSKI."

With a smile directed at Porn 'Stache, she proudly wore her strawberry blonde mullet haircut – short gelled spikes on top with ungelled and unkempt curls in the back. I felt almost guilty for being disgusted by her, since she was visionary enough to master two separate hairstyles into one. I had tried several different hairstyles during my life, but never did I possess the level of ingenuity necessary to mix two separate hairstyles into one.

"Yo Tommy, you ain't gonna believe what happened," the office lady said slyly. Apparently, Porn 'Stache had a name.

"Don't even tell me! Don't *even* tell me!" he responded, looking as if he was about to consider using his service revolver.

"Your mother's lottery number came in tonight – 538 straight!"

"Son of a fuck!" he shouted, "The one night I don't play it – Jesus, Mary and Joseph!" He said, quite confident that a higher authority comprehended his plight.

With a heavy laugh that could only come out of the mouth of a dangerously fat lifelong cigarette smoker, Wisniewski snickered, with the fatty flesh under her chin jiggling,

"Yo, Tom – guess who *did* play your mother's number tonight?"

"Don't you tell me that Smitty hit my mother's number!" He responded, with a fully reddened face.

As Wisniewski nodded her head affirmatively, giving me a full view of her spiky and corpulent scalp, Porn 'Stache, without hesitation, punched a corkboard that hung on that wall next to Wisniewski's window. A public service message from the Department of Homeland Security, advising citizens to report suspected terrorist activity, fell off of the board and onto the ground.

That such a sign hung in the Lower Salem Police Department was more than humorous. First, no terrorist would have the heart to wreak further havoc upon the depressed, uneducated vanilla environs of Lower Salem. Second, if anyone remotely looking like a Middle Eastern descendant ever set foot into either of the township's hotspots, Maggie's Pub or County Bowling Lanes, an impromptu lynch mob would probably be formed within seconds, and the olive skinned individual would be dangling lifelessly from a high branch before law enforcement ever knew what was going on.

After seeing Porn 'Stache react in such a manner, for the first time since being pulled over, I was truly afraid. This officer was not only crooked, but had a violent temper. I feared equally his superior or superiors who had directed him to bring me back to the station. If behavior such as this officer's was not unacceptable to display in the station house lobby, in plain view, I wondered what might befall me when I was taken out of the public view.

With a sullen face, his day ruined because he had missed out on the $80.00 jackpot, Officer Tommy said,

"Just buzz me in, would you, Maureen?"

At Porn 'Stache's direction, Wisniewski pressed a button and a loud sound emanated from a door with a plastic plaque that read, "PRIVATE." Officer Tommy jerked my arm and shoved me through the door. This was not going to be pleasant.

Now inside the inner sanctum of the Lower Salem Police Department, I was able to take in some of the classy relic surroundings. Next to a row of circa-1972 light orange colored file cabinets – half of which had broken handles or no handles, sat a Mr. Coffee machine and a water cooler from roughly the same epoch. Attached to the water cooler was a metal tube-like structure which dispensed conical paper cups.

"Counselor Brown, Chief would like to see you," Porn 'Stache told me. I had a feeling that he was talking about the Chief of Police, rather than former Boston Celtic, Robert Parish, or former Philadelphia Flyer, Bobby Taylor, the only two people, to my knowledge, who allowed themselves to be referred to as, "Chief." The thought of one of those two retired athletes actually being behind this affair gave me a brief moment of inward humor, though.

We walked down a long hall past one dead or dying plant after the next until we had apparently reached our destination. I knew that we had arrived when we came upon a closed wooden door with the painted inscription,

JOHN A. BOZZI
CHIEF OF POLICE

Porn 'Stache, upon our arrival, pointed to a chair that was positioned next to the Chief's door. He directed me,

"Sit."

After I complied, for fear that my hair would become misarranged if Porn 'Stache did to my face what he did to the corkboard, he added,

"Chief'll be wit you in a few. Sit tight, you hear?"

"I hear," I sarcastically responded, pointing to my ear.

Porn 'Stache walked away, looking at me over his left shoulder as if he wanted to pummel me. I had to get a barb in at him before he had transferred my custody over to the Chief.

Sitting on the chair outside of the Chief's office brought back some unsavory memories of sitting outside of the Headmaster's office at Presbyterian. I didn't like being subjected to authority back then, and I certainly was not enjoying it now – especially when I wasn't guilty of any wrongdoing.

After waiting seven minutes for the Chief, and in light of my not having been arrested or charged, the thought of leaving crossed my mind. I immediately dismissed that idea, though, once again coming to the realization that the consequences of leaving would be far worse that the consequences of staying.

Still waiting, I looked at my mobile phone, which indicated three missed calls from Julie. She had been expecting me at 7:30 p.m. and was probably worried sick at this point. I thought it best to hold off on calling her, until I knew what was in store for me.

As I was scrolling through my mobile phone, I heard footsteps from inside the Chief's door. I quickly put the phone in my inside pocket and tried to assume a posture and facial expression that didn't connote nervousness or anger. I wanted to appear confident, yet acquiescent, so as to portray the air of an innocent person.

After hearing the door handle turn, an imposing figure walked out of the office. The Chief stood at about 6'5" and, unlike Officer Tommy, he was wearing a short sleeved white uniform shirt with rank designations on his shoulders. Otherwise, their uniforms were very similar. The Chief had stark white hair, with a matching white mustache that was much fuller than Officer Tommy's. I wondered if there was a mustache hierarchy within the Police Department. Was Officer Tommy relegated to sporting a 70s porno movie-like mustache, by virtue of his inferior rank? What about this "Smitty" character? I wondered what rank he maintained. If he ranked in between Officer Tommy and the Chief, was he entitled to wear a handlebar mustache?

"Mr. Brown, sorry to keep you waitin'. Please come inside and have a seat," the Chief said to me in a much warmer tone than I had expected.

His office reeked of self-important photographs and memorabilia. Framed medals adorned the walls, with an incalculable number of signed commendation citations from elected officials. A sign on his desk read,

DO IT MY WAY OR HIT THE HIGHWAY

After I took a seat, the Chief closed the door, walked behind his desk and sat in his chair. The warped faux brown leather of the chair fit perfectly in the office of a third-rate suburban town police chief. He sat back in the chair, which reclined 35 degrees and looked dangerously close to toppling backward. The Chief's massive beer gut appeared to be significantly aiding the gravitational force that wanted to pull him to the floor of his office. He comfortably clasped his hands behind his head, revealing seven inch diameter circular armpit sweat stains, and said,

"Attorney Brown, thank you for agreeing to come in and meet with me. Sorry for the delay – I was attending to a few unlicensed *pharmacists* who made the trip over from Brandywine City to sell their goods to some of our 14 year old residents."

In my book, *agreeing* to "come in and meet" with someone entailed acting on one's own volition, rather than being pulled over under false pretenses and being forced to follow a crooked cop back to a police station.

He continued, angling forward, placing both elbows on his desk and resting his chin on his palms,

"Tell me, counsel, what's the *lee-gale-itee* (legality) of erecting a customs booth at the Route 927 exit to the Interstate, so that I can keep the undesirables out of my township?"

I smiled and began to tentatively laugh at his joke. The only problem was that the white haired mustached giant was neither laughing nor smiling. Seeing his reception towards my laughing, I quickly returned my face to a stern, stoic gaze. After a few seconds of feeling the Chief's gaze burning through my retinas, he unleashed a guttural, phlegm-enhanced chuckle.

"I'm just joshin', counselor! God Damn! I never understood why youse don't learn humor in law school. You shoulda seen your face!" he said.

With my heart pounding, I cautiously smiled, fearing another verbal backlash.

"Well, I bet you're wonderin' why you were brought in here tonight," he asked, once again reclining in his chair.

The moment of truth had arrived. The charade about my coming to the police station on my own accord was now over.

I briefly deliberated as to what my next words should be, and came up with,

"Well, Officer...err...Chief...I'm sorry, what is your proper title?"

"That's a damn good question. I'm glad you asked. It's actually Head Ass Kicker in All that I Survey, but if you'd prefer, you can call me what my wife and kids call me – Chief Bozzi," he responded, without a pause.

Judging by the manner in which his rejoinder rolled off of his tongue, it was clear that he had been asked that question at least once daily. There was simply no other explanation for the swift wittiness that accompanied the reply of this dolt.

Still afraid to laugh, I quickly said,

"To answer your question, Chief Bozzi, I'm really at kind of at a loss as to why I was brought here tonight. I think we both know that no one in this police department thinks that I've consumed any alcohol tonight. I think that you also know that I know that since I haven't been charged with any crime, I could have left this police station at any time."

With the widest smile that I had seen on the Chief yet, he shot back, gazing at his fingernails, instead of at me,

"You're very astute, young man. You should consider a career in the law." After pausing a moment, and once again shifting his gaze to me, he said, "I imagine that you also know that if you tried to leave my station house, the consequences might not be that appealing to you."

"That idea had crossed my mind," I answered.

"Counsel, let me do my best to fill you in," be began, stroking either side of his mustache with his hands. "May I ask you – what do you know about my history?"

Now I was on the spot. Until ten minutes ago, I didn't have the foggiest idea as to who Chief Bozzi was. Moreover, to the best of my knowledge, until Porn 'Stache began hollering his version of the English language at me about 45 minutes ago, I had never even partaken in a conversation with someone who hailed from this God forsaken hell hole. In fact, the only thing that I knew about the Chief was that he reminded me of every law enforcement official with whom I had ever come into contact. He was physically imposing, and chose his profession so that he could get paid for being the same bully that he was in high school.

Rescuing me after five seconds of my looking like an "undesirable" caught in the headlights of his squad car, the Chief said,

"Counselor Brown, you're understandably a bit bashful, so I'll just begin. Let me start by telling you that not everything that you've read about me in the Daily Post is true. While some of the things that they have written about my respect amongst my colleagues and the fear of me amongst criminals is true, that other horseshit ain't."

Holding his right hand at the side of his mouth, he then said at a whisper, "At least on the record it ain't." He then opened a drawer, pulled out a pack of Winstons and lit up.

As damaging as it may have been to the Chief's ego, I still had absolutely no idea what he was talking about. This unfamiliarity with his apparent bad boy rep was probably the result of the fact that I had never actually purchased a copy of the Brandywine County Daily Post, a suburban tabloid whose idea of news was a blood drive at St. Ignatius Church. I, as well as most people in the Philadelphia metropolitan area with a high school education, was a loyal Philadelphia Inquirer reader.

He continued,

"After I graduated from the police academy, I joined this Department and became the youngest lieutenant in its history. They put me on the ballot a few years later, and I became the youngest member of County Council. I was re-elected twice and served 12 years in total. Since this Department fell apart when I left, they begged me to come back and made me Chief. Here I am. I've been Chief for 20 years and counting. I run the tightest ship in the whole damn county."

I had absolutely no doubt that the "they" was the Brandywine County Political Machine. For the first time, I had an inkling of where this conversation was going and why I was there.

CHAPTER THIRTY

The silver haired American had become a nomad of sorts during the preceding few weeks. Since he left Véronique, and virtually all of his money with her, in the Place des Vosges on that day, he had been forced to change residences twice. He was now in the third and final safe house that he had purchased many years prior, anticipating one day being found. Unlike the two previous safe houses which were in charming neighborhoods in the 3rd and 14th Arrondissements, this retreat of last resort was located in the remote and industrial 19th Arrondissement on the Rue de Périgueux. Before the crisis had occurred, he had used it as a storage facility.

He sat on the rickety hardwood floor of the rat infested loft and smoked Marlboros. The silver beard that now covered his face was not a fashion statement. Rather, that and the tangled and grease-clumped hair were the product of there being no plumbing in the loft. His Glock 17 rested within three feet of where he sat. Five magazines stacked on top of each other were next to the gun.

For every waking second of every day since he left the last safe house, he had dreadfully regretted picking up and moving to the 19th Arrondissement. He equally regretted that he had never bothered to equip the place with living necessities. Then again, he never thought that he would have been forced all the way to the third of his three safe houses.

He was now past the point of no return and could not go back to the previous locations that had running water and beds. His undisciplined movements had left tracks. In his helplessly paranoid egocentric mind, both the governmental authorities and his extorters were now crawling all over the 3ʳᵈ Arrondissement and 14ᵗʰ Arrondissement properties. Returning to either location was not even a remote option.

At 11:34 in the morning, he heard four sequential honks of a car horn, each spaced two seconds apart, that sounded as if they had emanated from a Citroën C4 Coupé. Gilles was four minutes late. At least he had gotten the prearranged notification signal correct, though.

After picking up his loaded Glock and hobbling to an electrical panel affixed to the bare brick wall, he punched in a four digit code followed by the asterisk symbol. A loud buzzing from one flight below ensued. A heavy door creaked open. After another second or two, the door creaked again, until it slammed shut, shaking the entire edifice.

The silver haired American unbolted the steel door and, with gun in hand, shouted downstairs,

"State your business!"

Incredulous that Americans were so stupid, Gilles followed with the prearranged signal that was to verify his identity. Gilles could have thought of a hundred more efficient and, moreover, safer ways by which his identity could have been verified. Nevertheless, he did as previously directed, pulled out his iPhone, and after a few taps of the finger, the voice of the late great Gene Hart bellowed,

"Ladies and Gentleman, the Flyers are going to win...the Stanley Cup! The Flyers win the Stanley Cup! The Flyers win the Stanley Cup! The Flyers...have won the Stanley Cup!"

"You're late, Gil," he said with a vexatious tone.

"I am *sore-ree* – zee A4 autoroute – highway – was a nightmare – I do...did not know what to do wees myself...you have no *téléphone* – I coode not call," Gilles responded with fear in his voice.

"Easy, there frog boy, I'm not going to take away your government-mandated six weeks of vacation, O.K.? Come the fuck upstairs and bring me my shit," he said, relieved that his visitor was Gilles, and not the *Direction de la Surveillance du Territoire*.

Gilles walked up the stairs carrying a plastic crate full of provisions. Once Gilles had reached four stairs from the landing and the American could see his face, he walked back into the loft, lit up another Marlboro and put the gun in a back pocket of his dungarees.

"Did you bring me what I asked for this time?"

Gilles responded sheepishly, "Zare eeze no equivalent of 'white bread' in zeese country, nor eeze zare such thing as 'deli ham' or your American cheese. I have brought you some Jambon de Bayonne, a few delicious baguettes and some Emmental cheese."

"I know that, you worthless twit! I've been living here for a little while now. I meant that you should get me the closest thing you could find to white bread and deli ham."

He brusquely pulled the bag of food away from Gilles and inspected what he had brought. He unwrapped a brownish-orange paper package containing the meat and stuffed one of the paper-thin slices of cured ham down his throat. As the flavors circulated through his mouth, he made a violent facial reaction as if he had ingested drain cleaner and spit it out of his mouth. After it landed between Gilles' black leather shoes, he said to Gilles,

"What the fuck is the matter with you? This shit is raw and it don't taste a damn thing like ham. What else is here?"

He then opened a white paper package containing the cheese. Seeing what was before him, he pulled a switchblade out of the rear pants pocket not containing his handgun. Although Gilles was fairly certain as to what the silver haired American intended to use the knife for, the sight of this lunatic with a knife frightened him greatly. Gilles' senses caused him to involuntarily take two steps backwards.

Using his thumb to guide the knife through the tremendous hunk of cheese, he cut off a sizeable piece. After putting the cheese in his mouth, he chewed, swallowed, and said,

"Good God is that dreadful! That is the strongest damn Swiss cheese I ever tasted! It's cleared my friggin' nasal passages right out!"

Gilles interposed himself, "It's Emmental – it's actually a bit stronger than your Swiss cheese, I think that..."

With fresh blood rushed to his face, he responded,

"Gil, shut the hell up! Just shut the hell up! You've brought me raw pig, un-sliced putrid imitation Swiss cheese, three stale hoagie rolls and…and what's this?" he said, pulling a glass jar out of the bag, "is this supposed to be mustard? Since when does mustard have round pellets in it that look like bunny shit? No wonder youse fucks haven't won a war since Napoléon's second Italian campaign – you eat food that looks like it fell out of someone's ass. I can't eat this. I'll leave it on the ground, so at least the rats can have full bellies tonight. What's in the other bags? I sure as hell hope, for your sake, that there's something I can eat in there!"

With a flushed face and a twitching hand, Gilles furnished the two other bags.

"Ahh, good, at least you got my poisons right," he said with a juvenile beam, as he pulled three bottles of Johnnie Walker Black Label and ten packs of Marlboro Reds out of a handled plastic bag that read, "NICOLAS."

He pulled from the final bag a box of cereal, three boxes of room temperature milk and a package containing five Mars bars.

Upon finishing his inspection, he said to Gilles, "I know this is probably bad news to you, but at least I won't starve. The Mars bars and scotch will keep me going. Say, why do youse call Frosted Flakes, 'Frosties'? Tony the fuckin' Tiger is on there and so is the Kellogg's logo, yet it says 'Frosties'. What gives?"

Choosing his response carefully, so as to not upset this volatile maniac, Gilles answered,

"Uhh, maybe because zee French cannot pronounce 'Flecks'."

After pausing to take a swig of the sweet Scottish nectar, he said, "Gil, you're a fucking French genius! I hadn't even thought of that!"

Gilles temporarily caught his breath. At that moment, he remembered that he hadn't given his boss the most important part of the delivery.

"I forget to geeve you zeese," Gilles said, pulling a pink envelope out of the front pocket of his pants.

"Thank you, Gil," he said civilly, while taking the envelope.

He opened the envelope and, as usual, placed the sheet of pink paper in front of his face and took as deep a breath as his cigarette-damaged lungs would allow him. The scent, Jean Patou's Joy, was instantly recognizable to him. As the fumes ran through his nose, he closed his eyes and was immediately taken back to the identical bouquet that radiated from Véronique's pores on the many previous occasions during which they had been in the throes of passion. He then turned his back to Gilles and read the letter, which in black fountain ink, said,

le 11 juin, La Pomponnette

My love, all is well in the sleepy Pomponnette. I am missing you as much as ever.

The cargo will arrive the morning after next. I will execute the plan at the previously discussed time and location. I will await contact from you thereafter as to how to proceed.

Bises,

Véronique

After he was finished reading, the silver-haired man lit a match and set the letter on fire as he always did. He dropped the burning piece of paper in a metal bucket as it disintegrated.

"Gil, I've been awfully hard on you and I feel…well…awful about it. I'm going through a very tough time, and you've been nothing short of a godsend. I just wanna let you know that I'm thankful for all that you've done. I know that you're getting compensated well for your services, but sometimes I feel as if I don't give you enough recognition. Come over here and give me some sugar!" he said, extending both hands outward.

At that moment, as Gilles felt himself brought in to a gentlemanly embrace with his boss, he wished that he had been less sloppy, and knew that there was a very good chance that he was in immediate peril. With their bodies locked together, Gilles said,

"Thank you, Mr. ..."

In seemingly a millisecond, the American had retrieved the switchblade from his back pocket and plunged it into Gilles' back, barely missing his spinal cord. Gilles stumbled back a few feet, and fell to the ground.

"Please don't keel me!" Gilles pled, reminding the American that the French made very pathetic warriors.

"Gil, my boy, both you and I know that you're as dead as a doornail. Why don't you just try saving some face, here, O.K., and stop acting like a typical French Vichy collaborating pansy ass."

"I won't tell anybody of your whereabouts...I promeese!" Gilles shouted, with blood slowly trickling out of the left side of his mouth.

"Gil, please cut the crap," the American began, almost apologetically, "you had to have known that you were going to be eliminated eventually. And, if you didn't, then I'm sorry. I'm sorry because in that case, you will have lived *and* died as a very stupid man."

"But I have information that can help you! Véronique has been talking to...", Gilles beseeched the American.

"Oh, like hell you do and like hell she has. I know everything that there is to know about my unfortunate little situation. It's just that I was going to wait to kill you until after you performed your final task. Now, Gil, you've put me in a situation in which I have to place myself in harm's way, so that I can perform your previously agreed-upon job function. By reason of your being dead, Gil, I will now have to show my face in public and risk being caught. I'm very disappointed in you, Gil."

"Why do you aahv to keel me now? Give me one more chance!" Gilles shouted, now with his white tee shirt fully soaked in crimson.

"You can't possibly be that stupid, Gil, but if that's your dying wish – for me to tell you why I'm killing you now, then, well, here goes," the American began, lighting up another Marlboro Red. "When I hugged you, your cheek smelled like a combination of Jean

211

Patou's Joy, and the sweat from the area in between Véronique's thigh and crotch. Gil, I liked you. And, I may have been able to deal with your screwing the love of my life, if you hadn't been so sloppy. I can't have someone working for me who doesn't bother to wash his face of crotch smell before he comes to meet with the paramour of the woman to whom that crotch belongs."

The American took another long swig from the bottle of Johnnie Walker and ambled as best he could towards a cardboard box that was sitting on the ground. From that box, he retrieved a black steel silencer and promptly screwed it on the end of his Glock while Gilles looked on. He fired a single round through Gilles' heart, and placed the gun on the ground next to the meat and the cheese.

He broke off a chunk of the Emmental and wrapped a single slice of the ham around it. As he chewed on his makeshift sandwich, he felt bad that he had given Gilles such a hard time about the food. The meat and cheese, when consumed together, weren't half bad.

With two cheeks full of food, he looked down at Gilles' lifeless body, now surrounded in a pool of blood, and said,

"I've been dead, Gil – it ain't that bad. You'll get used to it."

CHAPTER THIRTY-ONE

"Mr. Brown, I'm not sure if you know how things work in this county, but I'll do my best to explain it to you," the Chief said to me. "People have always tended to take care of each other here. And we believe strongly in the adage that a hard day's work equals a fair day's pay. So, if someone gives money to your campaign, then you make it a point to support whatever charity or special project that the donor is into. And, if you get elected, you do whatever it takes to serve the best interests of your constituents."

By "special project," the Chief was probably referring to, among other things, fixing the minor criminal charges of members of political inner circles. The sad part was that the Chief, like so many elected officials, didn't consider such activity to be illegal or even unethical. The Chief was a public service lifer, and, therefore, felt an entitlement to fringe benefits – even if it meant that members of the non-connected general public were judged under a different set of laws than those connected. By "whatever it takes to serve the best interests of your constituents," I had the feeling that the Chief meant that when traditional diplomatic means failed, it was O.K. to use some old-fashioned intimidation. Case in point, my sitting in this office at this time.

"Mr. Brown, there's a corollary to those principles that I have just recited for you. If someone or something is acting contrary to the interests of one of your allies, then that person or thing is an enemy. Counsel, enemies tend not to last very long in this county. Do you see where I'm going with this?"

Playing dumb, and forcing the Chief on the spot, I responded,

"Chief Bozzi, I understand exactly what you're saying about how things work in Brandywine County, but I'm not sure how what you're saying applies to me. I was driving home, minding my own business, and here I am sitting before the Chief of Police. I couldn't be more confused."

The Chief clenched his cheeks and paused, clearly dismayed that I was forcing him to explicitly spell out why Judge Rolston had a vendetta against me.

"Counsel, this new client whom you've gotten yourself mixed up with is someone who did tremendous harm to this county a ways back. In this county, as I've hinted, when someone fucks you, you tend to not forget it."

Since I had landed three major clients recently, he could have been talking about any of them. I tended to believe, however, that he was not referring to the Lubranos or to Jean-Luc Le Guen. This conversation was 100% about George Ridgeway.

Still feigning confusion, I said,

"Chief Bozzi, if you're talking about my firm's recent representation of that rap star who was busted on drug charges in Brandywine County a few years ago, let me just set the record straight – Phil O'Brien, a partner in my firm, handled that matter from inception to conclusion. Plus, I think that all Phil did for him was to set up a corporation or two for his new sportswear line. I could confirm that with Phil, if you'd like – actually, he only lives a short distance from..."

The Chief stood up, pulled his billy club from his belt, and slammed it down on a stack of papers, creating a horribly loud and startling sound.

"Cut the goddamn horseshit, *Al-lugg-zander*! When you were cuttin' teeth, I was breakin' the kneecaps of people who pissed me off only about half as much as you're doin' right this instant. You've only been practicing law for a handful of years – don't think for one second that you're gonna outwit this old dago. If this were thirty years ago, you'd be sittin' in a cell with a black eye just for saying 'hello' to George Ridgeway. Do you know about that sonofabitch?"

Cautiously, I said, "I know a little."

"Alexander the Attorney *knows a little.* Do you know that by outing Judge Newton as a fag, he sent our county into quite a tailspin? Do you have any idea what that did to the establishment here? Do you think that the good wholesome Catholics, who, as you may or may not know, make up a majority of our populace, wanted to give money to our candidates after that went down? Do you think that the state reps wanted to throw any money to our county after that? Who do you think got left out in the cold after Ridgeway outed Judge Newton?" He asked, with a fully reddened face and saliva hanging from his wiry mustache whiskers.

Feeling that I could only damage my chances of getting out of the Chief's office alive if I so much as answered, I remained silent.

"Small law enforcement, that's who. Did you wonder why I didn't offer you a soda? Because we can't afford a refrigerator! Did you wonder why I have a hog sitting out there at the window? Because I can't afford to pay office staff who demand more than nine bucks an hour! Did you wonder why I ain't drivin' a Bimmer like you? The list goes on."

Now in a more conciliatory tone, the Chief said, "Alex, I'm kidding about them other things, but when money starts getting cut off from the police departments, criminals thrive. So, in the end, by George Ridgeway pulling his little stunt, a few more kids in my township bought dope, and a few more murders happened."

For survival sake, I acted as if I believed him. "Chief, look, I didn't seek out George Ridgeway – I just fell into this Physician's Justice client which is being run by –"

"Dr. Sanford Markowitz."

"Exactly," I said, a tad distressed that the Chief's people had clearly performed ample reconnaissance. I wondered what, if any, investigation they had performed on me.

"Chief, I'll be honest with you – I disliked George Ridgeway very much, before you even told me about the awful effect that his actions had upon the crime in your township. As far as I'm

215

concerned, he's a despicable human being. What you've told me about him only adds to that belief."

"What's that buzzing sound that I keep hearing from your direction? Did you bring your vibrator into my station, counsel?" the Chief said with a smirk.

"Chief Bozzi, that's my Blackber…that's my phone – I have it on vibrate mode so that it won't – "

"I know what a goddamn Blackberry is, counsel. This is Lower Salem, not West Virginia," the Chief snapped.

I failed to understand his point, in light of the fact that the average Appalachian West Virginia bumpkin was a hell of a lot more cultured than the average inhabitant of the Chief's township. Nevertheless, I moved on.

"Chief," I said, "my Blackberry probably keeps buzzing because my cell phone is turned off and my wife is trying to reach me. I was supposed to be home an hour ago with dinner for her and my son."

"Well why didn't you say anything? Don't keep that Julianna waiting. Shouldn't you know by now that it's unwise to piss off a female attorney – and a *paisan* at that? Here, use my phone – just make sure you dial '9' first. You're up in Thornley, so it's not a toll call – you won't need to enter a security code."

Now that the issue of the Chief having performed an investigation into my background was out in the open, I was somewhat relieved. If and when I left the station house, I would not have to lose sleep, wondering whether my family and I were being watched. It was an utter certainty.

After the Chief handed me the pale yellow rotary dial, I looked at the contraption, trying to figure out if I remembered how to use it, since the last call that I placed with such a device was to my late grandmother to tell her that I had lost my first tooth. As I stuck my index finger through the hole labeled, "9," the Chief said, "Wait!", grabbed my wrist, retrieved the phone and hung it up, causing a bell inside the apparatus to chime.

"I almost forgot," he said, "tell her that you witnessed an accident and that we're taking your statement."

Complying, I took the phone back off the hook and dialed our home number, which took about 20 seconds.

On the first ring, Julie picked up and, with a rapid and nervous inflection said,

"Hello...this is Julianna Brown – I'm Alexander Brown's wife."

"Jules, it's me – everything is O.K.."

On the other end of the phone, Julie began to cry hysterically.

"Julie...Julie, calm down, calm down..."

"Why are you calling me from the Lower Salem Police Department if everything is O.K.?" she screamed, having apparently detected the location of the call from the caller ID screen.

"Julie, I want you to take a deep breath. I witnessed an accident as I was getting off of the Interstate. The police brought me in to ask me some questions about it," I said, as the Chief was looking on with his arms folded on his chest.

"Well why didn't you answer my phone messages or e-mails?" She asked, having transformed her mindset from worried to agitated.

Lying through my teeth and feeling rather guilty about it, I shot back, annoyed,

"Julie, listen to me. I just witnessed someone probably lose their life. It could very well have been me if I were driving five miles per hour faster. I'm a little shaken up – so please excuse me for having left my Blackberry and phone in the car when I went into the police station!"

"O.K., honey," she comforted me, "I started to pack for you. I picked a Burberry suit, a Hickey-Freeman suit and a Ralph Lauren Purple Label suit. As far as shirts and ties, I chose all of your loudest combos from the things that you bought at Alain Figaret the last time we were in Paris. You'll get a good reception with those – they don't want to see you with a white shirt and a blue tie – you'll look too American. Did I tell you that you're totally buying me something obscenely expensive at Hermès, Louis Vuitton or maybe Cartier, since we're going to be rich after you seal the deal with this new French client? Oh my God, Charlie did the funniest thing in daycare today – it was written up on his daily report card – you know that cute little pigtailed blonde girl, Emily, who Charlie likes to play with? Well, she apparently took away his Wiggles book and he pinched her right on the ass! Emily was crying for a half-hour afterwards. We really need to stop horsing around in front of him – he's starting to notice things like that and is imitating what he sees. I don't mind if you pinch my ass – just try not to do it in front of…"

"Julie," I said, interrupting her in her giddy diatribe that followed her realization that she would be able to go the mall the following weekend instead of burying me, "I am in a *police station*. Thank you very much for packing my clothes for my trip, but can we have this conversation later?"

"O.K., fine. Why are you so fucking rude? I'm ordering a pizza from Andreoli's. Can you be there in 20 minutes?"

"Hold on," I said, then held my hand over the receiver, and asked the Chief, "Chief, is there any chance that I'd be out of here in time to pick up a pizza at Andreoli's in 20 minutes?"

"I'll call Tino Andreoli and tell him to speed it up. Your pizza will be ready in 12 minutes. We're done here."

"Jules, that's fine, I'll see you later. Love ya'"

After I hung up, the Chief said,

"Well done counsel. Very convincing. So, what time is the Paris Express leaving tomorrow night?"

A bit confounded, since I didn't remember verbally expressing to the Chief that I was going to Paris, I nevertheless responded, "Uhh, I think 6:30, or so."

"Good. Well, make sure to pack your passport, as well as your toothbrush and toothpaste because they don't brush their teeth over there," he said.

After politely laughing at his joke that might have been funny in the 1960s, he said, with a completely straight face,

"I am *not* kidding, counselor. My brother-in-law went over to that shithole a few years back for his honeymoon and forgot to pack a toothbrush. He told me that there's some environmental law against brushing your teeth over there. They clean their mouths with organic berries and shit. Trust me on this one."

Out of all of the nonsense that came out of the Chief's mouth this night, this comment was, by far, the scariest. I found it astounding that the head of a police force in suburban Philadelphia in the early 21st century legitimately believed that French people were precluded, by operation of law, from brushing their teeth by conventional means.

"Alright, counsel, I'm gonna part ways with you for the evening. But, before you leave, I will caution you that if you continue to associate yourself with George Ridgeway, you will be imperiling your career. You see what's going on with Rolston and your Bicentennial Lumber case? That'll be every case from now on if you don't disengage."

"I see what you're saying, Chief, and I fully understand," I said complacently.

"Good. Counsel, you will repeat no portion of the conversation that we had this evening. If you do, you will be placing yourself and your family in great danger."

The Chief shook my hand and walked me out of the station, commenting upon the Eagles' upcoming training camp, as if there had been no prior mention of possible harm to my family in the event that I blabbed. He seemed to be quite the seasoned veteran when it came to threats that were both violative of his office and illegal.

In a place where he and his allies were the law, his posture didn't seem terribly surprising to me.

CHAPTER THIRTY-TWO

Twenty-five seconds into my ride home, I made the affirmative decision to heed the Chief's warning and cut ties with Physician's Justice as soon as I returned from Paris. The only difficult part was that I would now be forced to invent for the firm's Partners some cockamamie explanation as to why the firm needed to immediately disassociate with Physician's Justice. Based upon the Chief's tone and what he knew about my family and my upcoming trip to Paris, I had little doubt that his people had already installed listening devices in my home, office and car. In fact, I now felt certain that the Chief was so up front about knowing those things so that he could effectively convince me that if I spilled the beans, he would know.

In addition to my suspicions about listening devices, I feared that the Chief's people had moles in other higher government offices. Thus, telling the firm, Julie, the Attorney General or the FBI about the threats was out of the question. The Brandywine County Political Machine was to win, without my putting up any fight. I wondered why such significant resources were being devoted by those powers to an old codger such as Ridgeway, who had run afoul of them so many years prior. I further wondered why, instead, the Brandywine County Political Machine wasn't focusing its efforts on trying to locate the stolen money that Ridgeway's former law partner had left in Spain after he was killed.

In any event, it didn't concern me anymore because I was going to do exactly as the Chief had said and move on with my career and life.

After picking up the pizza that Julie had ordered for us, I arrived at home, only to find the all of the downstairs lights out.

I didn't deserve this again – not after being corralled by the Chief's militia and having my career and life threatened. I had just talked with Julie 25 minutes prior and she was giddily bouncing off of the walls, telling me that she was packing the clothes for my trip and describing what presents I was going to buy for her. There was no way in hell that I was going to sleep on the couch again. I would rip open the lock to our bedroom if I needed to.

To let Julie know that I was approaching in ill-humor, I kicked each of the brass rods that harnessed the carpet covering the hardwood stairs. With each "ding" sound that my cap toed shoes made as they struck a rod, the angrier I got. Some of my rage was rooted in Julie's apparent presumption that she could freely exclude me from our marital bedroom and I wouldn't put up a fight. The other part of my rage was based upon my frustration in being unable to explain to Julie how I had blamelessly become entrenched in a Brandywine County political dispute that resulted in my being held captive in the Lower Salem Police Department for an hour.

After reaching the top of the stairs, and walking to the bedroom doors which, predictably, were closed, I knocked loudly, and said sternly,

"Let me in right now, I'm not kidding!"

From behind the door, Julie responded demurely,

"Why don't you try turning the handle?"

As I turned the handle and entered our bedroom, I expected to see a dark room with Julie buried under the covers, having retired for the evening. While such action would not have been as bad as locking me out of the bedroom, it would have been, effectively, an undeserved "F you!"

When I looked into the bedroom, though, I saw a sight that I would not have predicted. The room was illuminated only by candles and the television screen, which displayed the Phillies telecast. As I became engrossed in the pitch being delivered by Ryan Madson, I caught the sight of something more enticing.

Sitting on our bed, clad only in the French *tricolour* flag was Julie. She had apparently retrieved it from my storage box of childhood mementos in the basement. I had purchased it at a souvenir stand on the Champs-Élysées during my first trip to Paris in 1984. While I normally would have strongly disapproved of anyone breaking into my stash of memories, I had a policy of making an exception where the cherished article in question was affixed to the breasts and genitalia of my gorgeous wife.

Pathetically and wholly unconvincingly trying to play it cool and unaffected, I muttered, while not taking my eyes off of the television,

"Why would Madson throw a fastball there? It's 0 and 2, for cryin' out loud! An idiot would know that he's gonna sit on that pitch."

Calling my bluff, Julie responded,

"Uhh, do ya' think it might have anything to do with the fact that Chipper has hit four homers off of him this year, and they were all breaking balls?"

God, did I love this woman. At any point when I was angry with her, I would remind myself of comments such as that, and the far from insignificant fact that she had changed her baseball fan allegiance on my account. That any woman would voluntarily convert to being a Phillies fan is an undeniable testament to that woman's fidelity to her man.

When we had been dating for a while and things started to get serious between us, the thought of asking Julie to convert to Judaism never crossed my mind. The suggestion of religious conversion seemed to me an unreasonable imposition to be placed upon a loved one. To the contrary however, before I popped the question to Julie, I needed to know that she would be amenable to trying to become a Phillies fan, and that any children born from our marriage would be raised as Phillies fans rather than as Mets fans. After my steadfast refusal to bend, even slightly, on those parameters, Julie caved, agreeing without reservation to my prenuptial demands. I knew that that would be the last negotiation that I would ever win with Julie, but it was damn well worth it.

Seven years after I proposed to Julie, not only had Charlie been indoctrinated into the agonizing existence of Phillies phandom, but Julie, herself, had become a fan. If the Chief had put a bullet into my head earlier in the evening, the defining moment of my life, upon which I would like to have been judged, would have been my conversion of Julie from a Mets fan to a Phillies fan.

With my coolness fully expired, I said,

"Well, well, well, what a nice surprise."

"Oh, this?" she said, "this is only half of the surprise."

Although I generally only prayed for health and wisdom, I was forced to make an exception in this case.

"Did you, by chance, bring that hot blonde Summer Associate from your office home with you tonight?"

Judging by the fact she flung the remote control at my chest, I guessed that the answer to my question was an unequivocal "no."

"I was only kidding," I lied laughingly, while rubbing my left pectoral muscle to ease the pain inflicted by the remote control. "C'mon, tell me what the second part of the surprise is – I'm waiting with baited breath."

"You're such an asshole – if it weren't for the trouble that I went through to give you a proper sendoff, our evening would be over now."

After she was done speaking, Julie lay back on the bed and pulled the left corner and then the right corner of the flag away, exposing her tantalizingly bronzed body that was fully bare, other than an inscription, written in bright red lipstick across her amazingly firm six-pack abdominal muscles, which read,

BONNE
VOYAGE

I didn't have the heart to tell her that she misspelled *bon voyage*. It's a good thing, too, because otherwise I might have missed out on one of the most passionate evenings of our marriage.

While Julie and I were making love, I almost hoped that the Chief's people truly had bugged our house, so that he could be made aware that Jewish lawyers made better lovers than classless and corrupt law enforcement officials.

CHAPTER THIRTY-THREE

Since my plane was not scheduled to leave Philadelphia International Airport until 6:45 p.m., and Julie had packed my luggage the night before, I really had no excuse not to go into the office on Wednesday. Plus, I needed the distraction from the uneasiness occasioned by my ill-advised early morning dealings with Leon Richardson.

I had always found that the day before a vacation and the day following a vacation were the most hectic at work. Notwithstanding the fact that I had every intention of soaking in some of Paris' cultural and culinary treasures, the trip was not officially a vacation. Nevertheless, I would be out of the office for a few days and had to make appropriate arrangements for certain filings and court appearances to be handled in my absence. This proved to be no easy task since every time I inquired of a fellow Associate as to whether they would be able to so assist me, I was fed the quite annoying standard, "Oh poor you, you have to go to Paris and you need coverage for something" line.

Since dealing with such issues occupied most of my workday, I decided against broaching the issue with Krauss and Carlson of the firm's need to immediately disassociate with George Ridgeway and Physician's Justice. A firestorm would result in which I would be called a quitter and my integrity would be questioned. In light of that reality, I felt it best to avoid that inevitable confrontation so that I could be productive on the trip and not be concerned about what Krauss or Carlson had said to piss me off.

Not being forced to deal with such an altercation, I was able to timely depart the office and hop on a 3:50 p.m. SEPTA R1 Regional Rail train at Suburban Station to the airport. Knowing that I would be tuning out once on the plane, I elected to sneak in some last-minute preparations while en route to the airport. On the train, I reviewed my *Français des Affaires* Business French textbook from college that had been in the same cardboard box from which Julie had retrieved her *tricolour* body covering the previous evening. Although Véronique spoke English, I was uncertain as to whether Monsieur Le Guen did. So, although I was confident in my French language skills, I thought it best to give myself a refresher course of sorts.

After a short 20-minute ride, I was in the sparkling A-West International Terminal at the Air France check-in desk. Since Véronique had failed to e-mail my itinerary to me, instead simply sending me a cryptic e-mail stating that she had confirmed me for Air France flight 365, I had no idea of what my seat assignment was. When I arrived before the Air France representative, I prayed that she would not hand me a boarding pass indicting that I had a middle seat assignment. I could not bear the prospect of sitting on a seven and a half hour flight between snoring Frenchmen. After being directed to place my baggage on the scale and present my passport, the very pleasant forty-something French attendant said,

"Just two bags zeeze evening, Monsieur Brown?"

I nodded in the affirmative with a smile. She then promptly strapped destination tags reading, "CDG" to my two bags. Curiously, she also attached yellow paper cards to each bag which read,

PRIORITÉ

One did not have to be a French scholar to know that the "PRIORITÉ" tag designated certain luggage for special handling. The tag insured that if the plane didn't wind up in flames in the North Atlantic, my bags would successfully arrive at Charles de Gaulle airport and that they would be among the first off of the conveyer belt. I pleasantly nodded to the attendant, acknowledging her unnecessary act of kindness. I figured that she had noticed that I was a young and nervous business traveler and that I could use any bit of extra help that I could get.

Returning from placing my bags on the conveyer belt, she pulled a ticket out of a printing machine and placed it on the counter in front of me.

"Monsieur Brown," she said, "Your flight wheel be departing from Gate A-15. You are in seat 2B. I hope you enjoy your flight."

From previous experience, I knew that Air France flew only Airbus A330s out of Philadelphia, and that such planes had two classes of seating. The friendly French lady had clearly made a mistake, since seat 2B, in the very front of the plane, had to have been a Business Class seat. So that she wouldn't catch her obvious mistake, I high-tailed it towards the escalator that led to the TSA security checkpoint.

About halfway up the escalator, looking at the ticket jacket which contained Air France's blue, white and red logo, along with the words, "ESPACE AFFAIRES", the translation of Business Class, a light bulb went on over my head. The attendant had not made a mistake in ticketing me and placing the special tag on my luggage. Le Guen had paid for me to fly Business Class!

I could barely control my enthusiasm – so much so that when I went through the metal detector with a beaming smile on my face, I got a few suspicious looks from the security personnel who would ordinarily not move an inch if a Middle-Easterner with road flares strapped to his stomach had walked through.

By the time that I had cleared security and reached the gate, the boarding process was beginning. Armed with my Espace Affaires trump card, I took great satisfaction in being the fifth person to board the aircraft. I was so excited to have been flying Business Class courtesy of someone else that the two annoying Golf Assholes and their equally annoying wives who were walking down the jetway in front of me, were barely even making me grind my teeth. Ordinarily, being around Golf Assholes raised my heart rate 20 beats per minute and caused me to involuntarily clench my fists.

These guys, probably named "Jim" and "Bill," were typical, garden-variety Golf Assholes – 6'2", clad in collared golf shirts (one red and one orange) emblazoned with the name of a golf club on the upper left chest area, khaki shorts, and white sneakers with ankle socks. One of these jackasses was even wearing a visor that read, "Titleist" above the brim.

Even with the erosion of luxury in air travel fully complete, it was entirely inappropriate for grown men to be wearing shorts and golf shirts on a trans-Atlantic flight. Their wives, who were almost certainly both named "Kate" or "Katie," were 5'4", dressed in velour sweatsuits and carried designer handbags.

As I felt my heart rate begin to rise while my angst grew at these people's sheer existence, I closed my eyes, breathed in, and vowed not to even look at them for the balance of the flight.

As I sat in the gigantic seat 2B, I was enraptured by the size of the personal space that would be afforded to me over the next seven and a half hours. The private video screen, massage feature and flat-folding bed mechanism that surrounded me, permitted me to have one of those rare moments in which I felt proud of myself for reaching such a pinnacle – even if it was by virtue of pure luck in being the first guy whose name popped up on Jean-Luc Le Guen's internet lawyer search.

Just as I had finished stowing my carry-on bag, a dainty little number with her dirty blonde hair slicked back conservatively in a bun said,

"Sir, may I get you somesing to drink before zee flight? Some champagne or a mimosa, perhaps?"

"*Qu'est-ce que vous avez comme le vin rouge?*" I asked, in my throatiest and most virile French accent, inquiring into what the flight's red wine inventory consisted of.

"*Ahh, je m'excuse, monsieur...eh bien, j'ai un bon Bordeaux, un Beaujolais, et puis un Côtes-du-Rhône. Moi, je préfère, le Bordeaux, bien sûr,*" she responded, indicating that she had three red wines to offer, but that the Bordeaux was her favorite.

"Well, then, I'm just going to have to try your Bordeaux, aren't I?"

"Yes, you are," the knockout stewardess responded with a smile, angling her body downward ever so slightly, while bending her elbows inward as she scribbled my drink order on a plain white pad.

"By zee way," the stewardess said, "if you need any-sing during zee flight, my name is Delphine".

As she walked toward the front of the plane, I could see through the tight blue synthetic material skirt that covered her round, yet petite butt, that she was wearing "granny panties." While seeing the same spectacle on an American woman might have been a turnoff, there was something especially arousing about seeing the wide outline of the underwear on Delphine.

I sat back in my ultra-comfortable seat and began to read a copy of *Le Monde* that had been provided to me upon my entry onto the plane. Once a mere two minutes had passed, Delphine returned with a glass of Bordeaux and a smile. After properly thanking Delphine, I put down my paper, took a large swig of the wine, and stared forward, thinking happy thoughts of the lucrative prospects that awaited me on the other side of the pond. I envisioned Jean-Luc Le Guen making me an offer that I couldn't refuse: He would pry me from Krauss Carlson to be his personal attaché and counsel. I would drive a hard bargain for a fully furnished apartment in the 7th Arrondissement, as well as a tripling of my current salary and a four day recess every ten days. A supplement to my compensation would include Business Class seating on an airplane back and forth from Paris to Philadelphia. If Le Guen owned a private plane – a prospect that I wasn't currently ruling out – I wouldn't even need to negotiate the Business Class transportation.

My apprehension arising out of my recent bad behavior *vis-à-vis* Leon Richardson evaporated.

As I contently dreamt, I was loudly interrupted.

"Excuse me, buddy, could you settle a bet for us?" I heard a voice say from my left side.

Unless my father or one of the five living United States Presidents was referring to me as "buddy," I was not inclined to answer the verbal summons. Whether it was ego, or my simple belief and no human being past the age of thirteen should have to respond to being called, "buddy," I always resented being addressed as such.

"Yo – sir, excuse me. Sir?"

There, that was better.

"Sure, what can I do for you guys?" I said, in the direction of the Golf Assholes and their wives.

"Well, we heard you tawkin' tuh dat flight attendant in French and we heard you tawkin' tuh dat flight attendant in English, so we figured you speak French and all."

Bravo, Einstein! I speak French, and I also kiss that way, so you better watch out, or I'll have my way with your wife when you doze off two hours into the flight.

"Yes, I speak French."

"Cool, alright. Listen – my buddy over dare thinks dat dem crescent rolls are pronounced, 'CROY-sints.' I'm tellin' him he don't know shit and that they're pronounced, 'CREW-sahnts.' Now, do both of us a favor and tell us how much of a douche my buddy is..."

"You can't say that on an airplane, Jim! Watch your mouth!", one of the wives said, slapping her husband on his upper arm.

You really can't wear golf shorts or velour outfits on a trans-Atlantic plane either, so Jim's crass choice of words probably didn't worsen anyone else in the Business Class cabin's opinion of him.

"Owww, Stacy, what the fuck? Why'd you hit me? Just goes to show how much you know. 'Douche' is a French word that means 'soap.' So, everyone on the plane thought that I was talking about soap until you chimed in."

God, was I pissed that I had taken her for a "Kate" or "Katie." I should have known that she was a "Stacy."

"Oh my God, honey, I didn't know that you spoke French. How did you know that?"

"Stace – while some of us were doin' our lipstick and makin' dem origamis in school, others of us were studyin' French. How long we been together, Stace? Eight, nine years? And you didn't know that I spoke French? I took it, through, I think, like, 10th grade," Jim said.

"Actually, Jim, it's pronounced, *'croissant.'* And, in fact, *'une douche'* means 'a shower'", I responded.

As Jim tried to pronounce *croissant* three separate times, each rendition was progressively worse. Moreover, with each version, a greater amount of saliva shot from his mouth onto the seatback in front of him.

With a squinting brow and a confrontational look, Jim's friend, Golf Asshole #2 asked,

"By the way, what's your name, man?"

"Man" wasn't as bad as "Buddy," plus, I had, much to my displeasure, already begun a discourse with these idiots, so I had to respond.

"Gérard Depardieu."

"Lemme guess – people call you, 'Jerry'?"

"How'd you know?"

"I'm good like dat. Well, then wait a minute, Jerry, – if I call someone a...," he said, lowering his voice to a whisper, "a *douche bag*, then, am I really calling them a *shower bag*?"

Good Lord, did I need another drink.

"The phrase that you mentioned refers to a feminine hygiene... actually, let me just short circuit this – although the words sound alike, they don't quite equate when translated from one language to the other."

"Thanks, buddy," Jim said while laughing, "I appreciate you settlin' our bet – especially since I ain't gotta pay out!"

Now that we were friends, I figured that it would be O.K. for me to have some fun.

"Hey, Jim," I asked, "can you settle a bet that my left brain has with my right brain?"

With a puzzled look, genuinely mulling whether I had two brains, Jim said,

"Sure thing, bro."

"Did you guys win this trip from a hole-in-one contest or from a door prize at a golfing event?"

Before Jim answered, I momentarily considered the possibility that either Jim or Golf Asshole #2 was going to lunge across the aisle and pound both my left and right brains into oblivion.

Instead, Jim responded by slapping Golf Asshole #2 on the back and playfully messing up his hair and saying,

"Jerry, my boy Mikey over here is dumber than dogshit, but he's a two handicap."

Dammit, I should have known that Golf Asshole #2 was a "Mikey," rather than a "Bill." Although I had nailed Jim's name, I was striking out on everyone else. Plus, I probably shouldn't have been giving myself too much credit for guessing Jim's name. After all, if you're a Golf Asshole over six feet tall, there is at least a 40 percent chance that your name is "Jim."

Jim continued, "We were guests at some charity golf outing a few months back. On 15 – a par three – if you pay 10 bucks, closest to the pin for the day wins a trip for four to Paris. Long story short – I front the money – my boy Mikey five-woods the motherfucker in the hole and next thing I know, we're on plane to Paris! We're both 42 year-old salesmen who went to Catholic school and we've never been out of the country. Now we're in Business Class to Paris. Life is sweet, brother, life is sweet!"

Life would have been a hell of a lot sweeter if the Business Class cabin had not been contaminated with these vermin. Seizing an opportune time when there was a lull in the conversation, I picked my newspaper back up and shielded my face from the Golf Assholes. Pretending to read about President Sarkozy's tribulations with the French budget deficit, I felt my Blackberry vibrate on my left side. When I retrieved the handheld, the screen displayed a new message from Véronique. It read,

```
Mr. Brown:
If my calculation are
correct, you shoud be just
leaving Philadelphie now.
I hope that you enjoy
your flight and that the
accommodations are enough
spacious for you. You
meeting with Monsieur Le
Guen will not be taking
place until Friday.
```

```
However, I woud like to
meet brievley with you
tomorrow to provide you
with some document that you
will need to be reviewing
in anticipation of your
meeting with Monsieur Le
Guen. Please to call me
when after you have had a
chance to freshen up at the
hotel. My mobile phone is
+33-1-06-63-01-03. See you
latter, aligator!

Bises,

Véronique
```

I immediately regretted having packed my French to English dictionary in my checked baggage. While I could not be certain, I was fairly confident that the salutation, "*Bises*," was an expression derived from the French word for kiss, "*un baiser.*" I was a touch out of practice, but I seemed to remember that "*Bises*," used at the end of a letter, was the rough equivalent of, "Hugs and Kisses." My annoyance at being unexpectedly advised that my specifically-arranged jetlag recovery day would now be interrupted by a meeting with Le Guen's assistant was partially mitigated by the fact that that assistant was overtly flirting with me.

I couldn't wait to see what kind of a beast Véronique was. There was no way that this woman was even remotely attractive, given her tone towards me. While several images of Véronique were floating through my head, the one that was prevailing at this moment was that of a scrawny, chestless, medium height, frizzy-haired, hairy-lipped homely creature, who smelled badly of nicotine. It didn't matter, though.

Since I had been informed by Véronique that I would be required to use my brain cells one day earlier than anticipated, my air of leisure quickly evaporated. I began to fret about having to be on my game while under the influence of jet lag. So, when

Delphine brought me a second glass of Bordeaux without my asking, I was naturally relieved. Knowing that I only had a short amount of time to drink the wine prior to Delphine collecting the glass before takeoff, I took a hefty sip. The alcohol of the very dry and tasty wine flowed through my bloodstream quickly, once again placing me in a state of relative relaxation. I closed my eyes and had tranquil thoughts about some of my favorite places in Paris such as the cafés near the Panthéon, Napoléon's tomb inside the Hôtel des Invalides, and the artisanal mustard store near the Place de la Madeleine.

While I was mainly able to tune out most of the nonsensical banter coming from the Golf Assholes, when they started talking about the merits of the wine with which they had been presented, my ears unfortunately perked up, thereby disturbing me from my serene respite.

"This is a *really* good wine," Jim said, with serious conviction, to his wife, swirling the purple liquid in his glass, repeatedly smelling the bouquet, and looking at how it dripped down the inside of the glass, as if he knew what the hell he was talking about. "French red is nowhere near as good as the California varietals, but this is a fine, fine wine if I do say so myself."

"Jim," Stacy said, "I can't believe that you like this stuff. They didn't even give us any ice to put in the wine – it's so bitter this way."

Stroking the brim of his Titleist visor, Jim continued,

"Stace, listen to me. This is real wine, not that Alizé stuff that you buy at home. If you put ice in the wine, it releases hydrogen, which totally counteracts the sulfites and tannins. You really need to get an appreciation of wine if you wanna *hang* on this trip, Stace, O.K.?" Jim said, apparently unconcerned that his wife would detect the ridiculousness of what was coming out of his mouth.

"You think I could get a Bud on this plane?" Stacy asked.

"Stacy, the only place that they sell beer in Europe is in Germany and Ireland – you ever heard of Heineken and Guinness?" he asked indignantly, "Beer is not produced or sold anywhere in France, Spain or Italy. The only alcohol that's legal in those countries is wine, brandy and, I think, sambuca. Sambuca may have been outlawed too though, I'm not sure. Anyways, they don't got Bud outside of the U.S., so good luck finding it over in France."

"Jim, this Kronenbourg 1664 beer they gave me says 'Product of France' on it. You don't know what the fuck you're tawkin' about," Mikey said.

Befuddled, Jim shot back with a reddened face,

"All that means is that they use French water in the beer solution, you idiot – ever heard of Evian? It's the finest water in the world – that's why they use it in that beer you're tawkin' about. Plus why do you think that it's called 'Kronenbourg'? Does that sound like a *French* name or a *German* name to you."

While I half considered enlightening the idiot quartet that Heineken is a Dutch beer, that every European country, including France, produces and widely consumes beer within its borders, and that Kronenbourg is brewed in the Alsace Region of France, I thought better of the idea and swallowed the remainder of my wine in an effort to anesthetize my senses to these people.

The Bordeaux rather effectively took the edge off. As the plane taxied and eventually left the ground, I pondered only happy thoughts – mainly about how I was previously regarded at the firm as a fully replaceable cog in the machine, and here I was, on my way to Paris to court the business of an important French entity. The Airbus A330 took off to the north. I looked out my window and absorbed a dazzling view of the Philadelphia skyline, with the orange and yellow hues of the evening receding summer sun glistening off the glass-edifaced Comcast Center. Before the plane made a sharp right turn over the Delaware River, into New Jersey, I caught a superb perspective of William Penn, standing atop City Hall. I saluted Mr. Penn and silently asked him to tender me good fortunes, so that I could bring lucrative business back to his fair city.

Au Revoir, la belle Philadelphie.

CHAPTER THIRTY- FOUR

The plush sleep mask that Delphine had provided to me several hours prior did little to block the brightness when the plane's cabin lights were turned on. When I lifted the goggles from my face, I immediately regretted having allowed Delphine to persuade me to have the fifth glass of wine only four hours earlier. While the *tournedos de boeuf* nicely complemented the Bordeaux at 9:30 p.m., Philadelphia time, the effect was a bit more unpleasant at 6:30 a.m., Paris time. With my mouth dry and unpleasant tasting, and my mind disoriented, Delphine placed a French immigration card and hot towel in front of me. She was as chipper as she was hours before, probably because the alcohol demons were not having a fistfight between her ears, as they were between mine.

With a panicked feeling, knowing that I had had far too little sleep to be on my "A" game this day, I began to silently attack myself for having been so irresponsible as to get significantly buzzed the evening before the most important day in my professional career. In an effort to alleviate this mix of headache, nausea, anxiety and fatigue, I held the hot towel over my face and told myself that when I removed it, I would begin the day anew, would have a refreshed state of mind and wouldn't feel the hangover symptoms any longer. But for the Golf Assholes and their spouses jibber jabbering about "the hair of the dog" when they ordered their morning Bloody Marys, my strategy may have worked. Since I was forced to endure their inane and obnoxious sideshow, my symptoms lingered into breakfast and through the conclusion of the flight.

As I debarked the A330, I regretted having forced myself, in an effort to regain my equilibrium, to consume the entirety of the fresh fruit, yogurt, and *pain au chocolat* breakfast. I had assumed that the bland yogurt would soothe my stomach. Unfortunately, though, the effect was quite the reverse. So as I exited the aircraft past Delphine, I couldn't so much as muster a playful *"À plus tard!"*

Walking off of the plane into Charles de Gaulle's sleek newish Terminal 2E with only three passengers ahead of me was especially satisfying. Never before had I been one of the first to debark an international flight. This luxury meant that I would have a minimal wait time at the customs booth.

Indeed, when I exited the plane and walked through a short corridor into the über-modern minimalist glass and concrete building, I was presented with three customs booths from which to choose – none of which had a queue. Since none of the booths were occupied by a Delphine or similar-looking character, but rather by males in their thirties, I randomly chose the booth farthest to the right.

After handing my passport and customs card to the officer, he asked,

"Weycome to France. Zee lengse and purpose of your visit?"

Not willing to squander an opportunity to brush up on my language skills before my meeting later in the day with Véronique, I answered, indicating that I was in Paris on business,

"Deux jours – pour les affaires."

"Et, vous faîtes quoi comme travail?" He responded, inquiring as to my profession.

"Je suis avocat."

"Participerez-vous à un procès en France?" he further inquired, wishing to know whether I was taking part in a trial in France.

Responding in the negative, indicating that I was simply going to meet with a French client about the prospect of pursuing legal action in the U.S., I said,

"Non, pas du tout. J'ai un rendez-vous avec un client à propos d'un procès aux États-Unis."

Apparently sufficiently convinced that I was not going to stage a coup and that I was not planning on demonstrating against French military cowardice, he stamped my passport and waved me through.

Immediately upon arriving at the baggage carrousel designated for my flight, I caught sight of my two matching leather suitcases with the "PRIORITÉ" tags attached. Not having any items to declare for customs, I walked through the customs lane labeled, *"Rien à Déclarer."*

After passing through that lane, I walked past a set of motion sensor-activated sliding glass doors, into the public unsecured area of Terminal 2E. As usual, the scene in this area was a chaotic medley of foul smelling people from numerous worldwide origins, waiting to meet up with their family members and friends who had just landed. This first waft of international body odor nearly knocked me off of my feet as I looked upward for a sign directing me to the RER B train that would take me to my hotel in the 1st Arrondissement.

I had sworn by the RER B for many years, due to the exorbitant price of taxicabs in Paris and the simplicity of its public transportation system. Although I could most assuredly obtain reimbursement from the firm for taxi transportation, I was so used to taking the RER B from past trips to Paris, that I saw no reason to break tradition.

Bleary-eyed from the lingering effects of the Bordeaux and my lack of sleep, I had a bit of trouble locating the sign that would direct me to the train. As I squinted and swiveled my head like a lost owl, a 6'4" man with a sparkle shined bald head, whose complexion resembled a Hershey's Special Dark chocolate bar, approached me and asked in heavily accented English,

"You are lost, sir?"

Taking this character for one of the many illegal limousine drivers who worked Charles de Gaulle Airport for unassuming naïve foreigners who were duped and intimidated into paying 175 Euros for the 20 mile journey into central Paris, I frigidly tried to dismiss him, saying,

"Fous le camp – je prends le train."

"You are Meestair Brown, no?" he said, holding up, with his left hand, a white sign that had my name written in blue magic marker. I became immediately certain that this person was not a scam artist when I saw, in his right hand, a color printout of my bio from the firm's website, which displayed my headshot.

"Yes – yes I am," I responded.

"You think I was soliciting you for limo fare? Ha ha ha!" he bellowed comically in a monstrously baritone voice, "Dat eeeze dee bess one I've heard all day! No, no, no – Monsieur Le Guen send me to bring you to hotel. Deedn't Véronique tell to look for dee sign wees your name on it that big black guy holding? She so silly dat sometime she forget tings, you know?"

He picked up my suitcases and trial bag with one hand, for seemingly no reason other than to demonstrate that his inhuman strength allowed him to do so. He could seemingly have employed both hands to carry the bags, yet chose simply not to do so.

"No – she didn't mention that you would be picking me up. In fact, I was planning on just taking the RER B to the hotel."

As we exited the building toward a row of parked cars lined up on the curb, my new friend's jolly-looking expression changed to an inscrutable glare. He responded,

"Yes, you mention deese when you tell me '*fous le camp*' – get out of here, right?"

Feeling a combination of embarrassment and fear that I was about to be clubbed over the head with a lead pipe and stuffed into the trunk of this giant's car, I backpedaled in rapid fashion, pathetically managing,

"Uh – uh, when I said, '*fous le camp*', I thought that you were soliciting me for a limousine fare – I had no idea that Monsieur Le Guen had sent someone – you – to pick me up. I would never intentionally..."

"Ha ha ha!" he exclaimed again, "you shood aahv seen your face. I just busting your balls."

Before I had a chance to respond, he said,

"My name Alassane – I from Sénégal – you know, West Africa."

"*C'est un plaisir de faire votre connaissance, Alassane.*" I responded, hoping to smooth things over by telling him that it was nice to make his acquaintance.

After placing my bags in the trunk of an S-Class Mercedes-Benz, he opened a rear door of the vehicle, directed me in, and said, "You speak very good French, Mr. Brown. You aahv spenn time in France, no?"

"Thank you, Alassane. I feel as if I'm a bit out of practice, though," I said, adjusting myself to the almost uncomfortably spacious rear seat of the Benz.

"Normally, you be at dee hotel in 45 minutes. Wiss Alassane driving, you be dare in 28 minutes, O.K.?" He said, chuckling.

I responded with an appreciative nod as he looked at me in the rear-view mirror while driving the car towards the direction of the Autoroute 1 expressway.

In the elastic compartment attached to the back of the passenger seat in front of me were five newspapers: *Le Monde*, *Le Figaro*, *International Herald Tribune*, *Frankfurter Allgemeine* and *Corriere della Sera*. Already feeling a touch homesick, I reached for the *International Herald Tribune*, hoping to ascertain the score of the previous night's Phillies game. Before I was even able to find the miniscule sports section, I performed some rough math in my head and figured out that due to the time difference, the newspaper would have had to go to press no later than during the third inning of the Phillies' game the night before. Therefore, there would be no Phillies score from the prior night's game in the paper.

Since there was no baseball to read about, and I didn't feel like challenging my jet lag-affected mind with real news, I decided to just enjoy the scenery. The sight of the various Samsung, Daewoo, Stella Artois and other billboards with their French language slogans awakened my senses a bit and helped me to begin thinking in French. Unfortunately, however, Alassane's weaving of the S-Class in and out of the relatively heavy rush hour traffic, prevented my hangover symptoms from dissipating.

Aggravating his erratic driving was the fact that it was an extremely hot day, and Alassane had the windows of the vehicle closed, with minimal, if any, air conditioning flowing out of the vents. I cocked my head to the left, in order see what the digital temperature gauge read. When I saw a reading of 30.5°, I remembered how much I hated the metric system. I was sweating my balls off and I didn't even know how hot it was. Based upon the little that I had retained from high school science and the amount of moisture absorbed by my dress shirt, I surmised that 30.5° Celsius was somewhere in between 85° and 90° Fahrenheit. In any event, it was too damn hot to be in an un-air conditioned car with the windows up.

"Alassane," I asked, "would there be any possible way that you could turn the air conditioning up a touch? I'm really hurtin' back here."

"I from West Africa, man – deece eezn't hot!" he said, once again looking in the rearview mirror. "You look drenched back dare. You O.K.?"

"Honestly, Alassane, I had a few too many glasses of wine on the plane, and I have really important meetings tonight and tomorrow, so, to be honest, I've been better."

"O.K.," he said, turning on much welcomed artic blast of cold air, "lee-sin, man. You got nothin' to worry about. Monsieur Le Guen says dat you are great lawyer, he happy to have you workin' for him. I been workin' for him many, many years and he a good guy. You juss make sure your i's dotted and your t's crossed, O.K.? He gonna scrutinize your work even more dan most people, since he a lawy...since he always involved in lawsuits, you know?"

"O.K., Alassane, thanks," I said, dismissively, wondering if it would be in bad form to open the window and vomit out the side of the Benz, onto the A1. As I breathed in some more of the cool air and the nausea subsided, I replayed in my head what Alassane had said. Although I was concentrating more on the scenery and the thought of taking a nap in my hotel bed, I could have sworn that I heard him say that Le Guen was a lawyer. That made no sense. I would have thought that Véronique would have brought up that little tidbit during our e-mails and conversations.

"Alassane, I'm sorry, I couldn't hear what you said, with the air conditioning blowing so hard, did you say that – ."

Interrupting me, and speaking in a curt tone which greatly varied from his previous jolly, carefree Sénégalese vernacular, he said,

"No, sir, I deed *not* say dat he was a lawyer. I say dat he – Monsieur Le Guen – was successful beez-ness man and he gonna scrutinize your work 'cause he don't accept no bullshit. I deed *not* say dat, so I appreciate it if you don't start sayin' dat I say dat."

When he spoke the last sentence, his unyielding eyes, which sharply contrasted with his blacker-than-night face, were affixed directly on me, through the rearview mirror. I had struck a chord within this guy, and he wasn't happy. I chalked it up to something being lost in the translation. Maybe it was offensive in Sénégalese culture to accuse someone of saying something that they didn't actually say – even if that something was as innocuous as the issue of whether Jean-Luc Le Guen was or was not a lawyer.

For the rest of the trip, until we passed the Opéra Garnier and had just turned onto the Rue de la Paix, near the hotel, Alassane did not utter another word. That did not stop him, however, from driving like a complete asshole.

We arrived at the Hôtel Capdevielle at 8:08 a.m., exactly 23 minutes after Alassane left Terminal 2E at Charles de Gaulle. The sight of the hotel was welcoming for me, not just because I knew that I would be exiting Alassane's death trap of a Mercedes. This hotel, which I had selected for myself, maintained some sentimental value for me. During our third year of law school, Julie and I spent our spring break in Paris and had stayed at the Capdevielle, located off of the Place Vendôme. While on that trip, I proposed to Julie, a short ten minute walk away from the hotel, in the Tuileries Gardens. Returning to the site where we spent our first evening as an engaged couple made me feel a little less guilty for being in Paris without the love of my life. Besides, the hotel was on the less expensive end of luxury hotels in the center of Paris. Since Krauss, Carlson, et al, were footing the bill for the hotel, I knew that I would have an easier time in explaining a hotel invoice from the Capdevielle, than I would from the nearby Hôtel Meurice, Hôtel de Crillon or Hôtel Ritz.

Before a bellhop could make his way to the vehicle, Alassane retrieved my luggage, once again with a single hand, from the trunk of the Benz and placed the pieces on the curb. Alassane then opened the rear passenger side door and let me out of the vehicle.

As the bellhop arrived, Alassane pointed to the bags in a most condescending manner, as if he were higher up on the food chain than his fellow member of the service industry. He directed the young man,

"Une reservation au nom de Brown – Alexander Brown. Dépêchez-vous."

Alassane rudely told the nervous-looking lad that I was checking in and that he should hurry up with the bags. I was confounded as to why this previously gleefully genteel individual had become, seemingly in an instant, uneasy and now discourteous.

Nevertheless, the bellhop obliged and quickly took the bags into the lobby of the hotel. As I began to follow the bellhop, Alassane stepped into my path, once again with a very wide smile.

"Meestair Brown – eet was a pleasure meeting you," he said, extending his enormous hand. He clasped my hand extra firmly and did not let go when one would customarily do so during a handshake. After about seven seconds of shaking my hand, he finally disengaged. He then undid the top button of his shirt, loosened his tie and, in a continuous motion, unbuttoned his suit jacket.

He said,

"You know, I muss stann corrected – you were right – it *eeze* hot today."

After speaking, he pulled either side of the opening of his jacket in a fanning motion, ostensibly to air out his midsection. I expected to view the unpleasant sight of a sweat-drenched dress shirt stuck to the body of this large African. What I saw, however, was significantly more disturbing.

Clearly visible each time he went through the fanning motion was a gun holster that strapped over his hulking shoulders. The butt end of a handgun on his left side was more than apparent. In fact, the gun was so visible that I questioned myself whether he had opened his jacket for the sole purpose of apprising me that he was carrying. But why would he need to show me his gun? I never planned on seeing this person again, unless Le Guen hired him to drive me back to Charles de Gaulle in two days time. Maybe he wanted a tip.

"Goodbye, Alassane. It was a pleasure meeting you," I said, attempting to hand him a 20 Euro note.

Moving backward, he said,

"I cannot accept, but thank you, *Meestair* Brown. Enjoy your treep to Paris."

I walked into the hotel very confused. The friendliness followed by the fast driving followed by the standoffishness followed by the handgun didn't add up. It especially didn't add up, since I knew that licenses to carry concealed weapons were not obtained easily in France, and there was no equivalent of the Second Amendment in this country. In any event, I did not have time to worry about why a West African chauffeur needed to pack heat. I had made it out of his custody alive, and didn't wish to devote any more time to thinking about him. I needed to freshen up, take a brisk walk around the 1st and 2nd Arrondissements, gather my thoughts and ready myself to meet with Véronique.

CHAPTER THIRTY-FIVE

After cleansing myself of airplane germs with a handheld shower head in a curtain-less tub, I collapsed on top of the fluffy duvet cover of my bed. As I lay there, I told myself, as I had so many times after having arrived in Europe, that I would nap for a few short minutes. When I awakened six and a half hours later at 4:37 p.m., I realized that I had made the same mistake that I had committed virtually every prior time that I had crossed the Atlantic going east.

Not only had I squandered a beautiful summer day in Paris, but I had failed to reset my inner clock, thereby insuring that I would be faced with a sleepless night and a very tired following day.

Since Véronique knew my itinerary and was likely tracking the progress of my flight, I couldn't justly tell her that I had delayed in calling her because of a flight problem. So, I decided to come clean when I phoned her.

"*Âllo?*"

"Hi there, Véronique, it's Alexan..."

"You aahv taken a nap, no?"

"Regrettably, I have. Whenever I come to Europe, I always tell myself that I won't take a nap, but – "

In a sarcastic, pouty tone, Véronique responded,

"Well you are a very bad boy, and you will aahv to be punished, then."

Something was clearly lost in the translation, as I was certain that the words spoken by Véronique had never been uttered in the history of mankind in any context other than in a pornographic film. Adding to the mystique of her words was the fact that they were spoken in an extremely sexy French accent. Concerned that responding in an equally playful tone might endanger my business prospects with Le Guen, I said, simulating confusion,

"Uhh, I suppose so."

Continuing the sarcastic banter, Véronique added,

"Well, I *suppose* zat you better shower yourself and meet me at La Rotonde at seven surrtee. You know where zat eeze? On Montparnasse, at zee intersection of Raspail."

Thank God. She was giving me until seven surrtee – err – thirty, to get bright eyed and bushy tailed.

"That would be great, Véronique. I'll see you then. Should I bring anything?"

"No. It eeze I who will bring somesing. I will bring zee documents zat you wheel need to study before your meeting with Monsieur Le Guen. Until zenn. Ciao, *Ahh-lexx.*"

"Ciao."

I could not believe that the word, "Ciao" left my lips. In my experience, only those living in Italy and Hollywood wannabes from the 1980s said, "Ciao." I couldn't help it, though. The girl's voice was so enticing – it placed me in a quasi-trance, such that I just followed what she said without objection.

CHAPTER THIRTY-SIX

Finding the American in France hadn't been all that tough. All it took was a $10,000.00 bribe to a severely underpaid Brandywine County Courthouse I.T. employee. Within minutes, the computer geek, by combing through Judge Sebring's e-mail account, was able to locate numerous e-mails sent by the American. In one of those e-mails, the American listed what turned out to be a land line telephone number. With a bit more digging, by using the telephone number, the computer geek was able to determine the American's exact address in Paris' 5th Arrondissement.

George Ridgeway had waited an exceedingly long time for his just deserts. He had been villainized by the Brandywine County bench and bar and was left with virtually no means by which to earn a living. One man, and one man alone was responsible for his demise.

While others had accepted as fact the notion that his old law partner had died overseas, George Ridgeway knew better. His former partner was a crafty and vigilant man, and never would have allowed himself to have been slaughtered by Spanish thugs as the official report had suggested.

It was now time for George Ridgeway to get his money back. Despite Ridgeway's history with his former partner, he was not beyond striking a deal with him.

And so he had.

Since wiring the money or writing a check were not viable options, having a courier deliver the financial consideration was really the only choice. Through his ingenuity, he had hand-selected the most unassuming of all characters – a real boy scout – to bring the loot back to the States. By using the kid, George Ridgeway could avoid a face-to-face meeting and risk being killed. Since Winston was equally afraid of a sabotage, he quickly agreed to Ridgeway's suggested arrangement.

Once Ridgeway had received confirmation that the kid was on French soil, he decided to put in a call to his old partner to make sure that the plan was all systems go.

"Hello, James. How goes it?"

"Fuck you, you fucking parasite."

"James, who is the real parasite here? The thief and betrayer of trust, or the victim of the thief and betrayer of trust?" Ridgeway said, with his very evil hacking growl.

"I've got the plan set in motion. The kid will be on a plane back to Philly in less than 48 hours *with* your prize. As per our little deal, I keep the pittance that remains from the <u>Washington</u> case and I never hear from you again."

"You better make sure that your people at the Philadelphia Airport have a picture of that kid and take him through customs. If they miss him and he winds up going through the real customs line and they open his bag, then I'm out a lot of money and you're crossing the Atlantic shortly thereafter with the U.S. Marshal Service. Do I make myself clear?!"

"Georgie, I know what the hell I'm doing. Before I bid you a final 'fuck you', I'll remind you that once this is over, if you try to pull any funny business by alerting the authorities as to my whereabouts, in my first interview with the U.S. feds, I'll outline the exact details of how you extorted me and illegally moved the merchandise into the country by skirting the United States Customs and Border Protection Service. They might be interested in that one."

"How can I extort someone for money that rightfully belongs to me?!" Ridgeway screamed, losing his cool.

"Georgie, my law library is 4,000 miles away and I'm a little rusty on the exact definition of extortion, so – "

"Fuck with me and you're done, Jim. Try me."

After his old partner hung up, Jim Winston put the phone down, and laughed to himself, fully confident that George Ridgeway didn't have the foggiest idea of what he had gotten himself into.

CHAPTER THIRTY-SEVEN

As my hair had become misarranged during my extended nap, I quickly hosed my head down in the bathroom. At that moment, it occurred to me that the whole detachable shower head arrangement wasn't that ridiculous after all. I stood outside of the tub, angled my body over the tub and sprayed my head. In doing so, not even a droplet of water landed anywhere on my body, other than my head. The French were bloody brilliant. Since healthy and stylish-looking hair was an important virtue to the French, it made perfect sense for French households and hotels to have detachable showerheads. That way, they could wash their hair without going through the trouble of simultaneously cleaning their bodies. This arrangement allowed the French to maintain their trademark pungent body odor, while upholding their tradition of great hair.

Although Julie had packed a multitude of suits and matching shirt and tie accompaniments for me, I decided to go out on a limb and wear a sportcoat and dress shirt combination to meet Véronique. It was not uncommon for men to wear suits at La Rotonde and other adjacent Montparnasse establishments. In light of the tone that Véronique had taken with me, though, I felt it appropriate to don a more casual look. So, as I saluted the Capdevielle's doorman an *à tout à l'heure*, I was clad in a two buttoned navy blue blazer, a pink shirt that Julie had bought for me at Alain Figaret during our last trip to Paris and a pair of tan slacks. In my view, it said polished, confident and relaxed.

I could have taken a taxi to La Rotonde, but I rejected that option based upon my affinity towards the Paris Metro and RER system. It was quick, safe and direct. I walked a few short blocks away and boarded the 7 Line under the Opéra Garnier. After taking the 7 line a few short stops, I made an easy transfer at Châtelet-Les Halles, and boarded the RER B. I could have transferred to the 4 Line which would have left me virtually in front of the restaurant. Since I had 45 minutes, or so, to kill, I decided to take the RER B to the Luxembourg stop, so that I could stroll through my very favorite locale in Paris, the Luxembourg Gardens.

As the escalator from the RER B brought me to street level, the view of the Luxembourg Gardens' gates, the smell of its flowers and the diesel fuel from the vehicles on the Boulevard Saint Michel took my breath away. I was immediately transplanted into the year 1996, when I was a college junior, studying abroad in Paris. I looked upon that period with great fondness, in hindsight. Having been paired with an incompatible roommate, I frequently wandered the city alone and came to fall in love with it. Being forced to discover the city on my own turned out to be a godsend for my development into adulthood. For the first time in my life, I had ventured on my own, without friends or family.

Wherever my solo daily jaunts took me, I somehow always wound up in the Luxembourg Gardens in the late afternoon, puffing a cigarette and enjoying the scenery.

The Luxembourg Quarter reminded me very much of New York's Upper East Side. It was extremely refined and insulated from the hustle and bustle of the touristy spots. And similar to New York's Upper East Side, many affluent business people called this area home. The restaurants, cafés and, indeed, the Luxembourg Gardens, itself, were filled with locals.

After crossing the Boulevard Saint Michel, I entered the Gardens through an opening in an immense black and gold wrought iron gate. Breathing in the fresh air of the Luxembourg Gardens awakened my senses and immediately cured me of my previously lingering jet lag symptoms. Looking down at my feet, I realized that I had forgotten the hazards associated with wearing nice shoes in the Luxembourg Gardens. My Tod's loafers were sprinkled with the white dust that had covered the pebble and earth surface of the walking areas of the Gardens since the time of Marie de Médicis.

With the summer sun fading, I took a seat on a chair facing the awe-inspiring Luxembourg Palace, which houses the French Senate. I propped my feet on another chair, retrieved the pack of Gitanes that I bought earlier in the day, and lit up. Since I was never a habitual smoker and probably had not smoked a single cigarette in five years, the nicotine shocked my system and made me feel lightheaded for a few passing moments.

After the queasy feeling had subsided, I sat back, relaxed, and felt like a million dollars. The gravity of my sudden good fortune and skyrocketing career hit me like a ton of bricks. Just a few weeks prior, Lubrano Concrete, the Physician's Justice venture, and Jean-Luc Le Guen were not in my life. And now, here I was, in the Luxembourg Gardens, fresh off of a client-sponsored trans-Atlantic Business Class flight, getting ready to meet that client's personal attaché to discuss a lawsuit that was going to make me lots of money, win, lose or draw. Once word spread through the Philadelphia legal community that a youngster such as myself had amassed such an impressive client base at the age of 31, I would become famous. Businesses would be flocking to me for representation. Maybe I could upgrade the Bimmer to a 7-Series and tell Julie to quit her job and stay home to raise Charlie.

As I smoked the cigarette, I marveled at the immaculately-manicured green lawn, or *pelouse,* as the French liked to call it, in front of the Palace. Parisians would sit around the perimeter of the lawn for hours on end, read their newspapers and, literally, watch the grass grow. Incomprehensible to the average American, Parisians actually adhered to the *Pelouse Interdite* signs that were placed around the lawn, which indicated that entering the grassy area was forbidden. Parisians were more than content to look at the grass rather than frolic upon it.

With each exhale of smoke that billowed to the darkening Parisian summer sky, I became more and more confident that Jean-Luc Le Guen and his company were going to be my ticket to wealth and happiness for the rest of my life and the lives of my children.

CHAPTER THIRTY-EIGHT

At 7:15 p.m., I left the Luxembourg Gardens and made my way through the short and winding back streets of the 6th Arrondissement towards the Boulevard du Montparnasse, where La Rotonde was located. Although it was but a five minute walk, I wanted to make certain that I was a few minutes early, so that Véronique was not waiting for me when I arrived.

Boulevard du Montparnasse at nighttime was a spectacle. Its historically significant cafés were, once upon a time, frequented by the likes of F. Scott Fitzgerald, Ernest Hemingway and Pablo Picasso. The cacophony of voices of the café-goers, combined with the bright and flamboyant lights decorating each establishment always gave this strip a unique buzz found nowhere else in Paris.

Around Montparnasse's intersection with Boulevard Raspail were three of the most celebrated cafés on the strip, Le Dôme, La Coupole and La Rotonde. Véronique had chosen La Rotonde, which was more than acceptable for me. Set exactly on the angular intersection of Montparnasse and Raspail, La Rotonde provided some of the most picturesque café terrace views in the city.

I arrived at La Rotonde at 7:23 p.m. The very 1930s-looking multi-colored neon lights beckoned me by spelling out the name of the café in capital letters. Not knowing what Véronique looked like, I had intended to check in at the maître d' podium. Before I could even make it to the entrance, a voice from behind me said,

"*Ahh-lexx* – so you must have anozerr date tonight at zee same café, if you walk right past me, no?"

Date?

The voice was unmistakable. It was that of Véronique.

Before turning around, I made sure to put on my business greeting, wide smiling "sure is nice to meet you" face. Once I rotated 180 degrees, though, my face went numb and my previous expression had vanished.

The tanned, jet black haired specimen was wearing a solid cherry red cocktail dress that could have stopped a speeding RER B train. She sat with her legs crossed, elegantly holding a cigarette in the air between her left forefinger and middle finger, in a manner that exuded femininity from a bygone era. Next to her ashtray sat a champagne flute holding a pinkish-looking concoction. She had a chiseled jaw that looked as if it belonged on an exotic runway model. Her silky smooth and seemingly never-ending legs perfectly complimented her diminutive waistline and immodest breasts. From ten feet away, I could tell that this woman's bust was decidedly not store-bought. Véronique was a veritable living, breathing Chanel ad.

I didn't even bother trying to put the professional "sure is nice to meet you" face on again. My cheeks were still numb and were not responding to the urgent messages being sent to them by my brain. God knows what my expression looked like when I took notice of her. Judging by her world-class looks, though, it seemed apparent that Véronique would have been used to seeing such expressions on men's – and women's – faces on a daily basis.

"I sought zat you maybe were coming here to mitt someone else, since you ignore me."

"Oh my gosh, Véronique – or Mademoiselle Véronique..."

"Just Véronique, *Ahh-lexx*, remember?"

"Yes, yes," I said nervously, in extremely flustered fashion.

Calm down, she's going to think that you have no poise under pressure and that you're therefore a shitty lawyer.

"I'm sorry, Véronique. You see, I didn't know what you looked like, but I guess you knew what I looked like from my firm's website. Rest assured, I have no other plans for the evening, but you."

Oh God, that came out wrong. I was now sexually harassing the personal assistant of Jean-Luc Le Guen.

"Good. By zee way, calm down – you are too jet lagged. I was fucking wiss you."

I took a secret guilty pleasure in having heard this creature, who oozed sex, say the term, "fucking." Her invocation of levity into the conversation had an extremely calming effect on me.

"You are too stress. Let's get you a drink, *n'est-ce pas? Que désirez-vous boire?*"

"Umm," I said taking a seat at her table on the café terrace, "what are you drinking, champagne?"

"No, it's a Kir Royale – it has champagne in it, though. You're not getting that – it eeze a ladies drink."

"How 'bout a Kronenbourg?"

"No we wheel be drinking wine wiss dinner and zat eeze not going to mix well."

Only the French could place so much emphasis on the choice of an apéritif.

"O.K., then, how about a Pernod?"

"I deed not know zat zee Americans aahd heard of zeese."

"Well, Véronique, I like to think of myself as being atypical."

"Good. You wheel fit in well weese our company. *Garçon!*"

Eight seconds after summoning the waiter, he arrived at our table by power walking from the other side of the terrace. Clad in the traditional white shirt, black vest and bowtie, he asked,

"*Oui, mademoiselle?*"

"*Monsieur prend un Pernod. Et puis, on veut régarder la carte, s'il vous-plaît.*"

"*Bien sûr. Je reviens tout de suite.*"

That she had asked him to provide us with some menus was relieving to me. The combination of the nicotine and my unsettled nerves had me feeling that my blood sugar was low and that I needed a hearty meal.

"Can I offer you a cigarette?" Véronique said, opening the lid to her red box of Gauloises.

"Sure – thank you," I responded, not bringing to light the fact that I had my own pack of Gitanes in the inside pocket of my blazer. Due to the stigma to which I was accustomed in the States, I did not want to give off the impression that I was a regular smoker, for fear that she would adjudge me to have a weakness.

"I am surprise zat you are smoker. Not many Americans are anymore, no? Zay just pass a law in ziss country banning smoking inside bars and restaurants, but you can still smoke outside on café terraces. Our government get too many bad ideas from your government. I am waiting for zemm to ban a cigarette after sex – zatt wheel be next – how do you say – it wheel be a snowball effect, you know?"

She liked to smoke after sex. Not a bad thing for a loyally married guy alone in a foreign country to know about a woman after having been acquainted with her for five minutes.

I retrieved a Gauloise from her box – err – pack, and placed it between my lips. No sooner had I done so than she struck a wooden match to a rectangular box and placed the flame in front of my face. I inhaled. When she saw that the cigarette was lit, she blew out the flame, while locking her eyes with mine. As the air from her mouth hit my face, Israel One (as Julie liked to call it) involuntarily prepared itself for liftoff.

What the hell was I, a twelve year-old? *Get a hold of yourself. You're happily married to a knockout and Véronique is your client's attaché. Plus, she's not flirting with you – she's just French, and that's how they do things here.*

I crossed my legs to avoid severe embarrassment. During this uncomfortable development, I realized that Véronique did not appear to have brought with her the voluminous documents that she had previously mentioned. In fact, I seriously doubted that the Longchamp purse that she was carrying could have fit anything more than some money, a few credit cards, a lipstick and maybe five or six condoms. Good heavens. I needed to get a hold of myself and I needed to get a hold of myself in a hurry. When the next comment out of her mouth pertained to business, I was incredibly relieved.

"So are you ready for zee meeting tomorrow? Monsieur Le Guen is expecting a lot out of you."

"I'm as ready as I can be – I'll just need to look at those documents that you talked about, when I get back to the hotel tonight."

"Oh, zee documents. Monsieur Le Guen decided zat it would be insensitive to you, considering your jet lag, to ask you to look over zee papers. Zare are too many – like 12,000 – you woodn't even be able to make a dent in zem tonight. After zee meeting, we wheel ship zem to your office in Philadelphie."

Insensitive to me? No wonder the French economy sucked. Where I came from, if a client was paying money to an attorney, the client didn't care if the attorney had to bike across a tightrope to get the job done.

Hell, if that was their posture, I wasn't going to argue with her. But that begged the question: if she didn't bring the documents with her to discuss them with me, why was I sitting at La Rotonde with her? In light of the inch and a half of un-doctored cleavage that was staring at me, I wasn't inclined to call her out on that issue either.

The waiter arrived with my drink and placed it in front of me.

"*Un Pernod et la carte. Voilà. Je reviens prendre votre commande.*"

"*Merci bien,*" I responded, thanking the waiter for bringing the drink to me.

I sipped the flavorful anise liqueur, and didn't even wince as I had expected to do, as it traveled down my throat.

"Do you actually like zat?!" Véronique asked incredulously.

"Actually, I do." Lying through my teeth, in an attempt to convince her that I was worldly, I continued, "I always have a bottle of Pernod at home, in case company comes over."

In fact, although I had heard of Pernod before, and had seen it consumed in old movies, this was the very first time that I had tasted it.

"And who lives wiss you at home? You are married?" she said, looking at my gold banded left ring finger.

Now feeling extremely uncomfortable, I gulped some more of the Pernod and responded,

"Yes, yes I am."

"Does your wife know zat you aahr eehr?"

Was that a trick question?

"Uhh, do you mean *in Paris* or *here at this table with you?*"

"*Ahh-lexx*, you need to calm yourself. I was fucking wiss you again. Drink zat drink and we will order some food and wine. Do you know what you want?"

Did I ever.

"Sure."

"*Garçon!*" Véronique shouted, motioning the waiter over with her cigarette.

Once he arrived, Véronique quickly reeled off her order.

"*Alors, le saumon fumé pour commencer, et puis, le steak tartare*"

"*Monsieur?*" the cheeky waiter said to me, wondering what in God's name I was doing with a woman of this caliber.

"*Je prends les escargots, et aussi, le côte de veau.*"

"And, as wine, you will take what, please?"

I spoke much better French than this asshole spoke English. Yet he, like so many Parisian waiters and shopkeepers, insisted on answering Americans in English after being addressed in French. It was their little way of saying that no matter how hard we tried, we were Americans, and, therefore, of inferior blood, doomed to a cultureless and unenlightened remainder of our days.

Since my firm was paying for the dinner, and I figured that Véronique presumed as much, I opted for a fairly expensive Bordeaux, which had a listed price of 93 Euros on the *carte des vins*.

"We'll have the Château Calon-Ségur St.-Estèphe 2003."

Grabbing the *carte de vins* out of my hands in a huff, Véronique barked at me,

"*Ahh-lexx*, if you are going to meck me drink Bordeaux, I'm not going to drink zat shit zat you aahv chosen."

Now speaking towards the waiter and pointing at the page, so that both the waiter and I could see, Véronique commanded steadfastly,

"*Château Latour Pauillac 2003, s'il vous plait.*"

"*Très bien, mademoiselle.*"

After sending off the waiter to bring us a bottle of 575 Euro wine, Véronique smiled seductively at me and lit another cigarette. I did my very best to not display the nervousness that I was encountering, thinking of how I would have to explain to Nick Carlson why I spent over $900.00 on a dinner for two people.

Once again attempting to break the tension that she had engendered by making a series of puzzling suggestive innuendos, I decided to shift the focus of our conversation to business.

"So, Véronique, what sort of role do you play in Le Guen, S.A.'s tower crane operation? Do you stay mainly in the office, or are you generally at job sites?"

Véronique grasped the top of both of my hands, leaned over the table closer to me and said,

"*Ahh-lexx*, I sought zat I made it abundantly clear zat I do not want to talk about business tonight. I aahv aahd a very stressful couple of weeks and I juss want to – how you say – unwind – a bit tonight. Is zat O.K. wiss you?"

"Unwind? Sure, I can unwind."

"I mean, really, *Ahh-lexx*, you are een Paris – zee most beautiful city in zee world. And more zan zatt, you are on zee Boulevard du Montparnasse – zee most incredible café street in Paris, where everybody who's anybody goes to eat and drink. Let's watch zee cars. Let's watch zee people. Let's not talk about work, shall we?"

"Not another peep – I promise."

"Good."

***

After three hours, two bottles of Château Latour, a dozen snails, some smoked salmon, a veal chop, plate of raw hamburger meat, two crème brûlées, and two snifters of Rémy Martin XO, Véronique and I were having a good old time. In addition to being more than a little drunk, I had engaged in exactly the type of conversation with Véronique that I had hoped to avoid. We talked about our first relationships with the opposite sex, our pet peeves about the opposite sex, our respective views on the institution of marriage and many other similar topics that were patently inappropriate to discuss with an attractive young female who happened to work for my client. I had let my guard down, and was angry at myself for doing so.

Since the wine was gone and it had been about 20 minutes since any alcohol had entered my system, I was at the point where the alcohol-induced euphoria was fading and unpleasant reality was setting in. This emotion caused me to believe that I needed to get back to the hotel immediately, so that I could salvage some much needed sleep in preparation for my greatly-anticipated meeting with Jean-Luc Le Guen tomorrow.

"Véronique, what time will I be meeting with Monsieur Le Guen tomorrow."

"Ah-lexx, you are sick of *me* now? All you can sink about is Jean-Luc now?", she responded in a sloppily drunk, yet still flirtatious tone.

"No, not at all Véronique," I said, attempting to quash her playfulness, which was now causing me significant worry, "It's just that I want to be fresh for the morning, so that I can give my all to Monsieur Le Guen."

" 'Give eem your all?!' What are you, *Ahh-lexx-ondair* Brown, a television commercial?"

"No, it's just that I tend not to perform well when I'm sleep deprived. You understand, right?"

"You won't aahv one more bottle wiss me?"

"Véronique, I really can't."

I waved the waiter over and asked him for the check by saying,

"*L'addition, s'il vous-plaît.*"

"Well zen, you are no fun," Véronique stated, frustratedly.

"I have to agree with you there, Véronique – at least tonight I'm no fun."

"Are you fun on other nights?"

After taking a moment to carefully and honestly think that one out, I answered, while handing the waiter my credit card to pay for the obscenely priced dinner,

"You know, Véronique, that's actually debatable at this point."

"So what aahpens? You become a lawyer, you make lots of money, you get married, have a child, and all of zee sudden you are no fun?"

"Not exactly. It's a little more complicated than that," I said, now agitated at her questioning.

"O.K., whatever you say. I let you go home, but only eef you let me perform a scientific experiment first – but you have to go along wiss it and cannot question me. I promise I do nussing to get you or me in trouble."

Seizing the opportunity to get back to my hotel room alone, without saying anything that would jeopardize prospects with Le Guen, S.A. or my marriage, I agreed, declaring,

"Sure."

"O.K., *Ahh-lexx*, eehr's what you need to do: clasp your hands wiss my hands and close your eyes."

Oh shit. This was not a good idea.

She did promise that she wouldn't do anything to get either of us in trouble, though.

After I complied and I felt her body heat as she slowly moved her face towards mine, I failed to see how she could keep that promise in light of what I thought that she was about to do. My life flashed before my eyes as I prepared for her to affix her mouth to mine. I was about to betray my wife, my child and my upbringing and there was nothing that I could do about it.

As I readied my lips to be met by hers, Véronique stopped within a half inch from my face. I opened my eyes in shock, and she said, forcing her sexual breath into my mouth and nostrils.

"Close back your eyes, *Ahh-lexx*."

Once again, I complied.

"Do you feel my breath on you?"

"Yes."

"Do you smell my perfume?"

I did, and I had the entire evening. It was a delightful and sensuous bouquet of spring flowers mixed with spice.

"Yes."

"Do you hear my heart beating?"

I somehow was able to filter out the busy traffic sounds on the Boulevard du Montparnasse and the patrons at the other tables. I could, indeed hear her heart pounding.

"Yes, I can."

"Good. Now you know almost what it's like to fuck me. I hope you have a good night. Your meeting wiss Monsieur Le Guen will be taking place at 12:00 p.m. tomorrow. Please come to 230, Rue des Bernardins in zee Latin Quarter at zat time. Ciao."

With that, Véronique got up from the table, hailed a cab and was off.

For a good three minutes after she left, I stared at the pavement where Véronique's feet had left the ground and entered the cab. Breaking me out of my self-pitying trance, the waiter came back to the table and stood in the path of where my eyes were affixed. As I looked up, he said,

"Meestair – eeze everysing O.K.?"

"Another Rémy, please."

"I deedn't understand – are you sure zat you..."

"You understood me. *Un. Rémy. Martin. X.O. Tout de suite. S'il. Vous. Plaît.* Did you understand that, or do I have to say it in Dutch, too?"

"D'accord, monsieur. Comme vous voulez."

CHAPTER THIRTY-NINE

When both the hour hand and the minute hand on my Submariner were pointing due north, I figured that it was time to go home. Since the Metro was operating under a limited late evening schedule and I couldn't immediately find a taxi, I decided to hoof it back to the hotel.

I turned off of Montparnasse onto Rue de Rennes towards the Seine. Still smelling Véronique's perfume, I wondered what it would have been like to be rolling in the sheets with her at this very moment, rather than walking alone, back to a hotel two miles away. I kept telling myself that I had made the right choice. Nonetheless, I found myself agitatedly lighting one cigarette after the next, all the way home.

I passed Saint Sulpice, and, a few minutes later, Saint Germain des Prés, two of the most beautiful and celebrated churches in all of Paris. I stood in awe of both of the impressive structures, and told myself that I was one worldly and open-minded Jew for being so affected by the sight of beautiful churches.

After Rue de Rennes ended, I was funneled onto the tiny and ancient Rue Bonaparte. With the thought of the imposing churches still fresh in my head, a deeply religious feeling overcame me, giving me solace in the fact that I had chosen a path of morality rather that debauchery this evening.

I then crossed the Seine over the Pont du Carrousel, and then wandered into the Place du Carrousel. Behind me was the massive open expanse of the Louvre courtyard, with the gigantic glass-paneled Louvre Pyramid in its center. I stood under the center of the Arc de Triomphe du Carrousel and viewed one of the world's most impressive spectacles. Every time that I came to Paris, I made a point to stand at this exact location, in order to view the grand historic axis.

This so-called *"axe historique"* is comprised of a five and a half mile stretch that begins, at the west, with the Grande Arche de la Défense, and ends, at the east, with the central block of the Louvre. Connected by a virtual straight line between those points over the five and a half miles are, from west to east, the Arc de Triomphe, the obelisk of the Place de la Concorde, the Arc de Triomphe du Carrousel, and the Louvre Pyramid. Thus, standing under the Arc de Triomphe du Carrousel on this very clear evening, I could see all of the aligning monuments.

The French couldn't fight wars, but they sure as hell could put a damn breathtaking city plan together.

After I was done being enamored with the view of the aligning monuments, I made my way onto Rue Saint-Honoré and then to the Place Vendôme, adjacent to where the hotel was. I paid my respects to Napoléon Bonaparte, who stood at the top of the Vendôme Column in the center of the square, and turned in for the evening.

CHAPTER FORTY

All of that walking must have eliminated the Pernod, the bottle or so of wine and two cognacs from my system. When I woke up at 10:00 a.m. to the knock on the door of the man delivering the breakfast that I had pre-ordered last night, I felt quite refreshed. I quickly dug into my basket of *croissants* and *pains au chocolat.* A brown-shelled hard-boiled egg and a delicious five-ounce glass of seven Euro orange juice topped off my fulfilling culinary experience.

Not seeing ESPN or CNN as I flipped through the channels, I alternated between a Saudi man with a keffiyeh covering his head, telecasting the Arabian Peninsula's weather, and a Japanese soap opera-looking program.

I then hosed myself down in the tub, brushed my teeth and shaved. When I failed to nick myself with the razor, as I did most mornings, I had a funny feeling that things were going to come up aces with Le Guen later in the day.

My next stop was the closet. I perused the choices that Julie had provided to me. I deliberated for a few minutes, as my attire was a decision of paramount importance. Even if Le Guen had never worn a suit in his life and didn't appreciate fine clothing (which I seriously doubted in light of his wealth and his being French), I subscribed to the belief that 95% of the sale was made at the front door. So, in essence, if he thought that I *looked like* a refined, successful lawyer, he would necessarily trust me and want me to work for him.

I eventually settled on my black with subtle white pinstripe Ralph Lauren Purple Label suit. The ensemble was complimented with a pale pink shirt with white French cuffs and collar, and a diagonally striped tie of multiple hues of blue. I hoped to project a conservative, yet effervescent image. With a dab of pomade and some hand-sculpting, my hair was ready, and I was dressed to kill.

Rue des Bernardins, where Le Guen's office was located, was just on the other side of the Seine, on the Left Bank, in the 5th Arrondissement. Véronique had said that I was to meet Jean-Luc Le Guen at his office there at 12 noon. At 11:15 a.m., as I sprayed a healthy dose of Azzaro on my neck, and was readying to leave the hotel, the room phone rang. Since Julie could not figure out how to dial an overseas number if her life depended on it, and it was 5:15 a.m. in Philadelphia, I figured that it was room service, inquiring as to whether they could come up to reclaim the breakfast dishes. In a rush and not wanting to be bothered, I didn't greet the caller. Instead, I simply said that I was leaving the room and that they were free to come and get the dishes.

"Je suis en train de quitter la chambre. Vous pouvez récupérer le plateau quand vous voulez."

"Ahh-lexx, I deedn't know zat I was your butlair."

"Oh – Véronique – I didn't know that it was you," I said, ill at ease.

"In France, we say, *'Âllo'* when we answer zee phone. We don't just start talking. No, we don't do ziss," Véronique responded in a not completely serious, yet not completely unserious tone.

"Sorry about that, Véronique. You said 12 noon, right? I'm not late, am I? Oh my God, please tell me that the hotel clock is not broken," I said, looking at the Submariner and confirming that it was actually 11:15 a.m.

"No, no – I deed say 12 o'clock. Zare aahs been a change of plans, though. Zee plumber aahs to come to zee office and will be zare until 3 o'clock. So you go to take lunch wiss Monsieur Le Guen at 1:30 p.m. and zenn you come back to zee office to discuss zee case."

"Perfect. Where should I meet him?"

"You will mitt heem at Chez Poulin. Do you know zee Rue Mouffetard?"

"Of course."

"Zee restaurant eeze on zee Rue Mouffetard, at zee top, near zee Rue Ortolan. You will have lunch at Chez Poulin and zenn walk back to zee office. Eet eeze not far."

"Great. I'll meet him there in a little while. Will I be seeing you there for lunch, as well?"

"No, *Ahh-lexx*. You saw me last night and you aahd your chance."

As if I had forgotten. Attempting to dismissively make light out of her inappropriate and unwelcome response, I said,

"O.K., Véronique, I'll talk to you later, then. Take care."

"Adieu, Ahh-lexx."

"Adieu" is a farewell greeting that, in French, connotes the presumption that the speaker and recipient will never see each other again. I sensed that Véronique was a tad dismayed that I did not accept her invitation to commit adultery the previous evening. In light of her physical appearance, I found it quite confounding that she was so distraught that I had spurned her. The girl could walk into a room full of Hollywood actors or multi-millionaire professional athletes and be fawned over. What she saw in a 31 year-old fairly successful married commercial litigator from Philadelphia escaped me. I quickly dismissed her theatrics, for when it came down to it, I was after Le Guen's money, not his assistant's prime ass.

CHAPTER FORTY-ONE

Rue Mouffetard is a narrow and picturesque street in the Latin Quarter teaming with hollering produce, meat, seafood and other salesmen hawking their wares. Interspersed throughout the inclined cobblestone street are boutiques and cafés. The scene on Rue Mouffetard is genuine old European and can be found nowhere in the United States. I could not have picked a more agreeable locale in which to dine with Jean-Luc Le Guen.

Per Véronique's directions, I arrived just before 1:30 p.m. in my taxicab at Rue Mouffetard's intersection with Rue Ortolan. I quickly found Chez Poulin, a tiny bistro nestled in between a *charcuterie* and a flower shop. Men clad in bloody white uniforms hacked away at whole dead pigs in the adjacent outdoor storefront.

Before I was able to enter the scenic, quaint-looking restaurant, a short, spectacle-wearing, curly-gray haired woman carrying a ratty black bichon-frisé approached me and said, smiling,

"You are Monsieur Brown?"

"Yes, I am."

"Ahh, good, good. Your friend call and say he be five minutes late, but zat you should take a seat outside and he mitt you eehr shortly. Please," she said gesturing to one of the two outdoor tables.

"Thank you very much," I responded, placing my briefcase on the ground. The bichon frisé nearly jumped out of the lady's hand, as if it wanted to attack my bag. In light of the dog's physical stature and its French nationality, I liked my briefcase's chances in that fight. The lady then turned the dog around, pushed her nose up against the dripping wet nose of the dog and said, scolding him,

"Zizou! Qu'est-ce que tu fais! Alors, ça suffit!"

She then kissed Zizou's bare mouth three times, placed him on the ground and allowed him to run inside the restaurant.

"My leetle baby is bad boy sometimes, you know? *Alors*, will you take somesing to drink?"

"Just a Perrier, with a slice of lemon, please."

"You do not take whiskey?"

Whiskey was about the last thing that I was going to "take" in the early afternoon, just before I was to meet the client who would change my life. As whiskey was not consumed nearly as widely in France as it was in the British Isles and even in America, I was perplexed as to why she proposed that I drink whiskey – at noontime.

"No, why do you ask?"

"Well, you are friend wiss Monsieur Le Guen and he drink whiskey, so I figure zatt...well never mind, as you wish," she said, walking off and leaving me with a menu.

So, Le Guen was a whiskey drinker. My kind of man. My decision to wear a suit, rather than a business-casual getup was looking more and more like a good idea.

While waiting for Le Guen to arrive, I inspected the menu. To my enjoyment, it contained all of the great French café delicacies—onion soup, a *croque-monsieur*, a ham and gruyere baguette sandwich, and crêpes of all varieties. The only upsetting part was that I would not be ordering the onion soup that I so loved, for fear that I would look like a boob in front of Le Guen, trying to ingest the rubbery cheese encrusted around the crock.

My seat faced the downhill side of Rue Mouffetard. While waiting for my client, I watched business people, students and lovers amble up and down the street. I thought of how just about each and every one of the locals passing me by took the utter beauty of the scene that I was witnessing for granted. To them, Rue Mouffetard was just another street in their city. To me, the magnificent surroundings were so stunning and preoccupying that I was barely even nervous about meeting Le Guen.

At 1:41 p.m., amongst the rapidly passing people, I noticed a very slow-moving silver-haired individual arduously hobbling up the street. He had a noticeable limp and could not seem to be able to fully bend his left leg. I felt bad for the old man. From the looks of him, he was probably a lonely widower who had no family and had to journey outside every day to get his daily provisions. With a beet-red face, and veins visibly protruding from his neck, he was clearly encountering significant physical difficulties in walking up the fairly steep incline. The busy midday foot traffic on Rue Mouffetard was not aiding this man's efforts to get where he was going. Due to his slow pace, he was forced to dodge in and out of those not sensitive to his physical handicap.

When he got to within 15 feet of me, he began to look squarely in my direction. I looked behind myself to check whether anyone was sitting at the other outdoor table. Except for an ashtray, the table was unoccupied. When I turned back around, the man was still looking at me and was definitely approaching my table.

Could this be Jean-Luc Le Guen? I hoped not. This man looked to be in ill-humor, and did not give off the air of anyone who could afford to pay my fees on an ongoing basis.

When he was within four feet of the table and was still looking at me, it was clear that the man intended to sit down at my table. I stood up, put on my best and most beaming smile, extended my hand, and said,

"Monsieur Le Guen, c'est un plaisir de faire votre connaissance."

With a scowl on his face and highly labored breathing, he briefly grasped my hand, gave it a barely noticeable shake and let go. He placed two sealed letter-size yellow envelopes on the café table, sat down in a chair, reclined, and tried to catch his breath. Seeing that he was in decidedly bad shape on this very hot day, I asked whether he was O.K. and if I could get him a cold drink.

"Ça va? Puis-je vous commander une boisson fraîche?"

Instead of responding verbally, the old man indicated "no," by gesturing his right index finger back and forth.

The air was being slowly let out of my balloon. This was not the Jean-Luc Le Guen that I had imagined. He was wearing a white golf shirt with a red sauce stain on the abdomen area. The shirt was half un-tucked from his dark blue, non-designer blue jeans. His feet were covered by white athletic socks and tattered Nikes, that looked to be an early 1990s model. He had regal-looking combed-back silver hair. However, he looked to be two to three weeks unshaven. This man didn't look like he had enough money to afford the food that we were about to dine on, let alone fly me on business class to Paris.

After ten more seconds of collecting himself, he leaned forward, rested his elbows on the table and said gruffly,

"What's new in the world of law, kid? I've been out of that game for a while now – why don't-cha fill me in."

Oh thank God – this miserable old codger wasn't Le Guen.

He spoke in an American English accent that bore no indications of having a French inflection. In fact, at first, I almost thought that he sounded like a Philadelphian. I quickly dismissed that prospect by convincing myself that having not heard a native English speaker for a day or so, my brain had processed the accent as being familiar and I therefore interpreted it to be that of a Philadelphian.

"Uhh, not much," I responded in an obviously perplexed pitch.

"Astute answer, young man. With each passing moment, I'm becoming gladder and gladder that we brought you over here."

Although this man had not ordered anything, the gray haired proprietor placed a short glass with brownish liquid and no ice cubes in front of him. She left a Perrier for me.

"Do you work with Monsieur Le Guen?"

"You know what I miss most about Philadelphia?" he said, guzzling three-quarters of the drink that I adjudged to be straight whiskey.

After I moved my jaw and was unable to formulate a response, he said,

"Well, I'm gonna tell you anyway. I miss walking into a Wawa and ordering a hoagie. I miss mozying into a bar at happy hour and paying three bucks or less for my beer. God, what I wouldn't do for a Miller Genuine Draft. The only American beer they have here is Budweiser. *Donney-moi une Bood, see voo play!* What a goddamn joke. I hear that you drink Pernod. Holy shit – you couldn't pay me enough to ingest that garbage."

I desperately wanted to chime in, but this lunatic, in the middle of a rant, wouldn't allow me to do so.

"You know what else I miss? I miss a pitcher brushing back a batter when he's too close to the plate. In this hellhole, you get a piece of half cooked cold pig, some rancid cheese and stale bread coated in butter – and they call that a sandwich. A beer in a café is seven Euro fifty minimum – ten bucks to you and me. And, best of all, the only friggin' sport that I can get on TV is soccer. A bunch of pussies chasing around a ball and faking injury to get a free kick. That there sums up the French. A bunch of pussies faking it to get the sympathy of others. They *did* teach you about *double-you double-you eye eye* at The Presbyterian Academy, didn't they?"

Confused beyond belief, I was unable to ascertain why this man chose to sit at my table and how he knew that I was from Philadelphia and attended Presbyterian. With no explanation readily apparent, I surmised that this man was a Philadelphian ex-patriot who worked for Le Guen. Le Guen must have sent him to provide me with some sort of message.

"Where did you live in Philly? By the way, I didn't catch your name."

"Counselor, let's cut the shit and get to business, shall we?"

I had had just about enough of this old codger and would advise Monsieur Le Guen that he might want to consider hiring more amiable help.

"Sure."

"I understand that you have had the misfortune of making the acquaintance of George Ridgeway."

I paused for a moment and looked into this man's reddened eyes. How did he know that I knew George Ridgeway? Did the Chief have a spy following me all the way to Paris? If he couldn't afford a refrigerator and a desk clerk under 400 pounds, how could the Chief afford to send someone to France – and, why was my association with George Ridgeway worth going to such trouble?

"Yes, I do know George Ridgeway. How did you kn...'"

Interrupting me, he said,

"I feel bad for you – I actually do. You've gotten yourself into a world of trouble, really through no fault of your own."

"I'm sorry, I really don't know what you're talking abou..."

"Well let me enlighten you. While I was in practice with Georgie, I brought in all of the business. He worked the cases up, but I brought them in the door. We were 50/50 equity partners in the firm, but what I did for the business was so much more valuable than what he did. I could have found 5,000 other people in a heartbeat who could have worked up the cases like him. Yet, I ended up having to give him half of whatever rain I made. When he was poised to screw me out of a lot – I mean a lot – of money, I had to stand up for what I believed in and take my fair share. Do you see what I'm saying, young man?"

I felt as if someone shoved a dagger into my gut. I had been had.

"You're Jim Winston."

"And you're a fucking rocket scientist. I'm glad that our esteemed bar is turning out lawyers as swift as you."

"I take it that Monsieur Le Guen isn't coming."

"Right again, kid."

"Can I also safely assume that Jean-Luc Le Guen doesn't exist?"

"God Damn! Three for fuckin' three! I knew that kikes were smart, but you are absolutely off the charts."

CHAPTER FORTY-TWO

On a very rainy summer morning, she parked her Mercedes GL 450 next to a meter on South Johnson Street in Weston. She retrieved her tan plaid Burberry umbrella from the passenger seat and exited the SUV. What dumb luck. The day that the baby was to be photographed, both she and the baby would arrive at the shoot a rain-drenched mess.

She ran around to the rear passenger door and unbuckled the baby from his seat. Despite the baby's clear displeasure at having been dressed up in the overly-cutesy Janie and Jack garb, she knew that her son would soon come to appreciate what she was about to put him through. Clad in a madras suit and a light blue necktie, little Charlie was about to become a superstar.

With her left arm holding Charlie and her right arm holding the umbrella, Julianna Brown marched towards the door. Although the place didn't much look like a photo studio, she wasn't worried. On behalf of her child, she had already accepted the modeling offer, and, moreover, the $25,000.00 check that came with it. They couldn't back out now.

However, when she got to the door, the place appeared more and more as if it were an uninhabited commercial space. Decaying supermarket circulars, that looked like they had been delivered two months prior, hung out of the mail slot that was mounted next to the front door. Although she could see through the window just to the right of the front door, no lights were in that office and a dying plant's leaves rested on the other side of the glass. This looked like an ominous situation. Nevertheless, she decided to knock.

After twenty seconds with no response, she began to conclude that no one would be answering the door. Shielded from the rain, she placed the baby on his feet and began to look around. She confirmed that the address was correct and that the meeting date and time were correct.

When she was convinced that no one would be answering the door, her attention shifted to a white envelope that was taped to the door. It read, in typed letters,

JULIANNA A. BROWN, ESQUIRE

She promptly opened the envelope. It contained a single sheet of paper with a short indecipherable type-written message that read,

JOY. SEX MAD MALEVOLENT BEATER.

CHAPTER FORTY-THREE

"You look like you've seen a ghost, *Ale-ixx*," he said, laughing aloud.

"Why did you bring me here?" I said, matter-of-factly, as Jim Winston finished the remainder of his whiskey and motioned to the server for another.

"Well, you get right to the point, don't-cha?"

"You'll have to bear with me, Mr. Winston. My firm has allowed me to take time off from work to fly to Paris and meet with someone by the name of Jean-Luc Le Guen. I have just learned not only that Jean-Luc Le Guen doesn't exist, but also that I was lured to Paris by someone who is a federal fugitive for having run off with $12 million. Oh, and corrupt Brandywine County officials delayed a TRO hearing concerning the freezing of the $12 million to aid this fugitive in escaping with the money. Did I mention that I'm sharing a table with this very person?"

"God damn! I had forgotten what an instrumental role the courthouse folks played in my being able to abscond with the dough. I really should give them more credit," he said with a completely straight face.

Winston had brought me to Paris as part of some scheme that I surmised was both illegal and involved the threat of serious injury. I was sitting across from someone who was wanted by the FBI, and had decided to show his face to me for some reason. I doubted strongly that he had chosen to come out of hiding simply to fuck with a green lawyer. Something very big was going on, and I was deeply entrenched in it.

Knowing full well that he and/or others probably had guns pointed at me at this very moment, I was, nevertheless, about finished with the chitchat and was ready to force the issue with him.

"I have to apologize for my rudeness, but in view of there being no prospect of my getting any business for my firm out of this trip, I think that I'm going to run back to the hotel, gather my belongings and head to Charles de Gaulle, to see if I can catch a flight back home today – I think that you'll agree with me that there's no sense in my staying until tomorrow. I'm going to try to salvage something out of this trip – like, for example, my dignity," I said, beginning to rise from my chair.

"I'd say that there's plenty left for you to salvage, *other than* your dignity, *Ale-ixx*," Winston responded, firmly grabbing my left forearm and forcing me back down onto the metal chair. I was surprised and impressed by this man's strength. Although Winston's limp caused him to look infirm, the man had sturdy, stone-like hands, and evidently, was able to use them.

With his coy smile gone, his face was now red and he declared, under his breath,

"You keep your ass glued to that chair until I tell you otherwise. Take a look behind me to my right."

I did as he said. About thirty feet away, eating an ice cream cone with one hand and holding a metal briefcase in the other hand was a very tall and imposing black man clad in a black suit whom I recognized. When he noticed that I saw him, he pulled either side of his jacket in a fanning motion, as he had done yesterday. And, like yesterday, his gun was right there, in plain view. When he was done with his inane show of arms, Alassane smiled at me with a mouthful of light-colored ice cream that starkly contrasted with his black face. He mordantly waved his hand to me.

"Wave 'hi' to Alassane, *Ale-ixx*. He misses you."

Given my much weaker bargaining power, I did as I was told.

"Aww, *Ale* and *Ale* – ain't that funny. Youse guys should've been a team!"

The last time that I had heard such a similar statement was under more pleasant circumstances at the Capital Grille with

Vinny and his New Jersey bimbos. I seemed to remember not having guns pointed at me on that occasion, though.

Sipping on his second whiskey, Winston continued,

"*Ale-ixx*, I nearly pissed myself when Mary Rolston told me that she fucked up and called you 'Brownstein'. Then, I nearly *shit* myself when John Bozzi told me that you were arrogant with him, and thought that he didn't know what a 'Blackberry' was! Don't you know about John Bozzi?"

"Other than what I garnered during my meeting with him the other night, not really."

"Well, let me indulge you, *Ale-ixx*. He's the damn dirtiest local police chief in the whole Philadelphia area. You don't know how lucky you are that you didn't wind up with a bullet in your head that night. Half of the drug dealing niggers that his deputies bring in wind up with instant justice – no arraignment, no trial – nothin'. I guess he figured that unlike the garden variety nigger, some people might miss you if you didn't surface for a day or so."

"I don't understand – why did Judge Rolston and Chief Bozzi give me such a hard time?"

"Because they *work* for me, you idiot! Oh, and it really doesn't help your standing with Rolston that you're involved in that idiotic business relationship with my former law partner. Let's just say that she thinks of you as being a half-notch above the kiddy porn peddler who she sentenced last week, and a half-notch below the crack dealer who she sentenced two weeks ago."

Still perplexed, I carefully inquired further.

"But why did you tell them to give me a hard time?"

"It's really quite simple, *Ale-ixx*. I needed to give you a little taste of what's gonna happen if you're not a cooperative young boy. You see what Rolston's doing to you on that one case? What kind of a career are you gonna have when *all of my judges* – and believe me, I have judges in many places other than Brandywine County – start toying with you? You'll lose every damn case! Also, how are you going to feel when you're getting pulled over every night on your way home, and they plant weapons and heroin on you each time? Again, rest assured, Bozzi's not my only police guy. I've got people all over the damn state."

This guy meant business, and I was deeply concerned. It didn't make sense yet, though. The Chief seemed to be primarily concerned about Ridgeway. *How did he fit in all of this mess?*

"*Ale-ixx*, as I was saying before, you really do have more to salvage than your dignity."

Wishing that I had a gun, or my own West African henchman, I helplessly responded,

"Like what, for example?"

Jim Winston picked up one of the envelopes, opened its metal clasps, and pulled out a quarter-inch stack of what looked to be 8x10 photographs.

He looked through the pile for about fifteen seconds, cocking his head to get a better view and laughing at times. When he was done, he said,

"Oh, I don't know *Ale-ixx*, maybe like – well – your marriage, for example," he said, flinging the stack of photos in front of me.

I leafed through the 8x10s, which contained evidence damningly suggestive that I had committed adultery. The ultra-crisp appearance of the images made it obvious that they had been taken by somebody who knew what the hell they were doing.

What I saw were a wide variety of extreme close-ups, medium close-ups, and panorama shots of my three-hour encounter with Véronique the previous evening. One series of shots depicted my initial encounter with Véronique, when we exchanged the introductory cheek kisses. Another series depicted the dinner scene – my pouring wine for Véronique; Véronique laughing at something that I said; and Véronique feeding me a piece of her steak tartare with her bare fingers. The final series was the *coup de grâce*, and consisted of 18 shots, obviously taken at very fast intervals. The series showed Véronique's hands grasping my hands as my eyes were closed. Véronique inched closer and closer to my face as the pictures progressed. Eventually, the pictures showed what appeared to be Véronique and me kissing. Despite the fact that I knew that we had never kissed, the angle from which the photos were taken did not pick up the very small gap between our mouths. Since both my eyes and Véronique's eyes were closed in this series of pictures, to any casual observer, there could be no doubt that our lips were locked.

Cumulatively, the pictures told a very easy to follow story: boy meets girl at café, boy has long, romantic meal with girl at café (as evidenced by the light sky at the beginning, the darkening sky later on, and completely dark sky later yet), boy makes out with girl at café.

Winston was damn clever. He knew that I would come home and would eventually have to tell Julie about not having brought back Jean-Luc Le Guen's business. If I failed to perform whatever he was about to blackmail me to do, he would send the pictures to Julie – probably in electronic form, to her work e-mail account. She would receive the photos during the middle of a business day, while I was elsewhere and could not prevent her from looking at them. Julie would then conclude that the whole trip was a sham from the outset and that I had gone to Paris for no reason other than to bang my non-existent mistress.

Winston wasn't as clever as I was, though. I thought to myself that although he believed that he had me by the balls, he, in fact, did not. Once the guns were not pointed at me, and I was out of harm's way, I would take a cab to the American Embassy at the Place de la Concorde. I would explain to the guard that I was in imminent danger of death and was the subject of an elaborate multi-national blackmail scheme, in which high-ranking members of the Brandywine County government and local police were involved. Once being granted entry, the federal authorities would ensure my safety, and eventually fly me back to the States on a government plane. At home, I would be provided federal security detail protecting me from the Chief, and others. A probe would be immediately instituted, and heads would begin to roll in Brandywine County.

I would explain the whole story to Julie, including how Véronique attempted unsuccessfully to seduce me and advise her that the photos would be coming. I had done nothing wrong, and my story would appear credible to Julie. In other words, despite Winston's best efforts, once I was back in the States, I would neither fear for my life, nor the demise of my marriage.

With the best acting that I could muster, so as to prevent Winston from catching on that I had an exit strategy, I said,

"Just tell me what you want me to do – I'll do anything – just don't send those pictures to my wife – please!"

"I thought you might say that, *Ale-ixx*. There actually is a favor that you could do for me."

"Anything! I'll do anything!"

I wasn't going to win an Academy Award, but I felt that I definitely had Winston convinced.

"*Ale-ixx*, you may think that I'm the bad guy in this whole mess, but I'm about to enlighten you. You see, I'm only blackmailing you because Georgie Ridgeway is blackmailing me. We worked together for too many years. He knew everything about me, and I knew everything about him.

"I initially fled to Sénégal because during a hunting trip that I had taken several years prior, I became close with one of the tribal bigwigs over there. In any case, I threw his tribe about fifty grand, and that bought me a lifetime of protection and borderline idol status. I could have stayed there my whole life and no one would have found me. Only problem was, there were insects and vermin everywhere, it was 140 degrees morning, noon and night, and I could only eat antelope balls so many times.

"I needed to get somewhere that was not Third World, but where I could use my money to avoid detection. So, I made my way up to Tangier, Morocco with a forged passport and I hung out there for a little while. It was better than Sénégal, but it sure as hell was no First World. The people smelled like shit and that damn Arabic writing scared the shit out of me. I constantly felt like Osama was going to sneak up and roger me.

"Spain was 25 miles across the Strait of Gibraltar. I was so close to being back in civilization that it hurt. To make a long story short, I eventually paid an arm and a leg for some Spaniard to smuggle me in on a boat. I was back from the dead, in a country that had clean running water and where only half the people smelled like shit. I was also in a country that had very good diplomatic relations with the United States.

"Although I never sensed that anyone was on to me, I had trouble sleeping at night, for fear that the next day could be the end for me. I thought that I had covered my tracks pretty well on my various movements, but I couldn't be certain. So, I came up with a plan to set my mind at ease. I paid some sophisticated Spanish thugs to off some poor asshole who was about my age and about my build. After they killed him, they ripped his eyeballs out and beat his ass so badly that neither the coroner nor anyone else was able to identify the body. To be sure, they pulled his friggin' teeth out of his head, so that dental records couldn't be referenced. Oh yeah, these spicks were good. Guess what the poor guy was carrying in his pocket when he was found, though?"

"His passport?" I said, very troubled that he had given me this information, since his doing so likely meant that he had designs on eliminating me.

"Wrong. *My* passport!"

"Wow."

"You bet your ass, 'Wow!'. The spicks and the American authorities took it, hook, line and sinker. I knew how law enforcement officers – especially the feds – thought. A closed case for them is a good case. I was no longer a fugitive – I was dead.

"So, seven years after disappearing with $12 million, I was finally able to live the high life. I traveled all over Europe and lived like royalty. I finally settled in Paris when I met Véronique.

"By the way, kid, you didn't really think that she liked you, did you?"

"Mr. Winston, I'm a married..."

"Please, *Ale-ixx*, what's with the formal nomenclature? I'd say we know each other well enough to call each other my our first names, no?"

"Jim, I'm a..."

"You know what, *Ale-ixx*? Normally I'd say that you could call me 'Jim', but today, I feel like you should call me 'James'. You'll understand why, later. At least I think that you'll understand why later – you're a pretty sharp guy."

"O.K., James. I'm a married man, so the issue of Véronique liking me or not never entered my head."

"Oh, really? Did it enter your head when she was feeding you with her bare hand? Did it enter your head when she was about to play tonsil hockey with you? My friend, you are either a liar or a homosexual.

"Taking that issue aside, you missed the boat because her orders were to fuck your brains out while we filmed it with a hidden camera in a room in the Hôtel de Crillon, where she was gonna take you."

He continued, gesturing at one of the photos that appeared to depict a kiss,

"Tell you what, though, I think that these little snapshots serve the same purpose as if I had gotten you in a motion picture fucking her doggy style. I was married once – I know how women think. A kiss or a fuck – it's all of the same value when it comes to adultery."

Still playing along, I said,

"James, I think that I have to concur with you there. Now, if you don't mind my asking, what is it that I can do? Presumably, if I do something for you, you will forbear from sending these photos to my wife or anyone else, and guarantee my safety. Is that a safe assumption?"

"You know what counsel? For a young man, you sure as hell have a firm grasp of the concept of blackmail," he said, while emptying the remainder of his third whiskey down his gullet.

"O.K. Just let me know what I need to do."

"Let's not get ahead of ourselves. Let me finish. As I was saying, Georgie Ridgeway knew me too well to believe that I would put myself in a situation where I would get beaten up by thugs. While federal police on two continents and the whole world were fooled, Ridgeway probably knew that the whole passport in the pocket bit was contrived. So, he apparently never was willing to accept my being dead."

I momentarily forgot that I was in the process of being blackmailed, and was so captivated by this gripping story that I enthusiastically demanded,

"So, what happened next?!"

"So, I got dumb and undisciplined next. I'm an old fart and I don't know how this e-mail shit works. I thought that it was safer than phoning someone. Apparently, Georgie paid someone to break into Larry Sebring's e-mail. He found e-mails from me, and with those e-mails, he was somehow able to figure out where the e-mails came from. Next thing I know, George calls me on the phone."

Dumbfounded, I responded,

"*Judge* Lawrence Sebring from Brandywine County?"

"He's the only Larry Sebring I know. Why, did you have a case before him? I asked him about you, but he had never heard of you."

"No, I've never had a case before him. Are you telling me that there were *multiple* judges on the bench who knew that you were alive and kicking overseas?"

"No, *Ale-ixx*, I'm telling you that there *are* multiple judges – five to be exact – who know where the hell I am. Why is this surprising to you? Who do you think pays the most money for their election campaigns. It's quite simple, *Ale-ixx*, I pay, they make sure that no one starts reviving efforts to locate me."

"And that was working fine until Ridgeway learned of your whereabouts. Someone out of your inner circle now knows that you're alive."

"Again, *Ale-ixx*, your quick intellect is damn close to knocking me off of this chair."

"Why didn't Ridgeway just call the feds once he found out where you were? Why did he call you and give you a chance to scatter?"

"Because, *Ale-ixx*, he wants my money more than he wants me captured."

"Well, how do I fit into all of this?"

"My friend, you were in the wrong fuckin' place at the wrong fuckin' time. Georgie apparently made your acquaintance through a mutual business associate. Is that right?"

"It is."

"Well, being that he doesn't practice law anymore and seldom crawls out of his hole, let's just say that he doesn't often have the occasion to meet sweet and innocent looking young men."

I prayed that Winston was not about to tell me that part of this blackmail entailed my dressing up like Judy Garland.

"Come again?"

"He thinks that you're gonna smuggle millions of my dollars into the country and give it to him. Since you look innocent and can prove that you were in France for a routine business trip, he thinks that you will avoid scrutiny at the customs checkpoint, and that you won't get searched."

"Why didn't he just come to France and get the money from you?"

"For God sakes, *Ale-ixx*, use your head! For starters, because he knows that I would kill him, and I know that he would kill me. He would never accept any intermediary that I would send. Ordinarily, I wouldn't have agreed to his sending an intermediary of his choosing, but Rolston, Bozzi and others confirmed that you really were the boy scout that he said you were. That's why you're the perfect man for the job."

"Can I safely assume that I won't be carrying millions of your dollars back with me to Philadelphia?"

"You can."

"Can I also safely assume that you would like for me to eliminate Mr. Ridgeway – the only person out of your control who knows of you whereabouts?"

"You're still on a hot streak, *Ale-ixx*."

I was a Jewish kid from the suburbs. I had never murdered an animal, let alone a human being. While I didn't particularly care for George Ridgeway, a few photos that could easily be explained away were not going to force me to kill him. I would play along until I satisfied him that I was on board and then I would head to the embassy.

"James, how, exactly, do you propose that I carry out this task? Lets just say that I don't have much background in this field."

"*Ale-ixx*, I've thought of that. And, I've also thought of the fact that if you get caught, there's a decent chance of me getting caught

– with the possibility of you blabbin' and all. So, rest assured that it's in my interest for you to come out of this unscathed. If you don't fuck up this fool-proof plan, everything will turn out just fine. You'll be back at work, bringin' home the bacon to your wife and kid, and I'll be recommencing my retirement.

"John Bozzi is gonna handle everything. He'll give you your firearm and will assist you with the disposal of the body."

Firearm? Disposal of the body?!

"Looks like your association with the Lubranos is gonna work to my benefit, too."

"James, I implore you!" I cried, "Please do not involve the Lubranos. They are the only shot I have at redeeming myself to the firm after I come back from France without any business."

"Oh, don't be so dramatic, Sally!" he exclaimed, while looking at me with disgust. "It seems that the Lubranos are currently in the process of building some huge condo, just south of the Walt Whitman Bridge in Philly."

Good God. He was going to have me bury Ridgeway in the foundation – Jimmy Hoffa-style.

"Counsel, you look like you're gonna keel over any instant!" he said, chuckling and coughing out cigarette smoke at the same time.

Without my responding, he continued,

"Vinny Lubrano is gonna be looking for some assistance when you get back to Philly – and I have a feeling that you're gonna be able to help him with his predicament."

Not wanting to hear the remaining details, I nevertheless said,

"Continue."

"Don't mind if I do. You see, *Ale-ixx*, a couple of my people have been telling me that that condo is being built approximately five feet away from where the approved architectural plans had called for it to be built. You and I both know that them civic associations and politicians ain't gonna stand for it when that building is found to be set back five feet closer to the road than it was supposed to be. This is a problem, you see, because they're up to the 12th floor of the building, and, well, you're the concrete lawyer, you see where I'm going with this, don't you, son?"

I saw exactly where this demonic criminal was "going with this." He was going to get his crew of local government cronies to slap a stop work order on the job, for some bullshit construction defect that didn't exist. If the tower was deemed to have been constructed five feet off from the approved plans, such a scenario would have catastrophic ramifications. First, the sheer cost of the remediation, itself, if even possible without scrapping the entire building, would be in the millions. Second, Lubrano would be sued by the general contractor and its subcontractors for breach of contract, and with it, millions of dollars in damages, and a loss of its good name in the Philadelphia construction industry.

In fact, the scenario that Winston was describing was nearly incomprehensible. Had the footprint of building been constructed in a manner that did not conform to the architectural plans, this mistake would have been detected at an early stage of construction, which, in any circumstance, would have occurred before a single floor, let alone 12 floors, could have been fully poured.

It didn't matter, though. Winston was beyond connected in his world, and could dictate whatever course of events he so desired there. How Vinny was going to end up owing me a favor was escaping me, though.

"Let me guess, James. You're going to have a stop work order slapped on the entrance to the construction site."

"I'm gonna shut the motherfucker down, *Ale-ixx*," he said, taking another swig of the good stuff.

"Why, may I ask, are the Lubranos going to owe me a favor?"

"It's really quite elementary, *Ale-ixx*. You're going to tell them that if they assist you with the task, the stop work order will be removed instantaneously. I'm guessing that they won't be putting up too much of a fight. *Hmmm...lose $20 million and not hide body of dead asshole or keep $20 million and make a dead asshole a giant brick?* I'd say it'll be an easy choice."

The son of a bitch was trying to strong arm me into extorting my own client. The not-fully-incriminating photos of me with Véronique from the previous evening were certainly not enough to force me to break the law, shake down a client and guarantee myself that my law license would be taken away if I were caught. I silently wondered how such an evil genius couldn't plainly see that I would sooner have the photos exposed than go through with his plan. Nevertheless, I had to keep leading on that I was captive to him.

"Respectfully, they don't operate like that, James. The Lubranos know plenty of *goombas* and politicos in South Philly and elsewhere who will not only kick my ass, but may come after the Chief, too, if they believe that the stop work order is bogus. You don't know how these Italians operate, James."

He unexpectedly slapped my left cheek with his right hand and grabbed either side of my mouth with his left hand and barked at me, "who the hell do you think taught Mary Rolston that someone is disrespecting you when they begin a sentence with 'Respectfully'?"

I stared at Jim Winston's burning cigarette resting in a plastic ashtray that carried a Campari advertisement. The shock from his slap left me breathless and unable to shift my gaze.

"I can own the Lubranos as much as I own John Bozzi, Mary Rolston and you! Wake up and smell the coffee, *Ale-ixx*, and get the hell over yourself. Money talks and bullshit walks!"

"So that's why Rolston and Bozzi gave me such a hard time – because you told them to. Can I ask why you told them to do so?"

"Let me ask you this, *Ale-ixx*: do you have any doubt that I have the judiciary and the cops by the balls?"

I had no such doubt.

"No."

"As you sit here today, counsel, are you therefore inclined to fuck with me, or are you therefore inclined to carry out the tasks that I have bestowed upon you, so that you can keep your wife, kid and income?"

Actually, I planned to get the hell over to the American Embassy as fast as I could, so that I could ensure that I was safe and that this asshole was locked up.

"I am not inclined to fuck with you, James."

"And why is that, counsel?"

Lawyers sounded like such assholes when they conducted examination outside of the courtroom.

"Because you have sufficiently proven to me, in my recent encounters with Rolston and Bozzi, that you have the system by the balls. If I fuck with you, they will rain hell on my career and personal life."

Actually, I was going to rain hell on Rolston and Bozzi. When I got done with them, they would be under indictment and I would be on all of the national news broadcasts and have a tell-all book deal.

"*Ale-ixx*, my only regret is that we didn't meet earlier. You're a brilliant young lawyer. You would have liked working for me."

"Thank you, James, I appreciate your saying so."

"We're about done here, but before we go, I want to leave you with two very funny thoughts.

"First," he began, laughing uncontrollably with whiskey dripping from the left side of his mouth, through some white stubble and onto the table, "you never asked me how Georgie thinks that you're going to bring the money to him!"

I had given it some thought until it became apparent that Ridgeway was to receive nothing out of this deal. In any event, it seemed plausible that Ridgeway would insist upon high denomination bearer bonds that would take up little space and were not traceable.

"Not sure. Bearer bonds?"

"What the hell is a bearer bond? Hell no! He thinks that you're gonna smuggle a 100 carat flawless diamond through customs!"

I didn't know how big a 100 carat diamond was. I seemed to remember Julie's engagement ring being just over two carats, though.

"I take it that I'm not going to be smuggling a 100 carat diamond through customs?"

"Correct. You will be smuggling a diamond just over 45 carats through customs."

Once again, I was confused. He paused, laughing forebodingly, while sipping some more of his drink, and then continued,

"Georgie's always been a dumbass, but the diamond idea was actually a wily concept. What a great way to smuggle dough across borders – it's not like cash, where if the fucknuts decide to check your bags, you're busted. You can slip this little rock between your toes and no one will have a fucking clue."

"So, I *am* going to give the diamond to Ridgeway?"

"No, you damn nitwit!" he said, pounding the table, once again laughing. He looked both ways and said smilingly, at a whisper, "You're going to give the stone to John Bozzi. He's gonna keep some of the dough and dole out the rest to my other people. Protection ain't free, *Alex-ixx* – even if you're as well-respected as yours truly."

After he was done wiping away the tears occasioned by his hysterical laughter, Winston raised himself from the seat. Alassane quickly crossed the street and assisted his gimpy-legged boss.

"Give me the stone, Alassane," Winston ordered.

Without wasting any time, Alassane cleared away the ashtray and drink glasses and placed his metal briefcase on the café table. He turned the dual combination locks and snapped open the lid. From what little I was able to see of the inside of the briefcase, it appeared to be a virtual treasure trove for an on-the-lam fugitive. Two handguns – one black and one silver – were inside, next to what appeared to be decent sized stacks of U.S. Dollars, Euros and Swiss Francs. Alassane retrieved a key from his pocket and unlocked a separate compartment within the briefcase.

From the compartment, Alassane pulled out a small purple velvet sack.

"Hand it to him," Winston directed.

As Alassane extended his enormous hand in my direction, I cupped my palms to receive the diamond. Once the velvet sack made a thud in my palms and was in my possession, Winston snapped,

"Go ahead, kid, take a look-see."

I loosened the strings at the top of the sack and emptied the enormous stone into my hand. Although I wasn't a diamond aficionado, I had seen quite a few of the stones over the years.

What I was holding in my hand was, by far, the largest that I had ever seen in my life.

"That there is a D-colored, near flawless 45-carat job – street value four mil – U.S."

Uneasy and rattled that I would be carrying something on my person that could have bought a twenty-room mansion in the poshest of the Philadelphia suburbs, I thought that I should ask a few questions about how the stone should be handled.

"But...uh...but...what...should...," I began

"Uh...duh...huh...but...You sound like a damn LSD burnout. Is that how you speak in court? No wonder Mary Rolston hates your ass. Listen to me. Alassane and I – we gotta get going. Here's what you're gonna do. You're gonna put the rock between your toes before your plane lands in Philly tomorrow. You're gonna mosey through customs and nobody is going to say a damn word to you – trust me on this one. When you get home, you'll be contacted by John Bozzi. He's gonna tell you what to do from there. *Tu comprends?*"

"Yes, I understand."

As Winston and his African sidekick started to walk away, Winston, visibly intoxicated said, incoherently,

"*Ale-ixx*, I'm so upset that we must part ways! We barely even got to talk. You didn't even ask me what I like to do for fun."

After an awkward moment of silence during which Winston's happy drunkard smile morphed into a morosely neutral expression, I asked,

"James, what is it that you like to do for fun?"

"I'm glad that you asked, *Ale-ixx*," he responded sarcastically, "I think that you should know that I like to create puzzles and watch people solve those puzzles. That's what I really like to do."

Good to know, you psychotic drunken excuse for a human life.

As he took one more step away from the table, with Alassane keeping him upright, he exclaimed,

"Whoa! I almost forgot! You never asked me what the *second* funny thought was."

Before I had a chance to respond, he slapped the second of the two yellow envelopes on the table in front of me and said,

"*That's* my second funny thought. Here's lookin' at you, kiddo! There will be no backing out now."

His ominous tone gave me pause that my exit strategy might have just been rendered inoperable.

I pulled open the envelope and saw my life flash before my eyes. The contents of the envelope, which I instantaneously identified and fully comprehended, captivated me so much that I did not watch Jim Winston and Alassane turn their backs to me and walk away, down Rue Mouffetard.

The envelope contained the transcript of a recent telephone conversation in which I had engaged, as well as five 8x10 photographs. It read:

```
"Jules, I'm really trying to get
out of here as soon as possible.
Can we discuss this when I get
home?"
"Uh - I'm sorry, I must've called
the wrong number. I was lookin' for
Lawyer Alexander Brown."
 "I'm sorry, sir, I thought that
you were someone else. This is
Alexander Brown. How can I help
you?"
"My name is Leon Richardson. I
need representation. I was walking
through an intersection in Weston
a few months ago and some guy in a
Corvette ran a red light and hit
me. I fractured my skull and these
doctors say that I've got something
called neurocognitive impairment.
I don't know what the hell that
is, but all I know is that I spent
three weeks in the hospital, and
```

now I can't remember what I did five
minutes ago."

"I'm terribly sorry to hear that,
sir. I'd like to learn more about
this. Can I ask you first, though,
how were you referred to me?"

"Um, I'm not sure. I do janitorial
work at various businesses in
Brandywine County and I heard
your name from someone - I can't
remember who, though. Does it
matter? Can you still represent me
if I can't remember?"

"No, no, it doesn't matter at
all. Sorry. It's really not a big
deal - I was just curious. O.K., I
guess I'll have a few preliminary
questions for you. Do you know if
there was a police report generated
from the accident? Were you taken
to the emergency room after the
accident? Do you happen to know
if the person who hit you had
insurance?"

"Uh, yes, yes and yes. Actually,
I've got the case settled already,
but the insurance company suggested
that I hire myself a lawyer to look
over that paper thing-a-ma-jig, I
forget what it's called…"

"A Release?"

"Yeah, that's it, a Release."

"Are you telling me that you
already negotiated the settlement
with the insurance company and
you just want me to look over
the Release, to make sure that

everything is O.K.?"
"That's exactly what I'm telling
you. I'll pay you and all - I just
don't think that I want to pay you
a full 33 1/3% -- that's what I
paid my lawyer in a slip and fall
case I had a few years ago. We're
talking about a lot of money --
$200,000.00, so you guys will get
a nice cut, even if you lower your
percentage, you see what I mean?"
"Sir, did you say $200,000.00?"
"Yeah, that's what I said. Would
your firm consider taking 10% for
looking at the Release and dealing
with the insurance company the rest
of the way?"
"Uh, sir, I need to tell you that I
am just an Associate - an employee
- at this firm. I would need to run
it by my bosses."
"I ain't waitin' - I want to get
paid."
"Mr. Richardson, regardless of
what we decide to do, I'm not sure
that I could get you paid all that
quickly. They'll need to receive
the Release, cut the check, send
the check to me - it's a whole
long, drawn out process."
"Bullshit! That adjuster, or
whatever you call him at the
insurance company, he got the check
all ready to go. I just need to
sign the Release. Listen, I don't
have time to fuck around, so I'm
'aw make it worth your while. You

look at the Release yourself,
without your firm's involvement, and
I'll get you a 10 G kickback even
before I get mine. Shit - I'll meet
you tomorrow morning and give you
the cash."
"Sir, that arrangement constitutes
an unlawful diversion of funds
from my firm, is unethical and
would cause me to lose my job and
my license to practice law, if
detected."
"And who gonna find out? You mean
tell me you couldn't use an extra
10 G's?"
"Anyone could use $10,000.00, sir,
it's just that…"
"10G's. Yes or no. I'm callin'
someone else if you can't do it."
"I'd love to, but I…"
"10G's - now or never. You in or
out?"
"I'm in."

The photographs that accompanied the transcript showed me in the men's room of a fast food restaurant with Leon Richardson, as I had been on the morning that I left for Paris. The sequence showed Mr. Richardson opening a gym bag, presenting a few stacks of one hundred dollar bills to me, my examining the bills, then placing them in my briefcase, patting him on the back and then exiting.

Regrettably, unlike the pictures of me with Véronique, these pictures showed me engaging in an unethical and illicit transaction that had actually transpired. The photos were neither doctored nor taken at crafty angle so that they depicted something that hadn't actually taken place. Against my better judgment, I had taken the money and was now to be held accountable.

My plan of escaping to the embassy and having law enforcement come to the rescue was no longer an option. Appeasing Winston was now seemingly the only option that I possessed to secure an assurance that my secret would not come to light.

With Winston and Alassane gone for at least five minutes, my hands were still numb with pins and needles. Sweat was freely flowing down my forehead and had soaked through my shirt. I kept waiting to wake up from this dreadful nightmare, however, such relief was not going to occur. I was a captured criminal whose only chance at keeping his professional license, occupation, freedom from prison and family rested in the unenviable task of murdering another human being.

As I sat at the table, contemplating how I could extract myself from this disaster, my mobile phone rang. I answered the call.

"You're never going to believe this shit – please don't say 'I told ya' so' – I'm totally not in the mood for that..."

"Julie?"

"Yeah, it's me. You sound like shit. Are you sick?"

"No, just a little jet lag, still. What's the problem."

"The problem is that no one showed up for Charlie's photo shoot. The whole thing was probably a scam like you said."

Big surprise. Apparently, when it rains, it really does pour.

"Are you sure that you went to the right address?"

"Yeah, I used my GPS and everything. Plus, there was some cryptic letter waiting for me there – it was probably written by some pervert-psycho."

More layers of Winston's plan were being revealed, as it became apparent to me that he had involved Julie, as well. This "cryptic letter" was troubling to me.

"Julie, what did this letter say – read it to me verbatim – now!!!" I shouted.

"Alex, chill out! It means nothing. The whole thing was probably a prank."

"It is not a prank – they paid us $25,000.00 for God sake! Just read me the letter."

"How do you know that it's not a prank?"

"I just know. Now read the letter to me."

"It's not even a letter – it's a phrase that doesn't make any sense. It says, 'Joy' then there's a period. Then it says, 'Sex Mad Malevolent Beater.'"

I paused for a moment, trying to figure out what the passage meant and who had sent it. I pulled a legal pad from my briefcase and wrote the message down word for word, as she had spoken it to me. I realized that I needed to get off of the phone with Julie and onto the internet as soon as possible.

"Jules, I have to run back into my meeting. Can I call you later?"

"Do you have any idea what 'Joy Sex Mad Malevolent Beater' means?"

"Err...no, not really...no."

"'No' or 'not really'"

"No, Julie. No." I responded in a nervously perturbed tenor.

"Are you sure you're O.K., Alex?"

"Julie, I'm really in the middle of something and I have to go. Love you. Bye."

CHAPTER FORTY-FOUR

After hanging up with Julie, I placed both envelopes as well as the legal pad containing the scribbled message in my briefcase. I made sure that the diamond's sack was securely tied up and I put it in my right side pants pocket.

I needed to get to the closest internet café immediately, so that I could gain an edge – any edge – on Winston.

This son of a bitch was going to get his rocks off, thinking that I would toil night and day to figure out the substance of his parting hidden message. Although I could picture him deriving great "joy" out of "malevolently beating" someone in a "sex-mad" tirade, I had a hard time believing that the message given to Julie was, on its face, what he had intended to convey to me.

It was plainly apparent that the photo shoot ruse was selected as a means by which to ensure that I would not bring Julie with me to Paris and, therefore, Véronique's portion of the blackmail scheme could be carried out. After all, had Julie come with me to Paris, I wouldn't exactly have been in a situation where Véronique and I would be sitting alone at a café table. It seemed, however, that Winston was going to use Julie to do more than ensure that I be alone with Véronique long enough for a saucy photo-op.

You didn't even ask me what I like to do for fun...I think that you should know that I like to create puzzles and watch people solve those puzzles. That's what I really like to do.

The words that he spoke immediately prior to leaving resounded in my head. The message, "Joy. Sex-Mad Malevolent Beater" had to be some sort of anagram or puzzle. Since I had never even tried to solve a crossword puzzle in my entire life and was not particularly strong in the field of word games, I didn't like my chances of being able to solve the puzzle manually. So I wasn't even going to try.

I dashed across Rue Ortolan and quickly hung a right on Rue Gracieuse. I made my way into Place Monge, a vibrant, yet petite public square, by Parisian standards. I entered the square from its northwest corner. When I had lived in Paris, I frequented an internet café in the southeast corner, that bounded Rue Monge. I was banking on the internet café not having closed during the more than a decade period since I had lived in Paris. My view of that area was obscured by the stalls of merchants and their many patrons. With sweat saturating my hair, as I weaved in and out of elderly folks pulling their grocery carts, I caught several unwelcome looks.

When I arrived at the far end of the square, I could see that the Café Internet Place Monge was not only still operational, but was bustling. Still running at full stride, with the internet café not more than 20 feet away, I suddenly collided with something or someone very big and very solid.

My head hurt very badly and my mouth was pressed up against dark gray cobblestone. I looked upward and saw a very tall man in an official looking uniform, staring at me disapprovingly. An inquisitive crowd had gathered around the area in which I had collided with André the Giant. I felt my upper left thigh to make sure that the diamond was still in my pants pocket. Thankfully, it was.

After wiping away the blood that was flowing from above my left eye, I saw that André was unmistakably a member of the *Police Nationale*. His cylindrical gold-rimmed flat-topped hat made him look like the French Nazi-collaborator, Marshal Pétain. It was always a mystery to me why the French police continued the tradition of dressing like their collaborating predecessors. Lying on the ground, having collided with an armed national policeman, I figured that now was not the time that I might obtain an answer to that question.

"Pourquoi vous vous dépêchez? Il faut vous ralentir!" André the Giant exclaimed, asking me why I was speeding around and *telling* me that I needed to slow down.

"Pardon, je n'ai pas compris," I responded, playing the dumb American card, hoping to God that this was just a chance encounter and that I was not put on my ass as part of Winston's scheme.

"You were running too fast, why do you do zeese? Zare are old people shopping eehr. Zeeze is not Times Square, Monsieur."

He extended his Billy club in my direction, presumably to assist me back to my feet and not to beat me senseless. Considering that the only way a Frenchman could beat an American in combat was if the American was a business suit clad civilian who had just gone ass over tea kettle, I didn't fully rule out the possibility of him taking advantage of me in such a compromised position.

I grabbed the Billy club and he pulled me to my feet. As I rose, it became apparent that the back of my Purple Label suit jacket was shredded. What the hell else was going to go wrong for me on this day?

"Why aahr you een such a urry?"

Brushing dirt off of my suit pants that, apparently had a gaping hole running down the right leg, I responded,

"I'm not...I wasn't. I'm sorry – I just wasn't paying attention."

"Zeese eeze quite clear. Where are you going, Monsieur?"

"Uhh, just to the internet café over there," I said, motioning to the establishment just over his shoulder.

"What eeze so important zare?"

"No one...nothing, I mean. I'm traveling for business and I just need to check my e-mail."

"Well, why don't you do me and all of Paris a favor," he said, gesturing across the open air market with his Billy club, "when you aahr done checking your e-mail, try yourself walking in zee crowd eenstead of running sroo zee crowd, O.K.?"

"O.K., I'm sorry."

As he walked away, I momentarily considered desperately running back to him and explaining the whole blackmail situation, so that he could find and arrest Winston while he was still in close proximity. However, when I considered that this officer did not seem as if he would be inclined to help me in any way, and that I would be risking Winston leaking the layers of incriminating information, I thought better of the idea. While I could not be certain that Winston would even hold up his end of the bargain, the consequences of my defying him were too grave to dismiss.

I then turned around and walked in the direction of the Café Internet Place Monge. The place was just as I had remembered it: bespectacled, unbathed, leftist looking university students everywhere, drinking coffee and surfing the web. Except now, years after I patronized the joint, most of the customers were using the internet through their laptops on the café's Wi-Fi system, rather than using one of the fifteen, or so, PCs available.

At the front desk, I purchased a coffee from a petite young lady clad in a vintage KISS tee-shirt, sporting a purple-highlighted bob cut, thick brown circular framed glasses and a septum ring. Gene Simmons would have run away in fear of this lass. Although the urge almost overtook me to pull the girl around the café by the septum ring, I was thankfully able to resist. Doing so might have prompted my French law enforcement friend to be dispatched to deal with me again.

I sat down at the PC that was assigned to me, which was up against the storefront glass, facing Place Monge. Once I was able to acclimate myself to the French keyboard, whose key placement varied from that of English language keyboards, I immediately went to a search engine and typed in,

```
anagram solver
```

I clicked the hyperlink of the first responsive website that appeared. The page contained a box that allowed one to type in a word or phrase and the program would process a corresponding anagram. I quickly typed in,

```
Joy. Sex-Mad Malevolent Beater.
```

I hit "Enter."

The anagram that it provided to me seemed innocuous and even more nonsensical than "Joy. Sex-Mad Malevolent Beater." It read:

```
Joy. Vexed-lamentable maestro.
```

Was Winston sarcastically expressing shame at himself for being a "lamentable maestro" of this evil plan? If so, I was unmoved.

A button on the screen next to the computer-produced result read,

```
Formulate Another Anagram Out of Previous
                 Phrase
```

Figuring that it was worth a shot and wasn't costing me anything extra, I clicked.

The result was even more illogical. It read:

```
A Baa Ed Overjoys Elm Melt Next
```

"Baa?" Was there going to be a sheep involved in this crazy scheme? I certainly hoped not, but was not putting it past James Winston.

I would try once more. I was wasting precious time in this café – time that could have been used to walk around Paris until I formulated a brilliant plan of how to remove myself from this disagreeable situation.

I clicked my mouse again.

The computer generated response was not cryptic this time. It was neither difficult to understand grammatically, nor was it difficult to understand what Winston was attempting to convey to me via a letter delivered to my wife 4,000 miles away in the Philadelphia suburbs.

With my heart pounding through my soiled custom-made dress shirt, I rested my face in my hands and cried uncontrollably. Once again, I was probably making a spectacle of myself as onlookers admired me and the message on my screen that read,

```
Alex, don't betray me. Love, James.
```

CHAPTER FORTY-FIVE

Normally I'd say that you could call me "Jim", but today, I feel like you should call me "James". You'll understand why later.

Winston's words from an hour before resounded in my head.

It began to rain heavily. One of the merchants outside of the internet café sold umbrellas. With my suit and my life both destroyed beyond the point of repair, I decided to let mother nature piss all over me, as fate already had. Directly beneath Place Monge was a stop on the Metro's 7 line that would have taken me to within a few hundred feet of the hotel, without the necessity of making a connection. At this traumatic juncture in my life, I didn't need a fresh set of clothes and a shower. I needed to take a long walk in the rain, smoke a lot of cigarettes and think of what my next move should be.

I followed Rue Monge northward until it ended at Boulevard Saint-Germain. I then followed Rue de Bièvre down to the Seine.

On a normal summer day such as this, the quays along the Seine would be bustling with tourists and locals alike, examining the goods being sold by the ubiquitous *bouquinistes*. In this driving rain, however, every single dark green *bouquiniste* stall was padlocked shut. From my vantage point, which was greatly obscured due to the monsoon-like conditions, I detected not a single other pedestrian on the street. Many cars were even pulled over to the side of the street due to the limited visibility and flooding conditions on the roadways. I trudged forward, though, desperate for the magic solution to pop into my head while I battled this adversity. The Ferragamo shoes that I had bought especially for this trip were virtual scuba flippers at this point and were about as useful as sunscreen would have been on a day such as this.

As the rain was falling at a 45 degree angle towards my back, I was somehow able to create a tent over my head with my ragged suitjacket, which allowed me to consistently keep a cigarette lit.

Twenty-five minutes into my walk, I was passing the western point of the Île de la Cité and I still had not conjured up the magic resolution to my unfortunate situation. The choices were still simple and clear cut: risk being prosecuted for murder by killing Ridgeway and hoping that Winston kept his end of the bargain by not ratting me out; or, betray Winston by immediately alerting the authorities of his whereabouts and be subject to losing my job, my license to practice law, my wife and my child. I temporarily favored the second option until I reminded myself that I was professionally qualified to do nothing other than practice law. If I chose the second option, my house would be foreclosed upon and I would be relegated to a life as an unskilled laborer, making a miniscule fraction of what I would have otherwise made as an attorney.

With no resolution in sight, and the sharply ironic confluence of so many bad events, I decided that I no longer needed my suitjacket. I stopped walking and faced the river. I wrung out the water, which could have easily filled a dinner goblet, and rolled the Purple Label jacket into a ball. I held the orb of fabric with both hands at my chest, stepped back with my left foot while simultaneously bringing the jacketball over my head, and contoured by body to the right, kicked my left foot as high as Juan Marichal would have done in a similar situation, and fired it into the Seine.

Seeing the jacket rapidly flowing westbound towards the English Channel was enormously therapeutic for me.

With the rain still pouring down at a frenetic pace, I looked up to the heavens and began to laugh uncontrollably. My predicament was almost too humorously outlandish to be true.

I continued walking westbound. As I passed the Pont du Carrousel and was directly across from the Louvre, I thought of how, just a half-day earlier, I stood beneath the Arc de Triomphe du Carrousel, aligned in the middle of the *axe historique*. I remembered that as I had stood there just a short time prior, I fooled myself into believing that my standing directly on the *axe historique* was somehow a metaphor for the state of my life at that instant. A half-day before, I convinced myself I had been dealt an extraordinarily favorable hand and that all of the stars were aligned for me as Paris' *axe historique* monuments were. I was on the verge of turning a corner in my professional career that would have rendered me a very wealthy and important person at a relatively young age.

When I gazed across the river at the Arc de Triomphe du Carrousel this time, a markedly different emotion overcame me. Quite contrary to the previous evening, I felt most unfortunate at this juncture. I considered the reality that irrespective of which of the malevolent options I chose, I would most assuredly never, in this lifetime, achieve the level of wealth and importance that I believed, just hours before, to be looming.

When I reached the Quai d'Orsay, the rain most dramatically, and without warning, stopped. Brightness overtook the sky. I gazed at Les Invalides with its majestic golden dome. A brilliant rainbow arched over the remarkable structure.

On any other day, I might have felt inspired or even fortunate to have been in such a setting as a rainbow exhibited itself. To my great dissatisfaction, however, my emotions reacted in a most opposite manner upon the rain's disappearance.

Instead of feeling gleeful, I immediately encountered a depressed emotion, much like a hangover. While the rain was falling, I had begun to feel as if I had a companion in my melancholy. The sun was now shining and frolicking types began to reveal themselves. Seeing these very happy people made me a very sad person.

I walked away from Les Invalides onto the Pont Alexandre III, the most ornate and beautiful of any bridge traversing the Seine in Paris. I stared up at the imposing golden gilded winged horse sculptures. The Art Nouveau lamps surrounded by cherubs on the side of the bridge had always been a picture of stylistic perfection to me. On this day, however, they failed to brighten my spirits.

At the exact midpoint of the bridge, I stood on the eastern end, just over the famous nymphs statue. I unbuttoned the top button of my dress shirt, loosened my tie and leaned forward, resting my forearms on the side. As I lit another Gitane, I found it astonishing that my cigarettes, throughout my inundated trek, somehow managed to remain safe. I searched for a poetically symbolic message in this virtual miracle, but was not feeling particularly inspired and was unable to do so.

One lamp down from where I was leaning, I noticed a very handsome married Parisian couple in their mid-30s. I knew that they were married because they wore matching plain gold wedding bands on their left ring fingers. The man stood at about 5'11", had wavy brown hair, and strong, healthy looking face. The woman was about four inches shorter than him in flat shoes. She had straight natural blond hair that was pulled back in a pony tail and plump, pink, smiling lips. A picnic basket rested at their feet. They were probably on their way to enjoying a romantic lunch of fresh meats, cheeses and wine on the Champ de Mars. Something told me that the wet ground was not going to ruin their plans.

I got the feeling that the couple had been happily married for around five or so years. In an embrace, they spoke lovingly and stared in each other's eyes. They began to kiss passionately under the newly luminous Parisian sky. Their humble clothing told me that they were likely intellectuals and didn't care much for material possessions.

On this beautiful day, in this most wonderful city in the world, material possessions didn't count for much, though. Paris was theirs and they were, in my judgment, two of the happiest and most fortunate individuals in the world.

I would never again know happiness like these two people were experiencing at this moment.

Material greed had gotten the better of me and I was going to pay dearly for it.

CHAPTER FORTY-SIX

"Monsieur Brown? Monsieur Brown? Il faut vous réveiller. You muss wake up now. Meestair Brown?"

"Huh? Oh, yeah, yeah," I said, reaching for the blue United States Department of Homeland Security form that she was holding above me.

"Please return your seat to zee upright position. We wheel be landing shortly."

Before I had a chance to stop the snarky stewardess, she took away the breakfast tray that had apparently been left for me as I slept. This was a most unfortunate development because the calculations that my hazy brain was able to process suggested that I had not ingested any solid food in the past ten hours. Even the last solid food could not be counted, since I had vomited up the croissant that I tried to eat at Charles de Gaulle Airport.

Thankfully, my blackmailer had the decency to fly me back to Philadelphia in Air France's Business Class cabin, as he had similarly arranged for my flight to Paris. What a swell guy that Winston was. The spacious reclining chair came in handy since I hadn't slept much the night before.

After crying my eyes out for two full hours on the Pont Alexandre III, with my tears dropping into the Seine, I was escorted to a taxicab by two Parisian policemen. Although I was dangerously close to letting the cat out of the bag about Winston and his scheme, I balked and simply told them that I was heartbroken because my wife had just left me. Perhaps an accurate prediction, but, at the time, a white lie to law enforcement.

When the cab delivered me back to the Hôtel Capdevielle I quickly changed into fresh, untorn clothing. I then made my way back downstairs to the hotel bar. I ordered a Kronenbourg 1664. The time was approximately 6:15 p.m. I didn't recollect much about the ensuing seven hours. I did, however, remember that for a certain amount of time, I engaged in a cordial discourse with the bartender about French and American politics and sports. At some point thereafter, the bartender and my co-patrons became disinterested in what I was spouting out.

Oh shit, I had compared American slavery to the French cooperation with the Nazis in World War II. That was a big no-no – reminding the French of their recent collaborating past.

At the end of the evening, after having consumed about seven beers, a few single malt scotches and a cognac, I attempted to dismount my bar stool and wound up on my ass.

I remembered nothing more than those highlights, and that I had awoken on the floor of my hotel room's bathroom. When I arose at 10:15 a.m., two hours and forty-five minutes before my flight was scheduled to leave Charles de Gaulle, I was clothed in my vomit-covered button-down shirt and slacks from the previous evening. During the course of the ensuing 20 minutes, I showered, vomited, packed my suitcase, vomited again and checked out of the hotel. I miraculously made it to the airport, through the check-in line, and past security with 15 minutes to spare before the plane boarded. While in the boarding area, feeling physically and psychologically wounded, I realized that I was not hung over. I was still drunk from the previous evening.

Once in my cushy Espace Affaires seat, I evidently went into an 8 ½ –hour hibernation, only to awaken when the disembarkation card was shoved in my face. Although I didn't feel in tip-top condition, I was in much better shape than I had been before I fell asleep.

Panic overcame me when I realized that I had not stashed the diamond, as previously directed by Winston. It remained in its velvet sack in my pants pocket. Although the fasten seatbelt light had already been illuminated by the captain in anticipation of landing, I unbuckled my harness and ran to the Business Class lavatory before the *équipage* could direct me otherwise. Once in the lavatory, I removed the diamond from its velvet sack. The gem glimmered brilliantly, even in the scarce light of the lavatory. Notwithstanding the whirlwind that had materialized during the past 48 hours, I was still taken aback by the notion that I was holding an object that allegedly had a market value of four million dollars.

As Winston had told me to do, I took off the sock covering my right foot, and placed the mammoth rock in between my big toe and second toe. I quickly put my Gucci loafer back on my foot, splashed some water in my face and opened the lavatory door.

As I scurried back to my seat, the plane had already begun its descent. While strapping myself back in, the stewardess sauntered over and, while standing over me, said,

"Sir, you muss nutt get up from you seat while zee plane is being landed."

"Huh, what? I think you must have the wrong guy – I've been sitting here the whole time." I said.

"No, Monsieur Brown I juss see you get up and go to zee toilet."

Since there was a better than average chance that my life was going to be over, either literally or figuratively, within 72 hours, I decided to get some mileage out of the attention that this cuteish dirty blonde thirty-something Frenchwoman was giving me.

"Ma'am," I said seriously, "you must have me confused with another sexy American."

Not knowing how to react, the stewardess managed a half-smile, turned her head and walked back to cockpit wall and strapped herself into a jumpseat. I took solace in knowing that even though my life was going to hell in a handbasket, I still had the ability to make off-color remarks that made others not take themselves so seriously.

For the next 35 minutes, I relaxed and thought of the daunting decisions and tasks that lay ahead of me.

When I could see out the window that the A330 was over New Jersey, 100 feet inland from the Delaware River, with the Sports

Complex just off to the right on the Pennsylvania side, a sharp queasy feeling overtook me. I had arrived back in Philadelphia.

After a smooth landing, the plane taxied for about seven minutes, and parked at Terminal A-West. I gathered my carry-on baggage and quickly exited the aircraft. After wiggling the two toes that surrounded the diamond to confirm that it was secure, I took a deep breath and walked up the jetway. I was about to smuggle an inordinately expensive gemstone into the country, thereby skirting hundreds of thousands of dollars in taxes. If stealing legal fees from my firm and conspiring to commit murder weren't enough, I was now about to smuggle goods into the country in violation of federal law. Goddamn, was I going to be popular. The state and federal authorities were going to have to fight over who would get to prosecute me first.

At the end of the jetway, I walked out into the modern glass and steel international terminal. The secure pre-customs screening area led passengers to the right, down a long corridor. I was not looking forward to the lengthy underground journey to the customs checkpoint. The jagged edges of the four million dollar stone were hurting my toes with every step that I took. I worried that I would have a limp by the time that I got to customs and immigration, thereby causing the United States Customs and Border Protection officers' suspicions to rise.

When I was about thirty feet from an escalator that was to lead me underground to the customs and immigration area, I noticed that two uniformed guards with gazes of resolve on their faces, seemed to be focusing their interests in my direction. I initially attributed my concerns to paranoia and egocentrism, but as I further approached these gentlemen, I became certain that their stares were affixed to me.

Once I was ten feet away, the guards began to walk towards me in unison.

Oh shit. I was going to be arrested even before I had a chance to carry out Jim Winston's task and salvage my marriage and career.

The clone-like six foot dark brown haired, mustached guards were most certainly going to apprehend me. Their eyes locked on me as they marched to meet me with an apparent purpose. Once they were within spitting distance, I could see that they were not wearing Customs and Border Protection uniforms. Rather, patches on their shoulders identified them as being from the Brandywine County Sheriff's Office. While the presence of law enforcement meeting me as I debarked the plane was not completely surprising, I was perplexed by the presence of these Sheriff's Office personnel since they appeared to be out of their county jurisdiction.

"*Ale-ixx-an-duhhr Braille-n?*", one of them said in highly-accented Philly-speak.

"Yes, I'm Alexander Brown, can I help you?"

"Yes sir, you can," the other Deputy said, directing me to a door that read,

CUSTOMS AND IMMIGRATION ADMITTANCE ONLY!

"Can I ask what this is all about? I am being arrested?"

"Mr. *Braille-n*, it's definitely in your best interest to come with us – and no, you ain't bein' *arres-tit*," he responded in an accommodating and non-confrontational tone.

One of the Deputies scanned a magnetic card and the door opened. Although I was not handcuffed, I saw little alternative to following these people. I hoped to God that they were going to tell me that Winston was captured after I left, that they knew about the set up, and that in exchange for my cooperation, I would be granted prosecutorial immunity and that they would make sure that my firm wouldn't find out about the Leon Richardson affair. My cynical side, which controlled 95% of every fiber in my body, was telling me that these two knew that I was carrying a multi-million dollar diamond and that I was about to involuntarily disgorge that diamond, and in the process, be seriously injured or killed.

The door behind me closed loudly, and I was now in a very brightly lit corridor that had white linoleum floors, white-paint coated drywall, and a white tile drop ceiling.

I tried to make small talk to avoid appearing culpable.

"Are you guys from the *Brandywine County* Sheriff's Office? Aren't we in Philadelphia Coun..."

"Mr. *Braille-n*, we've got a nice little working relationship with our Philly counterparts, as well as the feds. Everything's been cleared and we have temporary jurisdiction here."

Temporary jurisdiction? If such a concept existed, I must have been daydreaming during that law school lecture.

"Well why am I..."

"We're here to help you, sir. Although we're not interested in the specifics, we know that you're carrying some important cargo, which might be placed in peril, were you to wait in the customs and immigration line with hundreds of others. The feds already checked your background out and OK'd us to bypass you through customs and immigration. We do it all of the time – we have an arrangement with Customs and Border Protection. One of our other deputies is having your bags diverted and will meet us on the other side with them. It was just the *two* bags, right, Sir?"

Incredulous that I hadn't at least been pistol whipped yet, and that these guys were going to spare me from having to sneak the diamond through, I responded, bemusedly,

"Uh – uh yeah, you're right, just the two bags. Wait a minute, did you say that you're going to bring me out *past* the customs and immigration checkpoints?"

"Yep. If you want to wait in line for 45 minutes and another half hour for your bags, we could certainly arrange that."

"No...no. This is great – very convenient. Thank you very much."

"Think nothing of it, Mr. *Braille-n*."

These two guys actually seemed believable. After all, if they were going to beat the piss out of me and steal the diamond, they would have done so already.

The Chief most assuredly had not told the Sheriff's Office that he was a co-conspirator in a plot to blackmail me and kill George Ridgeway. I was also fairly certain that the issue of my carrying a four million dollar diamond was probably not raised. The Chief probably just called in a favor to his point person at the Sheriff's Office and that person happily obliged. For all I knew, these guys could have thought that I was carrying a donor organ that needed to be taken to a hospital right away.

I knew nothing about how the law provided for federal and local authorities to interact in the setting of a secure customs area. However, it didn't seem implausible that the feds at Philadelphia International Airport had a working relationship with the Brandywine County and Philadelphia County Sheriff's Offices which allowed, say, a prisoner or a material witness to a criminal trial, to be intercepted before he reached customs.

The white hallway twisted and turned and seemed to never end. While we made small talk about how the Phillies' bats were slumping of recent, I wondered if I was being led to a secret airport interrogation area, rather than past the customs and immigration checkpoints.

After walking for three or four minutes, we came to double doors with push bar exit mechanisms. The Deputies stopped walking. One of them faced me, smiled and extended his hand to shake mine.

"Mr. *Braille-n*, this is the end of the road for us. As you might suspect, we have some *paperwork* to deal with on this end. So, we'll ask that you go through those doors and wait a few minutes for our colleague. He's dealing with his own *paperwork* and should have your bags out to you in a jiffy."

Although he stopped short of sarcastically winking at me, the way in which he said "paperwork" reeked strongly of sarcasm – as in "we need to talk to our federal counterparts so that they can tell us what type of a favor they'll be asking for the next time around."

"Thank you," I responded tentatively, as I pushed one of the double doors open.

As the door opened, I could see that I was, indeed, transported to the post-customs non-secure arrival area. My main indication was that numerous people wheeling luggage carts were being met by loved ones with the obligatory hugs and kisses.

I looked around for someone wearing a similar uniform as the two deputies, but saw no one. Since I had just deplaned five minutes prior and the aircraft had probably not even emptied itself of passengers, let alone baggage, I told myself to calm down.

After waiting another five minutes, someone piqued my interest but it was not the other deputy. Looking completely lost and nervous to be in a busy airport terminal was my bride, Julie. She stood about thirty feet away and was holding onto Charlie by his forearm. I had planned on taking a cab home, but, apparently Julie thought that it would be a nice idea to surprise me for my homecoming. Under normal circumstances, I would have thought the gesture to be heartwarming. On this occasion, however, I would liked to have had the opportunity to collect myself, decide what I was going to tell Julie and figure out where I was going to stash the diamond, before facing her. I was clearly not going to have that luxury and couldn't exactly run and hide at this point.

Still ignorant to my presence in the waiting area, Julie swiveled her head rapidly, presumably to ascertain from which door I might be exiting. My astute little boy saw me from across the hall, through twenty, or so, other people. Julie had him dressed to the nines for the occasion, with his combed and parted hair, a short-sleeved lime green Polo shirt, a pair of cream colored linen pants and penny loafers with no socks.

"Daddy!" he exclaimed, forcing his way out of Julie's grasp. He was holding the Dictaphone that I kept in my desk at home. He ran over to me quickly and awkwardly, the way only a fearless two year old boy can. Once he reached me, I lifted him up underneath his armpits, kissed him and hugged him tighter than I had ever previously done. Charlie flipped on the "Play" button of the Dictaphone. Out of the tiny speaker, I could hear Charlie's previously-recorded little voice saying,

"I love Daddy! Daddy come home today – have baseball catch with me!"

I could do little to curtail the tears that flooded down my face.

I disguised the tears to Julie as being happiness at having seen my beloved child and wife for the first time in several days. In actuality, however, the tears that I cried were tears of sorrow. Regardless of what scenario played out over the next couple of days, Charlie was either soon to be the son of a disgraced, disbarred and unemployed lawyer, the son of a murderer, or the son of a dead person. He had done nothing to deserve his fate, and would very likely endure a traumatic childhood, and beyond, solely due to the combination of my bad luck and bad decision-making. I had clearly failed as a father. This reality hurt badly.

I took the Dictaphone from Charlie, and put the device in my pants pocket. I placed Charlie back on the ground and kissed Julie on the lips while embracing her with both arms.

"Sorry – he found your Dictaphone in the desk this morning and has been making his own recordings since. *Peee-yew!* – God, do you stink! And what's that scab over your left eye? How much did you have to drink on the plane? Did you fall down and cut your eye after drinking too much?"

In actuality, I had not drunk a single alcoholic beverage on the plane. The fact that booze was still emanating from my pores from the previous evening's depressed bender was harrowing, and said a lot about the state of my liver and life at this moment. As for the scab, I probably should have invested in some cover-up to hide the evidence of having tripped to the cobblestone surface in Place Monge, during my haste to ascertain the meaning of Winston's anagram.

"Oh, sorry – the guy next to me was snoring and I had a few scotches to help me zone him out. And no, smartass, I didn't fall down – I nicked my eyelid on the bathroom door in my hotel – you can never tell where the light switches are in these damn foreign buildings."

"Well, you smell like you just got out of the distillery – and you're sweating. Why are you sweating?"

"Because you look gorgeous and I want to ravish your body."

"Not smelling like that, you won't," she said sternly, while smirking.

This was Julie's version of foreplay. Sex was about the furthest thing from my mind at this moment. However, it was very hard to ignore her snugly fitting yellow sun dress that exposed her delightfully petite frame. Her ample makeup was perceptibly freshly applied and her shiny and smooth brown hair, straight and voluminously blown out just as I liked it, was newly adjusted for the occasion.

I felt like crying some more when it dawned on me how lucky I was to have a wife willing to go to such lengths to surprise her husband at the airport. Julie had likely been planning this moment for several hours. Between getting Charlie and herself dressed and polished, as well as finding her way to the airport and the International Terminal, her task had not been easy.

"*Ale-ixx Braille-n?*", a voice bellowed from behind me.

I turned around and carrying my checked bag was another Sheriff's Office Deputy.

"Oh, oh – yes, hi – I'm Alex Brown – those are my bags – thank you."

Although this deputy was clad in the same uniform as the others, unlike his counterparts, he had no facial hair and was very young. He handed me the bags, patted me on the shoulder and said,

"Mr. *Braille-n*, you sir, are good to go! Enjoy your stay in the United States!"

I politely laughed at his attempt at humor and tried to dismiss him as quickly as possible, so that Julie's suspicions were not raised. Two seconds after the deputy turned and walked back into the secure area, Julie asked,

"What the hell was that all about? Brandywine County Sheriff's Office? Aren't we in Philadelphia?"

By necessity, I concocted something quickly.

"Oh, it's some Department of Homeland Security thing. They don't have enough DHS personnel here, so the various Sheriff's Offices from the surrounding counties apparently help out with things."

"O.K.," she said meditatively, "but why was *anyone* bringing your bags to you *outside* of the immigration area?"

"Yeah – I guess I didn't tell you – they flew me over to Paris and back – believe it or not – in Business Class. One of the perks is that if you declare nothing on your immigration form, they fast track your bag off the plane and bring it out to you."

"You are *such* an asshole!", she said fierily.

Oh no. She knew that I was lying and was going to make me tell her the whole story. I was not prepared for this scenario.

317

"They flew you in Business Class! How come you've never flown *me* in Business Class?"

Thank God.

"Jules, please – can we talk about this in the car? I'm so tired right now I can barely stand."

"O.K., let's go. Charlie, guess where Daddy is taking us for dinner?"

Thankfully, she allowed the subject to be changed.

"Where?!" my young son asked, intently staring at Julie as if her response held the secret of the universe.

"To the diner!"

"Julie, I'm really tired. Can't we just order hoagies?"

"No, we cannot *order hoagies*! You haven't seen your son or your wife for four days. We're going to have a nice family meal together, Alex."

"Yea! Diner! Diner!", Charlie exclaimed, jumping up and down and doing the cutest, most clumsy and ungraceful dance.

CHAPTER FORTY-SEVEN

Ordinarily, Charlie would eat his meals in a highchair. On this early evening at the local diner, I put Charlie on my lap and we colored the paper placemat with crayons together. Julie sat in a booth opposite Charlie and me.

To Julie, I was able to pass off my uncharacteristic clingy affection toward Charlie as being that of a father who hadn't seen his only child in several days. What Julie didn't know, however, was that I was savoring what might have been one of my last meals with Charlie. I even let him play with the Dictaphone, when he asked to do so.

"Do you think that we should sue that talent agency?", Julie asked, catching me off-guard?

"Huh?"

"The talent agency that scammed us, and left me that cooky message. Jog your memory at all?"

Putting Jim Winston out of my mind, even for this brief meal, was not going to be possible.

"Julie, let me make a deal with you. I promise not to play the 'I told ya' so' card, and talk about your indiscretion and naïveté involving this bullshit child modeling racket, if you promise not to bring it up ever again, O.K.? It's only gonna make me mad, and I just don't want to think about it."

"It's just that I'm so pissed off. I could have gone to Paris with you and we could have had the most romantic time there together."

Little did she know that powers beyond her control would never have let that scenario occur.

"I know, Jules. Can we just move on? I'm so tired and I just don't even want to contemplate the issue. Besides, we got 25 grand out of it, so who cares? Plus, I know that litigation is not your area of expertise, but you went to law school. Think about it – we've been paid – we have no damages."

With Julie working my nerves and Charlie repeatedly recording and playing back his voice on the Dictaphone, I became agitated and snatched the Dictaphone away from Charlie and put it back in my pocket. This caused him to cry. I felt guilty, but the constant sound of the recording being rewinded was grating on my senses and I could take it no longer.

"Fine," she said, dramatically sulking in an attempt to garner my attention. Speaking towards the hamburger that she was holding, rather than at me, she continued, "You're just going to have to take me to Paris to make up for it. Oooh! Maybe we'll go over there during Christmas! We'll take Charlie and get him a beret! Don't they have their big sales in December? Let's fly over there in Business Class!"

Even if I wasn't in prison or dead in December, I was very likely to be unemployed and would be villainized in the Philadelphia legal community. As such, it was probably not going to be in the budget to take a vacation to Paris at any time in the foreseeable future.

"Julie, I think that the sales in Europe are in August. Why would they have sales at Christmas time when the most shopping is done then?"

She didn't answer me. Instead, she seemed to just stare into space above my head to the left, in the direction of the entrance to the restaurant. I figured that I had struck a chord with her. Maybe she felt that it wasn't appropriate for a Jew to be lecturing a Christian about Christmas.

"Jules, what did I say? Why are you just staring at..."

"Sir, the hostess seems to think that you may be the owner of a silver Mercedes-Benz GL 450," a familiar voice spoke from behind me.

I turned my neck over my left shoulder to see someone who was, indeed, familiar – and unpleasantly so.

"Hello, sir – ma'am – I'm Officer Thomas Reardon of the Lower Salem Township Police Department…"

Porn 'Stache had an actual last name. He, apparently, wasn't Tommy Porn 'Stache. He was Officer Thomas Reardon. He was also about five miles outside of his jurisdiction, but who was keeping score?

"Oh my God! Did someone steal my car – we just got here 20 minutes ago, how did…"

"Ma'am, thankfully they didn't get that far. We maintain a regular patrol of this area and once we arrived, the criminals fled. They were a couple of bla – African American – youngsters. You see, they'll smash your windshield open if they see three pieces of loose change on the passenger seat. They use the money to buy crack down in Brandywine City."

What a piece of work Porn 'Stache was. He felt a need to make racial epithets even while inventing a story about a phony break-in attempt to Julie's car.

"Did they actually smash the window in? We'll need to have a police report prepared so that we can file an insurance claim."

"Mrs. *Braille-n*, since we arrived so quickly, the black kids didn't even get a chance to break your window open. I will, however, need your husband to come outside with the keys to the car, so that we can survey it."

With her cross-examination face displayed, Julie asked Porn 'Stache,

"I'm sorry, Officer – what was it…?"

"Reardon. Officer Thomas Reardon," he responded, while displaying a nervous visible contraction of his Adam's apple.

"Officer Reardon, how do you know my name?"

"Uhh…," Porn 'Stache struggled, "we…uhh…ran your plate on our computer. We do that as a matter of routine to see if gang violence is a possibility. You see, we needed to make sure that your car didn't belong to one of the high level drug dealers that roam these parts. If the plate came up as belonging to a drug dealer, we would have had to call in additional units to prevent any – you know – contingencies."

Porn 'Stache was a competent conniving liar, but he was no match for my wife, the lawyer.

"Officer, let me ask you this: how many of your drug dealers in this area – what is this, Somerville?"

"Yes, ma'am, Somerville."

"How many of your drug dealers in Somerville drive cars with baby seats in the rear and plush animal toys and children's books scattered in the front?"

"Ma'am, we need to take every possible precaution," he responded, now displaying some of the vitriolic anger that I had witnessed just a few days prior. "I'll need to speak with your husband outside for a moment or two, if you please."

"It's *my* car, not his. *I'll* come outside. Honey, you stay here with Charlie," Julie said, while rising from the booth.

I was not about to let Julie wander outside. I stood up right after she did and pressed on her shoulder, so that she would sit back down.

"Julie, I'm sure that this will only take a minute – just stay here with Charlie."

"Fine. But make sure you inspect the car to see if there is any damage – if there is, we need to get a police report!" she bellowed, as I walked with Porn 'Stache towards the exit.

Once outside, he directed me towards his squad car.

"Please, step into my office, counselor."

I was so used to the corrupt and twisted ways of Winston and his people, that whatever Porn 'Stache was about to say barely phased me.

"Don't mind if I do. Do you always patrol the parking lots of towns such as Somerville that are five miles outside of your jurisdiction?", I asked as we sat down in the police cruiser.

"Listen, asshole – if your cunty little lawyer-bitch wife ever talks like that to me again, I will pistol whip her ass. Who the fuck does she think she's talkin' to?"

Hmmm, let's see. A racist, uneducated, crooked, white-trash pawn of Chief Bozzi, that's who.

I felt it best not to answer his query.

"Counselor Brown, I am now in a very shitty mood because of you," he said, stroking his signature facial hair and cracking his neck. He retrieved a generic cigarette from a mangled soft pack that was clipped to his car's sun visor. He lit up, and only slightly cracked the window, presumably so as to not let the cold air from the climate control system escape.

"The only good thing you done for me was to stop for dinner near my township. I was gonna have to pull you over, so you saved me some trouble. Thank you kindly, counselor."

"Don't mention it."

"We ain't got a lot of time, so I'm gonna tell you how it's gonna go down on Monday. First of all, unlock your car."

I took the keys out of the pocket not containing my Dictaphone, and pressed the keyless unlock button. Julie's Benz, which was three parking slots to the left, emitted a beeping sound, indicating that the doors had been unlocked.

"Alright, good. I'm gonna put your weapon in the spare tire compartment. It will be loaded with one magazine – you won't need any more than that because you'll be shooting Ridgeway in the head from behind at close range. He won't see it coming, and he'll be drugged, so there will be no struggle."

I became short of breath listening to what he was saying to me. The carcinogens from the vapor of Porn 'Stache's sub-prime tobacco were not helping things.

"Here, take these," he said, handing me a raggedy pill container with a torn off label. "There are a few Rohypnol pills in there – you know, Roofies. You're gonna go to dinner with Ridgeway at the Atlantis House on Monday night at 8 p.m. You'll tell him that you're bringing the stone with you. As you know, that fucker drinks like a fish, so he'll be heading off to take a piss at some point. When he does, you pop a few of these pills in his drink. He'll be in la-la land in no time. You'll then cart his ass to the Lubranos' construction site on the river. Don't get there any later than 10:15 p.m. That shouldn't be a problem because the Atlantis House is just up Delaware Avenue from the construction site.

"You drag his ass to the bank of the Delaware River and pop him in the back of the head. Chief and I will get there at 10:30 sharp and will help you clean everything up. We'll spray the blood into the river with a hose that the Lubranos are going to leave there.

"You will obviously have the diamond in your possession and will hand it off to the Chief at that point. Any questions?"

I felt like asking him whether he could just shoot me right there, to put me out of my misery. Instead, I opted for a different question.

"Yeah – how am I going to gain access to the construction site."

"The Chief told me that Winston was going to explain the whole thing to you."

I did, actually, remember what Winston had told me about the bogus stop work order. I was hoping that they had changed their minds and that I would not actually be forced to extort my own clients.

"Uhh, no – he didn't mention anything."

"One of our Philly L&I people is going to slap a stop work order on the job when the foreman gets there at 5 a.m. Monday. The Lubranos will know about it at 5:30 a.m., and I'm guessing that you'll get a call from little Lubrano at 5:31 a.m."

"L&I" was the Philadelphia Department of Licenses and Inspections. The agency administered and enforced the city's Code requirements. A stop work order issued by L&I meant that the police department would physically prevent workers from entering the jobsite, if necessary.

"Now listen to me carefully," Porn 'Stache continued, "you don't breathe a fuckin' word about the deal to Vinny Lubrano on the phone. You tell him that you'll get right in your car, you'll make a few phone calls along the way to try to get the order lifted, and that you'll meet him at the site. End of story. Once you're down there, you take him to a secluded area, away from anyone. You tell him that the stop work order gets lifted as soon as he gives you full access to the site. You tell him that that fuckin' job will be shut down for a month if he don't wanna play ball."

"What if he asks why I need to use the site?"

"*Ale-ixx* – he's an Italian concrete guy. He ain't gonna ask you that. He'll get the picture – trust me."

"Why do we have to do this at his site? I don't understand..."

"*Ale-ixx*, let's get something straight, here: *We* ain't doin' nothin'. The Chief and I are pillars of the community. Last time I checked, you were the one who had a chance to keep his wife from seein' them pictures and to keep his bosses and the Pennsylvania Bar from seein' the transcript of the conversation with you and that nigger. So let's be clear: Chief and I call the shots, you pull the trigger.

Not that it's any of your fuckin' business, but Lubrano's construction site is *the* ideal place in the whole city to kill and dispose of someone. The site is in an industrial zone, three quarters of a mile from a house, passing car or pedestrian. And, it's right on the river, so we'll just tie weights around him, boat his ass to the middle of the Delaware and toss him in. You got any more questions?"

"No, not really," I said, clearly pregnant with a question.

"That didn't sound too convincing, counsel. What is it? I'd rather have you ask now, than have something get fucked up on Monday."

"Well, it's just – how do I know that after I've finished off Ridgeway, Winston isn't going to force me to perform some other seedy task, under threat of disclosing the photos and transcript."

Porn 'Stache smiled forebodingly.

"What? Did I hit the nail right on the head? Listen," I said unwaveringly, with no fear, "if that's the case, then I'm not doing the deed. You can just expose the pictures or transcript or whatever else you have on me because I won't be strung along like this."

"*Ale-ixx*, just calm your ass for a second," he said, laughing at me, "Chief told me not to say anything, but I guess it don't matter at this point. I think you can safely assume that *Winston* won't be blackmailing you any longer."

Curious as to why he was confident to speak in such certain terms, I asked,

"Oh?"

"Counselor, take a peak at them sombitches! Look at 'em! They're dead – deader than dead!"

Porn 'Stache opened his mobile phone, clicked a few buttons and handed it to me. What I saw was unexpected and gruesome, but not the least bit upsetting to me. Porn 'Stache looked on, nodding his head up and down with a smile, as if reveling in some sort of victory.

"Here – hit the right arrow button – that'll flip through the photos."

I followed his instructions.

Each picture was more ghastly than the previous one.

Jim Winston and Alassane had both been murdered by gunshots to the forehead. Some of the photos depicted them separately, and some of the photos depicted them together.

They appeared to be lying in pools of blood on a green and white tile floor. I felt no emotion in seeing the dead bodies of these two individuals. The fact that I had, in such a short period of time, become so entwined in this evil chain of events, and that I was insulated from feeling sorrow over death images of two people whom I knew was, in itself, disturbing to me.

After that series of photos was another series of photos depicting another dead person. This individual was an African-American whose throat had apparently been slashed. Although the amount of blood covering this man's face made it somewhat difficult to decipher his identity, and I had only actually seen Leon Richardson on one prior occasion, I was fully certain that it was his dead body that appeared on the cell phone screen.

Porn 'Stache pulled away the phone, wiped the smile clean from his face and assumed a stern visage.

"*Ale-ixx*, I hope that you take something from them pictures. Like – for example – do as you're told and don't give the Chief or me reason to believe that you're gonna say or do somethin' that you shouldn't. You be a good boy and everything should be just fine."

"O.K."

"After you leave, I'm gonna put your weapon in with the spare tire. It's gonna take me five or so minutes to take care of everything, so stall in there for a little while. Order your kid an ice cream sundae, or something."

I followed the officer's instructions and began to exit the vehicle without uttering a word. As I was swinging my second foot out of the car, he grabbed my left shoulder, forcing me back in the cruiser.

"You make sure you bring that fuckin' diamond with you Monday night!"

"I will, Officer," I said, pondering why Porn 'Stache didn't ask me to just give him the diamond then. After all, he knew that I was carrying it.

Then, it occurred to me that Porn 'Stache's dumbness aside, he could have had designs on disappearing with the diamond. That the Chief had allowed my one-on-one meeting with Porn 'Stache to occur was telling of the Chief's confidence in his mental control over his deputy. Porn 'Stache was too loyal to betray his crooked boss.

"Good. That's what I thought," he responded as if he were the high school bully and I had just agreed to give him my milk money for the rest of the semester.

"Now get the fuck back in there to your wife and kid."

I left the cruiser, this time unabated. I didn't turn around, but as I approached the diner, I could see, in the reflection of its glass façade, Porn 'Stache lifting the rear gate of the Benz. The man actually was going to put a loaded weapon in the vehicle in which my wife drove around our only child. These corrupt murderers expected me to use that gun to kill another human being in two days time.

As I walked back through the door into the diner, Julie immediately noticed me. If she were able to ascertain what was going on, she would force me to report the situation to law enforcement. However, the consequences of my reporting the blackmail to law enforcement would have been worse than if I had kept the scheme a secret. In order to prove that I was truly being blackmailed, I would be forced to disgorge the photos and transcript, which would then ultimately become known to Julie, my employers and the Pennsylvania Supreme Court. Those three entities, upon learning of the contents of the photos and transcript, would, respectively, divorce me, fire me and disbar me. Even if I had a fighting chance to convince Julie that the photos were misleading and that I didn't actually kiss Véronique, our marriage would certainly be in jeopardy after I was fired, disbarred and forced to find another career.

To prevent Julie from suspecting that anything was awry, I was going to have to try very hard to eliminate any outward visual signs of gloom from my body language. To preempt any observations about my demeanor that Julie might have had, I went on the offensive as soon as I got back to the table.

"Goddamn sons of bitches! It's not as if we parked the car in a bad neighborhood! This is ridiculous – you go in for dinner at a suburban diner and, in broad daylight, they try to break into your car. Julie, we're never coming here again. We're just going to have to find another place that makes cheeseburgers that Charlie will eat."

"What did they get? Did they smash the window open? Did they steal my radio?", she asked frantically.

"No, Julie. They didn't break the window and they didn't get to steal a thing. That's not the point, though! I feel like we've been violated. What the hell is this world coming to?"

"Alright, well, we're just not coming here anymore. Please pay the check and let's just get the hell out of here."

Since Porn 'Stache was probably still in the process of placing my firearm in the car, I decided to heed his advice about how to stall Julie.

"Jules, I could really use a cup of coffee. Charlie, how would you like some vanilla ice cream with hot fudge and whipped cream?"

"Yeaaaaaa!", Charlie responded with zeal. Julie couldn't deprive the child of his dessert now.

"Thanks a lot, hon," Julie said, glaring at me with a disapproving look.

CHAPTER FORTY-EIGHT

For Julie, the day after I returned from Paris was no different from any other typical summer weekend day. She met a friend at the mall and brought Charlie along. For me, though, this Sunday was possibly my last full day as an unimprisoned and undisgraced ordinary citizen. While I was home alone, I tried unsuccessfully to temporarily rid my mind of the tasks that lay ahead. Unable to follow the Phillies telecast, I paced throughout my house, repeatedly considering my extremely limited options.

During dinner, I spoke only when spoken to and pushed my food around my plate. When Julie asked why I wasn't eating or speaking, I responded with a familiar, dull barb about how she was a much better lawyer and lover than she was a cook. She didn't catch on that I was contemplating my life in ruin.

Bedtime with Charlie was uneventful, and Julie and I hit the sack at about 10:30. As Julie slept, I tossed and turned.

At 3:14 a.m., I was still awake, staring at the ceiling in our bedroom. For the first three hours during which I had attempted to fall asleep, I lay restless, feeling sorry for myself. I had gone from a budding young presumptive rainmaking attorney to a soon-to-be-disgraced father who would be collecting unemployment checks, or worse. I allowed for the fact that I was culpable for having irresponsibly accepted Leon Richardson's proposition. I felt like a victim, however, since this disaster would not have occurred, but for George Ridgeway coming into my life. When I really thought about it, Ridgeway was on the same plane of evilness as Winston and the Chief. He had hand selected me to be tricked into flying to Paris under demonstrably false pretenses, so that I could conveniently be used to courier his riches to him. I began to feel not so remorseful about the fact that I was going to take his life, albeit not fully voluntarily, in the near future.

Once my conscience became a touch clearer about the dastardly act that I would be committing in 19 short hours, my focus shifted to Winston and Alassane. Porn 'Stache had proudly shown me the photos of their dead bodies. It was, therefore, apparent that he and the Chief were at least somewhat responsible for or complacent in his murder plot. What I struggled with, though, was *why* the Chief had wanted Winston dead. Winston had kept his end of the bargain. Winston had dispatched me back to the Chief with the multi-million dollar stone. Maybe the Chief came to believe that the stone that I was holding was a fake. When the Chief realized that he had been duped, maybe he decided to exact his revenge. But if that were the case, why would Porn 'Stache have made it a point to tell me forcefully to not forget to bring the stone to the following night's rendez-vous? None of this muddle made sense.

After I had been tossing and turning for nearly five hours, I could hear a heavy summer rain beginning to fall outside. Strangely, the sound of the heavy raindrops pelting against our roof and windows had a soothing effect on me. After a few minutes of concentrating on the sound of the rain, with Ridgeway, Winston and the Chief out of my thought processes, I felt myself drift out of consciousness. My body was fully relaxed and I cared about nothing.

No sooner had I fallen into this comfortable state than an eardrum-shattering explosion, replete with blinding white light, violently awakened me. Our bedroom was momentarily illuminated to such an extent that I could see the artwork that hung on our walls, our dresser, and the pair of socks that I had left on the floor after undressing hours prior.

I sat up and realized that I was in a cold sweat. I was breathing as heavily as if I had just sprinted in a 40-yard time trial. I was not the only one whom the blast had awoken. Julie sat up just after I did, in a disoriented state. The frantic crying sounds that were being emitted from the monitor that sat on Julie's nightstand indicated that Charlie, too, had been startled by the lightning bolt that couldn't have touched down more than a quarter-mile from our house.

"Alex, honey, can you please go in there and rock Charlie? He's hysterical. Just go hold him for a few minutes and he'll be fine."

I tried to respond to Julie, but I couldn't. My senses were frozen and I suspected that I was hyperventilating.

Charlie had not stopped crying.

"Alex – please! I'm so tired. Please just go rock him!"

"Julie," I said, struggling for enough breath to speak her name, "I – I don't feel right…can—can you just get him?"

"You are *so* full of shit. You just lost sex for two weeks," she said, stomping off to Charlie's room, unpersuaded by my legitimately labored breathing.

The bolt of lightning had roused something within my brain and had provided me with a moment of lucidity. The situation, which was now clear to me, forced me into a state of nervous shock.

As was previously apparent, the Chief had Winston and Alassane killed. What was newly evident was that he was going to systematically kill, or have killed, every last person who knew about his scheme. Even Leon Richardson, who likely knew nothing about the plot was eliminated for good measure.

While Véronique also knew of the plot, I strongly suspected that she was the triggerperson for the French arm of the operation. She was likely given substantial financial consideration for eliminating Winston and Alassane. She would, therefore, have little impetus to ever come out of the woodwork. Porn 'Stache was too stupid to know that he, too, was going to be eliminated. The idiot sat there and laughingly showed me the death pictures of Winston and Alassane. He nevertheless failed to realize that those two were eliminated because of the extent of what they knew. It apparently did not dawn on the mustached moron that he, too, knew many of the details of the plot, and that he, therefore, was not much longer for this world.

I wasn't being told to bring Ridgeway to the Lubranos' construction site only so that I could kill Ridgeway cleanly. I was being told to bring Ridgeway to the Lubranos' construction site also so that I could be killed cleanly. They had provided me with a gun so that when I was shot, it would appear that I was threatening the shooter with deadly force. On its face, the notion that a married Jewish lawyer with a child and house in the suburbs would be threatening someone with a gun was outlandish. However, I had a feeling that the once all of the layers of this complex set-up were revealed, it would somehow make sense that I had a motive to kill.

Compounding this mess was my increasing hunch that the Lubranos were involved in this ploy to a greater extent than it appeared.

I couldn't figure out the rest and I didn't care. All of the sudden, losing my wife, my job and my law license didn't seem all that daunting. I had no choice but to spill the beans to the FBI, so that the Chief and Porn 'Stache could be arrested before I got killed.

CHAPTER FORTY-NINE

"Honey, get the phone...pleaaaaaase!"

"What?", I responded, in a confused state.

"Honey, get the phone – it's 5:38 a.m. – who the hell is calling the house this early?!"

My last memory, prior to hearing the sounds of the telephone and Julie's exasperated voice, was at 4:52 a.m., 46 minutes earlier, when I looked at the clock that sat next to my bed and concluded that I would not be sleeping even a wink that night. I had played out every possible scenario of the conspiracy in my head throughout the night and was resolutely convinced that the initial thought that entered my head upon being roused by the lightning bolt was correct. The conspiracy was designed to end with no one alive except for the Chief and Véronique.

When I heard the telephone and Julie's voice, I quickly concluded that I had dozed off for a few minutes at some point. God, was I tired.

"Hello?" I said, upon lifting the receiver.

"Alex. Vinny. Listen to me. These motherfuckers shut me down. They shut me the *fuck* down. I've got a fucking stop-work order and the cops just slapped a padlock around the fence. I've got 160 goddamn workers who are gonna be holdin' their lunchboxes and playin' with their dicks! I need you to do something – you guys have to know someone."

"Whoa – whoa – whoa, just take it easy for one second and let me digest all of the facts here."

"I don't have a fucking second – aren't you listening to me?! The stop work order says that the building is five feet off from the approved plans – I'm on the fucking 12th floor now. Do you have any idea what that means?! This is such bullshit. If the tower were an inch off, we would have known a week into the job. I'M ON THE FUCKING 12TH FLOOR NOW!

"Somebody in my company must have pissed off someone and now it's gotten political, or something. You need to get my job back running again. I'm going to lose a hundred grand for each day that the stop work order is in effect. And that's not including the penalties that the g.c. is going to assess me!"

Vinny's voice sounded surprisingly sincere. He did not have the requisite mental capacity to be able to dramatize what he had just conveyed to me. Maybe he and his father weren't involved in the conspiracy. That detail was of little consequence to me at this point. Once I was showered and dressed, I was going straight to the FBI's offices at 6th and Arch Streets in Center City, so that I could spill the beans. I was not going to play ball and, therefore, Vinny would not be getting his stop-work order lifted in the short term.

However, I wanted to give the impression that I was concerned about his dilemma, in the event that he was involved in the conspiracy, so that he didn't catch on that I was on my way to see the feds. Such a scenario carried the danger of one of the Chief's or Ridgeway's people cutting me off at the pass before I could get safely to the feds.

"O.K., Vinny, just hold down the fort over there. I'm going to make some phone calls. Once I see if I'm able to reach anyone this early, I'll call you right back."

"You've got to do someth..."

"Vinny – I just said that I was going to get right on it. You're wasting time by continuing to talk to me. Hang up the phone now and do whatever damage control you need to do and I'll be back in touch with you."

"O.K., bye."

Seeing that I was off the phone, Julie asked,

"Alex, was that Vinny *Lubrano*? What emergency could he have at five thirty in the morning?"

"Oh, not much. He just got to his project on the river and found out that L&I slapped a stop-work order on the job. We're only talking about 20 million in exposure here."

"Oh my gosh! What does he want you to do?"

"I suppose that he wants me to get the stop-work order lifted."

"How the hell are you going to do that?"

I didn't need to keep lying to Julie. I desparately wanted to come clean about Leon Richardson and Véronique. At this point however, I wasn't sure exactly what I was going to say to her. Also, I hadn't decided whether or not I should bring her and Charlie with me to the FBI offices so that they could be safe. Since there was a chance of my getting picked off before I even got to the FBI offices, I was presently leaning towards not doing so.

I needed to take a warm shower and decide exactly how I was going to break the news to Julie and how I was going to make sure that she and Charlie were safe prior to the Chief and Porn 'Stache being arrested. So, in the interim, before making these decisions, I decided to play along, as if I hadn't been expecting to receive Vinny's phone call.

"I probably won't be able to help Vinny, but after I'm done getting ready, I'll call Walt Krauss and see if he knows anyone at L&I – he's always bragging about how he's so connected."

Once again, screaming sounds came from the baby monitor, indicating that Charlie was awake, yet again. Charlie was going to be one pissed off, sleep deprived little boy today.

"Alex, since you have to get up now anyway to deal with Vinny's disaster, could you go change Charlie's diaper, so that I can sleep for another half-hour?"

"Sure."

Changing Charlie's diaper was the least that I could do for him. I was about to reveal something that would make me an outcast in society and ultimately make him an outcast amongst his schoolmates a few years down the road.

I walked down the hall to his room, hearing the crying getting louder as I approached.

"Hey, buddy, you O.K.? Didn't sleep so well, huh? Want Daddy to change that wet diaper of yours?"

When I entered the room, Charlie was standing up in his crib, with tears flowing down his bright pink face. In his left hand, he held his Phillie Phanatic doll and in his right hand, he held my Dictaphone. Despite the gravity of what was going on in my life, I still managed to be get perturbed about Julie allowing him to sleep with my expensive firm-issued technology device. I remembered that upon returning from the diner two nights prior, I had taken the Dictaphone out of my pants pocket when I was getting undressed, and that I had placed it on a table near my closet. Thereafter, while I was checking my e-mail, Charlie must have grabbed the Dictaphone. In order to prevent a crying-laced confrontation before bedtime, Julie must have allowed Charlie to take the Dictaphone with him when she put him in his crib. Apparently, it had remained in his crib on both Saturday and Sunday night.

"Charlie, you know that you aren't supposed to play with that. That's Daddy's special toy. Only Daddy can have that," I said, gripping the Dictaphone that was still in his hand.

"No, Daddy! I play with Daddy's toy too. Share! Daddy share with Charlie."

Since we had recently been attempting to instill in Charlie the virtues of sharing, the message that I was going to convey to my son by pulling the Dictaphone away from him was going to appear most hypocritical.

"Charlie, there are some things that Daddy can't share with Charlie," I said, unsuccessfully pulling slightly harder on the Dictaphone. For a two year-old, Charlie certainly had an impressive grip.

"No! Daddy share with Charlie!"

"Charlie, if you don't let go of Daddy's toy right now, you are going to sit in time-out. Charlie has never had to sit in time-out before six a.m., but I won't hesitate to put you in time-out right now!"

As I pulled harder, Charlie refused to relent, even going as far as to adjust his grip on the device, so that he had greater leverage. He was now holding the area over the "Play" and "Record" buttons.

I compensated for his adjustment and swiftly ripped the Dictaphone from his right hand. He let out an immediate shrieking cry.

A sound from a source other than Charlie caught my attention more than Charlie's crying, though.

When I pulled the Dictaphone from his hand, I must have forced Charlie to press down the "Play" button.

Instead of hearing one of the five or six correspondences that I had dictated the day before I flew to Paris, what I heard was entirely different. My voice was, indeed, present on the tape. However, there was another voice that spoke on the tape, as well. And, to be sure, the content of the recording did not include my dictating a series of correspondences for my cases.

The tape contained an inadvertent recording of my conversation with Porn 'Stache from Saturday night. The entire recording had been captured, beginning from when I took the Dictaphone from Charlie at the table in the diner. Instead of pressing the "Play" button as he had just done when I took the Dictaphone from him, Charlie must have pressed the "Record" button, when faced with the same situation two nights prior in the diner.

I listened to the whole tape. It captured the conversation immaculately.

Hello, sir – ma'am – I'm Officer Thomas Reardon of the Lower Salem Township Police Department...

Listen, asshole – if your cunty little lawyer-bitch wife ever talks like that to me again, I will pistol whip her ass. Who the fuck does she think she's talkin' to?...

I'm gonna put your weapon in the spare tire compartment. It will be loaded with one magazine – you won't need any more than that because you'll be shooting Ridgeway in the head from behind at close range. He won't see it coming, and he'll be drugged, so there will be no struggle...

There are a few Rohypnol pills in there – you know, Roofies... pop a few of these pills in his drink. He'll be in la-la land in no time...

You drag his ass to the bank of the Delaware River and pop him in the back of the head. Chief and I will get there at 10:30 sharp and will help you clean everything up. We'll spray the blood into the river with a hose that the Lubranos are going to have left for us...

You will obviously have the diamond in your possession and will hand it off to the Chief at that point. Any questions?...

One of our Philly L&I people is going to slap a stop work order on the job when the foreman gets there at 5 a.m. Monday. The Lubranos will know about it at 5:30 a.m., and I'm guessing that you'll get a call from little Lubrano at 5:31 a.m...

Last time I checked, you were the one who had a chance to keep his wife from seein' them pictures and to keep his bosses and the Pennsylvania Bar from seein' the transcript of the conversation with you and that nigger. So let's be clear: Chief and I call the shots, you pull the trigger...

I think you can safely assume that Winston won't be blackmailing you any longer...

Counselor, take a peak at them sombitches! Look at 'em! They're dead – deader than dead!...

Ale-ixx, I hope that you take something from them pictures. Like – for example – do as you're told and don't give the Chief or me reason to believe that you're gonna say or do somethin' that you shouldn't. You be a good boy and everything should be just fine...

You make sure you bring that fuckin' diamond with you Monday night...

I will, Officer.

When I finished listening to the recording of my conversation with Porn 'Stache, a vision overcame me. It dictated what course of action I was going to take, so that I could extract myself and my family from this ruinous state.

My strategy had been fully overhauled, and I would not be visiting with the FBI this morning.

With Charlie still crying, I rewound the tape about halfway through the conversation. I quickly found the portion of the conversation that needed to be edited. The tape counter read 743. I played the tape until the adverse portion was completed. The tape counter read 767. I rewound the tape back to 743.

"Charlie! Do you want me to show you how Daddy's toy works?"

"Yeah!"

"O.K. When I tell you, I want you to count all the way to fifteen like you did for Mommy and me at the diner the other night. Can you do that for Daddy?"

"Yeah!"

"O.K...ready...start counting...now!"

"Wann...toooooooo...sreeeeee..."

CHAPTER FIFTY

After showering and primping myself, I became even more resolute about the decision that I had made. I had gone from feeling helpless and victimized to feeling utterly invigorated that my proactive measures were going to leave me vindicated – and then some.

Wanting to avoid any surprises that might tamper with my plan, I decided to take State Route 612 all the way into the city. This route did not enter Lower Salem at any point. It was clear that the Chief and Porn 'Stache had no qualms about subjecting me to shenanigans outside of their home turf, as evidenced by the encounter at the diner. However, I felt that the odds were better that I would be safe if I kept out of their territory.

At 7:18 a.m. I arrived at the Breezeview Plaza construction site. Once on the dirt road leading from Delaware Avenue to the project, I was forced to slow the Bimmer down to about five miles per hour. Cigarette toting construction workers who had gotten an unexpected paid break were everywhere, making it very difficult for my car to pass. Little did these people know that the actions that I was about to take would ensure that they would be back on the job, earning their money very shortly.

The dirt road ended at a chain-link fence that had been padlocked shut. The entrance to the project was sealed off and a police officer stood guard. He wore a light blue short-sleeved shirt with a white hat. Aviator-style sunglasses covered his eyes and a cigarette hung out of his mouth, below his white mustache.

I opened my window and spoke to the officer in the most polite manner that I could muster.

"Officer, I'm trying to find Vincent Lubrano – Junior. You wouldn't happen to know where I might be able to locate him, would you?"

"Lemme guess, you're the new journeyman carpenter that the union sent over," he said with a mighty hacking laugh.

"I'm afraid not, officer. I'm his attorney."

"You don't say! Most of the workers here drive their Bimmers to the site – you just mixed right in! I'll be damned!"

"Where should I park?"

"Pretty much anywhere you want. Ain't no concrete or steel trucks comin' in here. Case you haven't noticed, the site's in lock-*dale-n* now.

"Tell you what – why don't you pull over there by my squad car. That way, none of them wiseguys'll end up eatin' lunch on the hood of your car. After you park your car, head *dale-n* there to the Lubrano trailer. Lubrano Junior should be in there."

"Thank you, Officer."

He put his cigarette back in his mouth, nodded his head and tipped the brim of his hat as I drove toward where his car was parked, about 50 feet away.

The officer's car rested on a dry patch of grass that was surrounded by wet mud chewed apart by tractor tires. Not wanting to get on the bad side of yet another police department, I opted to follow the officer's instructions and parked three feet to the left of his squad car.

I stepped out of my car and heard a squishing sound at my feet. With my mind swirling, it hadn't occurred to me that I should be careful when bringing my feet to the muddy surface. I looked down and saw that my cap toes were one inch deep in brown muck.

During the course of 72 hours, I had ruined two pairs of shoes. Strangely, I felt relieved after I realized that this latest pair was trashed. I thought back to a couple days prior when I was walking hopelessly alongside the Seine in a pair of waterlogged Ferragamos, caught in a torrential rainstorm. At that time, I had no idea how I was going to survive without a job or a law license. At this moment, once again with wet feet, I had a much better idea of how I was going to carry on.

I walked over to the trailer, muddy feet and all, climbed up four wooden stairs and knocked on the door.

After about ten seconds, a 5'6" basketball of a human being, wearing a green construction hard hat with the Philadelphia Eagles' signature wings on the sides answered the door.

"Can I help *yihh*?"

"I'm here to see Vinny."

"You from L&I?", he responded in an inhospitable tone.

"Sir, what's your name?"

The giant sphere inched a few inches closer to me, his bulbous gut now touching me.

"Bruno Montefiori. I'm da' foreman on dis job. Now lemme *aks* you again – are you from L&I, son?"

In light of what I had already been through during the past several days and the challenges that were facing me on this very day, Bruno did not scare me.

Without backing up, I looked down at Bruno and said,

"Mr. Foreman, let me ask you this: how many people from L&I do you know who wear $400.00 shoes – albeit covered in mud?"

He paused for a second, and then backed up so that he could see my shoes without being obstructed by his stomach. He then moved forward, so that his stomach was touching me once again.

"I'm not from L&I, Bruno. I'm Vinny's Jewish concrete lawyer. I'm the son of a bitch who's gonna get your job back up and running today, so that you don't have to pay those union pieces of shit over there for sitting on their asses. Now, if you want this job back up again, take your fat stomach away from my testicles, cut the South Philly tough guy nonsense and bring Vinny the fuck out here."

Taken aback, and realizing the gravity of what my role was, Bruno moved his fat stomach away from my testicles and said,

"Hey – yo, man I was messin' wit' chu! I knew you wasn't from L&I. Vinny is on duh phone. Come on inside – we got Dunkin' Donuts – what kind you like?"

"Bruno, I'll pass on the doughnuts. Do you have a hose somewhere and maybe a towel?"

"Yeah, yeah. Yo – those really $400.00 shoes?"

They were Testoni, and as I remembered, I had bought them for over $500.00 a year prior. I had made my point with Bruno and saw no reason to insult him further.

"Nah, I was just bustin' your balls. They're Florsheims – I got them on clearance."

"Damn, those are nice. I should have wenn ta' law school. My wife's second cousin is a lawyer – he does worker's comp, I think – He's got an office on Snyder Ave. Do you know Vito Santaguida?"

"Nah, Bruno – can't say that I do. Would you mind getting me that hose. I'm kind of in a rush."

"Yeah, yeah, no problem. *Vihhh-knee!*," he screamed into the trailer, "your Jewish lawy – uhh – your concrete lawyer is here to see you."

I was in utter amazement that I was still standing and did not have a bloody face that was being dragged through the construction site mud at that very moment.

"It's about fuckin' time! My fuckin' job is shut down – I'm makin' seven hundred phone calls and my lawyer takes his sweet ol' time gettin' here," Vinny bellowed from within the trailer. I couldn't yet see his face, but judging from the sound of his voice, I could gather than his disposition had not improved since I spoke with him earlier in the morning.

Bruno wobbled down the stairs to go fetch my hose. With him not obscuring the entryway into the trailer, I walked in to witness Vinny shouting on the phone at someone.

"You've surveyed my job every week since it began and have never found a problem. You do realize that I'm on the 12th floor now, don't you?! When I get off the phone, you're gonna call whoever you know at L&I and tell them that the setback conforms to the plans. Also tell them that based upon what you know about the quality of Lubrano Concrete's workmanship and management on this project, you have a feeling the something fishy is going on and that we're getting jobbed."

Vinny noticed my presence and motioned me to sit down. I continued standing.

"What? You're not gonna say what to them? Yes you damn well are! Do you ever want work from us again? Believe me, Rick, I can fuck your life up a hell of a lot worse than L&I can. Now get to fuckin' work on those assholes!"

Vinny hung up the phone and continued his tirade in my direction.

"I told you to sit the fuck down – you're making me nervous standing up like that. Holy shit! What happened to your shoes? Are they Ferragamos?"

"No, I ruined the Ferragamos the other day on the side of the Seine River, while caught in a rainstorm. I was outside, clearing my head, because I had just learned that I was being blackmailed. These are Testoni. Bruno just ran out to get me a hose and a towel."

"Bruno is getting *you* a hose and a towel?", Vinny asked incredulously.

"Yeah, we had a little misunderstanding. Then, I told him that I was your Jewish concrete lawyer and that I was going to make everything – well – kosher."

"You're out of your fucking mind – do you know what he does for money on the side when he's not workin' for me? Where did he go?"

"Vinny, I am not kidding. And based upon what I've been through during the past few days, I don't think that I'm mentally or physically capable of formulating a joke at this point. Here, why don't you sit down," I said, pulling an aluminum folding chair out for him.

Disinterested in having a seat, he swatted the chair away. It came to rest against the trailer's wall.

"Vinny – sit the *fuck* down right *fucking* now. I'm going to get your job back up and running within the hour – maybe sooner – if you just sit your ass down, stop talking and let me tell you what is going to happen," I said with a calm, yet forthright tone. I walked over to where the chair had landed, picked it up and unfolded it.

Once he arrived at the aluminum chair after a slow and calculated arrogant Italian-American strut over, I put my hands on his shoulders and forced him down onto the seat.

"Why should I believe that *you* are gonna get my job back up and running within the hour?", he asked patronizingly.

"Vinny, let me ask you this: Why did you hire me?"

Without hesitation, he responded,

"So that you could get me out of situations like this. Obviously, it was a mistake, since it took you a half a day to get here from when I called you."

"Vinny, do you remember when I said a few minutes ago that I was being blackmailed?"

"Yeah," he responded with a disbelieving sneer.

"Well, when I said that, I wasn't speaking in hyperbolic terms. I'm really being blackmailed and you're involved."

"What the fuck is 'hyperbolic terms?' Speak English – I'm a con-*shtruck-shinn* guy."

"You're also a Presbyterian Academy guy and have a B.S. from Drexel's engineering program. I wasn't exaggerating – is that better? I wasn't exaggerating about being blackmailed. Now tell me that you'll let me into your site tonight."

Vinny paused and looked away from me. He took a long sip of coffee from a paper Wawa cup and said with a wide grin,

"What the fuck did you get yourself into? Seems that the tables have turned, huh?"

Indeed, they had. I had failed to recognize the irony until Vinny had mentioned it. I was now the shady character and he was now the one being counted on for salvation.

From behind me, I could hear someone heavy ambling up the stairs to the trailer. The door opened and Bruno began to walk in, holding a hose and some rags.

"Bruno, take them shoes, hose 'em off, and stay the fuck out of here until we're done."

I unlaced my Testonis and handed them to Bruno.

After Bruno left, Vinny walked back to the door and bolted it shut.

"Assuming I let you do this, what's gonna go on at my site tonight? Do you just want a big place to hold your Passover cedar, but you're too cheap to rent out a banquet hall? What is it with you Jews? You'll pay someone to cut your lawn, but when it comes to..."

"I'm afraid I don't plan on having a Passover *seder* at the site. I may have an extra box of matzoh, though, from Passover a few months ago. It's probably stale by this point, so you may want to be careful.

"I'm going to do both of us a favor by not telling you what I need the site for."

Vinny took another gulp of coffee.

"Damn, *consigliere*, you must be in some pretty deep shit. Why my site?"

"Let's just say that the Breezeview Plaza's geographical juxtaposition allows me to effectively get done what I need to get done. It's completely isolated and right on the river. Nobody hears a thing, nobody sees a thing, and the evidence disappears into the river."

"What the hell are you talking about?"

"I was serious about being blackmailed. My blackmailers wanted me to commit the deed in a safe place. If I don't get caught, they don't get caught. Get the picture?"

"Yeah, but what does the job shutdown have to do with this?"

"You give me secure access to this site tonight – and Bruno's hose – and they get your job rolling again."

"And if I don't?"

I paused and pondered how my secret plan depended completely upon Vinny's complicity.

"If the job remains idle, how much will you be losing per day, again?"

"How do you know that I won't rat you out?"

"Because if I get busted, you'll be sharing the same cell at Graterford with me. Ever heard of conspiracy to commit murder?"

Now I was the conniving extortionist. It was an unsettling feeling.

CHAPTER FIFTY-ONE

After explaining to Vinny how he was going to get his job up and running again, I drove off in my Bimmer that Bruno had so kindly pulled out of the mud for me. With my newly sanitized Testonis, I symphonically worked the clutch, brake and accelerator and navigated my way through the streets of Center City towards my office.

I decided not to wait until I got back to the office to call the Chief, so that he would immediately get the stop work order lifted.

"Bozzi here."

"Chief, Alex Brown."

"Yo, counsel, how you doin'? Welcome back from France! You didn't eat any uh them snails over dare, did *yihh*?"

Actually, I had, while dining with a leggy French knockout whom I believed had committed two murders since she tried to seduce me.

"Chief, why don't we cut the shit, here, O.K.?"

Obviously not used to being spoken to in such a manner, he hesitated.

Understanding that my cooperation was essential to his plan, he then responded,

"Sure, pal, sure. Trying chilling *ale-t*, Kemo Sabe."

"I'm not gonna chill *ale-t*, you piece of shit," I said, proudly mocking his working class accent, "You have ruined my life and are a corrupt disgrace to your township, your county, your state, your country and your God."

"I been called worse, brother. I'd caution you, though, to be careful with your use of the word, 'corrupt'. Don't forget that that's what got Mr. Ridgeway into all that hot water years ago."

"Truth is a complete defense to defamation, you dirtball. In any case, the Lubranos are all in. You're gonna get your diamond and you're gonna get your dead man. Now call your fellow crooked folks in Philly and get Breezeview Plaza up and running again."

"I guess that I underestimated you, son. Well done. I can and *will* do that – pronto. Thank you, my brother."

I was more than slightly taken aback by his compliance and lack of confrontational response. This posture was out of character for the Chief and was therefore disquieting to me.

Sheepishly, and unsuccessfully attempting to sound poised, I asked,

"Are we done here?"

"So long as you ain't got any questions, we are. I'll see you later this evening."

Without responding any further, I hung up the phone.

I didn't like the Chief's conciliatory tone one bit. I hoped that he had not caught onto my plan.

CHAPTER FIFTY-TWO

"Ale-ixx, is everything O.K.?", Terri asked, over my intercom, "Everyone's waitin' to hear about how the Paris trip went. You walked into the office 15 minutes ago, didn't say 'hi' to no one and shut your door. You never shut your door – so I was a little worried. Now that you have a big French client, are you going to become one of them Partners whose shit don't stink?"

"Definitely not. Thanks for your concern, Terri, but everything is O.K. I'm just suffering from a little jet lag, that's all. Plus I need to tackle this ten-inch pile of mail that you so graciously left for me while I was gone. I figured that if I shut my door, I might be able to..."

Terri interrupted me and said at a whisper,

"Ale-ixx, Mr. Carlson is about to knock on your..."

Before she could finish her sentence, I heard a loud knocking accompanied by a simultaneous turning of my door handle. Nick Carlson was never one to wait for an answer before entering the office of one of his employees.

"A.B., why you hidin' from everyone this morning, bro?!", Carlson asked, displaying his trademark bleached-white teeth bearing grin that illuminated his miniature 5'5" frame.

"Sorry, Nick, I'm still a little jet-lagged. I've got to try and make a dent in this mail this morning, so that I can catch up on lost time."

His grin now fully evaporated, Carlson closed the door behind him and said forcefully,

"Don't gimme that shit, Alex. Remember a few months ago when I took Dugan and Walters to play at St. Andrew's in Scotland?"

I had no idea who "Dugan" and "Walters" were. I did know, however, that I was about to receive a lecture which included a gratuitous story from Nick about how well he played at the Old Course.

"We flew out on a Thursday, O.K.? We drink our asses off in First Class. We get to Fife on Friday morning, play a quick 18 on the Jubilee Course – I played like shit, but I don't care – it's Saint Fucking Andrew's, right? We drink our asses off Friday night, until the point where I've got Laphroaig running through my veins, instead of blood, O.K.? I shoot a fucking 72 on the Old Course! 72 – and I'm hungover. We fly back the following morning and I'm at my desk, bright-eyed and bushy-tailed on Monday morning. Meanwhile, Dugan and Walters owe me all of their respective companies' legal work for life because I got them on at St. Andrew's. That's how it's done, my brother, that's how it's done. Now what's your excuse for looking like someone just ran over your puppy? And you better not tell me that you're 'jet-lagged' this time."

"*Alex-ixx?*", Kristin's voice echoed over the intercom.

"Yes, Kristin, what is it?"

"*Concrete Buns is on the phone for you.*"

"Please send him through, Kristin."

"*O.K., and I wanna hear about Paris later. Did you get me one uh them Eiffel Tower figurines?*"

"I'll stop by later, Kristin – could you pass him through?"

My phone rang and instant later.

"Nick, could you just give me a second? I need to take this."

Carlson looked on, disapprovingly.

I picked up the phone and said,

"Vinny, I only have a second. Has the stop-work order been lifted?"

"*Damn straight, it has! You're the fuckin' man – I'll never doubt you again!*"

"Good, I'm glad. Happy to oblige. Are we all set, otherwise?"

"*Yeah, the site is all yours tonight. Bruno'll be there to take care of you.*"

"Good. Listen, I've got to run."

As I hung up, Carlson glared at me, in disbelief that I would have the audacity to take a business-related call while he was seated in my office.

"Sorry, Nick, one of my clients had a fire that needed to be put out this morning."

"*One of your clients?* Oh, I had almost forgotten that you are a regular rainmaker with Lubrano Concrete, Physician's Justice and the France thing. I'm surprised that you're able to find the time to service all of these clients – seeing as how you're now an international superstar and have businesses all over the globe jockeying for the opportunity to have you represent them."

"It *was* just one international client, Nick."

"That actually brings me to the reason for my visit. How *did* the client meeting in Paris go? The Partners have been sitting on the edges of their seats, waiting to hear whether you put the biscuit in the basket."

I could have lied and let Carlson learn the news later about how Jean-Luc Le Guen was actually Jim Winston, and how no additional money would be coming in from his fake company. But I wanted a confrontation with Carlson. Today was to be my very last day serving in his employ. I wanted to go out with a bang, so that I could, once and for all, let him know how I felt about him.

"Actually, Nick, things didn't quite work out in Paris. Looks like Le Guen, S.A. is not going to be compatible as a client for our firm."

After hearing me utter those words, Carlson inched up in his chair and angled his troll-like body over my desk. His facial expression morphed from a typical Golf Asshole smirk to an enraged money-hungry law firm partner scowl.

"Whoa, whoa, whoa, Alex. Who said that you're gonna be the one deciding what clients are and are not fit for representation by *my* firm?"

Now angling my larger body towards him, such that my nose was eight inches from his, I shot back,

"It was decided for me, Nick – it wasn't my decision."

"You mean that you flew to Paris on company time, stayed in a hotel on company money and are coming back with zero?"

Confidently, I retorted,

"Not exactly, Nick. If you'll remember, we received a $50,000.00 retainer. You're not going to sit here and tell me that my couple days away from the office cost the firm more than $50,000.00, are you?"

Now fully infuriated, Nick stood up from his chair and said,

"You are *not* going to talk to me like that! I sign your fucking paycheck! I'm also a veteran of 26 jury trials. Didn't you learn a damn thing in law school? We'll need to send those frogs back their $50,000.00, minus whatever work you did on their case – so make sure you inflate your hours for whatever horseshit work you actually did. We don't get to keep the full retainer, Alex – they get back the unused portion."

Seeing as how Jim Winston was dead and his attaché was probably a very rich murder fugitive, I felt compelled to advise Nick that the firm would not be needing to return the balance of the money.

"I'm not so sure that that's going to be necessary, Nick."

"You don't know shit, Alex. That's the problem with you Ivy League punks – you think you know everything. And guess what? I could care less about the money. The issue is that instead of being in the office and billing hours, you were in *Paris, France* on a boondoggle last week. Do you think that I was in *Paris, France* last week? Do you think that Walt, or any of my other partners were in *Paris, France* last week? The answer is 'no', Alex. The answer is 'no'.

"I told everyone at the firm that I knew this was going to happen and that we shouldn't let you go. No one listened to me though. Well guess what? They're going to listen now – because next time, you will have me expressly sign off on any client development activity that requires your being gone from the office for more than one hour. You got that, Mr. World Traveler?"

Carlson expected me to cave to him and beg for forgiveness, like any other Associate in his or her right mind would have done in this circumstance. I wasn't going to give in to him – not today. I was going to tell him what the score was and I wasn't going to hold back. Regardless of what happened later in the day, I wasn't going to need Nick Carlson or his firm tomorrow.

"Say, Nick," I asked, without even a hint of apprehension in my voice, "what makes you think that there's going to be a 'next time'?"

"I beg your pardon!"

"You beg my pardon – nice. I beg for you to think about how much time and money you are going to have to spend to find another Associate with my skill set, who's going to bill 2200 hours per year, win every piece of shit case you throw his way, and still manage to make rain. Taking into consideration what I bring in and what you pay me, I am more profitable for this firm than just about every Partner. You see where I'm going with this?"

Now borderline conciliatory, Carlson cut me off before I went any further.

"Whoa – just hang on a second – let's not get all excited here – you're having a bad day."

"No, Nick – I think that it would be therapeutic for us to *get all excited here*. I want you to answer my question, or I'm walking out this fucking door for good."

He backed up in his seat, ran his hands through his hair, focused his eyes on one of my diplomas and calmly said,

"Alex, do you realize the gravity of what you've just said, and to whom you've said it? Does Julie know that you're ready to throw away…"

I stood up from my seat, stared down and my soon to be former boss and said fearlessly,

"Nick, if I hear the word, 'Julie' leave your mouth one more time, I'm going to drop your munchkin ass on this floor, in this office."

Still staring at my diplomas, he said, devoid of emotion, as if he had experience in responding to physical threats,

"You've obviously been interviewing and you obviously have offers from multiple other firms – otherwise you wouldn't be speaking to me that way. What's it gonna take for me to keep you, Alex?"

"What?"

"I'll have to check with my partners, but I think I can get you a $20,000.00 raise."

God, did I regret never having previously spoken to him in such a tone.

"Nick, you just got finished telling me that my client development activities were effectively cut off. How can I expect to cultivate my client base?"

"Forget what I said."

"Then why did you say it, Nick?"

He was unable to formulate a verbal response.

"Let me help you out, Nick. Because you're a lifelong bully who suffers severely from the Napoleon complex, and gets off by inciting fear in others. Your existence is the precise reason that people hate lawyers.

"You were telling the truth when you said that you don't care about the money. What you care about is the fact that one of your employees got a free trip to Paris and you didn't. Am I on the right track?"

"Tell you what, Alex. You're having a bad day. Why don't you go home, pick up your son from daycare, take him to the park and toss around a baseball with him. When you come in tomorrow, we'll chat. I should be able to get that $20K for you, but you gotta promise not to tell any of the other Associates."

I was on a roll and was not planning on stopping until I got my last barb in. I wasn't going to be working for him or his firm tomorrow, but I was having too much fun to end the conversation.

"Tell *you* what, Nick. Let's make a deal. If you go door to door to each Associate's office and apologize for being a bully, I'll continue to work for you and you don't have to give me a raise. If not, I'm making no promises."

"Alex, let's not get carried away, here. You may be a star at this place, but you ain't irreplaceable."

The man was telling the truth and I had sufficiently made my point.

"Not so sure I agree Nick, but O.K."

"That's the closest you're getting to an apology from me. Why don't you take my suggestion and go home and play with your son. Here, take him to a nice lunch today," he said, as I accepted a 100 dollar bill from his tiny paw, cherishing my very last bonus from the Krauss Carlson firm.

"This doesn't mean I'm staying at the firm, Nick."

"I know, Alex. Go home and clear your head. Goodbye."

Carlson walked out of my office and closed the door behind him.

I could have sworn that I saw him stop himself as the words, "Off you go!" began to leave his mouth.

Even in light of my current precarious situation, I couldn't help but take satisfaction in what had just transpired with Carlson. This time tomorrow, I would not be his employee. Nevertheless, I had bested him once and for all. Regardless of how much longer I had to live, having put Nick Carlson in his place and quieted him, I had truly accomplished something during my time on Earth.

I had no time to revel in my accomplishment, though. More work needed to be done, and more undesirable people needed to be belittled. I lifted the telephone receiver and dialed the numbers inscribed on George Ridgeway's business card.

"*Yello!*"

"George, it's Alex Brown."

"Counselor, I was wondering when you were going to call. How the hell are you?"

"I'm fine, George. It's you who's the problem. You are a disgusting piece of garbage and an insult to the human race."

"Well let's be fair, Alex. What you did with Leon Richardson was most unethical. I wouldn't say that you're a model citizen, either."

I felt like exploding but didn't want to risk revealing that Winston and Alassane were dead. If he were to learn those small facts, he would simultaneously come to realize that the diamond was not destined to come to him and that he would be the next

355

one to meet his fate. Such a development would bring my plan to a screeching halt.

I needed to keep acting.

"George, you're a vile pig. I don't have time for your bullshit, so if you want the merchandise, here's what's going to happen..."

"I'm all ears, young man."

"You're going to meet me for cocktails at The Atlantis House, down on Delaware Avenue for dinner."

"Good show – I can't wait. I may even let you treat. Do they have Cutty Sark there, son?", he asked flippantly.

"Do you honestly give a shit, George? Have you recently looked in the mirror at your alcohol-abuse-induced exploding capillary collage of a face? I guarantee that if the bartender told you that all he had was low-grade wood varnish, you wouldn't hesitate to drink it. Am I right?"

I had to continue to let my emotions rage against him, so that he wouldn't consider for a second that I might be up to something. I needed to speak to him in the manner in which he thought someone in my position would.

"Alex, that tone is very unbecoming of a Presbyterian graduate – albeit that of a very non-Presbyterian Jew. I've struggled with alcohol for much of my life and you're sitting here mocking the way my face looks. Did you ever stop to consider that I may have feelings too?", he asked sarcastically.

"Not really, George."

"Well, I'm really sorry to hear that, young man," he said, punctuating the sentence with his signature phlegm-infused cough.

"George, you will meet me at The Atlantis House at 8 p.m. You will bring no one with you and you will tell no one where you are going. Since you have no friends or acquaintances, I don't imagine that this will be a problem.

"If I suspect that you have brought company with you, the deal's off. I don't care what you have on me. If I feel that my safety is compromised, we're done, O.K.?"

Ridgeway paused before responding, perhaps thoughtfully considering the possibility that he would not get the diamond if I got spooked.

"You bring that blasted diamond tonight, you fucking punk!", he snapped in a tone markedly variant from his prior lighthearted tenor.

After his outburst, I could hear that Ridgeway was breathing heavily. I immediately regretted angering him, since it sounded as if he was going to kick the bucket right there, on the other end of the phone. Since my plan was contingent upon Ridgeway not dropping dead before I could get him to the site, I was more than worried for a few moments.

"George? George? Hello? You there, George?"

I heard the sound of an asthma inhaler emitting its contents. Ridgeway's breathing slowly returned to normal.

"What are you trying to do, kill an old man?"

"Sorry, George. Don't go dying on me before I even get you the diamond, O.K."

"I bet you'd like that, wouldn't you?", he said, laughingly, in a renewed jovial tone.

Believing it best to change the subject as soon as possible, I said,

"I'll see you at 8 P.M., George. Goodbye."

"And goodbye to you, counselor."

CHAPTER FIFTY-THREE

I heeded Carlson's advice and picked Charlie up early from daycare. We ate lunch at Charlie's favorite hot dog joint and then threw around a baseball in the park. I pocketed the $89.75 in change from Carlson's 100 dollar bill.

When Charlie had had enough of the park, we returned home and ate ice cream while watching cartoons. As I observed my son's eyes fixated on the television set while he sat on the couch with ice cream all over his face, I thought about how very lucky I was, irrespective of the misfortune that had befallen me.

When Julie got home at 6:45 p.m., I explained to her that I had a dinner meeting with George Ridgeway back in town. In light of the fact that I had chosen to leave work early to spend time with Charlie, she gave me only minimal guff about leaving her for the evening. While she was feeding Charlie his dinner, I went upstairs to attend to some last minute preparations.

I locked the door to our home office and ran through my mental inventory of items that I needed to take with me to my meeting with Ridgeway. I needed the diamond, the pills and, of course, the gun. I inserted a key into the file cabinet, and opened its drawer. The gaudy diamond sat in its velvet bag, next to the bottle of pills and the loaded gun. On Saturday night, when I placed these items in the file cabinet, I had wanted to remove the bullets from the gun, to avoid any accidents in the house. After a half-minute of being unable to decipher how to execute this task, I gave up. I had figured that the odds of me shooting myself while jostling with the weapon were far greater than Charlie or Julie inflicting harm upon themselves, by opening this seldom used cabinet to which I held the only key.

Since the diamond was of greater import than the pills, I emptied the pills from their secure bottle and replaced them with the diamond. After fastening the childproof cap onto the pill bottle containing the diamond, I placed the pills in the velvet bag that previously contained the diamond. I dropped the pill bottle in my left outside blazer pocket and the velvet bag in my right outside blazer pocket. I secured the pistol in my rear waistband. My loose fitting jacket did not reveal the outline of the gun.

Before leaving the house at 6:58 p.m., I carefully took off my Rolex and discreetly placed it in the drawer of my night table while Julie was not looking. Controlling my overflowing emotions, I placed next to my watch the doomsday letter to Julie that I had written the previous evening. I deposited the $89.75 change from lunch into Charlie's piggy bank.

At 7:47 p.m., after an uneventful journey back up the Interstate, I entered the Atlantis House parking lot. A stylized white sign directed vehicles to the left for valet parking and to the right for self-parking. Taking into consideration what Ridgeway's condition was likely to be upon our exit, I deemed it advisable to opt for valet parking. This way, the parking attendant could help me place Ridgeway in the vehicle when we were ready to leave.

I left the Bimmer with the attendant and walked towards the building. Before entering the restaurant, I gazed upward at the Breezeview Plaza towers, which were no more that a half-mile away. An uneasy feeling overcame me as I looked at the construction project that I would soon be visiting under cover of darkness.

The restaurant, which sat on the Delaware River, was decorated with a decidedly cheesy under-the-sea 1980s-like theme. The Chief had picked the location for its proximity to Breezeview Plaza, rather than for its culinary reputation. I took some satisfaction, though, in the notion that Ridgeway would feel out-of-sorts in this very non-highbrow establishment.

Correctly surmising that Ridgeway was both early and had a drink in front of him, I walked toward the back of the restaurant where a bar sat in front of an expansive fish tank that occupied an entire wall. My dinner guest noticed my presence from about 25 feet away. He waved me over to the table. Once I got within earshot of Ridgeway, he said,

"Alex, my boy, come on over here – I've gotta get you one of these Mai Tais."

As I approached the bar, I noticed that Ridgeway was dressed markedly different from his usual central casting Brandywine County scotch drinking garb. With his baby blue linen blazer adorned with an off-white handkerchief in the breast pocket, a pale yellow oxford cloth shirt, light tan pants and braided leather loafers without socks, Ridgeway looked as if he were about to board the Love Boat. The man clearly thought that he was getting the diamond tonight and that he would be able to disappear into the abyss unimpeded.

"No thank you, George – I don't feel much like drinking tonight."

"Nonsense. Are you a lawyer, or a member of the temperance movement?

"Osvaldo, set the man up with one of your Mai Tais. These are really delicious. I mean *really* delicious. Do you drink a lot of these in Mexico?"

The bartender, who had a bright gold name tag that read, "Osvaldo" politely responded in flawless English,

"Sir, the Mai Tai is a *Polynesian-style* drink, it's not a Mexican specialty."

"Oh, horseshit, Osvaldo! Why didn't you tell me that? I would have had you make me one of them margaritas – now don't you tell me that you don't drink them bad boys south of the border because I won't believe it for one second!" Ridgeway shouted in a manner that he believed to be wryly humorous.

"Actually sir, I'm not even Mexican."

"Like hell you're not!"

"I'm Venezuelan."

"Venezuelan? Oh, for Christ's Sake! Osvaldo, what the hell are you doing tending bar? You should be bathing in gold, with all that damn oil you have down there!"

Osvaldo once again politely laughed. Notwithstanding the task at hand, I was still horribly embarrassed to be in the presence of this abominable creature. In an attempt to get Ridgeway to lay off of the bartender, I asked,

"George, did you have a chance to look at the menu yet?"

Undaunted, Ridgeway continued,

"Venezuelan, huh. Say, this may be a shot in the dark, but do you know Bobby Abreu?"

I grabbed Ridgeway's arm to cut him off.

"I'm serious, do you know him? He's Venezuelan. Helluva ballplayer. He was with the Phillies for the better part of a decade. Those idiot fans ran him out of town 'cause he couldn't take the Phillies to the playoffs."

Still firmly grasping his arm, I inched close to his ear and said softly,

"You're making a complete ass out of yourself. We are here to complete a transaction. The more of an idiot you are, the more suspicious people will be of both of us. Now shut your trap and pick out something to eat."

I moved back away from his Aqua Velva fragranced face and opened my menu. Thankfully, Osvaldo wandered to patrons at the other end of the bar, while I distracted Ridgeway's attention.

Without pausing, Ridgeway exclaimed,

"Classy place you've picked out, here, counsel. Remind me to cancel my membership at the Perennial Club – this is my new hot spot."

"Glad you like it."

Now at a murmur, Ridgeway said,

"I'm not real hungry, son. Whad'ya say we get on with the transaction and blow this pop stand? I've got places to go to."

"The vibe's not right yet, George. Your inane Bobby Abreu comments got people looking over in this direction. Do you want someone to club you over the head in the parking lot after they see me handing you a diamond the size of a boulder?"

"That's not much of a concern to me, Alex," Ridgeway said, carefully revealing the inside of his blazer. The unmistakable shape of the butt end of a handgun protruded out of the top of his inside pocket. In making known that he had a gun, Ridgeway was sending a warning message to me, as much as he was advising me that he could fend for himself in the parking lot while carrying a priceless gem.

"You know, George, I think I actually *am* going to have one of those Mai Tais. Did you have to ask for that pineapple slice, or did Osvaldo just put in there for you?"

With a reddening face, Ridgeway responded in a perturbed pitch,

"He just put the bloody thing in there, Alex. Now can you just give me the goods and let me be on my merry fucking way?"

"George, if you didn't act like such an idiot to the bartender, so that the whole restaurant was looking over here, I could have handed off the diamond to you already. You need to chill out for a half-hour, so that people are no longer suspicious of us. If you can accomplish that small task, I'll give you the diamond and we can get out of here."

"O.K., fine, you got a half-hour – no more!", he said, tapping the handgun from the outside of his jacket.

"See, now you're starting to think sensibly. I'm going to have Osvaldo set me up and give you a refill. Why don't you go to the pisser and splash some water in your face. You really look like shit."

"I do?"

"Yeah – your face is bright red and you look as if you're about to have a stroke. Just take it easy. You're going to get the merchandise and everything is going to be fine."

"I've got to take a piss anyway," he said, rising from his barstool, "don't go nowhere, Alex."

"George, if I were going to take off, why would I have even come here in the first place?"

Looking puzzled, he responded,

"Well – I suppose you're right. One half-hour, Alex – max!"

As Ridgeway walked in the direction of the restroom, I said,

"You have my word, George."

It was a comforting feeling to know that I was deceiving him and he didn't even suspect it.

He ambled toward the restroom with a confident spring in his step, as if he were marching in a conga line. Once I saw him disappear, I summoned the bartender.

"Osvaldo!"

"Yes, sir," he said, quickly racing over to my side of the bar.

"I need two more Mai Tais in a hurry. If you have them mixed within two minutes, you get to keep the change from this", I said, extending a hand, holding a $50 bill.

He took the bill and got right to work, feverishly mixing rums and juices. Within 45 seconds, he was garnishing the drinks with pineapple slices, flowers and mini-umbrellas. He placed the two drinks on the bar with pride and thanked me for the generous tip.

"Osvaldo, I like to stir my cocktail while I'm drinking it. Can you toss me a couple of those plastic doo-dads?"

Osvaldo happily obliged, placing in each Mai Tai, a kitschy plastic drink stirrer adorned with a colorful molded tropical fish. I needed to get to work in a hurry.

"One more thing, Osvaldo."

"Please, sir."

"Let's get one order each of the crab cakes, the fried calamari and the lobster spring rolls. My friend and I are in kind of a hurry, so if you would ask the kitchen to put a rush on it, I'd be grateful."

"Absolutely, sir."

I quickly retrieved from my right pocket the velvet bag containing the Rohypnol pills. Looking back towards the restroom, I dropped the pills into Ridgeway's drink and crushed them at the bottom of his goblet, using the fish stirrer. Thankfully, the Mai Tai was opaque in color. So, even though my prodding with the stirrer told me that the pills were not fully dissolved, Ridgeway would never be able to visually detect that he had been slipped a Mickey.

While waiting for my guest to return, I took a sip of my cocktail and chewed on the wedge of pineapple. Maybe Ridgeway was on to something. Osvaldo poured a damn tasty Mai Tai. The mixture of light rum, dark rum and fruity-tasting accompaniments gave the drink a quality that both quenched the thirst and satisfied a sugar fix. If I survived the night, I resolved that the Mai Tai would be my new drink of choice. Dewar's and Pernod were ancient history for me.

In mid-gulp of the liquid gold, I felt a sharp thump on my back. The impact caused the Mai Tai to go down the wrong pipe, which forced me to cough.

I turned around to see the raving loon behind me, dancing the mambo with an imaginary partner.

"Jeez, George, I didn't even hear you coming. What are you trying to do, kill me?"

"Well, for your own good, pay attention next time," he responded jovially.

While I was still coughing, Ridgeway retook his seat at the bar. Noticing the gift that I had bestowed upon him, he exclaimed,

"Holy shit, Alex, what are you doing to me? Tomorrow's Sunday and I've got to be at mass! Father Dunleavy doesn't like it when his parishioners come to church all boozed up. I know you Jews don't believe in hell, but come on son, I'm a Roman Catholic. I ain't gettin' any younger and I'm running out of free sins!"

Ridgeway didn't know how close he really was to standing before Saint Peter.

Accommodating his puerile attempt at humor, I played along and said unenthused and monotonically,

"George, tomorrow isn't Sunday, it's Tuesday."

"Well I'll be damned! You're right, son! Ozzie, keep these bad boys coming, this baby is about to go down the hatch."

He then held up his glass, gestured for me to do the same and said,

"Alex, I know that you think I'm a miserable old bastard who screwed you over real bad. But when this is all over, and I'm sippin' these babies all day on a beach and you're winnin' juries over, you'll thank me. What did Nietzsche say? What does not destroy me makes me stronger? You're gonna come out of this predicament a stronger man. Son, it was a real pleasure knowin' you. *La Hymie!*"

George downed his toxic brew in three gulps, as I took a small sip.

"Actually, George, it's *L'Chaim*, but I'm touched by the gesture."

Although I hated myself for feeling any empathy towards the man, I actually was somewhat touched by his attempt to toast in Hebrew. If nothing more, he was one funny old son of a bitch.

"*La Kay-imm...La Key-imm...*", Ridgeway torturedly attempted, as his jugular vein swelled.

"That's O.K., George. You gave it an honest effort."

"How the hell do you make that sound?"

"*You* don't, George. If you've ever eaten Spam or worn green polyester pants, you're just not going to be able to pronounce the *chhhhh* sound – sorry to be the bearer of bad news."

We laughed as Osvaldo placed three platters of appetizers in front of us.

Ridgeway gorged himself with crabcake after calamari ring after spring roll. Had he known this to be his last supper, he might have taken more time to savor his meal. Instead, he proceeded like a ravenous dog, with grease on his fingers and crumbs dangling off of his face.

"So, George, where's this beach with the free-flowing Mai Tais that you're headed to?"

"I meant that metaphorically, young man. What I was getting at was that for the first time in my life, I'm a free man. No more corrupt judges and law enforcement riding my ass. No more being blackballed by society...", he said with his voice trailing off.

Only I knew that Ridgeway's expectation for the future was more than a touch overconfident.

Although I could see that the Roofies were beginning to work, I still felt compelled to play dumb with him so that he wouldn't suspect anything.

"Seriously, George, where are you headed to – I'm jealous."

"Parts unknown, my boy, parts unknown," he said, while stuffing a crab cake in his mouth.

He stood up from his chair and took his blazer off. With his knees wobbling, Ridgeway sat back down.

"Is it hot in here, Alex? Holy shit – I think I'm drunk! Ozzie, what kind of lighter fluid you puttin' in them Tai Mais?", he said, slurring each and every word.

"George, how many of those things did you have before I got here?"

"I dunno – I'm really – just – so – tired."

Ridgeway undid two more buttons on his shirt, leaving nearly his entire chest exposed. He sat on his barstool with his eyes closed and his chin pointing upward.

Seeing Ridgeway's condition, Osvaldo walked over.

"Sir, I'm sorry – I cannot serve your friend anymore, but you are free to still drink."

"You make a very good Mai Tai, Osvaldo, and I thank you, but that's really not going to be necessary. I think that I'm just going to take the check. Here – run my credit card and give yourself 25%. I need to get my friend out of here before something bad happens."

"Yes, sir."

Osvaldo quickly swiped my card and handed it back to me.

"Say, Osvaldo, out of curiosity, how many did my friend have before I got here?"

"Four. He got here about an hour before you."

Hell, I didn't even need the Roofies. The man had consumed six or seven oversized mixed drinks during an hour and a half timeframe.

"Osvaldo, do me a favor. Could you come around to this side of the bar and help me get my friend out of here?"

"Of course, Sir."

The last thing I wanted was for Ridgeway to fall on his ass and for his gun to go flying across the marble floor of this crowded restaurant.

Osvaldo got to Ridgeway just in the nick of time. As Ridgeway listed to the right, Osvaldo wedged his hand underneath his right shoulder while I secured his left side. When we lifted him to his feet, it was clear that he was in very bad shape. All of the restaurant's diners stopped what they were doing and watched Osvaldo and me carry this man out of the building. Although Ridgeway still had use of his legs, had he not been supported on either side, he would have staggered about and would have eventually fallen to the ground.

Osvaldo and I placed Ridgeway on a bench next to the parking attendant podium. I thanked Osvaldo for his assistance, and he returned back into the restaurant.

While I was waiting for the Bimmer to be pulled around, Ridgeway's rubbery body slouched to the left and he slowly tumbled. Before I could stop his momentum, his head met the metal armrest of the bench. The cliché, "that's gonna hurt in the morning" ordinarily would have come to mind. However, in Mr. Ridgeway's case, I didn't envision him feeling much of anything in the morning.

After the Bimmer pulled around the restaurant's front circle, a goateed teenager with a mohawk haircut and a red nylon jacket that read "VALET" on the back emerged from the car. For a few moments, I mused over whether this kid's stupid germs could have infiltrated my car, and whether I could possibly contract them. Once that emotion passed, I turned my concerns to how I was going to get this wretch into the car.

I retrieved a ten dollar bill from my wallet and handed it to the valet freak.

"Thanks for getting my car, man. Hey, would you mind helping me get my buddy into the back seat?"

"Dude, he's wasted! I just saw him come in here a little over an hour ago – he was fine then. He must have been doin' some serious drinking. Were you guys funneling beers in there?"

We placed Ridgeway on the back bench of the Bimmer. Given the circumstances, I didn't feel it necessary to secure him with a seatbelt.

"He was, I wasn't. I don't use a funnel to drink on weekdays."

"Dude, you gotta be a player if you're gonna hang with the big dogs. I funneled three beers at once last week in my buddy's basement – it was awesome!"

"Sounds like a tremendous accomplishment. Well, I've got to get my friend home."

As I pulled away towards Delaware Avenue, I reminisced with a heavy heart of the days when life was about funneling beers and having fun. Now I was on my way to commit murder in the hopes of retaking control of my humdrum life as a father, husband and lawyer.

After a two minute drive southbound on Delaware Avenue, I passed under the Walt Whitman Bridge and came upon the entrance to the Breezeview Plaza construction site. When I reached the area where I had turned in earlier in the day, I was met with a sealed chain-link fence which displayed rectangular white signs with red writing that read, "CONSTRUCTION SITE – KEEP OUT" and "ALL PEOPLE ENTERING MUST WEAR HARD HATS."

Five seconds after I parked the Bimmer in front of the obstruction, Bruno appeared behind the fence, clad in a badly-soiled wife-beater tank top, a pair of cut-off dungarees and his Eagles hard hat. An Italian horn and a near-life-size crucifix hung from chunky gold chains around his neck. He held a cigarette in one hand and the dwindled remains of a hoagie in the other. It was nice to see that Bruno could loosen up when he was working on after-hours special assignments for the Lubranos.

"How ya' doin' Bruno?"

"I'm doin' good," he said, swinging open the fence and approaching the driver's window.

"Here – take deeze and dis," he said, handing me an extremely heavy chain and a pad lock, while projecting his onion and lunchmeat-infused breath into my face.

"Thank you," I said, incredulous as why he was giving these items to me.

"Your insurance company photographer looks like he's a little tired back dare," he said, pointing to Ridgeway.

"I'm sorry?"

"Yeah, *Vihh-knee* tol' me about how you had ta' bring da' photographer here ta' take pictures to prove dat dare ain't no problems wit' da' building's setback or nothin'"

Attempting to cover my mistake, I responded,

"Oh, I though you said *pornographer*. Yeah, yeah – that's George back there. He had a long ride down from Hartford today, so he's catching some z's."

"Yeah, I hear dat. Listen, when yous're done wit' dih pictures youse gotta take, lock up dih fence and give *Vihh-knee* back dih key tomorrah, O.K.? *Vihh-knee* tol' me to get lost once youse got here. So, yous're here and I'm getting' lost. Dih ol' lady's makin' lasagna tonight, so if you don't mind, I'll be on my way."

"Great, Bruno – thanks for your help."

Bruno waved goodbye and I drove my car down the same dirt road upon which it had traveled earlier in the day. I passed the muddy area where I had damaged my shoes and drove through the gate to the construction area that had previously been guarded by a police officer. I dodged stationary boom cranes, bulldozers and backhoes, and found a clear parking area immediately adjacent to the tower that was under construction.

I turned off the ignition and got out of the car. The construction site was hauntingly quiet. I could hear nothing except for the gently blowing summer wind and the rippling waters of the Delaware River, some 50 feet away. The only illumination was from the brightly shining full moon and a series of sparsely scattered light bulbs hanging in plastic cages from the ceiling of the first floor of the tower. The light bulb cages gently swung with each new waft of putrid river air.

I opened the rear driver's side door and looked down at Ridgeway's weathered visage. Copious amounts of drool were pouring out of the right side of his mouth onto the supple leather seats of my Bimmer. Between the parking attendant's stupid germs, Bruno's hoagie breath and this old codger's 80 proof drool, I made a mental note to get the car fumigated if I survived the evening.

Feeling my presence, Ridgeway awakened slightly from his slumber and began to mumble.

"Venezuela! I ain't goin' to no Venezuela! Get me off the barge, Osvaldo, or I'll have your neck! I shoot 'em all, I tell you! I'll shoot every last one of them bastards!"

Although I initially found Ridgeway's impaired rant humorous, his mention of shooting people abruptly brought my attention to a crucial omission on my part. Realizing that Ridgeway could still be dangerous with a loaded gun, even in his weakened condition, I delicately reached to retrieve the gun from his inside pocket. While doing so, I pointed my own gun at him, so that I could protect myself in the event that he made a sudden move.

I was able to successfully extract the gun from Ridgeway's person without incident. While doing so, I felt an exhilarating rush of adrenaline, having for the first time pointed a loaded weapon at someone. Ridgeway's gun looked very similar to mine. Both were black and roughly the same shape and size. I harnessed his gun on the left side of my rear waist band that was covered by my blazer. I moved my gun from the center of my back to the right side of my back.

It was now time to pull Ridgeway out of my car. I clasped both of his hands, extended them over his head and pulled. He slid easily off of the drool slickened leather. Seeing no practical reason to handle him delicately, I dropped him on the ground with an audible thud. The impact apparently roused him, as he began to mumble again.

"Would somebody get me a drink already?! I asked for a Cutty Sark hours ago! What the hell do I have to do to get a damn cocktail? Wait a minute – what the fuck am I doing lying on the ground?"

With his eyes now open and looking at me upside down, he seemed to be coming out of his impaired state. Since I had both weapons, I was not worried. However, I didn't want to shoot him at this specific location. I needed to get him onto the ground floor of the tower. I briefly considered hitting him with the gun to knock him out again, but he presented me with a better alternative.

"George, you fell down, but I think that you're O.K."

"Well don't just stand there, Alex, help me the hell up!"

After I lifted him from the ground, Ridgeway asked, thankfully still very much affected by the pills and booze,

"Where the bloody hell are we?"

"George, don't you remember? You asked me to take you to that new bar. They're doing some construction in the parking lot. The bar's over there," I responded, gesturing to the tower.

"Well now you're talkin'! I need a damn drink – take me there!"

Although his walk was more of a stagger, Ridgeway was able to put one foot in front of the other during his death march. I walked a few feet behind him and a few feet beside him to ensure that he could not make any abrupt movements to disarm me. As we made the 20 foot journey to the to where the ground floor's concrete slab began, it became clear that in his disoriented shape, Ridgeway truly did not know where he was and that he did not suspect that I was up to any high jinks.

"I need to get to the airport by 10:30, so this is gonna have to be a quick drink, ya' hear me?"

"I hear you, George. I promise – we'll be in and out."

"Well O.K., then – and I'm not payin' $12.00 for a damn drink!"

"Don't worry about it, George, the drinks are on me. Walk this way," I said, pointing to the far end of the ground floor, which abutted the shore of the Delaware River.

"Why the hell are we goin' over there? It's dark, and I don't see nothing."

"George, how many times am I going to have to tell you? They're doing construction – we need to walk through this area to get to the bar. You're the one who picked out the place, so stop complaining."

"Well that's because it's a damn good place! I come here all the time!"

As he continued to babble absurdities, I stopped walking, but allowed him to continue stumbling towards the edge of the foundation. When I could see that he was five feet from the rim, I instructed him to stop.

"George, hold it right there."

He stopped just shy of the end of the concrete.

"Oh, good heavens! Stop. Go. Stop. Go. What the hell are you doing to me?"

I took a deep breath and prepared to execute phase one of the series of ungodly acts that were necessary to regain my life. Ridgeway turned around from the edge and faced me.

"George, you've jeopardized everything that I care about in this world, and you've done so solely for your own financial gain. You hand-selected me to be your pawn in this dreadful scheme, and you have no remorse in having done so. Because of that, I have no remorse or trepidation in separating you from your pitiable excuse for a life."

Hearing my message loud and clear, Ridgeway responded,

"What is it that you're gonna do, son, call the cops on me? Good luck finding a way to earn a living for the next 50 years!"

"Not exactly, George. I'm going to kill you. After I'm done killing you, I'm going to kill Chief Bozzi and whoever he brings with him tonight. And I'm going to get away with it, too. You know why?"

"Why?"

Once it became clear that the Chief had designs on eliminating me, I had decided that I was going to refuse to cooperate with the blackmailers. By going to the FBI, I was going to allow the Chief to leak the transcript of my dealings with Leon Richardson and the photos of me and Véronique. I was going to take the fall, get disbarred, divorced or whatever, and start again from square one. Charlie's inadvertent foresight had changed that defeatist strategy.

"Because my two year old son, who's a hell of a lot smarter than me, had the presence of mind to hit my Dictaphone's 'Record' button when I went to speak with Bozzi's deputy Saturday night. I realized that instead of having my life ruined, I had the opportunity take your diamond away from you and secure my financial future, while ensuring that none of the damaging information got leaked. Thanks to my boy, I've got a taped recording of Bozzi's deputy explicitly outlining the conspiracy to blackmail me to kill you. I had to tape over a particular portion where he referenced Leon Richardson, but other than that, I've got a virtual full confession of all of the details of the plot on tape.

"Once I allow the authorities to listen to that tape, I'll easily be able to sell my story of killing the two cops in self-defense. After all, I have incriminating information about the two cops and it will make perfect sense that they would have a motive to eliminate me. As for killing you, I may be able to get the Chief to do his own dirty work – albeit after he's dead.

"After I'm cleared of any wrongdoing and you and the piece of shit cops are dead, I'm going to keep the diamond for myself. Of course, I'll tell the cops that the diamond wound up in the river during the tussle that left you, Bozzi and Bozzi's sidekick dead."

Now bearing almost no sign of impairment, other than his paranoid dementia, Ridgeway exclaimed, with the reddened face that I had come to know,

"Now wait just one goddamn minute! We had a deal! You lousy conniving son of a bitch! You're a fucking liar! Bozzi wasn't gonna kill me – I was gonna give him a cut of the loot from the diamond!"

"You're really just not that smart of a person, are you now, George? Why would Bozzi want *some* of the loot when he could have *all* of the loot?"

Ridgeway clenched his face and gritted his teeth, realizing that my analysis was on-target.

I continued,

"Also, George, did you ever stop to consider that Bozzi might not want you alive, for fear that you might let the cat out of the bag about him?

"What's more, I bet you think that your ol' partner Jimmy Winston – the one whom you tried to convince me had his eyeballs ripped out by Spanish thugs – is the driving force behind all this, right? Well guess what? He *and* his African henchman are both dead. So, as it turns out, you weren't had by a retired lawyer. You were had by a two bit, brainless, corrupt Brandywine County police chief, and his bigot deputy. How does that make you feel, George?"

In an instant, Ridgeway reached inside his blazer for his missing gun and lunged at me. As I easily moved out of the way, and Ridgeway fell off the edge of the foundation and landed three feet below in a pool of thick mud.

At that moment, a high-intensity lamp flashed on, forcing both Ridgeway and me to cover our eyes with our forearms. The light was so bright and startling that it momentarily caused me to lose my balance. Ridgeway wore a frustrated look on his face, as he desperately searched inside his jacket for the gun that I now possessed.

Once I regained my balance, a familiar voice belonging to someone standing on what appeared to be a police boat said,

"*Two bit, brainless, corrupt Brandywine County police chief? Bigot deputy?* Yo Tommy, seems that our white collar friend ain't got no respect for law enforcement," the Chief said, with his gun drawn, as he stepped off of the police boat onto land.

"Ungrateful motherfucker!," Porn Stache added, also with his gun drawn, "Youse professional types don't appreciate what we law enforcement do for you. Who the fuck do youse think keeps the niggers from breakin' into your houses? Without us, some Mexican mushroom picker would be parkin' his low rider on your driveway and eatin' chimichangas with your wife while you were tied up in the basement with his bandanas!"

I thought it best not to respond.

The Chief and Porn 'Stache helped Ridgeway out of the mud and back onto his feet. With the Chief pointing his gun at me and his deputy pointing his gun at Ridgeway, they lifted Ridgeway onto the concrete foundation where I was standing. His light-toned island outfit was a muddy brown mess. When they were done helping Ridgeway, with guns still drawn, they both ascended to the ground floor level.

Attempting to sound like someone different from the buffoon that he was, the Chief said,

"*Ale-ixx*, I'm very disappointed in you. I gave you the opportunity to save your career and your marriage. All you had to do was carry out a simple task for me. What do you have to say for yourself?"

For a few seconds, I carefully thought out my words. As my mouth opened to speak, the Chief preempted me,

"Hang on *Ale-ixx*, terribly sorry to interrupt you. I've got a small housekeeping matter to attend to. Tommy, we both know that *Ale-ixx* is carrying, but I think we'd be remiss if we didn't pat down Mr. Ridgeway. Go check if he's got any weapons."

Upon receiving the Chief's command, Porn 'Stache walked away from the Chief, toward Ridgeway. The deputy wore an ominous smile. He patted down Ridgeway and found nothing. Still facing Ridgeway, he walked backwards towards the Chief.

Before I was able to take cover, the Chief extended his enormous arm parallel with the ground, paused for the briefest of moments and squeezed the trigger. An explosion of sound and cacophony of echoes, the likes of which I had never previously heard, rocked my senses and sent me to the ground. I didn't know whether I or Ridgeway had been shot.

When the echoes ceased, I saw Ridgeway gasping for breath, standing up with his hands on his knees. Seeing no blood emanating from his body, I was convinced that I was the victim of the gunshot. I felt no pain, though, and was easily able to rise to my feet. As I dusted myself off, I quickly realized that it was neither I nor Ridgeway who was on the receiving end of the Chief's gun blast.

Porn 'Stache's body lay approximately five feet from where he stood prior to being shot. He came to rest on his side. Blood flowed rapidly out of a gaping mass of bare flesh in the back of his head, as well as from his nose and mouth. This was a gruesome sight, especially in light of the fact that I considered the odds of my lying next to Porn 'Stache in an identical condition in the immediate future to be high.

I felt as if I should draw my gun immediately and stop the Chief from killing me. Since his gun was pointed at me, though, such a task was presently impossible.

"Well that's a monkey off my back, *Ale-ixx*! Tommy was so damned undisciplined!"

I was very confused. *Why hadn't he disarmed me, when he knew for a fact that I had brought the police-issue gun that Porn 'Stache had given me?*

"*Ale-ixx*, before that little interruption, I think that you were going to say something, weren't you?"

Trembling with panic, I was unable to formulate words.

"Let me help you out, son. Seems like with all that distraction, you forgot what you were gonna ask me. In that case, I think I'll just fill you in on the situation here.

"Jimmy Winston was an important ally of mine when he was the king of Brandywine County. He made sure my department was always properly funded and, well, made me feel like I had job security. When he disappeared to the black continent and then on to Europe, he still called upon me for favors, but never really gave me anything in return. I had pulled all the strings to make sure that any effort to track him down was immediately suppressed. When it really became a one-way street, with me givin' and him takin', I just got tired of him talkin' to me like I was his boy. Also, with his erratic behavior and drinking problem, I was obviously concerned that he might turn me in during a moment of weakness.

"So, when I caught wind of him havin' a purchasable lady friend who was scared shitless of him and wanted him dead, I seized the moment. Once the lady friend found out that Jimmy had killed her French side dish, I didn't need to convince her no more."

"Véronique kills Winston and Alassane – Véronique gets to keep the balance of the loot that remained after the diamond was purchased. You aren't worried over Véronique blabbing about your involvement because the money will keep her quiet. Plus, you've employed your usual brand of Lower Salem Township intimidation, which has caused her to believe that if she so much as thinks of blowing the whistle, your people will hunt her down, no matter what corner of the Earth she's inhabiting."

"It took a while, but Ol' Veronica decided to listen and do what was best for herself. That young lady got a very good deal from me because my connections in the State Department made sure them Frenchies allowed her to escape justice and get to a safe place to hunker down.

"Your parents must be proud, counselor. You are one sharp Jew."

That Véronique had killed Winston and Alassane was not the only one of my suspicions that had now been confirmed. If the Chief had shot his own man and commissioned the killing a political ally overseas to eliminate any link to his involvement in a crime, he sure as hell had no designs upon allowing me out of this construction site in any way other than in a body bag.

As such, the gun that he knew that I was carrying was undoubtedly loaded with blanks, or was not loaded at all. He knew my pedigree well enough to be able to correctly predict that I would not attempt to verify that the gun given to me was operable. As far as the Chief was concerned, I was not armed with any deadly weapon.

"Did you bring a present for me tonight?"

"Do you mean the diamond?"

"That's my fucking diamond, you bastards!", Ridgeway cried, still out of breath.

I expected those words to be George Ridgeway's death sentence. Instead, the Chief laughed, and said,

"Never mind him, *Ale-ixx*. Let's see my diamond."

I took the pill bottle out of my left pocket, and placed it on the ground in between where the Chief and I were standing.

When the Chief holstered his gun at his side, I became instantly certain that my previous theory was correct. Confident that he was in the midst of two unarmed men, he squatted down to pick up the pill bottle containing the diamond, without the protection of his weapon.

"Creative packaging, counselor."

Still in a crouch, he attempted to open the child-proof lid to the bottle. He jostled with the cap, to no avail. Desperately trying to connect with his prize, and with his eyes distracted from me, I quickly reached behind my blazer and pulled out the gun that was strapped to the left side of my back.

"Freeze, you piece of shit – don't fucking move an inch!"

Still unable to open the pillbox, the Chief gazed up at me and initially displayed a surprised look. This expression was replaced, in rapid fashion, with a confident smirk that gracefully bent his white mustache. He rose to his feet.

"I told you not to move a fucking inch! Stay right there!"

I became immediately concerned as to whether I had pulled from my rear waistband the harmless gun or Ridgeway's presumably loaded gun.

Still boldly sneering, with no detectable nervousness, the Chief sarcastically retorted,

"Whoa, there, chill out, you're the boss. I ain't doin' nothin.'"

"I want you to place your hands behind your head. You're gonna stay like that until some *real* cops get here."

"And what makes you think that I'm gonna do that?"

"Because I'm gonna kill you otherwise."

"Oh, you are? How sweet," he responded, without a tinge of seriousness.

"I will shoot your ass dead right here, right now. This is your last chance."

"You know what, *Ale-ixx*? I don't think you're gonna be shooting anyone tonight," he said, opening the pill bottle at last.

The Chief turned the pill bottle upside-down, emptying the gargantuan diamond into his palm.

"Now that's a beauty," he said in awe, with his eyes fixated on the gem.

He was completely disinterested in the gun that was pointed at him. He tossed the pill bottle aside and placed the stone in his pocket.

"So, what's it gonna be, concrete lawyer?"

I looked to Ridgeway. He winked at me and nodded his head, as if to signify something. I interpreted the gesture as Ridgeway telling me that I was holding his gun, and not the dummy gun. If I was misinterpreting his signal or had simply grabbed the wrong gun, I was a dead man.

The Chief began to walk towards me with a gleaming smile. I backtracked slightly.

As the Chief casually began to reach to the side to retrieve his gun, I fired a single shot.

The recoil of the gun and the sound of the shot stunned me and left a frantic ringing in my ears.

With adrenaline and fear running through my system, I walked over to where the Chief's body lay. My gun was still drawn. As I stood over him, I pridefully watched blood stream from his forehead wound and out of his nose, onto his mustache and eventually onto the virgin concrete surface.

My euphoria at seeing the Chief in this state was troubling to me. I felt absolutely no guilt or regret for having taken the life of another human being. This exhilaration associated with having killed someone who was such a detriment to society made me feel validated as a man. That I had such a satisfying feeling caused me significant pause.

What had I become? What had these loathsome people turned me into?

"Nice shot, cowboy," I heard Ridgeway say from about ten feet away, my eyes still affixed to my fresh prey.

I didn't answer. I just looked at the two corpses. Their blood dripped over the edge of the concrete foundation and into the Delaware River, and along with it, the damning details of my indiscretions.

Only one obstacle remained to my slate being wiped entirely clean.

"I'd say it's a good thing you had my gun, huh, partner?"

I couldn't remove my eyes from the lifeless bodies – the very demons that had been exorcised from my life.

"You were an ace, Alex, an absolute ace!"

"George, give me your handkerchief."

"Sure, son – if you need to get emotional, go right ahead. I know you've never done nothin' like that before."

I took the handkerchief from Ridgeway's hand and walked over to where the Chief's body lay. I pulled the diamond out of his pocket with my bare hand. I then covered my hand with the cloth and retrieved the Chief's gun.

George Ridgeway's rosy face turned white. He stared at the Chief's gun, now in my right hand and pointed at him, in disbelief.

"Son, you're not still thinkin' of shootin' me, are you?! Bozzi's dead – Winston's dead for Christ's Sake!"

"I'm not going to shoot you, George. The Chief is going to shoot you."

"Oh sweet Jesus, son – just wait one minute. Why in God's Name would you…"

"Don't you realize that you are the unfortunate holder of damaging information concerning me. You know all about Leon Richardson. In fact, if my guess is correct, you hand-selected him to take part in this mess. Am I correct?"

"So, fucking what?! We're even now. Before you made your move, I let you know that you were holding a live pistol – my Smith & Wesson 945 – rather than the one with blanks in it that Bozzi gave you. I figured the whole thing out when they pat me down but didn't pat you down. He brought you here, saying that if you wasted me, he wouldn't tell on you. Alex, you should have known that he wouldn't have given you a live weapon."

Ignoring his pleas for his life, I responded, still pointing the Chief's gun at him,

"I'm gonna guess that the Chief didn't load any blanks in his gun – what do you think? Do you have any last words?"

"Don't do it, Alex! What are you gonna do – hunt down and kill the French broad too? She knows just as much as I do! You're not a murderer, you're a lawyer and a family man! You've got your life back – just as it was before this mess started. Take the damn diamond and move your family into a mansion in Gladwyne or Bora Bora. It's over son. I'm sorry to have put you through all this."

I hesitated after I heard Ridgeway's words. I thought of the sensation of Julie's breath in my face immediately before I kissed her. I thought of how Charlie proudly wore his tattered Phillies hat every evening when he ran to me upon my return home from work. I thought of the elation in hearing a jury foreman reading back a verdict in my client's favor. I thought of how much I loved my humdrum life before I became sucked into this debacle.

Ridgeway was right, I was not a murderer. I was an ordinary guy who had studied hard in school for the purpose of ultimately earning a comfortable living. I was well on my way to achieving everything that I had ever wanted in life.

The mansion in Gladwyne would come, in time, if I used all of my God-given resources effectively.

"George, I'm not taking the diamond. You are."

He looked up at me with disbelieving eyes which displayed a glitter of positiveness upon an otherwise wretched soul.

"I beg your pardon?"

"With this diamond," I said, placing the stone in his hand, "I am buying my life back. I have been to hell, and I have the chance of returning to heaven. The mansion in Gladwyne is no good if I constantly have to worry about prosecution for killing you or about you or your slimy designees showing up at my door with a militia. I love my family. I love lawyering. You represent an impediment to my enjoyment of my favorite things. If I kill you without having to do so, then I am just as soulless as you.

"You will take this diamond and will leave this time zone tomorrow, before 10:00 a.m. You will never return to this time zone and you will never contact me again. You will obviously not disclose the Leon Richardson situation to anyone. If I find out that you have violated any of these conditions, I will consider the same to be a threat upon my life, my family and my livelihood. If that scenario arises, I will hunt you down and I will kill you."

"Are these terms acceptable?"

CHAPTER FIFTY-FOUR

The day after I killed the Chief and didn't kill George Ridgeway was a happy one. Julie, Charlie and I had played hooky from work and daycare, and had gone to the park for a picnic.

The trip to the park was a much needed diversion after Julie had come to meet me at the police station the previous evening and I had told her the entire, unadulterated truth about everything, including Véronique.

My Blackberry was incessantly chiming with e-mails and voicemails being left by the local and national TV, radio and print media. Everyone wanted an exclusive from the young lawyer who had shot a corrupt police chief in self-defense after that police chief had orchestrated an international blackmail scheme involving sexually suggestive photos of that lawyer and another woman.

According to the inquiring reporters, the public had a right to know the details of the claim of self-defense and why I had been released from custody within two hours after arriving at the Philadelphia Police Department's central "Round House" headquarters. To them, the story embodied salaciousness – Presbyterian Academy, University of Pennsylvania, blackmail, marital infidelity and dead people on two continents.

No one asked, though, about the death of a middle-aged African American man named Leon Richardson, who had been randomly killed on the streets of Brandywine City a few days prior. In fact, the story had not been mentioned on any of the network TV broadcasts and was barely reported in a 12-line story on page 26 of The Philadelphia Daily News. If I had my way, the two stories would never be connected.

"Alex, turn off the Blackberry already. I thought that we decided that you're not responding to any of the interview requests."

"We did, and I am," I said catatonically, as I read e-mails from reporters for the France2 network and KABC in Los Angeles.

Mindful not to upset the woman who had within the previous 12 hours, without reservation, fully exonerated me from any marital or other misconduct, I thought it best to not test her nerves. So, I finished reading the e-mails and placed the Blackberry in my left side pants pocket. Immediately upon doing so, it vibrated, indicating that I had received yet another message.

I'll read one more and then I'm turning it off for the rest of the day. Period.

I retrieved the device from my pocket. Who was it this time? Barbara Walters? Geraldo Rivera? Although this situation was unenviable, it was kind of cool to be in such high demand.

Once my eyes were able to combat the reflection of the sun and focus upon the screen, I was able to ascertain immediately that the e-mail was not from a news reporter.

I lost my breath.

The subject line read:

```
Desrosiers, Marguerite A. - Your Secret
Will be Safe
```

Oh my God! Véronique was back and she already had an alias – Marguerite Desrosiers. Or, maybe Marguerite Desrosiers was her real name. What did she want from me?! My life was supposed to be falling back into place!

I quickly opened the message. It read:

```
Have you ever dream of
being millyonaire? You,
Honourable sir needing
to wait no longer. My
```

```
company needing to
deposit $9.5 millions
dollar (U.S.) into
American bank and will
pay 20% commission to
account holder for
transfer fee. You will
have no tax rammificashion
and your secret wil be
safe. Utmost discretion
applied.

Please call immediately:

Marguerite Desrosiers
World Secure Investments
of the Democratic
Republic of the Congo
8008 AVENUE DE LA GOMBE
KINSHASA
DEMOCRATIC REPUBLIC OF
THE CONGO
+243-8926560
```

Air began to flow through my lungs again.

Although I was not fully out of the woods, today would not be my day of reckoning.

My life would never be the same, but on this day, I decided to think only optimistically.

Once the whole story came out, minus the Leon Richardson chapter, to be sure, the media would go away and my 15 minutes of fame would be over. However, I would never live another day in which I didn't think about an ugly head rearing itself. Each day when I rose from bed, I would wonder whether that day would be the one during which Ridgeway or Véronique would resurface, to tear my life back into shreds. And indeed, every time henceforth that I opened up a foreign scam e-mail or answered the phone from a party with an undisclosed caller ID, I would, for at least a second or two, fear that my possessions, livelihood and family would be taken away from me.

I took solace, though, in knowing that my two living foes were mainly neutralized. Véronique was now very rich, likely living in a remote corner of the world. She would have very little reason to reveal my dealings with Leon Richardson. As for George Ridgeway, although he personified evil, I felt confident that with the proceeds from the diamond and his nemesis, Jim Winston, dead, he would leave me alone. Besides, I meant what I said about killing him if he ever breached one of my directives.

Despite intuition telling me that the Ridgeway/Chief/Winston/Véronique chapter of my life was closed, I knew that one day, things could change dramatically.

But life was full of uncertainties. That's what kept it interesting.

I resolved to become a better husband, father and attorney after my brush with death and career destruction. I had decided to follow Nietzsche's guide, as so eloquently conveyed by Ridgeway the previous evening. The unfortunate sequence of events in which I had become immersed did not destroy me. I was, therefore, going to be a stronger person in the future.

***

When Charlie had tired of kicking around his soccer ball with Julie and me, we sat on a blanket and ate lunch. A soft and moderately cool breeze blew, signifying the end of summer. The chill in the air made me think of autumn's approach, and its falling foliage and football. I would welcome the upcoming change in seasons, just as I would welcome the excitement and uncertainties that would come with the next chapter in my life.

Charlie awkwardly held and chomped down upon his bologna and cheese sandwich. As I saw the brown mustard dotting his cheeks and his Phillies hat covering his eyes, I smiled and thanked God that I was alive.

Julie sat across from me, basking in the sun, with the wind pleasingly allowing her silky brown hair to flow. While she was looking away from me, I gawked at her beautiful body and face, and could not wait until later in the day when I could once again feel her breath in my face.

Looking at my family in that instant, I knew that I had made the right choice.

"Daaa-deee! More mustard!"

"Alex, please – I think he's had enough mustard for the day."

"It's O.K., Jules, I'll clean him up afterwards. If the kid wants mustard, I'll give him mustard."

"O.K., honey, you got it – knock yourself out." Julie responded with a smile, eager to see me regret my decision.

I scooped a giant dollop of mustard onto Charlie's sandwich.

"Charlie, you know where they have really good mustard?"

Charlie lifted the bread from his sandwich and licked off a giant heaping of mustard. He looked at me and turned both palms skyward, to signify that he didn't have an answer to my question.

"Charlie, the best mustards in the world come from Dijon in France. How 'bout maybe we all go there together someday – you, me and Mommy?"

"Yeah!"

"O.K., and when we're done in Dijon, we can go to Paris – the capital of France. Guess what they have in Paris?"

Charlie once again titled his palms skyward.

"They have a store in the Place de la Madeleine that sells *nothing but mustard!*"

"Whoa!"

"Do you know that in Paris, they also have a bridge named after Daddy?"

"Daddy's bridge!"

"That's right – it's called the Pont Alexandre III and it's the most beautiful bridge in all of Paris."

As the words left my mouth, I thought of how I had been standing on that very bridge a couple of days earlier, a continent away, contemplative of disbarment and murder. Where I sat, at this moment was a continent away from the Pont Alexandre III, literally and figuratively.

I had my life back, at least for the time being, and I resolved to take full advantage of it.

ACKNOWLEDGMENTS

I owe a tremendous debt of gratitude to the many wonderful people who inspired me to write this book and who were kind enough to offer invaluable editorial analysis.

The following people read and critiqued at least one version of *The Concrete Lawyer*: Anthony Andreoli, Vikki Cherry, Lance Donaldson-Evans, Stephen Frishberg, Jan Koziara, Inez Markovich, Elliot Menkowitz, Marc Menkowitz, Chris Nickels, Jon Petrakis, Christina Rideout, Francis Albert Sinatra and Igor Stravinsky. Quite simply, without the assistance of these individuals, this book would not have been possible.

I feel particularly compelled to single out certain individuals for their support.

In my humble opinion, Lance Donaldson-Evans is the very best professor at the University of Pennsylvania. Apart from stoking my passion for the French language and all things French while I was his student, he greatly exceeded the call of duty in meticulously scrutinizing both the French and English portions of my manuscript.

Vikki Cherry is the Babe Ruth of legal assistants. Words cannot describe my appreciation to her for devoting significant portions of her precious time away from work to monitor multiple drafts of my manuscript for technical and substantive issues.

Stephen Frishberg and a particular individual who wishes to remain anonymous are my mentors in the practice of law. Along with their much-appreciated unflagging efforts to sculpt my development as a lawyer, they were both kind enough to provide helpful detailed appraisals of my work on this book. In addition those two individuals, I am privileged to work alongside some of the Philadelphia area's most accomplished and well-principled lawyers.

I must also thank fellow authors, Michael Diamondstein, Saira Rao, and Richard Sand, who graciously spoke with me at length concerning the ins and outs of the publishing industry.

As a child and young adult, I never idolized a particular actor, athlete or politician. My hero was a baseball announcer by the name of Harry Kalas. During the production of this book, Mr. Kalas sadly passed away. His death has left a void in my life and in the lives of all others who, like me, marveled on each occasion in which they were able to listen to a Phillies game narrated by the baritone grand master. I was fortunate enough to be in Harry the K's company on a number of occasions and was even provided the opportunity to interview him and write about him several years ago. His gentlemanliness, articulateness and perpetual optimism have inspired me in the writing of this book and in life, generally.

I would be remiss if I didn't take this opportunity to personally thank the 2008 World Champion Philadelphia Phillies. Your purveyance of a championship to our fair city after a quarter-century title drought has proven to me and countless others that anything is possible. After being able to appreciate a major sports championship from a Philadelphia team for the first time in my life, I have a newfound confidence that world peace and cures for our most deadly diseases must not be far behind.

I express my sincere gratitude to my wonderful in-laws, Joann and Bill "Willy the Fixer" DeSario. Without Joann's culinary delights, I could never have mustered the energy to see this project to completion. Willy the Fixer taught me everything that I know about being a degenerate thoroughbred horse player and provided the context for the Turf Club scene in this book.

I cannot adequately articulate, in this limited space, the extent to which my parents, Lynn and Marc, and my brother, David, are responsible for shaping my life, so that this book was ultimately able to come to fruition. I am grateful beyond words for their love, compassion and placement of honorable ideals in my life.

Finally, I thank my beautiful bride, Joy, and our loving children, Alexander and Dominique. Independent of her good looks and even better taste in men, Joy is one of the finest transactional attorneys in the Great State of Delaware. While I was writing this book, countless weeknights and weekend days were spent tapping away at the computer, while Joy was continually attending to my share of the household tasks. Joy, I thank you and love you for your undying commitment to and support of this several year-long project.

Breinigsville, PA USA
02 February 2010
231797BV00001B/3/P